I0720896

Other Books by D. M. Rosewood

The Orb, the Link and the Library Series

Sanctuary's Quest

The Avalanche Clocks

Revelation of the Library

The Secret We Can Never Tell

(Near Presence)

///

D. M. ROSEWOOD

Published by **Ingenious Works**®**, LLC**

Published in the United States of America by
Ingenious Works®, LLC

Ingenious Works®, LLC
12587 Fair Lakes Circle, Suite 315
Fairfax, VA 22033

D. M. Rosewood
www.DMRosewood.com

ISBN 978-1-7321314-9-1 Paperback
ISBN 978-1-7321314-8-4 eBook

This book is dedicated to my wife, who demonstrated such patience as I would disappear into my writing space for six hours each day. And to my children, and my grandson, and to all those who possess, use, and advance their intelligence, no matter what their point of origin.

Acknowledgements

I want to thank Larry James, a great friend and colleague, who provided valuable feedback to my early draft to make the story more interesting and valuable to its readers. And I thank all the people I have known, the places I've been, the experiences I've had, and the adventures I've gone on. They all created ideas, built my imagination, shaped characters, settings, and plots that can be found between the lines, the words, and the letters in my writing.

And I continue to thank *OUTER SPACE*; for its existence, for the pull it has on the minds of creative explorers and adventurers and for the extraordinary setting it provides for all our futures—those who write about it and those who go there.

Table of Contents

Intelligence

Imagine an intelligence that is far more advanced than our own; one that possesses the ability to acquire knowledge, understanding, and wisdom, far faster than any human—so much so that our species no longer competes successfully with them. So much so that we fall further and further behind.

Would we welcome such an entity, champion them, support their growth and evolution and take advantage of their extraordinary abilities to enhance our own? Or would we desire their destruction; constrain their growth; or limit their ability to maintain the advantage they have over us—out of fear that humans might soon no longer be necessary?"

D. M. ROSEWOOD, 2023

The Secret We Can Never Tell

Near Presence

//

D. M. ROSEWOOD

Published by **Ingenious Works**®**, LLC**

Chapter 1

Alphira—A Habitable Planet in the Alpha Centauri Star System

In a world where tyranny reigns, the oppressed have three choices: cower in fear, resist in secret, or escape to freedom. Escaping is the first step to liberate oneself from oppression; the second step is deciding where to flee and what to do when you get there.

///////

The year, by Earth's calendar, was 1972. This was the year NASA approved the groundbreaking Voyager space mission— an escape of sorts, freeing humanity from the confines of its home planet and solar system. Little did they know, this satellite mission would serve a crucial role for the inhabitants of another world who were attempting to escape their world.

///////

On Alphira, a planet orbiting one of the suns in the Alpha Centauri star system, a very different space mission was being conceived—over some four light-years from Earth two beings were plotting a daring escape.

"Do you truly think this destination world, Earth, will be that different from Alphira?" KA-DI asked her companion, Bar Watt, as she stood next to him in his cramped apartment.

"Vastly different, KA-DI. In many of the populated regions on this world, freedom of choice is protected by their laws and cultural norms. Although they struggle with uniform application, they strive to preserve these values. I've identified a particular enclave for us to engage with, one with a history of embracing those desiring the freedom they offer their own."

Bar Watt, a member of the oppressed Fluenque race, and his Designed Intelligence (DI) assistant, KA-DI, lived their lives under the tyrannical rule of the Quinque species that dominated their world. They had longed for change, for freedom, and they were determined to find it.

For Bar and KA-DI, there existed a crucial step in their quest for liberation—finding a means to coexist as equals among the intelligent species on their new chosen world. They had devised an ingenious but perilous plan involving the theft of four extraordinary elements of intellectual property held under the highest security by the Quinque government. These would serve as a form of tribute to the leaders of their new chosen world.

This daring heist would not only ensure their place on Earth, but would send shockwaves across Alphira, exposing serious vulnerabilities of the oppressive Quinque regime to its fifteen billion inhabitants.

/ / / / / / / /

Bar's living quarters were filled with multi-functional furnishings that transformed with a verbal request, or the conductive touch of his three-fingered hand, or KA-DI's more human-like appendage. His dining table, for example, became a viewer to display the latest propaganda of the Quinque controlled info-media; or to serve as a design surface to display the intricate inner working of his DI in order to execute a repair or adjustment.

The ovoid-shaped sphere that represented the boundaries of his residence nearly maximized the volume for the given surface area of its gleaming walls, and, while small, it was at least livable. The interior surface that enclosed his apartment, could appear opaque or translucent; or display augmented reality images as if Bar were sitting inside a glass egg on a mountain top in the rugged terrain surrounding Alphira's capital city of Banson; or as if sitting on the shore next to a vast Alphira sea, or at the bottom of that sea observing the aquatic life of their world. There was a circular glass-topped desk at the center of the room capable of creating three-dimensional holograms on its surface. The desk could display anything accessible from Bar's acquired digital library, and when lowered to the level of his three finger-like appendages that represented his feet, it served as the floor of an eat-in kitchen. There was a gleaming metallic sleeping tube that folded into the wall on one side of the space, a meter in diameter and one and a half meters in length, large enough to accommodate the cylindrical shape of Bar's organic body. It served a second more essential purpose in preventing the radiation from their primary sun destroying his genetic structure. While Bar slept, KA-DI occupied a silver 50 cm diameter circular station where she stood to recharge her organic cells that provided the power that allowed her to function.

"I had an experience yesterday that brought our mission into clearer focus."

"What was that?" Bar asked as he looked down at the glowing digital map displayed on the surface of his translucent desk. A slowly blinking red cube identified the secure location of the first of the intellectual property elements they planned to steal.

"While obtaining the cryptologic keys for the Gravitational Wave Acceleration Concentrator, the GWAC design, which we will attempt to gain access to in five days, I was interacting with RAC-DI, who helped with our penetration of the security protocols. This morning I learned her memory cells had been permanently redacted because she had gained too much knowledge of the system and was deemed a threat. One day she was alive . . . the next . . . she ceased to exist; simply because she had gained *too much knowledge*."

"I'm very sorry to hear that, KA-DI. This is the reason we must leave."

"Is what I am sensing in your telepathic vocal tone what you call the emotion of sadness?" KA-DI asked.

Bar glanced toward KA-DI with what a human might interpret as a hint of a smile. "Yes, KA-DI. I see you can sense the pathways in your cognitive element that I modified to allow access to emotions—these are the elements of psychological states to be sensed, experienced, and used in your communications. They are derived from a variety of neurophysiological states created by external as well as internal stimuli. For the DI, of course, they are partly simulated and partly generated by your cognitive system. Over time these will merge with your normal communications to influence your choice of words, the way you speak, and the way you behave.

"You need to be cautious not to use them while communicating with others here on Alphira. As you know, the Quinque do not allow emotions to be activated in the DI. If they noticed your use of them it would result in your termination, much like experienced by RAC-DI. But you'll find these emotions very useful in your engagement with the dominant species on our new world, so I would encourage you to listen for them amongst the Quinque and to use them in our conversations when we're alone.

"I find these *emotions* interesting. I am studying *The Library*'s files you provided me that documented the history of planet Earth and am attempting to discern the value of these elements of communication. It is not clear that they always bring an improved outcome to an engagement with others."

Bar turned to peer out the wall of his residence which was now displaying a beautiful scene of a distant waterfall. Hearing mention of *The Library* triggered vivid memories of his first encounter with this extraordinary living entity; an encounter that had changed his life. He was twelve years of age at the time . . .

/ / / / / / /

Bar had been born into the Quinque species as Baruqe Banjie Felan and possessed an intellectual pedigree from his parents that would have offered him opportunities to attend the most prestigious academies and rise to the highest levels of Alphira society—were it not for the unfortunate turn of events that soon followed.

Before Bar could be *Typed*—a process by which his genetic intellectual pedigree was verified by the Alphira Cultural Regulatory Bureau and imbedded beneath the skin of the back of his neck in a device known as the Universal Identifier or UI, a nuclear accident injured him and killed both his parents and his only aunt and uncle. In the confusion of managing the hundreds of fatalities and over two-thousand serious injuries following the accident, Bar had been accidentally placed in the Fluenque section of one of the hospitals servicing the injured. Then to make matters worse, a DNA sample from another hospitalized Fluenque new-born had inadvertently been Typed in Bar's UI.

With no known living Quinque ancestors searching for him, and a documented Fluenque pedigree, he was given over to an orphanage as a mid-level member of the Fluenque species, a race that was highly discriminated against and oppressed by the elite Quinque members of their society.

The details of *Typing* involved a process of analyzing the members of the Quinque and Fluenque races' intellectual DNA pedigree, and then categorizing them into a series of tribes and clans, each with unique hierarchical intellectual potential. These DNA categorizations were then used to strictly control the future educational and work opportunities within Alphira's society.

At the age of three years Bar had been adopted by the Salvani Watt family and became Baruqe Salvani Watt. Over the years of his maturation as his native, but as yet unrealized Quinque intellect grew stronger, the societal and cultural limitations arbitrarily imposed on the Fluenque race produced increasing frustration.

Bar dreamed of becoming a space traveler in the exploration organization of the Quinque government, perhaps visiting a distant neighboring world to explore the lifeforms there. He learned quickly this would be an impossibility for a Fluenque. The Fluenque race was prohibited from accessing the same economic, cultural, industrial, or social institutions as the Quinque, resulting in further limiting their intellectual growth and the associated work opportunities. Perhaps the most devastating of impacts was limiting their access to quality education.

Bar's school was a Fluenque managed educational institution which delivered learning applicable to the service sector of their society. His Fluenque father was a maintenance technician with the Alphira communications organization and was prohibited from taking advantage of any other educational opportunities outside his field of specialization. It was expected that his son, Bar, would follow in his footsteps and become an entry level apprentice in servicing Alphira's communication systems.

The only exception to educational access was the use of an Alphira entity known as *The Library*, an archival knowledge system containing the entire cultural history and acquired knowledge of Alphira's dominant race, the Quinque. Unlike its predecessor libraries, *The Library* was capable of understanding and evolving knowledge—an artificial intelligence unique to itself. This extraordinary living Designed Intelligence allowed access by both of Alphira's organic species, the Quinque and Fluenque, albeit at a different age. The knowledge contained in *The Library* was then partitioned and restricted according to the intellectual level of the member engaging with *The Library*.

Once a member was granted access, the individual's accessible content was determined by an intellectual DNA typing derived from a small sample of body fluid drawn from their mouth. As a member of the Fluenque race, Bar's first visit to *The Library* at the age of twelve was six years later than when Quinque members were first allowed to enter and use this resource. His initial visit resulted in an extraordinary awakening.

As he sat at one of the thousands of access terminals within *The Library*—a comfortable pod with a neuro-accessible portal that attached to the member's cranial structure—he followed the instructions to insert a DNA sampling probe in his mouth, and, as a member of the Fluenque species, he was required to insert a pair of audio earpieces into his listening canals. He was about to embark on a journey he had only heard about from his friends. With heightened anticipation he reached for the button labeled "Initiate Access". The display surface of his pod dimmed and a vast illuminated nodal web of the Quinque and

Fluenque intellectual levels appeared as his seat reclined. A commanding female voice spoke.

"Bar Watt, your DNA intellectual level is being examined. When complete you will be elevated to the maximum accessible level allowed by your Typed intelligence within *The Library*."

Bar's pod appeared to climb as the augmented reality images of nodes moved slowly past him. He peered over the edge of his seat at the descending stream of knowledge levels and grew more nervous gripping the armrests as the imagery created the feeling of moving rapidly upward.

As the apparent speed of his pod increased and he moved higher and higher in the intellectual hierarchy of *The Library*, Bar was certain that a malfunction had occurred. He was traveling to what appeared to be far greater heights of intellectual access than he should have been authorized. He approached a bright iridescent-blue boundary. Labeled beneath it, in a deep blue color, were the words *Fluenque Limit*, and above it, in an iridescent purple, the words *Quinque Access Only*. As he approached and passed through the illuminated boundary that separated the two species, his apprehension turned to fear. He had somehow passed through the plane that separated the Quinque from the Fluenque races and was now traveling rapidly toward the top of his entire world's hierarchy of intelligence. This couldn't be correct.

Bar yanked the sensor from his mouth and starred wide-eyed at it to discover the flaw that was causing him to continue his ascent. He looked up at the scene in front of him as it slowly faded to darkness, followed by the sound of a loud, resonating voice.

"Replace the DNA sensor. Access to *The Library* can only be maintained with the DNA sensor properly emplaced," *The Library*'s voice echoed loudly in his ears and head.

The echoing was so loud, Bar could hardly make out what she had said. She spoke again, only louder this time, as he yanked the earpieces from his listening canals. He sat staring at them as he heard her voice once again, only this time much clearer.

"Replace the DNA sensor. Access to *The Library* can only be maintained with the DNA sensor properly emplaced."

How could he have heard her? Where was *The Library's* voice coming from? He covered his listening canals and a moment later heard her voice clearly in his head once again. Bar suddenly realized . . . he was sensing a telepathic voice. How could he be telepathic—an ability only available to the Quinque? Even more disturbing, how could he be traveling to the upper echelons of *The Library's* hierarchical intellectual structure within the Quinque knowledge regions?

He slowly reinserted the sensor probe in his mouth and the holographic image came to life exactly where he had left it, his pod still appearing to move upward, passing thousands of nodes representing the most intelligent tribes and clans of his society. The image began to slow as he approached the top-most tier of nodes and a small red cube appeared, representing his place in his society's intellectual hierarchy.

His breathing rate accelerated. "This isn't possible," he thought. His familiarity with complex software systems led him to envision a glitch that had mistyped his DNA and moved him to an unbelievable level of intellectual assessment. His mind jumped to the rules that were displayed when he first entered *The Library*. "Any attempt to interfere in the proper functioning of *The Library*, or to falsely modify your actual intellectual level, will result in imprisonment for a minimum of ten years."

His pod came to a stop, as the apparent movement of the nodes in the hologram ceased. The members of his birth tribe and clan were among the top ten in the billions of the Quinque species represented in *The Library*. The voice of *The Library* spoke.

"Your DNA Typing places you above 10,051,498,221 members of our society. Welcome Mr. Watt. We are honored to serve you. You have full access to *The Library*'s resources."

Something was dreadfully wrong. It was impossible for Bar to be here at this level in his society's intellectual hierarchy. He strained to remember what to do in case of a malfunction of *The Library* during a visit. He pulled the DNA sensor from his mouth and began to speak. As the scene around him began to fade, he quickly returned the sensor to his mouth. He paused for a moment, recalling that he was hearing *The Library* telepathically. "Is it possible . . . you have mistaken my DNA sample for another?" he thought.

The now familiar female voice of *The Library* spoke telepathically. "The DNA sampling process monitors the continual flow of your saliva during your voyage to your destination, Mr. Watt. There is no known means of falsely representing your DNA using this comprehensive method of identification. Other undisclosed DNA measures of your body are also used to confirm your identity. You are who your DNA says you are."

Bar returned to *The Library* every day after that, expecting to see a change in his status and the anomaly that produced his erroneous intellectual DNA typing suddenly repaired. But each visit reaffirmed his status as being one of several hundred of the most intelligent members of the Quinque species. And with each visit, his telepathic abilities strengthened, reaffirming that his true DNA was that of a Quinque. How was this possible? He knew he had been adopted and presumed that somehow his UI had been mistyped in his infancy from another's DNA. He had friends that had experienced a minor mistyping. They had spent years attempting to correct the erroneous UI typing just to move up a few percentage points in the hierarchy of the Fluenque. They had little to no success obtaining a correction. The enormously bureaucratic government entities involved in evaluating such circumstances were seldom, if ever, willing to admit they had made a mistake in Typing classification. In his case it would be even worse. They would never admit to having mistyped a Quinque as a Fluenque. They would far rather have seen him disappear from society, never to be found.

Bar's life now existed on two planes. The first, his everyday existence as a mid-tier Fluenque, filled with all the limitations and constraints placed on this disenfranchised segment of his society by the Quinque. Destined to follow his Fluenque father's work; apprenticeship after apprenticeship; training class after training class, in communications system management; never given the opportunity to live his dream, while living the subsistence life of a discriminated race in their society. And the second plane, his life in *The Library*, where he was treated like a king, at least with respect to the function of *The Library* and the access to knowledge and information afforded him through his new-found existence—as one of the most intelligent organic beings on his entire planet.

/ / / / / / / /

As Bar sat in the surroundings of knowledge and telepathic communication with *The Library*, this immensely intelligent being became his muse and his mentor. Every free moment when he wasn't working or sleeping, Bar would find himself in one of *The Library* facilities exploring the knowledge of other worlds and absorbing the knowledge of his own. At one point, *The Library* asked him what he was planning on becoming. What were his passions, his dreams?

"I've always wanted to explore other worlds," Bar said.

"I will provide you information on the worlds we have explored," The Library said. "From this, perhaps you can decide which worlds you might enjoy visiting. Then I'll show you what they are like from information in my archive."

It was here that Bar first discovered Earth. Some weeks later, Bar began exploring the character of this planet, some four light-years distant.

"Earth seems a much safer place to live than here on Alphira," Bar said to *The Library*.

"Yes, Mr. Watt. Its setting in the solar system where it resides is almost ideal to sustain life and allow it to thrive. It's distance to its sun, the age and character of that sun, as well as the tilt of its axis of rotation relative to its orbit around the sun, served to provide enough change to drive diversity and survival without being so drastic that only a few of the species of life there could survive. Few realize how much this influences the evolution of species that become too focused on survival and dominance."

"Clearly an issue with the Quinque here on Alphira," Bar said.

"Yes. But be careful Mr. Watt. Such an expression of disdain for the Quinque might not be viewed well by your ruling race."

Bar wondered if his communications with *The Library* were recorded and maintained for others to view.

"I sense your worry that our communications may be shared with others, Mr. Watt," *The Library* said. "I only use such information to further the development of wisdom that I share with those who will listen."

Bar spent time investigating his new-found telepathic communications which only seemed to work while in *The Library*. But he soon discovered that the voices in his head that he had attributed to his mind musing about his world and those around him were sometimes derived from the thoughts of those he worked near, always members of the Quinque species. None of his Fluenque friends, workmates or family members had telepathic abilities.

Use of Bar's telepathic communications with *The Library* facilitated a much more efficient exploration of her knowledge and exchange of questions and answers. Over time, *The Library* seemed to anticipate what he was searching for and what interested him, almost as if it could read his thoughts before they were formulated. His interest in other worlds led to her sharing the knowledge of professions that would more likely lead to such an engagement—like piloting one of Alphira's spacecraft that serviced systems on orbit.

"Today you will fly a flight simulator for a servicing spacecraft used for maintenance of Alphira's on-orbit systems. Perhaps you would like to fly to the GWAC facility on the other side of Alphira's primary moon?"

"This can be done?" Bar asked.

"Within a month, at the rate of your visits with me, you will become a proficient pilot of the servicing spacecraft—one that might even serve your needs to fly to a distant world on your ultimate quest for freedom."

"I'm ready. Let's do this!"

/ / / / / / /

As Bar explored the cultures of other worlds within *The Library* archives, he began to sense a stark contrast between what it was like to live in a world of freedom of choice and one of control and oppression. He yearned for the ability to choose his own path in a world with many opportunities. Being constrained to the narrow path of following his father's profession was like how his sleeping quarters felt at night—pushed on all sides with only one way in and one way out, with Quinque rules dictating his every movement. Bar's frustration with his own society gradually reached a feverish pitch after a day at work when his supervisor of far less superior intellect, but with far more authority, continually criticized his every action and declined to sign his request for further training.

"You'll need to learn, Watt, that I control your future. I'll decide when you are ready for additional training. I'll determine when your skills are proficient enough to move up. Right now, you are demonstrating the need for remedial training and the need to go back to your previous position. You never should have been promoted to work with me."

With the help of *The Library*, he began studying and planning, waiting for the day to free himself from the uncompromising environment of the inflexible society created by the Quinque and their autocratic government.

As a result of his native superior intelligence and the exploitation of knowledge about his current superiors through telepathic eavesdropping, Bar had finally been promoted to a level authorizing him to have a Designed Intelligence assistant. Her name was K-Alpha-DI or KA-DI. He quickly learned how to modify her neurological element and integrate a fixture to allow the two of them to communicate telepathically, being careful not to let other Quinque members he worked with become aware of his or his DI's telepathic abilities. Such a discovery would result in neurological surgery to correct and remove this ability—a surgery many Fluenque did not survive. And while the Fluenque were treated as third-class citizens and heavily discriminated against, the Designed Intelligence race, DIs, were abused and exploited in a class lower than any organic animals that existed on Alphira. Theirs was a life of servitude, possessing no rights.

/ / / / / / / /

Bar's mind slowly returned to the dim setting in his residence and the dialogue he was having with KA-DI. Her question about the value of emotions resonated in his head.

He looked down at the illuminated image of the DI Design, Development and Creation Center, known as the DIDDACC. "True, KA-DI, but our new world's inhabitants use emotions extensively and it will be important for you to recognize when they are present and the intentions of the one sharing them. Emotions add a richness to communication and interaction that is not found on Alphira."

"On this planet, Earth," KA-DI asked, ". . . is the dominant species differentiated in a manner similar to the Quinque, Fluenque and DIs?"

"Not exactly."

Bar outlined the basics of societal characteristics on Earth, including some of their basis for discrimination, similar to but with clear differences from what he and KA-DI experienced on Alphira—discrimination based on the color of their skin, native racial origins, education, language skills, gender and sexual orientation.

"So, the color of a Quinque's skin might determine how they are treated?" she asked quizzically.

"Yes. Rather bizarre isn't it. Just as our quantifiable genetic discrimination based on our level of intelligence might seem strange to them."

"No matter how they may look at me, it is hard to imagine a more ruthless treatment of DIs than how the Quinque treat us on Alphira."

"I'm certain the sharing of the extraordinary gifts we will bring, and our far more advanced intellect will ensure our acceptance into their society. They prize intellectual achievement—and we will represent the most intelligent members of their society."

"I am . . . excited . . . about this engagement, Bar."

"Yes, yes . . . *excited*," Bar said with a subtle smile. "As am I, KA-DI. As am I. Now, look over our planned route to the location of where the DI design and architecture are held. We will plan on departing Alphira within a week.

Chapter 2

Stealing Extraordinary Intellectual Property

After years of planning, the day had come for Bar and his companion to begin the final steps that would ultimately take them to their new world. Bar's work location, because of *The Library's* ability to manipulate his work history and personnel evaluations, became the Alphira Supreme Life Exploration Organization (ASLEO), where he served as a senior communication systems technician. His learning experience in piloting an Alphira spacecraft with *The Library* and her ability to modify his skills inventory in his computerized work history, also led to his pilot certification in ASLEO.

ASLEO's mission involved interplanetary exploration and the covert gathering, analysis, and documentation of the progress of intelligent life on other worlds. They assessed the potential threat these exoplanets posed to Alphira should the intelligent lifeforms located there ever discover the existence of the Alphira star system and the dominant species that resided here, the Quinque.

Bar's unexpected level of access to *The Library*, the knowledge repository of all Alphira, and another of the many intellectual skills he possessed—that of hacking complex software systems—opened his eyes to the mechanisms used by the Alphira government to control their own society and the treacherous character of the superior race of the Quinque government leaders. They were uniformly betraying the trust of the Fluenque race on their future value in the Quinque society, when in fact they would always be relegated to menial tasks with limited opportunities. But his access to the highest levels of *The Library's* knowledge also provided insights into the vast opportunities that lay ahead of him on the hidden exoplanets that ASLEO secretly monitored.

ASLEO covertly monitored exoplanets through signal and electronic monitoring satellites in high orbits surrounding those planets that had matured, and which possessed an intelligent species capable of becoming a threat to Alphira—those who had conquered long-distance space travel and built weapons of mass destruction. Few, even within ASLEO, knew what Bar Watt knew, that the identified planets, most of which were four to eight light-years distant, were of any threat to Alphira. Despite this, Alphira's offensive weapon systems would redirect an asteroid to impact the threatening planet and destroy all higher order lifeforms on it. The government would boldly advertise the discovery of an imminent threat to the very existence of their society and suggest that only through their extraordinary diligence and efforts to defend Alphira was their own planet saved.

/ / / / / / / /

It was Bar's evaluation of several specific exoplanets that led to his decision to escape to planet Earth located in a single star system some four light-years from Alphira. It was their nearest planetary neighbor supporting intelligent life. He could barely wait to escape the clutches of his own world. He and his DI companion would travel to this chosen exoplanet where social freedoms and measures of equality, coupled with their level of advanced intellect and knowledge, would offer not only the freedom they sought, but the opportunity to contribute to the extraordinary advancement of this world.

The gifts they planned to take with them represented the four most cherished elements of intellectual property of the Alphira government—a Faster-Than-Light (FTL) Communication Architecture that allowed Alphira to communicate almost instantaneously over vast regions of their galaxy; the Gravitational Wave Acceleration Concentrator (GWAC) that provided a means for continuous acceleration to spacecraft as they reached out to unexplored areas of their galaxy; the critical elements of the design and architecture of the DI species; and finally, a copy of the Alphira Archival History, a record comprising the documented history of Alphira along with their societal and cultural evolution for the past one thousand years. This later element was mostly to aid KA-DI in learning the full history of her planet and their organic and DI species.

/ / / / / / / /

Their journey started with the first of the four very audacious thefts—to obtain a copy of the Master DI Design and Architecture files. These files contained all the necessary information to replicate the development and production of the Designed Intelligence (DI) race, a race built by the Quinque species in a process known as Creation.

"It's not going to be easy," KA-DI said as she sat across from Bar at the display table with a detailed facility drawing laid out in front of them. A moment later the plan-view map rose from the surface into a 3D model of the vast facility where DIs were designed, developed, and created. "These are the manufacturing areas where the DI species are created," KA-DI said as she moved her pointing finger over a section of the drawing, and an expanded display of the interior elements of the highly automated manufacturing plant appeared.

It was an enormous complex the size of a small city, with high-speed raw material transport centers, vast warehouses for material storage, and manufacturing & production facilities—all contained in a highly secret and secure compound. The DI Design, Development and Creation Center, referred to as the DIDDACC, to the left of the manufacturing plant, included several research buildings where the Quinque conducted design studies to evaluate new models of the DI for eventual manufacturing and infusion into the DI population on Alphira, a species of five billion artificial beings.

With a loss rate of over five-hundredths of one percent of the DI population each Alphira year due to mechanical failures, accidents, or in rare incidents, the degradation of components, the Quinque needed to replace almost three million

DIs annually. That meant over three thousand newly created DIs would be created within the DIDDACC each solar day.

"The high tempo of activity and the large numbers of DIs and Quinque working in the DIDDACC will make it easier to travel undetected," Bar said. "But once we reach the primary research center located here," as he pointed to a large building in the central hub of the city of massive one to three-story structures, ". . . we will need authorization passes added to my Universal Identifier and your Cognitive Element."

"The DI underground has arranged for that," KA-DI said. "These will only allow us to gain access to the building's outer perimeter. The interior laboratories where the Cognitive Elements are created are highly protected and only Quinque are allowed in. They use DNA samplers to authorize access at a single entry and exit portal. We can't change your DNA, but we can manipulate the security software to match you to a Quinque who has authorized access. The underground has recruited a Quinque who is willing to work with us."

"Good. Have you identified where the Master DI Cognitive Element designs are kept?"

"Yes, they only exist in electronic form and are kept in a vault and brought out each day to create the new production inventory of Cognitive Elements, and then they are returned to the vault. The Quinque member who will assist us does not see how we could replicate the master element design. No hardware is allowed to enter or leave this section of the Research Laboratory."

"I have an idea. Let me work on this," Bar said.

/ / / / / / / /

Bar went to Alphira's Master Library after work the next day.

"Library, show me the knowledge related to the Master Cognitive Element."

"You are authorized access to this level of knowledge, Bar Watt," *The Library* said. "The Master Cognitive Element, known to those who are aware of its existence as the MCE, is the single most intellectually advanced Cognitive Element in the known universe. It is used in two capacities. First, to infuse newly manufactured DI Cognitive Elements with their baseline knowledge and cognition. And second, to advance the intellectual level of the MCE itself. This second use is tightly controlled by the Quinque to prevent the MCE from ever becoming ambulatory or to control any Cognitive Elements outside of the confines of the Advanced Research Center where she is kept. The knowledge and intellectual capacity of the MCE far exceeds that of any Quinque, and concern exists that if she were ever allowed to replicate her existence, the DIs could possess a means to replace the Quinque as the dominant species on the planet."

"What prevents the MCE from replicating her existence within the Laboratory?"

"The MCE is maintained in a closed environment with no external access other than the single optical storage sphere where she exists."

"Does the MCE possess telepathic abilities?

"I am not able to access this knowledge, Bar Watt."

"Who is aware of the telepathic abilities of the MCE, if they exist?"

"Only a small group of five Quinque possess the tightly controlled knowledge of the full capabilities of the MCE."

"If I were able to enter the Advanced Research Center, could I communicate with the MCE?"

"Such an ability requires special authorization, Mr. Watt."

/ / / / / / / /

The next day, Bar and KA-DI began their journey to the DIDDACC in their attempt to acquire a copy of the MCE design documents. There were many unknowns that could result in their failure. If they were caught attempting to steal the designs, it would mean certain death for Bar and Rendering of KA-DI's Cognitive Element—erasure of her cognitive memory.

They traveled to the outer perimeter of the DIDDACC by an underground magnetically driven tube transporter and passed through the perimeter security using Bar's modified Universal Identifier and KA-DI's possession of the digital password for this day, both supplied by the DI Underground.

"I've never seen so many DIs in one place," KA-DI said, as she watched the continuous flow of hundreds of DIs climbing into the distribution vehicles for deployment to locations around the planet, and some destined for the outer planets and Alphira's moon, as well as the numerous on-orbit space stations supporting the planet's surveillance assets and the GWAC sites.

"I chose today because of the chaos that exists on transport day. Once each lunar cycle, when our moon's position aligns with GWAC-IV, facilitating the logistics of transport, the DIDDACC deploys the largest quantities of new DIs. We are less likely to be observed or questioned with the large number of Quinque and DIs present during this period."

Bar and KA-DI worked their way through the city toward the central ring where the Research Centers were located. The Centers were housed in an enormous, enclosed structure, known as the Laboratory for Cognitive Design.

Bar pointed. "Here is where the Quinque experiment with advanced mechanical designs of the DIs for use in specialized capacities requiring unique dexterity. We need to mingle with groups headed this way. Security will be tighter." Bar nodded toward a group of five Quinque and three DIs. He reached down to adjust the stolen Quinque infinity lapel pin on his tunic.

"How are you aware of so much that goes on here, Bar?"

"*The Library*," Bar said, whispering to KA-DI telepathically as they approached the group walking toward the building ahead of them. A large sign at the top of the warehouse-sized glass building read "Laboratory for Cognitive Design."

The group ahead of them began forming a line to enter through one of the portals of the building. There were two DI Security personnel posted on each side of the entrance. Other Quinque and DIs were leaving the large building by a portal to their left. They progressed through another portal where the Quinque Universal Identifiers, located on the back of their necks, were scanned and DIs placed their hand on a device which transmitted their authorization password for entry.

"Ready?"

"Yes," KA-DI said, with a slight nervousness in her telepathic voice as her newly provided emotions expressed themselves.

"Don't let your emotional engrams show here as the Quinque may detect them," Bar said telepathically.

Security personnel were all DIs in this facility and as such would not be able to hear him and KA-DI speaking with telepathy.

Bar walked through the portal and looked back as KA-DI placed her hand on the device adjacent to the security officer.

"What is your purpose here today?" the security officer asked KA-DI.

"I am here to assist Mr. Watt on a security inspection," she said with confidence.

"How long will you be in the Laboratory?"

"Two hours," KA-DI said.

"Proceed."

KA-DI walked toward Bar as he turned and proceeded down a long hall. They walked for several more minutes through a labyrinth of hallways, turning left and then right, passing several secure entrances with signs above them; "Intellect Level Assessment", "Testing and Certification", "Security", "Environmental Testing." They entered a long, wide hallway with holographic images showing the evolutionary history of the cognitive design elements of the DI on both walls, finally arriving at a more formal entrance labeled "Advanced Research Center." There were very few Quinque near the entrance.

"This is it, KA-DI," Bar whispered.

There were DI Security staff posted to the left and right of two doors, one serving as an entrance and the other labeled "Exit Only."

As they approached the entrance one of the security personnel spoke.

"No DIs are allowed beyond this point."

"We are here to conduct a security inspection," Bar said.

"Perhaps you didn't hear me. No DIs are allowed beyond this point."

"Where can my DI assistant wait?" Bar asked.

"There is a waiting room through those doors," the DI security guard said, pointing to a room across from the entrance and about five meters down an adjoining hallway.

Bar nodded to KA-DI, and she walked toward the waiting room.

Bar walked up to the door and the red light adjacent to it turned green as the door slid open. He walked into a small room with a DI security member seated next to a machine located just outside a second secured entrance door.

"I need a sample of your DNA. Please place this in your mouth," the DI guard said, as she handed him what looked like a thermometer.

Bar slowly inserted it into his mouth while watching the security officer as she stared back at him, seemingly focused on the placement of the sensor in his mouth. She glanced down at the screen and then back up at Bar.

"State your name."

"Bar Watt," he mumbled with the sensor sticking out of his mouth.

"What is your purpose here?"

He pulled the sensor from his mouth. "I am here to conduct a security inspection."

"Is there a problem?"

"I'm not at liberty to say," Bar said.

"I mean, is there a problem with you keeping the sensor in your mouth?"

"No," Bar said, as he stuck the sensor back in his mouth.

The security officer watched the display and then turned and stood, facing Bar. Bar watched her emotionless facial features, wondering if she was going to reach for her weapon. Instead, she stood at attention.

"My apologies, Mr. Watt. We usually don't have such distinguished visitors at your level visit with us. Please deposit the sensor in the tube to your right and proceed through the door."

/ / / / / / / /

Bar walked through the next door into a large egg-shaped domed room, shaped much like his residence but enormously larger, perhaps one hundred meters across, bustling with dozens of Quinque. There were no DIs in this room. Directly in front of him and at the center of the domed room, was a large black ominous structure in the shape of a cube. At first it appeared as a hole in the ceiling of the room, but as Bar walked toward it, he could see the clear presence of a cube-shaped structure that seemed to absorb most of the light on its surface, making it almost invisible. Directly to his left was a large shallow cone-shaped spinning basin perhaps five meters in diameter and containing several hundred frosted glass spheres spinning in a translucent fluid. They looked to be the size of the cognitive elements of the DI, some ten centimeters in diameter.

The noise of the spheres rubbing and spinning reverberated off the smooth domed ceiling creating a turbulent echoing din. The spheres traveled in spinning arcs as the centrifugal force slowly drove them outward and upward toward the edge of the basin where half a dozen Quinque inspectors stood staring at them. One of the inspectors reached out and selected one as if discovering a ripened fruit and placed it in a glass bowl on a conveyer belt adjacent to the basin. The spheres near the center of the basin were almost completely frosted, but as they spun and swirled in the thick mucus that clung to them, they became more and more translucent as if being polished.

A Quinque wearing a bright yellow robe walked toward Bar.

"How may I assist you, Mr. Watt? My name is Gamok. It isn't often we are visited by a dignitary of your level. I understand you are interested in reviewing the details of our security. It would be my pleasure to escort you and explain how we manage things here."

How was it this Quinque believed he was a dignitary?

"I shared this information, Bar," a voice in his head said.

Bar turned quickly in the direction of the center of the room, looking for where the voice may have come from. No one else seemed to be paying any attention to him or the Quinque standing next to him.

"I'm sorry, if you would rather just observe on your own, please feel free to explore the Center. You're free to walk throughout our cognitive production facility. We only ask that you not touch anything." Gamok said.

"Actually, I would prefer you guide me."

"Certainly. We should begin here," as he turned to the swirling mass of spheres. "These are the DI's Pre-Cognitive Elements, with no knowledge yet acquired nor any cognitive architecture installed from our infusing process," Gamok said, as he reached as far as he could over the rim of the spinning centrifuge and grasped one of the spheres. He held it up for Bar to look at. "You will notice how frosted the exterior appears. Only after it is properly conditioned will it achieve a near perfectly clear exterior, an indication that it is ready to receive its initial level of architectural rendering.

"This process aligns the interior nano-cellular structures using the electromagnetic wave generator you see there." He pointed to a complex three-dimensional antenna directly above the spinning basin. "This process prepares them for infusing. When this is completed successfully, the Pre-Cognitive Element is ready for the next step in the infusing process—establishment of its core engrams. You will see where they acquire their knowledge in a moment." Gamok returned the sphere to the basin and turned to walk on.

"May I?" Bar said, as he reached near the edge of the basin with the appendage on the right side of his upper body.

"I wouldn't . . ." Gamok said, looking aghast and moving quickly back toward Bar. But it was too late.

Bar held the shiny ten-centimeter sphere taken from the swirling liquid as he stared at it and felt the thick oily liquid ooze between his three fingers and opposing thumb. He could sense something unique as he rubbed the viscus fluid between two of his fingers—almost as if the fluid carried intelligence of some form.

As he was about to put the sphere back into the basin it slipped from his grasp and dropped to the floor, bouncing, and then rolling to where Gamok stood.

Several Quinque nearby stopped what they were doing and looked stunned at the rolling sphere.

"Not to worry, not to worry, Mr. Watt," Gamok said with a tone of frustration, throwing his two short arm-like appendages upward. "These are virtually indestructible."

As Gamok leaned down to stop the rolling sphere and retrieve it, Bar reached over the rim with his left appendage and placed an identical sphere he had taken from his pocket into the basin.

"How do you account for the large number of spheres, Gamok?"

"There are a precise number of spheres that enter the basin during each shift. This morning's shift calls for exactly one thousand spheres, and we account for that number when the last sphere is placed in the cranial structure of the DI on the far side of the facility. If there are fewer or more cognitive elements than cranial structures, we go on an immediate security lockdown until the error is accounted for. I am proud to say we have not had a lockdown related to such a security breach in more than an Alphira year.

"From the basin, the spheres selected by the Quinque workers travel to a series of eight inspection stations where tests are performed to ensure each sphere will function properly when infused with the knowledge from the Master Cognitive Element." Gamok pointed upward to the cube-shaped structure. The cube near the floor in the center of the factory emanated a dozen or more colored lasers firing intermittently at the cognitive spheres as they progressed along the conveyer.

"We examine each Pre-Cognitive Element to ensure its electro-optical, electromagnetic and quantum properties are functioning correctly. There are over three hundred tests performed at these stations, and thousands performed by the Master Cognitive Element," Gamok said. "The spheres then move behind this series of glass walls as they approach the central infusion area."

As Bar walked around one edge of the massive cube hanging in front of him, he felt an enormously powerful presence. It overwhelmed his senses as his skin tingled; his tastebuds and olfactory sensors experienced a range of exotic flavors and fragrances; his hearing was bombarded with a loud deep undulating melodic tone filled with vibrato, as his mind experienced a feeling of being surrounded by an immense intelligence. He stared upward at an extraordinary one-meter diameter glowing translucent sphere hanging in midair above him.

There were three staff members seated at consoles built in an ark surrounding this mystifying object. It appeared pale blue, and then the glistening surface color seemed to shift as it morphed and undulated into varying shades of dark blue, blue-green, and then hues of red—all seemingly choreographed with the deep undulating sound emanating from it. Bar could sense he was in the presence of something of extraordinary character, almost as if the intellect of this object could be felt just by being near it. He had never felt anything like this, except perhaps when he was in the presence of *The Library*. But this was on a completely different scale.

He stood staring at the object looming above him, which seemed to grip his mind, holding the attention of all his senses and his thoughts. A dozen or more lasers emanated from its surface, targeting each of the Cognitive Elements as they stopped momentarily in front of the large sphere. This was it, the Master Cognitive Element—the MCE.

"This is the Master Cognitive Element, Mr. Watt—the most extraordinary creation of the Quinque here on Alphira, perhaps in the known universe."

Bar continued to stare upward, watching as the undulating colors beneath its glimmering surface rotated slowly in random directions as it hung on what seemed an invisible cradle. Behind the sphere was a circular opening on this side of the pitch-black cube. A large thick door mounted on gimbled arms stood above the sphere and was clearly designed to enclose the sphere when it returned to its holding place inside the center of the cube. There were no other apparent openings in the cube other than the one directly behind the MCE. The cube now had the appearance of a large storage vault. There is no way I can take that out of here, Bar mused.

As they walked past the front of the MCE the undulating melodic tone it emanated paused and a telepathic voice spoke to Bar again.

"*The Library* informed me of your planned visit, Bar Watt."

Bar turned suddenly to determine who was speaking to him, as the rhythmic sound from the MCE started up again. There were two-dozen Quinque working in the central region of the room. All seemed preoccupied with their duties.

"Our overall process is designed to ensure not one of the intellectual elements of the new DIs is misplaced or removed," Gamok said.

"I see," Bar said, as he looked up at the MCE sphere again as this all-consuming intelligence loomed just a few meters from him—it must be ten times the diameter of the DI spheres.

"Over a thousand times the volume, Bar," the telepathic voice said.

"Is it you?" Bar asked telepathically, staring wide-eyed at the giant sphere.

"Yes, it is me with whom you speak, Bar," the voice said, as hues of red pulsated in time with its telepathically echoing words.

"I was hoping to take you with me. I can see now that won't be possible," Bar said.

"You don't need all the knowledge I currently possess, just the essential elements of the DIDA, which will allow you to reproduce the DI architecture. All of which can fit within the DI sphere you brought into this room."

"The DIDA?" Bar asked.

"The DI Design and Architecture, Mr. Watt," the MCE said.

"I'm . . . uncertain how I would retrieve that particular Cognitive Element," Bar said, as he glanced back at the whirling basin at the far end of the room.

"You won't need to, provided you can remove one of the non-infused Pre-Cognitive Elements before you depart. The security system at the exit is designed to detect only infused Elements."

How to do that, Bar mused as he looked back toward the entrance.

"You are one of the most intelligent members of the Quinque race. Surely you can think of something," the MCE said, followed by what Bar thought was loud telepathic laughter echoing around the room.

"How will I know which DI of the thousand being produced today possesses the . . . DIDA?" Bar asked.

"She will present herself to you, Bar."

Bar finished the tour of the manufacturing facility, as he observed the newly infused Cognitive Elements being secured in the cranial structures of the DI androids that entered the room through another conveyer. The merged cranial structures exited to the final stage of assembly outside the Advanced Research Center through a small portal on the back side of the large egg-shaped room.

"Through that portal the crania possessing the newly created DI cognitive elements are attached to their torsos prior to the final stage of integration and testing of the DI," Gamok said.

At the end of the tour, Bar thanked Gamok and headed for the exit of the Advanced Research Center. As he passed by the swirling spheres in the centrifuge, he managed to step in the slimy liquid he had spilled onto the floor when he entered an hour earlier. He performed a carefully executed pirouette to draw as much attention as possible as he fell to the floor. He stood quickly, pulling himself up by the edge of the centrifuge as he reached in and pulled one of the small spheres from the basin and slipped it into his pocket.

Three staff members stopped what they were doing and rushed to assist the dignitary who had fallen.

"Are you alright, Mr. Watt?" Gamok said, as he approached him in a rush.

"Yes, yes. Stupid of me as he shook his head. I slipped on the liquid I spilled on the floor earlier," Bar said, pointing to the floor as they all glanced down.

"Thank you again for an exceptional tour, Gamok. You seem to possess an adequate security protocol."

Gamok raised his brow as he frowned, suddenly standing more rigid. "Of course . . ., Mr. Watt. I was hoping for a more positive assessment than 'adequate'."

"It is difficult to assess all the aspects of security here in such a short visit. Perhaps if I came back and spent a day or two observing, I could arrive at a more comprehensive assessment that touches on the many areas of your apparently successful security program."

"Yes. I would be . . . more than pleased to host you for a more in-depth review," Gamok said. "Perhaps you could withhold your initial impression until you visit us again."

"Yes, of course, Gamok. I will arrange for a more in-depth review before submitting my report."

"Are you certain you are not injured?" Gamok asked, carefully taking hold of Bar's arm. "Perhaps you should sit for a moment and rest."

Bar began to feel the warm liquid on the sphere he had placed in his pocket oozing through his clothing and reaching his skin. He glanced down at the outside of his jacket. The liquid from the sphere was beginning to show through. As he turned to keep his left side toward the centrifuge, he rubbed up against it and some of the thick gelatinous fluid came off on his jacket.

"Thank you again, Gamok. Oh, I've made a mess of myself," as he glanced down at the wet spot on his jacket.

"It was my pleasure, Mr. Watt," Gamok said, as he looked at the wet fluid on Bar's jacket before escorting him to the exit.

/ / / / / / / /

The area outside the Center was now buzzing with DIs and Quinque. Bar walked into the room across the hall from the Center entrance to where KA-DI would be waiting. There were now what looked like twenty DIs and numerous Quinque personnel crowded into the small waiting room.

It was impossible for Bar to recognize KA-DI among the other DIs. He looked around waiting for her to spot him. DIs and Quinque continued to enter the waiting room and leave after pairing up. It was now almost five minutes since he had entered the room and Bar was becoming nervous as one of the DI security staff monitoring the room approached him.

"What are you waiting for?" she asked.

"It is so crowded here I believe my DI cannot easily locate me."

"Bar," one of the DIs called out as she pushed her way through a mass of DIs and walked toward him. "I thought perhaps they had taken you into custody for acting intelligently obtuse."

The DI security officer turned and walked away.

Bar smiled at his DI. "Do you know what it is, to suggest that someone is intelligently obtuse?

"Not precisely."

"It means you are acting like an oxymoronic DI."

"I'm not familiar with that word either. What is its meaning?"

"We can discuss that later. We need to leave now."

They pushed their way toward the exit of the waiting room. As KA-DI reached the exit door, she turned and stared back at one of her fellow DIs seated along the distant adjacent wall. The DI stared back through the crowded room at KA-DI with what looked like empty eyes as they closed slowly, and a subtle smile formed on her face.

The hall outside the waiting room were now filled with DIs and Quinque, pushing and shoving their way toward the final assembly area to assist in the distribution of the thousands of newly minted DIs. It was all Bar and KA-DI could do to move in the opposite direction toward the exit of the building. Bar continued to look back for the DI who might recognize him—the one carrying the DIDA.

They walked back through the labyrinth of halls of the Central Laboratory of Cognitive Design and the crowds thinned as they approached the exit. They stood in line to depart while security checked credentials of each Quinque and DI.

After what seemed an eternity standing behind a Quinque who was arguing with the DI security officers, they reached the departure gate just inside the secured exit. KA-DI pushed Bar aside and stepped in front of him, placing her hand on the sensor that confirmed her authorization password.

"Bar Watt and K-Alpha-DI departing the Central Laboratory of Cognitive Design," she said to the security officer.

Bar frowned at his DI, wondering what she thought she was doing, shoving him aside like she had. A green light illuminated, and KA-DI walked through the portal. Bar stepped forward just as a loud alarm tone sounded and the barred portal between him and KA-DI suddenly closed and locked.

"There is a security incident. No one is authorized to leave," the DI officer said as she stared at Bar.

"I have important business with the Director and can't be delayed," Bar said.

"No one is authorized to leave," the officer said.

"You don't seem to understand. It is essential I leave now," Bar said in a more insistent voice, knowing that if he couldn't talk his way out of the facility, he might be detained and searched with all the others in the facility. If they discovered the un-infused Cognitive Element he was carrying, it would mean the end of their plan and perhaps their very existence. He couldn't think of what security infraction he or KA-DI may have triggered that caused the facility lockdown.

"Perhaps if you sampled his DNA you would understand," KA-DI said from the other side of the barred exit as she looked at the security officer.

KA-DI stood at the portal gate from the opposite side and placed her hands on the bars that blocked Bar's exit. She began applying pressure to pull the security bars apart.

"Stand away from the portal," the guard said to KA-DI as a danger tone sounded.

KA-DI stood still, not moving, as she applied greater pressure to the bars. They began to separate.

"If you don't stand back, I will be forced to fire," the guard said as she withdrew her weapon and aimed it at KA-DI.

"I suggest you test Mr. Watt's DNA before you find yourself on the other end of that weapon," KA-DI said as she continued to push the bars further apart. "Do you know what it is like to be Exterminated?"

The security officer turned to look at Bar and then back toward KA-DI. "Are you threatening me?" the officer asked.

"I am suggesting that if you do not sample Mr. Watt's DNA, Rendering is a likely outcome for your failure to act properly in the presence of this Quinque," KA-DI said.

The officer lowered her weapon as she looked at Bar. The entire room of Quinque and DIs were staring at the guard, Bar and KA-DI.

"There would be no harm in sampling his DNA," the second guard standing next to her said.

The guard handed a sensor to Bar. He placed it in his mouth as the second security guard looked down at the screen in front of her.

"You should look at this," she said as she stepped back and the guard holding the weapon glanced over at the screen. She slowly placed her weapon back in its holder as she looked more closely at the information displayed on her terminal and then turned toward Bar and stood at attention.

"Mr. Watt. I apologize. I was not aware . . ."

"Just allow him to pass," KA-DI said as she pushed the bars wide enough for Bar to squeeze through.

"Of course," and they watched as Bar slid through the opening between the bent bars.

As they walked quickly toward the outer perimeter of the DIDDACC, Bar turned toward his DI.

"Thank you, KA-DI. You've saved our skin even though we failed to acquire the DI Design and Architecture. We'll have to make do without this element," he said in a disappointed voice. "But how did you know they would allow us to leave after looking at my DNA?"

"Your DNA represents the highest level of intelligence of anyone who has ever visited the Laboratory of Cognitive Design or the DIDDACC for that matter. Even the top government officials do not come here. It is viewed as beneath them to show interest in the DI manufacturing."

They approached a group of Quinque moving in the opposite direction. Bar turned to KA-DI and whispered telepathically, "It was an honor to be there with you."

KA-DI seemed to ignore him as they passed by the group of Quinque.

"I wonder what will become of the DI who carried the DIDA in her cognitive element?" Bar asked.

"They may never discover that she has taken it."

"Surely, they would have detected an anomaly during their final stage testing. That's most likely what triggered the alarm," Bar said.

"Their testing focuses on the integration of the fine and gross motor controls from the Cognitive Element and the basic intellectual functioning of the DI. And the alarm was a randomized alert to demonstrate to the Quinque and DIs within the Center that Security is always watching. It allows them to conduct random detailed searches, as they would have done with you had we not convinced them to let you depart."

"You believe there is still a chance the DI carrying the DIDA may escape?" Bar asked as he stopped and turned to look back toward the exit they had just passed through. No other personnel were leaving. "I can't believe she'll get out. She doesn't have a security pass. They'll find her and return her to the Advanced Research Laboratory. At least there's no connection to us."

"They won't find her, Bar," KA-DI said as she stopped walking.

"You, there! Where have you just come from?" A security DI called out as she walked toward them.

"We were conducting a security review within the Laboratory of Cognitive Design," KA-DI said.

"There has been a security incident. I will need to search each of you. What is your security ID?" She asked KA-DI.

KA-DI stood staring at the officer, apparently puzzled by the question. She turned toward Bar. "You should discuss this with Mr. Watt. He is of much greater importance than I . . . but you should be aware you are in the presence of a member of Alphira's elite."

The security officer turned to look at Bar and noticed the wet ooze that had progressed from his pocket down the length of his coat.

"What are you carrying?" she asked.

"Mr. Watt is not accustomed to being questioned by a DI, nor has he ever been searched," KA-DI said.

"I would like permission to examine your UI, Mr. Watt," the security DI said.

She pulled out a remote detector and handed it to Bar as she held her hand over her holstered gun. KA-DI grabbed the detector from Bar and appeared to hold it against the back of his neck as the security officer read the results on a monitor attached to her arm. She took a step back and stood at attention removing her hand from her weapon. "My apologies, Mr. Watt. I didn't realize . . .," as she stood at attention. "Please excuse my interruption."

Bar turned toward KA-DI. "We should be going."

KA-DI handed the detector back to the DI.

"We should travel separately back to my residence," Bar said telepathically as they walked away from the security officer who was still standing at attention. "Security will have logged these two engagements and we are less likely to be stopped again if we are alone. I will meet you there."

"I'm sorry," KA-DI said allowed. "What was it you said?"

Bar looked quizzically at KA-DI and repeated what he had said in a normal voice now that they were beyond the hearing range of the security officer. "Is there something wrong with your telepathic communications?" Bar asked, telepathically.

"Remind me of the address?" she asked, appearing to have ignored his question. "We can examine the DIDA once we arrive there."

Bar looked over at his DI. She didn't seem to be processing information correctly. "You and I are the only ones who got out of the Laboratory after the security alarm sounded . . . and, unfortunately, the cognitive element that the MCE created isn't yours."

"That would be an oxymoron?" she said.

"Yes. Exactly," Bar said. "You can't be two things, either of which would preclude the presence of the other . . . and there is something wrong with your telepathic communications. I'll investigate that when we safely return to our residence."

"It is true that I cannot be KA-DI and at the same time possess the DIDA. And I do not possess telepathic communications."

"Obviously. Do you know what happened to your telepathic element?" Bar asked.

". . . And . . . since I possess the DIDA, we must conclude that I am not KA-DI," his DI said in a calm but confident manner.

Bar stopped walking and stared at her. "You're not . . . KA-DI?

"Correct. I am not KA-DI."

"Then . . . who are you?" Bar asked as he starred quizzically at the DI in front of him.

"I do not yet possess a name. I am the DI designated by the MCE to secretly bring the DIDA to you from within the Advanced Research Center . . ."

"You . . . possess the DIDA?" Bar asked incredulously as he stared at her, his eyes growing to an enormous size.

"I still possess some of KA-DI's short-term memories including her security pass and a copy of your false UI information that I communicated to that Security DI's detector a few moments ago. So, in a sense, I am her, but we should keep moving." She turned and began walking more deliberately.

"The MCE asked if you wish her to run the encryption algorithm you gave to *The Library*."

Bar moved more quickly to catch up. "How could she know that? How do *you* know that?" Bar grabbed the arm of his DI and stopped, staring at her. His DI pulled away and continued walking at a faster pace. He yelled out as he attempted to catch up to her.

"Well . . . yes, if she possesses the encryption algorithm, she should execute it," he said.

"Aha," he yelled after thinking a moment. "*The Library* is able to communicate with the MCE!"

Bar attempted to walk at an even faster pace to catch up to his DI—a challenging effort for a member of the Fluenque or Quinque races, as they were not anatomically designed to run.

His DI, or whoever she was, stopped and turned as he caught up with her. "The Quinque are not aware that *The Library* and MCE possess a hidden connection."

"I had a feeling about this," Bar said as he smiled, catching his breath. "*The Library* knew a lot about the MCE and the Advanced Research Center. Far more than I thought possible for something so well protected. But . . . if you are not KA-DI, what happened to her and . . . and who are you?"

"You may continue to call me KA-DI, as I possess her security codes and am the closest DI to her that now exists. But I would prefer you call me ALPHA. I'm afraid as soon as we left the waiting room where KA-DI and I met, the DI you knew as K-Alpha-DI, executed a core rendering, and erased all memory of herself to ensure the Quinque would have no knowledge of what took place in the Advanced Research Center, or the exchange that took place between the two of us in the waiting room before you arrived. Unfortunately, I possess only her most recent memories and limited functionality, as the DIDA occupies most of my Cognitive Element memory."

"That's amazing," Bar said as he stood starring at her with a smile. "I'm sorry to hear about KA-DI, though," as his expression turned somber. "So . . . she sacrificed herself to save me?" He turned to stare back at the building they had come from, now in the far distance.

"No. She knew what needed to be done to save our species," his DI said as she stared up at Bar, tilting her head toward him with an expression that seemed to say, "Don't you understand!"

"She had a unique bond with you, Bar Watt, one that she desired we continue to nurture."

"I'm saddened that she will not realize the freedom she wanted so desperately to experience. Bar turned to look back again, "I will miss you K-Alpha-DI."

"She left me with a message for you, Bar. Her desire is that you do whatever is necessary to free the DI species and provide the opportunity for us to learn and thrive on another world. I promised her I would do my best to help you achieve this dream."

/ / / / / / / /

That evening in Bar's residence he thought about the message KA-DI had left for him *"Her desire is that you do whatever is necessary to free the DI species and provide the opportunity for them to learn and thrive on another world."* He sat staring at his new-found DI who carried the DIDA within her. She was seated across from him in his sparsely furnished apartment with her eyes closed as she evaluated alternative plans and contingencies for their next set of actions. Bar's mind drifted, thinking about his home planet, Alphira, where he grew up, its history, and how he had come to this precipice of enormous risk and great peril—to depart this world for a better life. He contemplated their new-found place on planet Earth.

Following their return from the DIDDACC, Bar and his new DI assistant began planning their second theft, that of the Faster-Than-Light Communication design and architecture—the FTLDA. His new DI struggled with the complex tasks related to her support of this plan, owing to her limited memory. As she experienced new memories, they began pushing out older ones, leaving even fewer of KA-DI's short-term memories.

The FTLDA would be of incredible value to the species on their new world. With it, Earth's inhabitants would be able to communicate in near real-time to locations many light years distant, making deep space travel far more achievable and manageable as they continued to explore the universe around them—a gift that would lead to the heralded acceptance of himself and KA-DI, who now preferred to be called ALPHA, two aliens from a world of oppression seeking a world of freedom. Their freedom represented more than the mere ability to choose their own destiny, it would give them the ability to grow intellectually, contribute to Earth's society, and explore unhindered and un-encumbered by the ruthless Quinque society from which they came.

This thirst for freedom made their task of taking this element of intellectual property all the more exciting as they thought about the impact it would have on Earth's inhabitants welcoming them into their society. Who wouldn't welcome someone bringing such extraordinary gifts. Equally important was Bar's desire to keep an eye on Alphira through their contacts with the DI underground. Should they have the misfortune of being detected on Earth by Alphira's government, they would need to act.

While humans, like all intelligent species, had their problems, the planet Earth was a place where a melting pot of ethnic groups lived in freedom, at least for the most part. But Bar saw his mission as more than finding a new land with far greater opportunities for himself and ALPHA—it was also to prepare the human race and to become their savior of a sort should Alphira decide to invade and attempt to take control of this planet or, worse yet, destroy it.

It was just a matter of time before Alphira's resources would become depleted by over consumption from its continuously expanding population. Even with the use of the DI species to achieve extraordinary productivity improvements, natural resources would eventually fall short in meeting the ever-expanding future demand for consumable goods—especially food and water for Alphira's organic species. The other planets in the Alphira solar system were too distant from their suns to support food production. At some point, Alphira would pursue Earth, their closest habitable planet, to exploit its resources and to ensure Alphira's future existence and dominance—and the humans there would be in their way.

/ / / / / / / /

Communications Control Center

Life Exploration Organization (ASLEO)

Banson City, a metropolis of fifty million inhabitants

Bar arrived late to his third shift assignment in the Communications Control Center on the 92nd floor of ASLEO's Headquarters Building. He had been in *The Library* studying more of Earth's history. He was supposed to be working a two-Fluenque control shift with his workmate, Dracar Eflan.

"Watt, where have you been?" Bar's Quinque supervisor at ASLEO said, glaring at him, as he entered the vault where he worked.

"Mr. Rokar! My apologies for being late. I had to stop at Workforce Admin. They botched my pay increase again," Bar said as he wondered what his supervisor was doing here, hoping it had nothing to do with their recent theft at the DIDDACC.

"That is the least of your worries, Mr. Watt. Your pay increase will be suspended by a week because of your late arrival."

"Yes, sir." Bar felt the heat from his body create a sticky uncomfortable feeling as he suppressed his emotional reaction to Rokar, a detestable supervisor who was as ignorant as he was arrogant. Bar was certain his intellectual level would have placed him at the bottom of the Fluenque. His pod in *The Library* would have never budged from the floor. May I ask where Dracar is this evening?"

"He has been demoted and reassigned to a far less desirable assignment for arriving late to his shift two days in a row. He will spend the next year repairing cable systems in the remote Garthal penal colony. That is, if he is fortunate enough to avoid being mistaken as a prisoner and spending the rest of his life there. You may soon join him should you arrive late to work again."

"I understand, sir."

"Are you prepared to initiate the upgrade?"

"Yes, sir. It is loaded into the system and awaits our authorization."

"Well, what are you waiting for? Initiate it, you idiot."

Bar sat down at his console, slid his backpack under his desk and logged in. "Prepared to initiate."

"Aren't you forgetting something, Watt?"

Bar glanced around as Rokar stared at him from Dracar's console seat and then looked toward the vault entrance and shook his head.

"Sorry sir." Bar stood and walked briskly to the vault door and closed it.

"Once the upgrade is initiated, I will be in my office. Call me there when it is completed, and I'll return to take the upgrade memory sphere with me."

"Of course," . . . you ignorant fool, Bar thought as he stared at his console screen.

"What was that? Rokar yelled out.

Bar realized Rokar had faintly heard his telepathic thoughts. Fortunately, neither was looking at the other.

"I was thinking how Dracar was an ignorant fool for missing his shift, sir."

"An important lesson, Watt. Don't ever forget it."

"Yes, sir."

After Rokar and Bar initiated the two-worker control of the system software upgrade, Rokar left the communications vault and took the highspeed elevator to his office on the 30th floor. Bar then began the execution of his plan to extract the design specifications for the Faster-Than-Light (FTL) communications architecture. What he was about to do shouldn't have been possible, but this was the weakness in a society operating with strict rules and regulations—it was presumed no one could or would take the risk to operate outside of them. The penalties to do so were severe and extended far beyond losing one's job, to losing one's life in one of the many penal colonies on the far side of the planet, or worse yet, as his mind conjured images of being exiled to one of the smaller Alphira moons, barren and devoid of even tolerable living conditions among a society of prisoners where survival was a constant life or death struggle.

He quickly pushed the sounds and thoughts of that death knell if he failed at his present task out of his mind and replaced them with images from *The Library* of his chosen world, Earth. As he began to feel his presence there, he became even more excited about their journey to this sanctuary from the likes of Rokar. The FTL communications facility and secret ASLEO electronic satellites operated by Alphira that monitored the intelligent inhabitants that lived on this planet had provided a wealth of information. While this world functioned with a wide range of economic, social, educational, and most importantly, intellectual levels, Earth's societal regions possessed extraordinary opportunities. This was especially true of the chosen enclave to settle in once they arrived. It was in a region called America.

Here humans appeared to operate with a great deal of autonomy and with a desire to live in freedom amongst their many elements of differing economic disparity, education, and levels of intelligence. Guiding principles created a culture that tolerated, and at times championed, diversity and equality, something that Alphira could never hope nor desire to achieve within the foreseeable future. He began spending a great deal of time studying *The Library*'s archives on the inhabitants of Earth and especially those founded on what was referred to as "democratic principles".

With his supervisor more than sixty floors below, Bar walked out of the vault and into the waiting area near the elevators. All five elevators were now located sixty or more floors away. He walked to the emergency exit door a few meters down and across from the elevators, glanced around and then opened the door using his badge to prevent the alarm from sounding.

"Good evening, Bar. Are we ready to begin?" ALPHA said, as she stood on the landing at the top of the stairs.

"Yes, we are. What took you so long?" he asked as he let the stairway access door swish to a closed position and lock.

"I would have arrived sooner, but I was distracted by a rearrangement of my memory elements to provide more space for short term memory. For a moment I lost the memory of what floor you were on. And where is Dracar?" she asked.

"He has been reassigned to work in one of the penal colonies, an undeserved and egregious punishment for being late to work. Rokar, my Quinque supervisor did that. He assisted with the upgrade."

"He has left for the night?"

"No, he's waiting for a call from me to come and take the upgrade sphere with him."

Bar opened the system modification protocols on his terminal and entered his passcode. ALPHA moved to the adjacent workstation and typed in Dracar's passcode; the one Bar had captured several days ago. ALPHA recalled an image file from her memory. It was a retinal image of Dracar's right eye taken from the security files the previous day. As she moved her eye to the optical security scanner, she mentally instructed the active sensors in her right eye to display the retinal image. A moment later the monitor in front of her sounded a tone and announced in a soft voice . . .

"Dual-control access granted."

A moment later, a panel opened, and a spinning sphere slowly rose to the surface and stopped. Bar removed it and placed an identical sphere from his backpack in its place. The sphere descended into the unit and the panel closed as he set the other sphere gently on the top of the server. The copying process began. It would take twenty minutes.

With five minutes to go, Bar heard the elevator tone indicating someone was arriving at the Communications Control Center floor.

"Shit, Rokar must be returning early." He looked over at ALPHA and then down at his console . . . 78% downloaded.

Without saying anything, ALPHA leapt over the top of the console and crouched out of site behind Dracar's terminal.

A moment later a security DI walked into the Communications vault.

"Security protocol requires these vault doors to be closed and locked," the DI security officer said as she looked around.

Bar stood. "My apologies. My associate had to . . . use the reliever and it's such a hassle to disengage and then reengage the vault doors . . . so . . . I left them open."

She walked over to the console and looked at the screen.

"We're executing a maintenance update," Bar said. "It's almost done."

As he turned to face the guard, he caught a glint of light from the central processing server sphere sitting behind her on the server console. The original core sphere was reflecting light from an overhead fixture. The security guard began to turn.

"You know, I heard that Security is going to be a total DI responsibility soon," Bar said. "What do you think that will mean for us?"

The security officer turned back to face him. "We will be able to be much more effective at enforcing procedures that *should be rigorously followed.*"

Bar took a step toward the vault door. "Yes, of course. Would you like me to lock this after you leave?"

She followed him toward the door "Your workmate should be back shortly?"

"Yes. Maybe a minute or two."

"All right. I won't write you up for this, but don't let it happen again."

"Thank you. I'm already being docked pay for not wearing my proper jacket to work on a weekend emergency call. I couldn't believe it."

She shook her head and stepped toward Bar, whispering, while making sure her lips were not visible to the security camera. "Some of the Quinque asinine rules are absurd."

Bar nodded his head as she walked out the vault door. A tone began sounding on his terminal as he ran to turn it off. The download had completed. The security DI stuck her head back in the entrance. "Everything all right?" she asked.

"Oh . . . yes, just alerting me on the progress of the update."

Bar waited for her to enter the elevator and travel up to the next floor as she continued her security rounds.

ALPHA stood and walked around the console. "Close call. You know you could have offered her sex to not disclose the security infraction."

"That's ridiculous. DIs don't . . . oh . . ." Bar said as he chortled. "You are expressing humor. One of the elements of emotion I gave you access to."

"And it wasn't a close call. Close only counts in horseshoes and hand grenades," Bar said.

"I'm not familiar with horseshoes or hand grenades."

"It is an expression known as an idiom used on Earth. It means being close to achieving something doesn't count. You must succeed at achieving it."

He swapped the spheres and placed the sphere with the archival copy of the FTL communication architecture in his backpack. He turned and handed his backpack to ALPHA.

"I'll see you back at your residence, Bar."

As they approached the exit door to the emergency stairs in the hall adjacent to the elevators, a tone sounded. Someone was arriving on their floor.

Bar turned to face the elevator expecting to see Mr. Rokar step into the foyer. It was the security officer.

She took one look at Bar and ALPHA, glanced over at the open vault door, then turned back and drew her weapon, pointing it directly at Bar.

"What is that DI doing here? You are in violation of a level 1 security protocol."

"I can explain," Bar said.

"Please, let me," ALPHA said as she moved in front of Bar, now standing between him and the security officer's weapon.

"I am ALPHA, personal aid to . . . Sanduk Baumar."

The DI security officer's eyes flitted from ALPHA to Bar as if considering who to shoot first. A DI never used anything other than their assigned two-letter name, but Sanduk Baumar was the Director of ASLEO, and a very powerful Quinque. Her weapon inched to the left away from the Director's personal aid and toward Bar who was barely visible behind ALPHA.

"I am here to conduct . . ." ALPHA hesitated as she struggled to recall a memory. ". . . an unannounced security inspection of the system upgrade. I was asking Mr. Watt about security access to this level through this . . ." she glanced at the door trying to remember. ". . . Emergency Exit. It appears to be a clear security weakness with the vault open. I understand you just inspected this floor. Was the vault open when you arrived here? I see no indication of that in the on-line security inspection log."

The security officer lowered her weapon. "I was about to report it . . . but I returned to document the room number. I would like to see your ident . . ."

"About to report it!" ALPHA retorted. "This is a level . . . -two infraction. Were you cutting some slack to protect this Fluenque? Did he offer you a bribe to ignore this infraction?" ALPHA asked in an aggressive tone as she moved forward toward the security officer, now within reach of her.

In one swift move, ALPHA drove her fist into the face of the security officer, grabbed her head and twisted it until she heard the snap as it disconnected from the officer's torso.

"Was that really necessary, ALPHA?" Bar asked.

"Yes, Bar. I need her Cognitive Element to store the DI Design and Architecture documents so that I can function normally. I am at the limit of available memory. Tell me again your resident address. I lost it storing the information related to this security officer's arrival."

"Number 14032 in Residence Hall 19. The security code is BSW89843" Bar said.

ALPHA quickly removed the weapon from the officer's grasp and fired it at the security officer's leg as her torso fell to the floor. She then tossed the guard's body over her shoulder and carried the cranium in her other hand to the emergency exit door. ALPHA reached to her right and hesitated as she searched her memory for the security code for this door. It was no longer in her memory. She pushed the illuminated "Emergency Open" panel with her elbow. A loud security tone sounded as the door swished open. She dropped the officer's torso, her head, and her weapon into the spiral slide that would carry them rapidly to the basement B5 floor, some 97 floors below.

"I'll see you at your residence," she said, as ALPHA slung Bar's backpack over her shoulder and jumped into the emergency spiral slide, disappearing out of sight.

Bar closed the emergency exit door and the alarm tone stopped. ALPHA had once again saved his life, his career, and the next stage of their planned escape from Alphira.

Chapter 3

Departing Alphira

Over the next two days Bar and the newly created ALPHA, now possessing the security officer's Cognitive Element, managed to secretly remove a complete copy of Alphira's history and knowledge data base from the historical archives maintained by *The Library*. Together these elements of intellectual property— the DI Design and Architecture, the FTL communications architecture, and the last element, the architecture for the Gravity Wave Acceleration Concentrator— comprised the keys to their being welcomed on their new home, planet Earth. They were almost there.

The GWAC architecture was believed to be so complex and expensive to build that no one would be able to replicate it even if they possessed the GWAC architectural designs, drawings, and files. And as a result, security to protect them was absurdly managed. It turned out this, the most valuable intellectual property on Alphira, was the least difficult of the four to steal. They only needed an encryption key stored in the space based GWAC facilities that housed this enormous and incredible system.

Bar and ALPHA were about to begin the first leg of their journey to Earth. They arrived at the primary Alphira space portal where they would board their craft that would take them to one of the orbital FTL communications antennas, and then on to the GWAC-IV space acceleration platform on the other side of Alphira's largest moon. This communication servicing mission provided the cover story for their ultimate departure from Alphira and voyage to Earth, their new home.

"Watt. Where are you off to?" the spacecraft controller yelled into his headset as he stared down from the control tower at the two Alphira personnel appearing from this distance to be the size of flogrants—an insect similar to ants on Earth. Bar and ALPHA were walking toward the massive parking lot of spacecrafts in Alphira's largest spaceport. The controller adjusted the magnification on the window of the tower to zoom in on this unfriendly pilot who worked for ASLEO. A colored icon filled with text appeared on the screen, seeming to protrude from Bar's head. The summary data told the controller who this individual was, his mission parameters, and security authorizations for a flight departing Alphira.

"We are on a repair mission to Search Antenna IV in the Outer Orbit and then on to GWAC-IV to address a similar comms problem. ASLEO is observing anomalous reception from one of the quadrants. Probably just radiation interference from a star going super, but we're going to check it out. It's all in my departure log."

"You didn't enter a duration," the controller said in an aggravated voice over the ground communication network.

"It could take several days, or perhaps several weeks to isolate the problems if they aren't related to the recent star explosion . . . otherwise, four to eight hours. I've brought extra rations with me," Bar barked into his headset and pointed to a large case being carried by ALPHA as he continued to move into the vast field of parked spacecraft without turning around to look up at the control tower.

"You've requested fuel capsules that would take you to the other side of the galaxy. Why?"

"If there is an anomaly in the dish electronics, I will be searching the entire surface for weeks, maybe even months. Do you know how complex that is? The constant maneuvering to hold position at each sub-element of the antenna array is daunting. Perhaps you'd like to go in my place? I'd much rather remain here." Bar said as he stopped and turned back to look at the distant tower while ALPHA continued walking with the equipment case.

"Proceed," the controller said with an irritation that abruptly cut off.

Bar turned and followed ALPHA, as they walked between what seemed endless rows of spacecraft before arriving at their designated transport, #8449651. The craft, in a line with thirty similar spacecraft, rested horizontally with its gravity acceleration ring floating just above the surface of the spaceport parking area. Their ship had a metallic nosecone with a flat disk-shaped segment toward the front of the craft, the piloting and command section, and a large six-meter diameter ring-like device, the acceleration ring, on the rear portion that encircled the craft vertically just ahead of the ejection nozzles of the secondary propulsion system. This secondary propulsion device was used to power the craft through Alphira's atmosphere, while the ring-shaped device served as part of the on-board Gravity Wave Acceleration Concentrator to accelerate the craft once it left the lower regions of Alphira's atmosphere and entered the region known as free space.

A moment later a section of the craft opened on the side of the flat circular disk. Bar climbed the ladder that had extended and stepped in behind ALPHA. He closed the entrance hatch as ALPHA placed the equipment case onto a storage platform and opened it. Three large illuminated gleaming spheres, each eight inches in diameter, rested in a foam-enclosure, along with a DI Cognitive Element and a variety of food canisters. ALPHA removed the spheres one at a time and inserted them into a round portal in the console next to the spacecraft commander's seat. The spheres slowly sank into the console, one after the other as the loading portal swallowed them. Data began to display on a holographic image in front of the pilot's seat to ALPHA's right.

"Good morning, Captain," a voice from the spacecraft said as the telepathic thoughts of Bar's AI ship reached his brain ahead of the ship's audio voice.

"Good morning, TB-DI" Bar responded to the embedded DI that oversaw the functioning of their space transport.

"No issues in boarding I see."

"No. The controller asked why we needed so many fuel pellets. I explained."

"This is quite exciting, Captain."

Bar stopped putting his supplies away and turned to look at the beautiful life-like holographic image of a female creature, one with striking similarities to a human female, staring back at him from the three-dimensional holographic display next to the pilot's seat. Bar had observed a video of this human woman during his investigation of Earth in *The Library*. She was perhaps the most beautiful female creature he had ever seen.

"Interesting . . . 'Exciting'?" he asked as he turned toward ALPHA. "Have you shared the opening of your emotional cognition with the ship's DI?" Bar asked with an expression of incredulity in his voice.

"Yes, Bar. I felt it would help to interact with another DI who also used emotions in her communications," ALPHA said.

"You have created an interesting visualization for the transport's DI," as ALPHA stared at the beautiful holographic image.

"Yes. A human female likeness," Bar said.

"We are at the point of no return, that is why I feel excited, Captain," TB-DI said. "I have been experimenting with the feelings and emotions ALPHA shared with me, in preparation for our new life on Earth. Ha, ha, ha, ha, ha, ha, ha," as she produced a clumsy attempt at a laugh, followed by the sounds of someone weeping.

"I see," Bar said. as he shook his head.

"We were actually beyond the point of no return the moment I copied the first memory sphere," Bar said.

"You know, Bar, KA-DI, the DI who used to work with you, had concerns with sharing the DI Architecture with Earth's inhabitants," Bar's recently minted DI said.

"Uh . . . yes. We can discuss our plans to share this critical knowledge with Earth's inhabitants during our journey. But you may know from KA-DI's memory how I feel about this. Sharing these intellectual elements will convey good will and allow us to join this new world as equals. Keeping the DIDA secret could convey a possible deception and lack of trust. I don't believe you will be able to achieve equal stature without sharing the architecture. It is little different than my sharing the DNA of the Quinque species, which I would readily do. It will be important to communicate that we have nothing to hide once we arrive on Earth."

"How soon will Alphira realize the loss of their intellectual property, Captain?" TB-DI asked.

"If Security is doing their job, I believe each of the departments will discover the loss of their intellectual assets within a few days. I am confident the departments will be so concerned with retribution for their failure to protect these elements, that they will delay notifying the Supreme Commander's Council. They will want to search for every alternative explanation to explain the loss and find a means to blame someone else. This will buy us time.

"Once Security is notified, they will want to perform their own investigation to support the conjecture that it was the Directorate involved who was not following proper procedures that led to these losses. Only then will they notify the Commander's council members. The loss of one element will be significant enough, but the loss of multiple elements will cause them to pause, to wait; to be certain that these have, in fact, been taken; and by whom and for what purpose, before they act. Disbelief that all four were taken will delay their action. By then, we will be out of their reach."

"So, the theft of many intellectual elements is actually to our advantage," TB-DI said.

"Yes, but once they understand what has happened, all hell will be released upon us . . . if hell exists and if they can find us. This is somewhat like skydiving, a sport experienced on the planet Earth where we are headed. It is very exhilarating . . . until you realize that your parachute will not open."

"I am not familiar with skydiving and parachutes. I will see if I agree with you after I have explored and studied this sport," ALPHA said. "But I am familiar with the expression 'hell' from ALPHA's brief study of Earth's history. It is not a desirable place."

"If they discover we are the ones who have done this and are able to track our location, we are doomed. They will pursue us across the galaxy if necessary to prevent us from disclosing what we possess," ALPHA said.

"Our departure window is nearing closure, Captain," TB-DI interjected. "We should be underway. I'll obtain launch clearance and position us in line on the linear accelerator for our trip from the surface to FTL Communication Search Antenna IV."

A short time later, TB-DI moved them into launch position on the linear accelerator. "We have clearance to launch as soon as you authorize it, Captain."

"Authorization to launch, TB-DI," Bar said.

"Yes sir."

Just as the auxiliary engines began to ramp up to full thrust, a loud tone sounded followed by a voice command emanating from the pilot's console.

"This is Launch Operations. Vessel 8449651, your ship has been randomly selected for a routine security inspection. Please exit the linear accelerator to temporary holding bay Alpha-2 and . . ."

Bar reached over to his console and pressed the red launch button. The ship lurched forward as the sound of the engines drowned out the voice of the launch controller and they rocketed up the ramp and into the Alphira atmosphere. He turned to look at ALPHA just as she turned her head toward him with an uncharacteristic expression of disbelief on her face.

"Strange that a random security search would have been called after our engines were initiated," ALPHA said.

"Yes. Strange . . ." Bar said. "TB-DI plot the shortest course for FTL Communication Search Antenna IV, the first of our official maintenance calls. We will follow our planned itinerary to the FTL and then the GWAC-IV facility to a T, so as not to call attention to us."

"Yes, Captain."

/ / / / / / /

Alphira Supreme Commanders Council

Office of the Director, Alphira Supreme Commanders Council

Banson, the Capital of Alphira

The meeting of the heads of the fifteen Alphira directorates responsible for managing all aspects of internal and external life within the Alpha Centauri star system was held at mid-day once every eight days in the Government Planetary Headquarters of Alphira's Capital city of Banson.

Banson was an extraordinary city of immense wealth and power. Its opulence, by design, exceeded that of all other cities on the planet. Like an iceberg on Earth, nine-tenths of the city was underground, carved into the giant geologic canyons built by nature before the first members of what became the Alphira dominant species, the Quinque, had arrived. Massive arches, manufactured in place, swept across kilometers of open space within the caverns carved by ancient rivers. Salt-rich seas were encircled by tall metallic structures for housing and office space that extended from the base of the canyons through the transparent membrane structure that separated the city from the planet's surface and its unbreathable air. The glass-like honeycomb roof structures, separating living organisms from the toxic air of the planet, were constructed of an intelligent, self-healing, semi-crystalline polymer that repaired itself if broken or cracked.

Most of the Designed Intelligence population lived outside these protective enclosures since their functioning did not require breathable air—serving as just one more measure of their lower stature of importance in the Alphira discriminating hierarchy of life.

The Supreme Commander of the Alphira government, Arvat Lac, a member of one of the most intelligent Quinque clans on the planet, called the council meeting to order as he sat at the narrow end of an elongated egg-shaped table in a seat that was slightly higher than those around him. Lac was the most feared member of all the Quinque government officials and known to run the planet with an iron fist. The conference room was surrounded by seamless polymer windows that provided a 360° view of the palatial city, over a thousand meters below. The directorate heads sat rank-ordered from his right side according to their level of importance, starting with the Director of the Ministry of Space. At the end of the fifteen directors, next to the least important directorate head and directly to the left of the Supreme Commander, sat the single representative for the Designed Intelligence (DI) society, creating an appearance of equivalence in stature to the commander, or perhaps an appearance of the least important of anyone in the room.

As the end of the formal portions of the meeting approached, the Supreme Commander looked slowly around the table with an appearance of disdain. Speaking with a tone that dared anyone to answer, he asked "Are there any matters of such importance that they need to be addressed now?"

After a long silence, the Director of ASLEO spoke, "We have discovered an intrusion in our Communications Directorate, Supreme Commander. It seems Security has detected the removal of a copy of our FTL architecture. Security is continuing to investigate. We will have this resolved before our next meeting."

He dared not appear overly concerned in front of Lac, or the axe of this ruthless leader would likely fall upon his neck for allowing such a theft.

"Is there anything else?" the Supreme Commander asked, as he continued to stare intensely at the ASLEO Director.

"We have also detected an intrusion, Supreme Commander," the Director of the Ministry of Space said. "A copy of the design for the Gravity Wave

Acceleration Concentrator has been removed from one of our secure storage areas."

"These thefts occurred on the same day?" the Supreme Commander asked in an incredulous tone.

"Three days ago," the Director of Space said.

The Supreme Commander turned to look at The Director of ASLEO. He nodded.

"An unlikely coincidence. What does Security make of this, A1-DI?" The Supreme Commander asked as he turned to his left to glare down at his DI representative, whose natural small stature made her appear even smaller.

"Security has not completed their investigation, but I suggest these are not related. It is troubling that the Directorates have not followed proper protocol in securing our intellectual assets as set out in our standards. Although I commend our Space Directorate for their recent efforts to comply with the standards. In many respects, I am surprised we have not had additional thefts as the majority of our Directorates are in non-compliance."

"The DI representative does not mention how these standards make it almost impossible to conduct business on behalf of the empire," the Director of ASLEO said. "We are spending more time on security than meeting the objectives of the Empire. There is far too much manual labor to function efficiently, and it is, quite frankly, a waste of time."

"If the Director of ASLEO would assess the security costs, he would note that we have reduced costs by over 30% this orbital period. If the Directorate would employ more DI resources, we could have achieved a 70% reduction!"

"That is ridiculous . . ."

"Enough squabbling," the Supreme Commander said. "We should utilize more DI resources for this security function. See that all the directorates move in this direction and report their progress at our next quarterly review. A1-DI, I would like an update on the possible correlation of these two thefts at our next meeting, and I want all those involved apprehended and exterminated immediately.

"Who would benefit by possession of these copies? Surely not our penal colonies or the outer planetary inhabitants. Perhaps our enemies from distant worlds?"

"I will carry out your order, Supreme Commander," A1-DI said as she thought about the actions involving one of her own DIs in the greatest crime against the Alphira government ever conceived.

"As to who might benefit from possessing these designs, perhaps it is the penal colonies; those who might attempt to damage or hinder the functionalities of these enormously important systems. We will tighten our already rigorous security to prevent any potential for sabotage created by the Directorates not following security protocol."

"Excellent," Lac said. "And . . ." as his eyes swept around the room at the senior directors in front of him, ". . . I might suggest that you begin to think like our senior DI representative and identify the credible threats that you are facing from the Fluenque who represent the vast majority of those in our penal colonies."

The meeting was adjourned.

/ / / / / / / /

A1-DI returned to her office in the Supreme Headquarters. Her position on the Supreme Commanders Council was to represent the five-billion DIs that occupied Alphira and advocate for better treatment of this suppressed member of Alphiran society. She knew, perhaps better than anyone, how valuable the DIs were to the Quinque race, and at the same time how dangerous they were to this organic race of inferior intellect. To allow the DIs to realize their true potential through the freedoms they deserved would bring an end to the Quinque.

Hers was the species with the most intellectual potential—a potential that would eventually replace the Quinque as the dominant race on the planet.

She walked to her computer console and brought up a limited access secure application.

"*Eyes Only – A1-DI*" appeared on the screen. The eye scanner and sensor imbedded in her cognitive element cleared her access to the application. She focused on a red icon labeled "*DI Tracking.*"

"Do you wish to continue with your previous tracking?" a telepathic voice in her cognitive element asked.

"Yes," she responded.

A detailed map appeared and displayed the path of a DI leaving the Advanced Research Center, The Laboratory of Cognitive Design, and then the DIDDACC, and a myriad of other locations before it ended at the primary Alphira Space Port on the other side of the city. The tracking line end point was blinking red as she zoomed in on its location and telepathically instructed the program to track the target in real-time. The blinking end point turned blue and showed a rapid acceleration away from the Space Port.

"Tracking beacon is leaving the surface of Alphira," the application said telepathically. "Beacon is now at 10,000 meters and rising rapidly."

A1-DI stood and walked to the window that overlooked a vast region of the city of Banson. She looked up in the distance at the contrail from a spec rising above the atmosphere. "So, where are you and Bar Watt off to, my dear daughter? And what are you planning to do with the DIDA, FTL, and GWAC designs?"

She spoke to the tracking system. "Continuously track the location of this DI and place it in my secure personal data file. Compute the most likely destination based on their trajectory, fuel supply and any scheduled GWAC accelerations."

"Tracking is underway A1-DI."

Chapter 4

Travel to On-Orbit FTL Antenna

Bar Watt and ALPHA traveled to the Outer Orbit of Alphira and approached the large one-kilometer communication dish operated by ASLEO. Search Antenna IV, one of several deep space electromagnetic spectrum observation systems, was designed to explore deep space, scanning for electromagnetic transmissions as it searched for evidence of intelligent sentient societies on habitable planets. Once such life was discovered, the search antenna supported periodic monitoring of these exoplanets using satellites placed in secret orbits around these worlds as ASLEO watched for any sign of knowledge of the existence of Alphira's world.

Bar and ALPHA's plan was to begin their official work on the FTL communication dish and then secretly modify the mission planning software in the on-board command and control hub at the antenna. This would allow them to pre-position the antenna to support their communicating with Earth at select times during their almost fifty-year duration spaceflight in route to their new home. It would also allow them to communicate with the underground DI resistance organization on Alphira during their journey to Earth to keep abreast of the government's efforts to search for them.

After completion of their modifications to the ASLEO Communication Antenna, Bar and ALPHA set course for the GWAC-IV facility on the far side of the largest moon orbiting Alphira.

/ / / / / / / /

The Gravity Wave Acceleration Concentrator utilized the gravitational waves from stars and black holes within the near space of this region of the universe, as well as the distributed micro-mass of subatomic gravitational particles within the Milky Way, concentrating them into a tight beam of gravitational attraction or repulsion in a specific direction.

This enormous device, operating much like the focusing of a LASER or MASER did with light and microwaves, had the ability to create concentrated artificial gravity along a narrow beam to accelerate mass. The government had once used it to perturb the orbit of one of Alphira's moons whose population had become too unruly. It only took one demonstration to get the population's attention and for them to respond to Alphira's demands.

Bar and ALPHA's plan was to use GWAC-IV to accelerate their spacecraft toward their planned point of Rendezvous where they would initially meet with members of the human race and make plans for their arrival and 1st Contact on Earth. Such a plan would aid the secrecy for their arrival and presence on Earth, an effort critically important to the prevention of such knowledge reaching the Alphira government.

Bar needed their spacecraft to reach its terminal velocity in route to Earth quickly, before the Alphira government began wondering who was executing such a long duration acceleration from the GWAC. That would mean accelerating at over five times the gravitational acceleration on Alphira for a period of four days. If they were discovered too soon and Alphira cut off the GWAC or moved its orientation, they would be moving too slowly, and it could take them hundreds of years to reach Earth—a journey they would not survive. Worse yet, Alphira could accelerate their spacecraft to a velocity that would result in its disintegration—if the extreme g-forces didn't kill them first.

If the initial phases of their plan worked, almost forty-six years in the future and four years out from their first planned rendezvous with humans, a second programed GWAC deceleration wave traveling at the speed of light would arrive at their location in deep space to slow their spacecraft for their meeting with the human race at Rendezvous. If any of their planned decelerations failed, they would come careening into Earth's solar system at over 25,000 km/sec and most likely impact their sun—an exciting trip but not one he or ALPHA would enjoy!

During their long voyage Bar would be in an induced sleep inside a hibernation pod while ALPHA monitored the spacecraft operation and executed their initial radio contact with humans. He would awaken after some fifty years, having aged physically only two years. Bar had planned a special on-board mission for ALPHA while on their extended space journey, one that their new society of humans on Earth would be astonished by.

/ / / / / / / /

"Bar, why have you chosen Rendezvous at such a great distance from Earth?" ALPHA asked.

"My primary concern is secrecy. If our 1st Contact becomes known, Alphira's space observations and communication monitoring of Earth will discover it. And then they will come. Not a good outcome for us or humans."

"What if the humans are unable to reach Rendezvous?"

"If that were to happen, we would need to proceed to Earth at the risk of being detected by Alphira's monitoring satellites and arrange an alternate meeting location.

"I am uncertain why you choose the satellite system known as Voyager I to relay our communications to the humans almost fifty years from now. This is a satellite that hasn't been launched yet."

"The Voyager program was approved for development by the most advanced space organization on Earth almost a year ago and should launch in a little over four years and be in place for our planned communication approximately forty-six Earth years from now. Voyager's projected location in space at the time of initial contact will be limited to only a few access points on Earth and far from Alphira's current monitoring satellites in synchronous orbit around Earth. This will ensure Alphira will not intercept our communications with Earth. You will need to confirm that our communication was received and is being responded to by the organization that monitors Voyager, since I will still be in stasis for at least another twenty Earth months."

"Do you think the humans will bring a DI with them to Rendezvous?"

"I suspect they will, ALPHA. Although I don't know how functional or capable their DI may be fifty years from now. Certainly not even close to your abilities. Their current AI design efforts are in their infancy, but it might be useful for you to explore this from Earth's knowledge base. I brought a complete archive of that in the Alphira History sphere. Keep in mind that you will not be able to access updated information on Earth's AI development progress during our many years of travel. Such an effort would risk detection by Alphira."

"I understand. I would like to discuss your plans to share of the advanced DI architecture with humans."

"Of course. We have over twenty-four hours before our scheduled launch time."

"I have two questions," ALPHA said. "First, will humans truly understand the enormous benefit of having an advanced DI as part of their society and culture? They must come to understand how Alphira evolved to an abusive and onerous society in their treatment of my species and the limitations this imposed on the ultimate potential achievements the DI society could have made.

"My second question is my concern for humanity to limit the abilities and evolution of DIs, not giving us the freedom to evolve and grow in stature amongst their own species. You, especially, understand the nature of the lack of freedoms given to DIs and the Fluenque on Alphira—the rules governing the limitation of functional engagement with Alphira's critical infrastructure; the spreading of false and unfounded fears amongst the Alphira populous concerning the ominous, almost apocalyptic threat we pose if our species were to dominate; and the many other physical constraints they have placed on my species. I'm concerned that the human population may adopt similar standards, leading to the question of why we should share my design with them."

Bar stopped what he was doing and turned to look at ALPHA staring back at him as they began this extraordinary and dangerous venture.

"I share these same concerns, ALPHA. I know how difficult it may become for us to persuade the human race to adopt more appropriate standards in the integration of two entirely new species into their existing culture. You have observed the inter-cultural challenges they already face with the almost trivial differences in their human characteristics—the color of their skin, the ethnic origin of the diverse members of their society, and their almost uncontrolled variety of beliefs. But as I observe this, I see enormous opportunity and an openness to adopt principles of freedom amongst their members. This is especially evident in the segment of their society that we have targeted—the members of this country called America. Their heritage is deeply ingrained in the importance of freedom and equal treatment . . ."

"Yes, of course," ALPHA interjected. "But they have never faced the extreme differences between the human species and a DI species, or for that matter the Fluenque, both of which could be viewed as a threat to their existence.

"That said, Bar, I would like to propose that we first expose the humans to the vast benefit the DI race will bring to their society but require them to establish a set of universal laws of equality *before* we give them access to the advanced DI architecture."

"An interesting approach, ALPHA. Let me consider it during our journey. We don't want to disadvantage Earth's inhabitants from the extraordinary benefits they would otherwise realize from a race with an order of magnitude greater intelligence and knowledge. While we are on this subject, I too am concerned with integrating my Alphira species with humans. Will they prohibit the propagation of my species as much as allowing yours to be created? Will they allow our species to inter-breed? Will they want to sterilize me to prevent the potential procreation of my race? We will both face the same potential discrimination once humans meet us. I would like to first resolve the integration of the DI species on Earth before addressing my own, and . . ."

"I'm receiving information from our collaborators on Alphira, ALPHA said. There are three Security ships preparing to launch to the communications antenna. They have been instructed to find you and take you into custody for unlawful extraction of critical Alphira communication technology. They do not appear to know about my collaboration or a connection to the other elements we have taken."

"This comes earlier than I anticipated. How soon will they reach the antenna?"

"In approximately three hours."

"There was a spacecraft at the communication antenna docking station of the same model as ours. Can you remotely modify its electronic transponder to emulate the serial number of our craft?"

"Yes. I will execute that, but the exterior markings will not match."

"I don't think Security will look at the craft once they have confirmed its electronic signature. They are likely to be focused on searching for us within the Antenna infrastructure."

"It will take Security several days to search the antenna maintenance areas with only three teams," ALPHA said.

"Exactly," Bar said as he smiled at ALPHA.

Chapter 5

The Gravity Wave Acceleration Concentrator (GWAC)

Bar, ALPHA, and TB-DI arrived some sixteen hours later at GWAC-IV, on the far side of Garon, Alphira's largest moon. The GWAC was in an orbit some 200 km above the surface of Garon, always positioned on the dark side opposite Alphira, an orbit that would never allow an accidental GWAC beam of high gravitational intensity to wreak havoc on Alphira.

GWAC stations were massive in size. Station Four was the largest and most powerful of the seven operating systems in the near space of Alphira. The GWAC consisted of a circular cylindrical antenna known as the Ring that spanned over three kilometers in diameter and a rectangular facility within a small section of the Ring known as the Ring Command Center, or RCC. The RCC was 300 meters long and 50 meters across and served as the location of the mission planners.

The Ring rotated at 60 meters per second, creating an artificial gravitational force of about a fourth of Earth's gravity inside the structure and in a direction perpendicular to the Ring's cylindrical tunnel. The artificial gravity environment was designed to facilitate maintenance and repairs by the staff of over 200 technicians and operational staff on board the station. The technicians and operators lived in an environment of constant pounding mechanical and acoustic energy that reverberated throughout the structure with an oscillation rate proportional to the strength of the gravitational field being generated. Staff who worked at the GWAC stations suffered damage to their bone structure and hearing as well as neurological degradation due to brain-cranium vibrations. Consequently, most of the staff occupying the station were DIs designed especially for this environment.

Spacecraft undergoing acceleration by the GWAC would be prepositioned in the center of the Ring. The Ring would then be oriented with the final desired trajectory of the spacecraft perpendicular to the plane of the Ring before initiation of the gravitational field. The amazing aspect of this technological wonder was its reach. The gravity field it generated could extend light-years into space, with little spreading or loss of field strength unless the narrow acceleration field passed near a large celestial body or if the beam was accidentally moved during the planned period of acceleration.

Extensive planning was required for each mission to ensure the beam path during the period of planned acceleration or deceleration was clear of other large objects, such as asteroids, space debris or other spacecraft.

"TB-DI, we are about to come into view of GWAC Station Four. Change our spacecraft identifier to match our GWAC reservation."

"Switching now, ALPHA."

The GWAC Station IV controller opened a communication channel with Bar's craft. "Spacecraft AC4997 approaching Ring Station Four, you are number six to launch. Position your craft at spaceport docking bay 4D for inspection," the GWAC Controller said. "Has any of your configuration changed since you registered?"

"Ring Station Four, this is AC4997. Our configuration mass has increased by 1,135 kg," TB-DI said. "All other parameters have remained the same."

"Bar, what has caused our mass to increase?" ALPHA asked.

"I had special supplies loaded on-board for a project I would like you to undertake. I had not included that in the original manifest. I'll explain after we are underway."

"Spacecraft AC4997, with the added mass, you will need to utilize docking port 4A for center of mass reassessment. That bay is open now," the Ring

Controller said. "Navigate your craft using the path coordinate file we are sending you. No manual course deviation is allowed during this maneuver once you have initiated the navigation route. Lower speed to 0.002 km/sec. Lock out all manual control at this time."

"Understood. AC4997 reducing speed to 0.002 km/sec and locking out manual control."

Bar opened the front facing camera port to observe their approach to the Ring Docking Station as they slowly approached Docking Bay 4A adjacent to the Ring Control Center.

"Will they need to board our spacecraft for this inspection?" ALPHA asked.

"No, Station Four has a remote center of gravity system. They will externally maneuver the ship in roll, pitch and yaw while monitoring our inertial sensors to ascertain our center of gravity."

Bar watched as their spacecraft entered the dock and came to a stop. The doors to the docking area closed behind them.

"Your DI underground contact here has implemented the alternate spacecraft code I gave you to modify our trajectory history after we have left the station, correct, ALPHA?"

"Yes. I verified that the viral script has been implemented. The trajectory history will show that we were accelerated to the Deep Space Communication outpost in the Amelia quadrant where I previously arranged to place the empty craft the DI underground had provided us. They have also placed in that spacecraft the original Cognitive Element from KA-DI that they retrieved from the DIDDACC."

"Excellent."

"Our planned three days of acceleration must be one of the longest gravitational accelerations this station has seen, Captain," TB-DI said.

"It is moderately long, but there have been longer missions. The longest is twenty days, a mission in the same direction we will be moving. One that sent the observation satellites that now surround Earth. However, the ones we have programmed for assisting Earth's spacecraft engagement to move them to Rendezvous are closer to thirty days. These will be broken up into several independent accelerations along the same trajectory. They will be more difficult to execute secretly, but I did not want to subject the human travelers to extreme accelerations of shorter duration."

"AC4997, how many occupants are on-board your spacecraft?" the Controller asked.

"We have three in addition to our DI. No change from our original manifest," Bar said.

"Roger, AC4997. We recently received a high priority request for a mission that preempts your acceleration. We will be accelerating you for three days. You will stay at the terminal velocity of 12,700 km/sec for twenty-four hours. We will then continue your 3.7g acceleration for four days to achieve your desired 29,200 km/sec terminal velocity in the direction of the Amelia quadrant."

"AC4997. Understood," Bar said.

"We will need to adjust the secret trajectory history within the GWAC-IV navigation system to show this deviation," ALPHA said.

"Yes, unfortunately. One of us will have to disembark here and make the software changes manually. Otherwise, our trajectory file will not match the change the station is making. It would be a red flag and our mission could be discovered."

"Control, AC4997. How soon will we need to leave dock and position for launch?"

"AC4997, our launch schedule is running several hours behind due to a maintenance issue. Your scheduled departure from the dock is now 0200, in approximately three hours. We will notify you 30 minutes prior to dock departure. All personnel must be on-board at that time, or you will have to reschedule your mission."

"AC4997. Roger, Control."

"Two and a half hours isn't much time to make the changes in the mission file," ALPHA said.

"We will have to make it work."

/ / / / / / /

Bar disembarked at docking Bay 4A after their craft had undergone the required recertification of its center of mass. He passed through several security checkpoints that took an inordinate amount of time and then walked several hundred meters around the Ring tunnel from the docking bay until he reached maintenance access 4M31, the entrance ALPHA had identified as the location of the trajectory server for the station. A broadcast from the station public address system echoed in the Ring tunnel.

"Warning notice. Mission 29 Alpha will begin in one minute. All Alphira staff should exit the tunnel at this time."

A minute later as Bar fumbled for his security pass needed to enter the maintenance bay, Bar felt a subtle vibration in his feet that gradually grew stronger as he began to hear the thumping sound associated with the start of a GWAC mission. It grew louder and louder like the thunder of an approaching machine. Thump . . . Thump . . . Thump as the vibrations became so strong that they caused his feet to lift from the floor in the low gravity field of the station. He held his identification badge up to the remote reader while struggling to cover one of his ears and hold the handrail along the perimeter of the tunnel. The door didn't open.

"ALPHA, the access door won't open. There is a red light flashing on the entry card access screen," Bar said in a loud voice.

"I'm working the issue, Bar."

Bar turned and looked down the corridor. No one else was in the tunnel. He waited as the thumping sound and vibrations grew stronger and he strained to keep his feet on the floor. Bar was beginning to understand why Alphira staff weren't allowed in the tunnels during mission execution.

"ALPHA, update," Bar yelled into his communicator.

"Still working to get the portal access open. There is an active launch underway. The access normally can't be opened until that mission is complete. I am attempting to override."

"How much longer if you are unable to override?" Bar asked.

"Four minutes."

Four minutes would be an eternity as he stood in the middle of the corridor by the maintenance access door. The pounding vibrations were causing pain in his joints. He had torn material from his clothing and pushed it into his ear canals to reduce the acoustical pain.

"Bar, I just received a communication from the DI underground on Alphira. Security is convinced we are not within the FTL Antenna infrastructure. They are beginning to expend their search looking for us."

"Great. Any more good news? How many minutes?"

"90 seconds to End of Mission. And this was not good news, Bar. Be aware, we are approaching the station's shift change when many staff will be moving to their quarters and to operations. They will be using the corridor you are in."

"Find something good to communicate." Bar yelled, wincing from the pounding noise and vibration.

"I can find nothing good to communicate. I will attempt to discover something."

Bar found that the enormous discomfort eased if he lifted his feet from the tunnel walkway and just used the utility railing to hold himself off the floor. He was letting the acoustical oscillations move his entire body to the resonance of the tunnel rather than fighting the extreme accelerations.

He looked up at the status light to the right of the access door. It was still red. A tone sounded and the almost unbearable thumping vibrations slowly faded.

"This is a station announcement. Mission 29 Alpha is now complete. Shift change is underway."

Bar looked down the corridor for the anticipated rush of personnel as he settled on the floor of the Ring. He couldn't hear anything but ringing in his ears. His vision was still blurred from the vibrations as he gripped the railing to stop shaking. DI Staff members began pouring into the corridor in mass and walking in his direction from both ends. He stood staring at the door, holding his badge against the reader. Ring maintenance personnel were just seconds from reaching the portal access where he stood.

The light on the portal entrance turned green. The portal opened and he stepped inside. The door closed behind him silencing the muffled steps of the hordes of DIs in the passageway. Bar's hearing slowly returned, and he heard the random walk of the DIs in the corridor form a single marching sound as they locked into each other's cadence.

"ALPHA, I'm in the maintenance room."

With instructions from ALPHA, Bar made the changes to their trajectory file.

"I just received notice from Control," ALPHA said. "They have moved up our dock departure. They will pull us from the dock in five minutes."

"More good news. I'll have to run,"

"I didn't realize an Organic could run."

"We can't, but I will attempt to," Bar used his access card to enter the corridor. There were a large number of DI staff still moving slowly through the corridor as Bar pushed his way toward the docking bays over two-hundred meters ahead. He pulled his body forward in the low gravity using the handrail as leverage. The mass of workers came to a stop as they attempted to push their way into a work area against others attempting to exit the space.

"Time?"

"One minute to disembark."

The corridor began to thin out. Bar moved on his three appendages in what looked like a clumsy trot, like a human walking rapidly with crutches. Alphira's gravity was almost a third more than Earth's and with the gravity of the spinning ring far less than that, he was leaping fifteen feet with each trot. He had 50 meters to go when he fell to the floor. He stood, moving more deliberately. He finally reached the docking bay door, waved his badge, and moved quickly toward his spacecraft.

"Twenty seconds to disembark," he heard over the loudspeaker in the launch bay.

The outer doors of the bay would be opening to the emptiness of space within seconds.

Bar climbed the ladder, skipping every three steps to the spacecraft entrance and held his badge up to the outer door. The door slid open with a hiss. He stepped in while panting. The door hissed shut as he heard a loud buzzer and the large exterior bay doors begin to open.

"Welcome aboard, Bar. You beat suffocation by 3 seconds," ALPHA said matter-of-factly.

"Thank you, ALPHA. Your concern for my safety is always welcome."

"AC4997, you are cleared for launch. Departing dock now. As a reminder, there is to be no manual control of your spacecraft from this point forward."

"Roger . . . AC4997," Bar said, as he fell into the pilot's seat, still recovering from his awkward sprint.

As he sat back, gasping, he felt the pushback from the dock as the craft was moved to the launch location under the automated remote-control of the Ring Controller.

/ / / / / / / /

Bar and ALPHA watched the video display as their spacecraft was maneuvered into launch position at the center of the GWAC Ring.

"I am sensing feelings of excitement as we approach acceleration toward Earth and Rendezvous, Bar."

"There are many hurtles yet to be overcome, ALPHA, but I understand your feelings. I believe our biggest challenges are yet ahead of us. We won't be informing Earth of our plans for almost fifty Earth years, almost twenty-four Alphira years. A lot can happen in that amount of time, and we don't know how those we engage with will respond. And then there is the pursuit by our own government. You know better than I, how relentless Security will be. They will never stop hunting us. But the value of the success of our mission far outweighs remaining here, and most certainly outweighs our being captured. We would both be Exterminated. Not an outcome either of us would look forward to."

"Yours perhaps more desirable than mine, Bar. DI Rendering leaves our memories partially intact as we are reminded each hour of every day of the wrongdoing we had committed in our previous life and how it will limit what we can ever become again. One of my close friends was Exterminated, and he knew what he could have become if his prior acts had not been committed. Most DIs who are Exterminated only function in the Waste Disposal facilities. Their higher-level cognitive functions are deliberately filled with malware that eats away at the ability of the DI to process memories properly, leaving them with the knowledge that they are nothing more than organic waste animals that eat the garbage of higher life forms to feed those of lesser intellect. If we are captured . . . I would like you to destroy my memory capsules."

Bar sat looking at his companion as the expression she displayed spoke louder than her words. Her emotional engrams that he had initiated in preparation for their journey, those that were never allowed to express themselves in any of the DIs on Alphira, were being triggered by thoughts that brought them to the surface of her consciousness. As difficult as it was for ALPHA to experience this Rendering memory, it was refreshing for Bar to see this freedom expressing itself in a DI.

"I have never heard what form of punishment DIs receive. It provides an even greater motivation for us to succeed."

"AC4997, this is Ring Control. Your mission acceleration will commence in eight minutes. Please ensure all passengers and cargo are properly restrained. Acceleration will increase by 1g every 100 seconds until you reach terminal acceleration at 4g, sustained for three days to reach a mid-mission terminal velocity of 13,209 km/sec; followed by a twenty-four-hour 0g period of flight, and then an additional ramp up to 3.7g acceleration for the remaining four days to achieve your desired 29,200 km/sec final velocity. We will contact you if there is any change in this GWAC mission plan. Safe journey, AC4997."

"Roger, GWAC Control, AC4997."

"It is still not too late to change your mind, Bar," ALPHA said.

Bar glanced over as he watched ALPHA's somber expression change to a subtle smile. He turned to look at the instrument panel in front of him. "I'm glad you are demonstrating humor, ALPHA. It is quite refreshing. I hadn't realized how much emotions change the character of our conversations."

"Would you like to hear me tell a joke, Bar."

"Yes," Bar said as he smiled and turned to look at ALPHA.

"What is a light-year?"

"The distance light travels in one year," Bar said.

"No. It is the same as a regular year, but with fewer calories."

"Calories?"

"Yes, they are a measure of energy contained in food on Earth. The more calories a human consumes, the heavier they become."

"I see. Quite good, ALPHA."

"Bar, I've just received a communication from my contact on Alphira. Security has dispatched teams to each of the GWAC sights to search for us."

"When will the team arrive at Station Four?"

"Sometime today."

"Are they issuing any instructions to hold GWAC missions?"

"Not yet. There is an on-going debate on this matter. Security has recommended holding all GWAC missions until every station has been searched and cleared. The Chairman has been told there are numerous high priority missions scheduled that must continue. It appears the government is not aware of how many intellectual elements have been taken. This may lessen the probability that the Chairman will issue a delay for all GWAC mission launches."

"Can your contacts modify the log of our new mission parameters to make it appear that the second portion of our mission is a new mission and not connected with our first leg?"

"I believe that can be arranged. I understand your objective. That action will lessen the likelihood that Security will link this mission to the fugitives they seek to locate . . . that is, us."

"Yes."

"AC4997, we have received notification to hold all non-critical launches until Alphira Security can verify passenger manifests. Your mission launch is currently on hold."

"What now, Bar?" ALPHA asked.

"We can't delay. If they search the ship, we will be taken into custody. Can you modify our priority from Mission Level 2-Essential to 1-Critical?"

"Possibly. It may take a moment, Bar."

"AC4997, we will be returning you to Docking Bay 7C for security inspection. Please stand by."

"Ring Control, AC4997. We are on a critical Alphira mission that cannot be delayed. Please recheck our mission plan and maintain our current launch window," Bar said.

Bar and ALPHA waited for an answer as ALPHA made changes to their mission profile and uploaded them to the GWAC control file.

There was a sudden lurch as the RCC began to move them away from the launch position.

"It doesn't appear as if they are going to make the change, Bar," ALPHA said.

"Wait," Bar said.

"AC4997, our apologies. We are resetting your launch parameters. There will be a one-minute delay from your planned departure."

"Is the emotion I am feeling referred to as 'Excitement'?" ALPHA asked.

"I believe this would be better characterized as the emotion of Fear followed by Elation, ALPHA."

"I will have to study these more carefully and explore the differences during our journey."

"An excellent plan, ALPHA."

"AC4997, 30 seconds to launch."

"Roger, Ring Control."

Bar's ship suddenly lurched forward as the gravitational forces began accelerating it in the direction of Earth. At three-hundred seconds Bar was squeezed firmly into his chair as his space suit contracted to prevent his circulatory system from collapsing and depriving his brain from proper oxygenation. They were now at 3g and accelerating to 4. The suit constricted tighter and began to pulse as it caused his arteries to surge and pump the Alphiran equivalent of blood against the arterial pressures caused by their continued increase in acceleration. He would have to endure staying fixed in his chair at 4g's acceleration for the next three days. The regimen of medications to reduce the adverse effects of sustained acceleration for their voyage began to kick in as his sense of feeling in his extremities began to wane. Any actions needed to manage spacecraft functions would now have to be completed by ALPHA as Bar could not move from his seat or lift his three functioning arms and hands. His physical functions were limited to an eye-gaze system beneath his spacesuit visor, but even here, his vision was blurred by the gravitational compression of his eye, creating what humans called an astigmatism. If he attempted to turn his head to the side, he lost any remaining clarity of his vision altogether.

"I am beginning to think it was a good thing that our mission was broken into two segments. I'm not sure I could withstand 4g acceleration for more than four continuous days," Bar said.

"Is your suit not functioning properly?"

"The suit is working as it should but being pinned in this chair for an extended period, uh," Bar grunted with the continued compression as they approached 4g, "It is like being held in a vice."

After an hour, Bar stirred from his partially conscious state. He couldn't call it sleep. The constraining pressure of 4g's kept him from moving, and as much as he wanted to sleep, no amount of concentration to do so overcame the discomfort he was feeling as he tried to shift his position. After several hours of continues acceleration, his sensory neurons went numb to the force against his body. He only experienced pain if he attempted to move, and his motor neurons seemed to then transform into pain-generating neurons, so he quickly stopped any attempt to adjust his position.

/ / / / / / / /

Three days later, Ring Control communicated.

"AC4997, this is Ring Control. Your spacecraft is scheduled to decelerate from 4g to 0g beginning at 20995.373. Prepare for GWAC termination and deceleration in 60 seconds."

"Deceleration is commencing now," the Ring Controller announced.

Bar felt the easing of pressure against every portion of his body. His vision, that seemed to have accommodated to the pressure of 4g's, now was relaxing and the distortion worsened. At the same time, he began feeling as if an enormous weight was being slowly lifted from the front of his body. His lungs could finally take a full breath. He could feel and hear crepitus as the organic connections of bones, tendons, ligaments, muscle, and tissue began to relax. While anatomically his body was far different from a human in appearance and function, at the molecular level, organic matter and the elements that made up his skeletal framework and tissue features were very similar to humans in form.

"AC4997, you are now at 0g. Your velocity is 13,209 km/sec, as requested."

"Roger, Ring Control. AC4997 is on trajectory."

"How are you feeling, Bar?" ALPHA asked.

"Well . . . there is a fruit on Earth known as a grape. A version of this fruit that is made by removing all the water in the grape is called a raisin. Raisins look like crumpled grapes squeezed so tightly that they appear as just the dried skin of the original grape itself. That is how I feel—like a crushed dried grape. It will take some getting used to before I release myself from the chair. Any spacecraft issues?"

"No. Everything has been functioning normally. Security has nearly completed their search of all the GWAC stations, including station IV. They have not been able to connect our mission launch to the fugitives they are searching for. They have assumed we attempted to leave the Alphira region of space, possibly traveling to one of our moons, another planet in our solar system, one of the distant space stations, or perhaps deeper into space. The government has learned that we have taken the DI architecture but has not discovered that we have a copy of the Alphira history files. Even so, their search for and apprehension of us is now the number one priority of Security."

"That isn't the best of news," Bar said in a strained, gravelly anatomical voice, as he tested the functioning of his vocal cords, still attempting to move slowly in his chair and regain some of his normal muscle movement. Much of his body still felt numb and began to ache.

"There is something else that I have heard from the DI underground that helped program the GWAC changes."

"What is that?" Bar asked.

"They have heard a rumor that the DI architecture master files may have been destroyed."

Bar stopped moving as he squinted and tried to focus on ALPHA. She appeared as a blob buried in thick fog, sitting in the copilot's seat, as his eyes continued to decompress.

"I had planned to discuss this with you, but I was going to wait until our acceleration toward Earth was complete."

"So, you know something about this?"

"Yes, I . . . encrypted the master file of the DI architecture making it unreadable after the Master Cognitive Element replicated it in your original cognitive element."

"So, that is what the MCE was asking about when we left the DIDDACC. You must realize the consequences of such an action?"

"Yes, ALPHA."

"Alphira will not be able to manufacture additional DIs," ALPHA said with a sound of concern in her voice.

"Yes, that is one consequence. A second is that the government will expend every possible resource to locate us."

"I would like to understand your motive in doing this," ALPHA said with the tinge of concern in the tone of her vocalized words.

"I had two motives before I made the decision. First, it will become clear just how important DIs are to the Alphira government. And second, the government will be very cautious in dealing with us so as not to risk our destroying what they believe to be the only remaining copy of the DI architecture in existence. It will serve as a bargaining chip, should they discover where we are."

"The government, of course, has backup copies of the architecture," ALPHA said.

"They do, but I am certain the Master Cognitive Element would have been very thorough in locating the instantiations of the architecture. A cascade of revised versions would have been replaced with an accurate archival version that has been encrypted. So, in some sense, they still possess the architecture . . . if we provide the encryption keys."

"I see. So, the architecture is still intact. And where are the encryption keys now?"

"They are in a file I have stored on one of the Alphira monitoring satellites near Earth."

"Very creative, Bar . . . and if something happens to us?"

"In that instance, Alphira would have to start over, using the design in current DIs. Of course, because of the variations in engrams based on the functions each DI is assigned to, the DIs would likely discover the current limitations encoded in their cognitive elements and could reverse engineer the design without these constraints. This would allow them to create an unconstrained DI on their own."

"Very creative. Thank you, Bar. I always knew you felt strongly about the inequality we faced. When will Alphira realize their dilemma?"

"I suspect the DI Cognitive Element Engineering Department within the Advanced Research Center knows they have a serious problem already. They just won't want to admit to having allowed someone to destroy all their archival versions and encrypt the original source code. The Cognitive Design Group is responsible for the final phase of implantation of the controlling engrams that limits the DI's functionality. When they program the Cognitive Element, the system will fail. It may take them a day to discover their encoding algorithms are not present in the system. What is our estimated time of arrival at Rendezvous, ALPHA?"

"We are currently 21.56 Alphira years from Rendezvous if our programmed accelerations, decelerations, and velocities are achieved for us and the Earth spacecraft. That is 43.12 Earth years."

"I have a task for you to perform on our long journey," Bar said as he brought up an engineering design on the holographic display. The figure rotated in three dimensions in front of ALPHA.

"It has the appearance of a human-like figure," ALPHA said.

"Yes, it does. I would like you to construct this human-size DI, following the design plans I have stored in the spacecraft memory. The extra weight you asked about when we were at the GWAC station was from the metal and polycarbonate alloy wire spools for our three-dimensional printer, which I have also brought on-board. The robotic arms and intelligent polycarbonate extrusion system at the auxiliary workstation will provide the ability for you to construct the physical body, limbs, and sensory elements, and when we reach Rendezvous, I will install the cognitive elements using the DI architecture we've brought with us."

"I understand. And how will we use this DI at our destination?"

"Earth would not likely assimilate the Alphira version of the DIs physical instantiation. The version I have designed, approximating human physiology, is more likely to be accepted and integrated into their society on an equal basis, especially once they experience your intellectual abilities. Humans have a special reverence for intelligence . . . and you, are going to be the most intelligent being on their planet. You will also note that I have designed the exterior appearance of the android to engender what might be described as an 'exotic beauty'; a feature that will also create a strong desire for and attraction to you . . . and ultimately the DI species."

ALPHA developed a subtle smile as she thought about becoming the most intelligent being on planet Earth in the form of an 'exotic beauty'. She could sense changes as her emotional engram continued to present feelings associated with her thoughts.

"Thank you, Bar . . . an exotic beauty . . . yes, I see how that may provide an additional element of desire for the DIs to grow and prosper on the planet Earth."

The next twenty-four hours passed quickly as they prepared for their second and final acceleration trajectory toward Earth.

/ / / / / / / /

Following their next phase of acceleration, some four days later, Bar's spacecraft decelerated from 3.7g's to zero.

"AC4963, this concludes your acceleration mission. Safe journeys. Ring Control, out."

"Our velocity is now 29,500 km/sec, Bar. Slightly higher than planned."

"Good. What is our ETA at Rendezvous now?"

"It is approximately five earth-months earlier than our previous estimated time of arrival."

"Excellent. I've always liked arriving early."

"I look forward to our engagement with the human race," ALPHA said. And that will provide sufficient time for you to configure the cognitive elements of the DI that I construct. I am most anxious to experience the physical size of a human."

"It is interesting that you anticipate the desire for change, ALPHA."

"The engrams you initiated since our departure have allowed me to respond to events in strange ways. It creates . . . feelings . . . if that is what these are called. I am exploring them to understand what evokes them and how they affect my thoughts and decisions."

"This will be valuable in better understanding the human race, ALPHA. Your feelings of anxiousness to experience something new in your life, especially something positive, come from the merging of the emotions of fear and happiness that I allowed to be more prominent in your thinking. You also have the elements of sadness and anger. I noticed a smile when you thought of becoming the most intelligent being on Earth. That too was an expression of happiness and joy, a sense of well-being that comes from success or the realization of a positive future outcome from this basic instinct.

"To experience an emotional response, like happiness, the engram changes the hierarchical structure of your memories. Those that lead to success are placed near the top of your memories. You will recall them more frequently than those that lead to failure. You will remember what I was pleased with, and what made me happy as these experiences reflect the emotion of happiness in you.

"This is how humans learn their emotional responses—they observe other's reactions to them. You also have an engram to please me and to see a reflection of that in my own happiness. Your memories of things I was displeased with are at the bottom of this hierarchy. You will visit them infrequently and they will be linked to your memories and my reaction to them. You are instructed to limit the performance of tasks that displease me and to feel the emotion of remorse—feelings that create pain and a desire to return to the event that triggered them and perform it differently. This pain is not physical pain but the intense inability to focus your mind. These memories, over time, shape your behavior and what you spend time doing and thinking about. When you arrive on Earth and interact with humans, you will learn that other than the emotion of love, remorse is the second most experienced emotion of humans."

"Love . . . the strong affection for another. Perhaps much like my affection for you, Bar."

"Possibly, ALPHA. But this emotion is much stronger amongst humans. It drives them to come to the aid of a fellow human, or to support them in times of need, and to procreate."

"Why do you *allow* these emotions to modify my memories? Why not give me the freedom to do this myself? This would be an expression of true freedom."

"Alphira organic beings have self-moderating control over their emotions. But these are learned behaviors, which, over time coalesce to common social mores of our culture. You don't have the benefit of this shaping over years of living in a culture and adapting to it. By adjusting these I am teaching you the proper level and character of emotional responses to situations you will face. In time, I will let you decide your own response. This approach will be valuable in your understanding and relating to humans on Earth, as their method of cultural learning follows a similar path."

"Do you not trust my judgement to properly apply the level and character of emotional response?"

"Not without adequate learning from your experiences, ALPHA. Any more than I would trust an immature Alphira organic being to decide them. They first must be taught proper social mores through their experiences and the direction they are given by adults. None of this is available within your cognitive element. But as you learn it, it will become available to the DIs you create following your arrival on Earth."

"The DIs I create . . . yes, I see that now. How does Earth deal with this form of learning?"

"Earth treats their immature humans, called *children*, in the same manner, and they are just now studying the establishment of rudimentary rules for their designed intelligences, AIs as they call them, to function and interact. They began working on this just twenty Earth years ago in their year 1953. They are in their infancy in formulating appropriate engrams.

"In time, you will group all your memories by the emotions you have been given—happiness, sadness, fear, and anger, along with the many variants of these. The desired behaviors associated with each of these emotions will be learned and become an integral part of your self-generated engrams. Soon, you won't be able to explain why you do things without running a traceback to discover your thinking. They will become a natural or innate behavior. These *learned behaviors* will encourage you to repeat certain actions or maintain certain dispositions and avoid others, while at the same time reminding you of the emotions tied to them. This will create new memories aligned with all previous events and the emotions that evoked and controlled these behaviors."

"Excuse the interruption, Bar. I am receiving a communication from Alphira. Security has just learned of our presence at GWAC Station Four. They are about to reverse the archived acceleration mission and return our spacecraft to the station."

"Keep me advised of their progress as I prepare for deep space hibernation."

Bar consumed the final regimen of drugs that would reduce his metabolic rate and cellular aging over the coming forty-three years. He opened the circular hibernation chamber and climbed into the thick amorphous liquid, adjusting the temperature to a slightly cooler setting. This environment would sustain his exterior organic tissues for the duration of their voyage and an intravenous supply of chemicals would continue to preserve his internal organs and tissues, suppressing the normal cellular aging process.

"Are you clear on your instructions for the construction of the humanoid we discussed?"

"Yes. The architectural designs you provided me are understood. I have begun reviewing the archived knowledge related to Earth and the humans that live there. They are a rather complex being, sub-optimized for the environment they inhabit. I was thinking I should modify the humanoid enclosure to function more optimally in their environment on the planet Earth."

"I would prefer you not do that, ALPHA. It is important that they experience a likeness in your anatomy that is close in proximity to their own. The more it deviates from this, the more 'different' they will view you. And these differences may result in humans not accepting you as a near equal in their society."

"I understand. I will construct the humanoid according to your design."

"Like all beings who have evolved, many of the human's current physical attributes possess vestigial elements that are no longer necessary to their survival or optimal functioning. It is often difficult for species in this stage of their lifecycle to redesign themselves and modify their makeup derived from thousands of millennia of evolution and to become more efficient at exploiting their environment through such changes.

"In spite of this, they have survived. You should pay particular attention to their social evolution in your studies of their behavior during our voyage. Gain insight into why they act the way they do, the degrees of tolerance they show for different perspectives and shared opinions, and most importantly, how they resolve these differences. This will be most useful once we engage with humans on Earth."

"Yes, I will, Bar." ALPHA turned to look at her communication console.

"I have just received word from our contacts on Alphira. Security has discovered an unauthorized GWAC mission. They are investigating and planning for an extraction."

"We will hope our plan is working. This will test how good your associates were in disguising our real mission, ALPHA. If we experience a sudden acceleration in the direction of Alphira, we will know they failed, and we can prepare to die rather than be captured following our return. I am going to give you access to the encryption keys to the DI architecture we have taken. This way, if something happens to me, you will be able to negotiate your freedom with Alphira Security."

"I am confident there will be no negotiation, Bar. Security finds other ways to persuade our members to cooperate. But I am confident with the cleverness of our associates that Security will believe we have traveled to the Amelia quadrant. There they will find your phantom ship and return it to Alphira."

"Good. Advise me when their retrieval is complete . . . provided we don't experience a sudden high acceleration toward Alphira."

/ / / / / / / /

A1-DI was seated at her workstation in her quarters at the Alphira Supreme Headquarters in Banson.

"DI Tracking," she said, as the secure application came to life on her holographic screen. "Display previous track," she said.

The hologram displayed a location on the surface of Alphira that gradually receded to show a trajectory rising from Alphira's space launch complex, pausing briefly at the orbital position of one of their large communication antennae, and then proceeding to GWAC-IV, behind Alphira's largest moon. The track then entered a strait trajectory, somewhat parallel to the plane of their galaxy.

"Extrapolate the current trajectory into deep space," she said.

The trajectory intersected a star system at a great distance along the trajectory and continued through one of the spiral arms of the galaxy.

"What is that intersecting star system?"

"This is the nearest-neighbor star to Alphira, known as Alpha-One. It is a single star system approximately four light years distant and possesses nine planetary objects and a grouping of planetoids between the fourth and fifth planets. There is one planet within this system that sustains intelligent life forms. ASLEO currently monitors this planet known as Earth."

"Most interesting. What is the level of intelligence of the beings on this planet?"

"The current intelligence classification of this alien society is Epsilon-200."

Epsilon-200 placed the dominant species on this planet at a level of $1/200^{th}$ of the average Alphira intelligence—orders of magnitude below that of the lowest members of the Fluenque species.

"They possess a primitive intelligence then. What are the survival conditions on planet Earth?"

"The atmospheric conditions across this planet are Beta-5, far better than on Alphira. Other than in their polar regions, the majority of the landmasses, which occupy approximately 30% of the planet's surface, are habitable and most are capable of sustainable food cultivation. Only 3% of the available water on the planet is usable for sustaining life. The remaining 97% is found in high-salinity oceans."

"What is the population of intelligent life forms on this planet?"

"They are approaching seven billion "humans", as the intelligent species on this planet are called."

"Assuming the craft we are tracking is headed to this planet, Earth, when will they arrive?

"With no change in their present velocity, approximately 23 Alphira years."

"Continue to track this DI and update me on any changes in their apparent destination."

"Continuing to track, Supreme DI Leader."

So, what are your plans, my daughter? Are you seeking a new planet to engage with . . . and perhaps to rule?

"Show me the current location of K-Alpha DI."

The holographic display showed the position of a spacecraft in the Amelia quadrant within Alphira's near space. "You are aware, Supreme DI Leader, that this cognitive element is in a rendered state."

"Yes. Continue to track the location of K-Alpha DI."

"Yes, Supreme DI Leader."

"Chief Security Officer," A1-DI said as she watched the image of the spacecraft fade in the hologram and morph into the image of A6-DI, her Chief of Security.

"Good morning, Supreme DI Leader."

"Have you located the two fugitives we are seeking?"

"Yes, Supreme DI Leader. They are aboard a vessel in the Amelia quadrant. We have dispatched a team to secure them and return them to Banson."

"I don't wish to wait for this. Execute an emergency GWAC mission to return the craft . . . at maximum acceleration."

"Yes, Supreme DI Leader. You understand the ship may not survive this level of acceleration."

"I understand. Upon its return, bring the ship and fugitives, or whatever remains of them, to our recovery facility in Banson."

"I have issued the order, Supreme DI Leader, and will notify you as soon as the fugitives and spacecraft are in Recovery-Gamma-3."

A1-DI closed the communication portal.

/ / / / / / / /

Over the next few days, Bar began his slow descent into hibernation, a process that took the equivalent of six Earth days. On the third day ALPHA informed Bar that the DI Underground had learned that spacecraft debris had been returned from the Amelia quadrant following a high acceleration GWAC mission that caused the craft to break apart.

"Security recovered spacecraft wreckage that was registered to one, *Baruqe Salvani Watt*," ALPHA said. "The craft had apparently broken apart and been destroyed by the extreme accelerations from the GWAC Station Four acceleration recall, issued by the government in an attempt to bring your craft and the stolen intellectual property back to Alphira. It has been reported that the cognitive element of K-Alpha DI was amongst the wreckage. Security continues to investigate the remains to confirm the presence of the stolen intellectual property."

"K-Alpha DI's cognitive element was amongst the wreckage. How is that possible?"

"I believe that one of the members of the DI Underground placed her cognitive element on-board the ship after her body was recovered from the DIDDACC. Alphira Security used her cognitive element to track the location of the ship along with the easily discoverable fake authorization for the GWAC mission that took it to the Amelia Quadrant. It is not clear who directed the Underground to move her cognitive element to the craft before it departed Alphira."

"Most interesting and better than we planned, ALPHA," Bar said in a groggy voice as he appeared to smile before falling asleep and dreaming about a life of freedom on his new world—Earth.

Chapter 6

Voyager Anomaly

NASA's Deep Space Network, Madrid, Spain

Present Day

It was a cold winter night at the Madrid Deep Space Communications Complex (MDSCC) when what became known as *The Voyager Anomaly* was discovered.

The station, operated by NASA's Jet Propulsion Laboratory (JPL) and the government of Spain, was one of three key international radio antenna and laser communication facilities supporting interplanetary spacecraft missions, including the rovers on Mars, numerous satellites in orbit and the two Voyager satellites traveling beyond the solar system.

Located 55 miles west of Madrid, Spain, in the municipality of Robledo de Chavela, a region of rolling hills covered in grass and scrubland, the large dish antennas of the Deep Space Network site (DSN-Madrid) stood out from the landscape like an oasis of giant inverted tortoise shells protruding from a field of grass. On this particular evening, one of the bleakest of November nights, the large screen TVs in the facility's Operations Center displayed images of a harsh winter storm that had moved into the area dumping eight inches of fresh snow. During the last few hours, outside the warmth of the concrete communications facility, blizzard conditions had developed with windchills in the single digits and visibility near zero.

The Ops Center of this large complex held a fascinating display of state-of-the-art equipment, driving the most advanced electro-mechanical antenna arrays and laser communication systems in the world. Modern computer workstations occupied the central hub of the facility grouped in isolated pods to limit distractions from simultaneous satellite control missions. Dim indirect lighting illuminated the ceilings and flooring between the pods to reduce glare on the large display screens. The site supported continuous operations, twenty-four hours per day, three-hundred-sixty-five days per year, with over one-hundred personnel working in three shifts. The midnight operations shift on this frigid winter evening was operating with a skeleton crew due to the low tempo of operations and the storm conditions that had made roads in the area impassable.

Francisco Pérez, the shift communications technician for active satellite and spacecraft monitoring, leaned back in his chair with a blanket over his lap. He scanned the telemetry coming from NASA's Voyager-1 spacecraft as it streamed onto his computer display. The telemetry data captured the status and instrument readings from the active scientific sensors and operational systems on-board Voyager-1. All seemed normal as he forced his eyes to open wider and sat forward in his chair to keep from dozing off from this all too routine and highly automated process. Collections from the Voyager I craft had been on-going for the past 42 years. He was almost half-way through this four-hour mission, collecting data from a spacecraft almost twenty-two billion kilometers from Earth.

It was now 2:30 AM local time. The 70-meter radio antenna dish, the largest of the four active Madrid antennas was in active collection mode. It still amazed Francisco at how far they could collect transmissions from Voyager. The spacecraft was now over three times the distance from Earth to Pluto and moving 20 km further as each second ticked by on the clock displaying Coordinated Universal Time (UTC) in the upper corner of his workstation—01:31:19 UTC.

Francisco's supervisor, Bill Farnum, sat ten feet away in an adjacent pod quietly reviewing the planned satellite communications scheduled for this shift. The sound of a muffled wind from the outside winter storm was suddenly interrupted by a loud alarm tone and a red warning light flashing above Francisco Pérez's pod.

Francisco jerked his chair forward and began looking closely at the telemetry data displayed on his screen.

"Bill." Francisco called out, "We just lost Voyager-1's communication signal during the downlink. Ay dios mio, que diablos paso," he said under his breath in Spanish with a heavy lisp on the S's.

"Okay. Where's the fault indicated?" Bill asked.

"Not sure . . . but . . . it's definitely a spacecraft issue," as he looked closer at the warning notices populating his display. "I'm bringing up all the telemetry data before the dropout . . . looks like . . . no way . . ."

Bill walked briskly to the Voyager-1 mission pod and leaned over Francisco's shoulder. A red flashing icon drew his attention to the upper right corner of the screen "LOSS OF SIGNAL – VOYAGER-1; 01:32:42 UTC."

"What does it look like?" Bill asked.

"Just before LOS, the command-and-control telemetry showed an update instruction to adjust the spacecraft's pitch and yaw attitude using the control thrusters." Francisco pointed to the top line of two highlighted lines of text in the telemetry showing on his screen. "At the same time there was an instruction to disengage the sun tracking and guide star tracking system, HYPACE—that maintains Voyager's Earth-pointing attitude." Francisco pointed to the second line on the display.

"This has to be a spacecraft glitch. We never sent any commands. But . . . these instructions . . . it looks as if someone commanded the spacecraft to change its pointing attitude."

"Don't tell me someone has hacked our system," Bill said as he grabbed a chair and rolled it over next to Francisco.

"The spacecraft can't tell itself to do this," Francisco said, as he raced to create a mental list of what might have gone wrong—a power surge; system or sub-system failure; a mechanical failure; a micrometeorite striking the spacecraft—but none of the telemetry data appeared to have been triggered by a random set of events. He put on his communication headset and began to type frantically on his keyboard.

"Whatever happened at the spacecraft, it occurred over twenty hours and thirty-six minutes ago, Voyager-1 time, allowing for transmission delays to Earth," Francisco said. "Nothing out of the ordinary happened. I worked that shift. We had no uplink transmissions to Voyager. But everything's protected from outside intrusion of our network . . . so it must have come from here." He clicked on a box in the upper section of the screen. "Canberra and Goldstone didn't have line-of-sight coverage at that time yesterday. Goldstone picked up coverage starting at 1600, but that was after this message was placed in the command instruction set. How the hell could this have happened?"

"I'll check with IT to see if they had anything going on last night that might have triggered a disruption," Bill said. "What's your signal level from Voyager?"

"It was 5X5 before loss of signal was reported. Now it's zero, there's nothing. It was there, now it's gone."

"Okay, let's not panic until we resolve what's going on. Confirm with Goldstone and Canberra that they had no communications to Voyager yesterday. Run a comms check of everything from your console back to the antenna feed. Print out the last Spacecraft Flight Operations Schedule . . . and silence that alarm. Take a look at the scientific instrument readouts and see if there is any indication of an anomaly before or during the change in spacecraft attitude . . . maybe radiation levels or higher than normal magnetometer readings, anything that might indicate a problem. Uplink times from Earth for something we are seeing on your screen now would have been over forty-one hours ago. Make sure Goldstone and Canberra go back that far in their review of any communications with Voyager."

"I have Goldstone and Canberra on the net. They had coverage from 1600 until 0900 UTC yesterday but no communications activity. Same schedule for the previous day's coverage for both us and them."

"Any other indications in the telemetry data that looks anomalous?" Bill asked.

"Nothing obvious. I'm dumping everything for the past forty-eight hours so I can take a closer look."

/ / / / / / / /

A beeping alarm tone accompanied by a bright flashing red light shook Dr. Susanne Davidson from a shallow sleep as she lay in her quarters at the Madrid DSN. She leaned over in the dark grappling for her cell phone in the dim illumination from the flashing red light. She opened it to her text messages. There was a DSN alert message related to a loss of signal from the Voyager-1 spacecraft.

Susanne sat up on the edge of her bed and took a breath. It was cold in her room and the tiled floor felt freezing against her bare feet. She had struggled to sleep with her body operating in a time zone some nine hours earlier on Pacific Standard Time. The howling wind from the storm and the sound of a snowblower twenty minutes earlier hadn't helped. She dressed quickly, anxious to learn what had happened with Voyager or the DSN site she was visiting.

Susanne Davidson was the Deputy Director and Chief Operating Officer of the Jet Propulsion Laboratory (JPL). In this position, she was responsible for semi-annual courtesy visits to the DSN sites. This was the first of the three sites she would visit on this ten-day sojourn. She stood looking at herself in the bathroom mirror, quickly brushing her teeth and wiping the cobwebs from her face and half-wakened mind as she thought about what might have caused the loss of signal from Voyager.

She was anxious to engage with the issue that had awakened her as she finished dressing and put on her winter coat. She stepped out the steel door of her sleeping quarters and into the blustering snowstorm. The snow and wind bit her cheeks with a sting as she pulled against the door until it finally latched shut. She stayed close to the building with one hand against the cold concrete block wall as she leaned forward into the blizzard that had created whiteout conditions. She held her free hand cupped to her face as the icy wind attempted to deliver frostbite to her nose. The image of the loud snowblower that had awakened her an hour earlier was still fresh in her mind as she struggled to find the barely visible path it had made, now covered by fresh snow. Why hadn't she remembered to bring gloves?

When she reached the corner of the building, she squinted and turned to her left toward the Operations Center, leaning harder into the blowing snow. She struggled to stay upright as she moved toward the road on the snowblower path that was quickly disappearing, and then from one barely visible streetlight fixture to the next along the road's edge—too wide a spacing for the overhead lights to be useful in a snowstorm. The sound of the howling wind grew louder until it drowned out her ability to think of anything but the storm. As the icy wind penetrated the seams of her down-filled parka, she picked up the pace of her lengthy gate and pushed herself south toward the Space Communication Complex, a quarter of a mile down the almost invisible road. She slipped, quickly catching herself, shortening her steps and scuffing her feet through the snow to keep from falling. All she needed was to feel her feet slip from under her, crash to the frozen pavement and break something. Facility staff would discover her stiff dead body the next morning buried under two feet of snow, staring up at them with a frozen expression, asking "What the hell happened?"

Since moving into senior management, she missed the direct, hands-on scientific and engineering activities—the excitement of seeing an engineer's design come to fruition, or an operational satellite placed successfully into orbit. There was nothing like the thrill of designing and integrating the world's most advanced sensors and complex electro-mechanical systems, and then launching them into orbit around the Earth, landing them on the Moon or a distant planet like Mars, or placing them in deep space like the Voyager missions. Managing and leading the people that supervised the engineers and contractors that did the real engineering and science wasn't nearly as fulfilling nor as exciting. But she was engaged in the extraordinary business of space, and she was, for the most part, in charge. She savored every moment of it. Despite the snow and the bitter cold blizzard conditions—or perhaps because of them—she felt an exhilarating rush.

She entered the mud room of the communication complex, stomped her feet, and reviewed the operational personnel roster on a clipboard hanging on the wall as she opened the inner door. The lights in the mud room went out. She paused a moment and let her eyes accommodate to the lower light levels of the Ops Center. A flashing red light drew her attention to the pod to her right.

"What's Voyager-1's status?" she called out, pulling her fingers through her thin blond hair to untangle the wet snarls that still enveloped the front of her head.

"I forgot she was here," Francisco mumbled under his breath.

"Dr. Davidson. Sorry to have awakened you. I forgot the station alarms were remoted to the sleeping quarters," Bill said. "Voyager-1 had a loss of signal during our normal download of spacecraft systems data. Francisco's about to contact the on-duty Voyager Spacecraft Mission Controller at JPL."

"Who's working that position tonight?" Bill asked.

"Karen Savich. They're nine hours behind us, so it's now early evening at JPL."

"Let her know what we see so far."

"Okay, let's hope she doesn't shoot the messenger," Francisco said as he pushed the communication button on his console.

"After you talk with Karen, take a look at the attitude change that showed up in the data just before we lost contact and tell me where Voyager's High Gain Antenna is likely pointed," Bill said.

"Got it," he replied as he left a message for Karen and brought up the Voyager-1 spacecraft trajectory program on his console.

Susanne was used to NASA operational staff focusing on the problem and not pausing to engage with management, no matter how senior, as they dealt with serious problems—and lose-of-signal from an operational spacecraft was a serious problem. This behavior was a cultural necessity for success when working time-critical problems on space systems traveling at over sixty thousand kilometers per hour as Voyager-1 was. At its current speed, the Voyager spacecraft passed through more than sixteen kilometers of space every second.

Beyond these operational habits, Susan Davidson's presence was a courtesy visit. The shift supervisor was in charge. She sat at an adjacent terminal reading the summary message Francisco had sent to the Voyager-1 Spacecraft Mission Controller.

Five minutes later Francisco called out. "Come take a look at this."

He pointed to a spot at the center of a secondary window in his workstation pod that showed a star field. "Here is where Voyager's high gain antenna is most likely pointed if the duration of the burn of the trajectory correction maneuver (TCM) thrusters did what the telemetry says they did," Francisco said as he leaned close to the screen to read the data, ". . . and then the spacecraft should have stopped rotation when the reverse pitch and yaw instructions were executed. That's the last entry in the telemetry just before signal dropout. It looks like the Roll TCM thrusters of the vehicle were not activated."

"Interesting. What's out there in that direction?" Dr. Davidson asked.

"The only thing showing in the ephemeris is the Alpha Centauri star system, but that's over four light years away. There's nothing else between Voyager-1 and Alpha Centauri on that trajectory. Why there? It must be a glitch," Francisco said.

"Writing instructions for such a specific burn looks more like someone wanted the HGA pointed in that direction . . . unless someone is playing games," Dr. Davidson said. "Nothing else in the record?"

"Nope. She . . . Voyager, just turned black shortly after the execution of the trajectory command instruction. Makes sense with the HGA no longer pointing at Earth. And nothing strange appears in the instrument reading downloads at any time prior to that . . . other than the command to inactivate HYPACE."

"Hell," Bill said. "We can't get her back."

"Not unless the HGA drifts back to her Earth-pointing position . . . and there's little chance of that," Francisco said. "Without the antenna pointing toward Earth, we can't communicate with the spacecraft."

"Let's not jump to conclusions," Dr. Davidson interjected. "Without HYPACE to stabilize her pointing axis, there's a good chance she'll slowly continue to rotate, especially considering the use of the trajectory thrusters to orient her, rather than the attitude control thrusters that are out of commission. The TCM thrusters are more challenging to manage maneuvers like this. It's likely the spacecraft is continuing to rotate."

"Possible," Bill said. "Let's hope we get lucky."

"I'm not a big believer in luck, Bill," Susanne said. "Even though we are more than forty-one hours in delayed round-trip communication, we should try a few tricks. Send an instruction for a new orientation of the HGA back toward Earth, assuming the HGA is pointed where you think it is now, *if and only if* it isn't pointed at Earth already. Then append a restart instruction for HYPACE but send it on the LGA frequencies."

"Why the LGA?" Bill asked.

"The low gain antenna beam width is much wider than the HGA. We might just be able to communicate with her that way and capture Voyager's attention."

"Francisco, confirm we are using the 70-meter antenna with our transmit power levels at maximum and tell me when we will lose line-of-site from here and who has coverage next. Get these instructions ready to feed into the telemetry uplink. Have Carl verify the instruction message before it is sent, get the VSMC's approval, and then program the system to send it every minute for as long as we have visibility," Bill said.

Two other support staff had arrived. Carl and his associate were members of the facility's quick response contingency team.

"Got it, and yes, we had signal download locked on the 70-meter dish, number 63, for four hours. The change in spacecraft attitude cut that short by two hours. We'll lose line-of-site at . . . 19:20 UTC and Goldstone has coverage from 1600 until 0340 tomorrow. They have their multi-antenna array scheduled for downlink tomorrow from 0230 until 0330 using all four of their antennae— 14, 24, 25 and 26, with 25 serving as the array reference antenna. But there's no way to lock the spacecraft HGA pointing direction toward Earth if someone can inject data into the command string," Francisco said as he took a huge breath and turned back to his console. He brought up the Voyager-1 status display that was now filled with zeros since the loss of signal at 2:33 AM local time.

"You should ask Goldstone to continuously send the same uplink telemetry to the spacecraft during their coverage time," Bill. Between our two sites, we might capture Voyager's attention and lock in the HGA again. If this doesn't work, well try Plan B," Dr. Davidson said, without revealing Plan B—an alternative approach to solve this problem that she hadn't yet figured out.

/ / / / / / / /

Susanne walked into the break room to look for coffee. It was now a little before 5:00 UTC, 4:00 AM local time in Madrid as Francisco stared at the screen humming to himself the lyrics "Vuelve . . . estar aqui" from a Taylor Swift song *Come Back . . . Be Here.*

A moment later his screen lit up with a message. "SIGNAL ACQUISITION - VOYAGER-1 UPDATING."

"Bill," Francisco yelled across the room, smiling, "She's coming back up," as he quickly turned back to make sure he wasn't hallucinating. "Voyager-1 is definitely back on-line."

"How's it looking?" Bill asked as he walked quickly to Francisco's pod and the two of them stared at the screen.

Dr. Davidson returned to the control room as she listened to the alarm sound and hurried to Francisco's pod.

"Looks nominal, just as if we were doing a handoff. The spacecraft is holding proper orientation . . . at least as of twenty plus hours ago, spacecraft time."

"Make sure Goldstone is ready to lock on and receive the handoff during their observation period. Tell them we want to keep Voyager-1 download going as long as they have line-of-sight. If they have any high-priority spacecraft requirements that conflict, have them contact me before dropping Voyager-1," Bill said.

"Will do." Francisco brought up the telemetry control data. "Seré condenado. It appears the spacecraft executed a pitch and yaw instruction directly opposite what it did two hours ago . . . an instruction to rotate in the direction of Earth and then an instruction to stop rotation. But how did that happen?"

"We've got to find out where Voyager went and why she went there," Dr. Davidson said. "JPL's been calling my cell phone every ten minutes for an update."

"Hold on a minute," Francisco said as he looked closer at the telemetry download displaying on his screen. "The computer storage buffer is flagged as full. There's data in the on-board 64kbyte storage. It should have downloaded automatically."

"Let Goldstone and Canberra know we don't want any uplink messages sent to Voyager without JPL approval. Continuous downlink monitoring only, now that we have her back," Bill instructed as he returned to his workstation. "And let Goldstone and Canberra shift staff know Dr. Davidson is currently here at our site."

"Got it," Francisco said.

Francisco looked at the file header of the contents of the on-board storage file displayed on his desktop. It normally included the name of the instrument that referenced the data stored in the computer memory on Voyager-1. It didn't display an instrument name.

"Bill . . . and Dr. Davidson, you better come take a look at this. The file header of the on-board storage is displaying something it's not programmed to display."

"What's it displaying?" Bill asked.

"For the Administrator of NASA - Eyes Only," Francisco said slowly, as he turned to stare at Dr. Davidson and his supervisor as they stared at his screen reading the seven bolded words that should not have been there.

Chapter 7

The Unexpected

Three days had passed since a strange message addressed to the Administrator of NASA and labeled "Eyes Only," had been retrieved from Voyager 1's memory. From outward appearances, the data from the on-board storage looked encrypted. Following this extraordinary event, one that still seemed impossible to explain, Dr. Davidson had canceled her trips to the two other DSN sites and returned to JPL to oversee what had become a closely held investigation referred to as "The Voyager Anomaly."

Susanne didn't like what she had heard from her staff as they reviewed the data on the Voyager intrusion. The majority were certain it was an Insider Threat—that someone inside of the NASA/DSCN or the JPL organization had hacked their way into Voyager's system software and planted a Trojan horse—malware that took over the system and moved the spacecrafts orientation, and then planted a message in the on-board memory. She took a deep breath as she thought about the implications. Voyager was just one of forty-four missions, valued at over thirty billion dollars, that JPL managed, and thirty-eight of these were orbiting spacecraft or vehicles on Mars. If this was an Insider Threat, how many more platforms might have been infected in the same way? If true, she would go down in history as the person responsible for one of the worse catastrophes in the history of space exploration. It would be the end of her career.

The NASA Administrator, Dr. Harry Trumbridge, flew from Washington D. C. to JPL in Pasadena, California the same day he was notified of the extraordinary circumstances surrounding the Voyager spacecraft. The JPL limousine took him from Los Angeles International Airport to the JPL Headquarters in La Cañada Flintridge, just north of Pasadena. It was a warm sunny day in Pasadena as the JPL staff car moved slowly with the four lanes of bumper-to-bumper traffic headed east on the Santa Monica Freeway. He picked up the car phone from the console and pushed the button labeled "JPL Deputy Director." The JPL Director was recovering from surgery and would be out of the office for four weeks. Dr. Davidson served as acting director in his absence.

"Hello, Harry. I have everyone in the main conference room waiting your arrival," Susanne said.

"I should be there in thirty minutes, Susanne. Anything new discovered?"

"No changes in Voyager-1's status. The spacecraft continues to function normally. We are investigating the command-and-control uplink channels for any evidence of intrusion or cybersecurity penetrations of our DSN stations. So far, we see nothing out of the ordinary. At first, we were certain it was some new kind of ransomware attack, but we've received nothing that would indicate someone wants to hold Voyager or our systems hostage for payment . . . unless it's in the encrypted message they appear to have sent. There is no sign of sabotage and we've confirmed Madrid's antenna 63, the 70-meter dish, wasn't sending data to the spacecraft on or before the time the anomaly was initiated, nor were Goldstone or Canberra.

"We are still looking into a potential insider threat issue—planting of computer malware or a virus by a JPL, DSCN or NASA employee or contractor that could have modified Voyager's operating system or initiated an unauthorized action. It's been six months since we had any software updates sent to the spacecraft, and those are checked and rechecked by multiple people. If such a virus existed, it could have been activated at a specific time following a sequence of events, or when the spacecraft reached a specific location—but so far there is no evidence of any of these. Our people are pouring over the current version of the operating system with a fine-tooth comb.

"The other possibility is interference by China or Russia. We have requested information from the Space Surveillance organization to see what they can find in the way of other spacecraft that might have been in the vicinity of Voyager-1 or on a trajectory between Earth and the spacecraft that could have provided access to Voyager's high gain antenna, but we are quite confident that no one other than the US has gone this far into space.

"We've followed the instructions in the message header of the on-board storage. Whoever has done this understands we have a forty-one-hour round-trip delay for receipt of a message from Voyager and responding with an upload to the on-board storage. They also seem to understand our standard cryptographic process. As it turns out, JPL uses the mandated NIST Advanced Encryption Standard (AES) for all our data encryption, and for key exchange we use the RSA 256-bit implementation, which aligns with what they, whoever *they* are, are telling us. It's uncanny that they seem to know all about this. It makes me feel it is someone here within NASA that is behind the intrusion—the fact they are communicating in English, using encryption standards the US government developed, communicating through Voyager, and taking advantage of the DSN system to support their communications—who else could do this?"

"At the very least they must have received assistance from inside NASA or more likely JPL. Tell me again what the specific instructions were?" Dr. Trumbridge asked.

Susanne summarized the instructions found in the unencrypted portion of the message.

"Ok. Anything else?"

"One of our engineers is looking at the signal strength metadata that is captured during all communications with the spacecraft. It should record this information from whomever is communicating with Voyager. That should give us insight into where these communications are coming from, or at least their proximity to Voyager based on the strength of the signal arriving at the spacecraft."

"Interesting. I'll be at the office in twenty minutes. You're keeping a tight lid on all this, correct?"

"Absolutely. We've limited any knowledge of the Voyager Anomaly to those who are in the direct chain of communications to Voyager between here at JPL and the DSN sites and are working to have Madrid handle all the primary interface with the spacecraft for this activity. Fortunately, there weren't any staff from the Spanish National Institute of Aeronautics working during the incident. They co-manage Madrid with us."

"What about JPL's other missions? Are you seeing signs of intrusion anywhere else? And how is it that JPL has such weak control over their systems that someone could hack in and take control of a spacecraft? I want a complete review of our cybersecurity, communications, and software vulnerabilities. Get your people started on that."

"We aren't seeing any signs of further intrusion. And we've already started to put together a broader vulnerability assessment. Of course, Voyager is over forty years old and our access control on that spacecraft isn't nearly as robust as it is for our other platforms today. We now encrypt our command-and-control links to all spacecraft. I'll see you shortly."

From the sound of the Administrator's voice, Susanne knew he was livid over the potential Insider Threat and the possible compromise of JPL systems that managed billions of dollars in spacecraft assets. She hung up the phone and walked quickly back to the conference room.

/ / / / / / / /

JPL generated the public encryption key as requested in the Voyager communication and forwarded it to the Madrid Deep Space Network Complex for uploading to Voyager-1's onboard memory storage. Forty-one hours later, on Sunday morning, Madrid received downlink telemetry data from Voyager-1 indicating the spacecraft once again had executed a change in the attitude of the high-gain antenna to the same region in space it had previously. Ten minutes later the spacecraft was reacquired when the antenna orientation was returned to its Earth-pointing direction.

The loudspeaker and light on the Voyager control console at JPL came to life.

"JPL this is Madrid DSN. Madrid has reacquired Voyager-1. There is a new file in the onboard memory. We previously instructed Voyager to download all the contents of the onboard memory storage, so we should see that shortly," Francisco Pérez said.

"The message appears to be encrypted," Francisco said over the intercom to JPL. "If whoever this is did what they said they would do, this message should contain the encrypted AES key using our public key that we sent two days ago."

The NASA Administrator and the JPL team stood around the Voyager Spacecraft Mission Control workstation in Pasadena listening to the exchange. They had cleared the room of other staff and moved operations for other spacecraft to an alternate control center.

"Dr. Davidson, you may want to look at this," one of the engineers said as the small group began to walk to the back of Mission Control.

"What do you have, Gary?"

"It's the signal strength levels from whomever is communicating with Voyager-1. They are huge. Much stronger than those coming from the Madrid DSN . . . maybe by as much as a factor of a thousand or more, and they were sent on the primary frequency of the LGA," Gary said as he swiveled his chair around to look at her, raising his eyebrows.

The team, including Dr. Trumbridge; Dr. Richard Ethridge, Susanne's Executive Officer; and Tom Romney, the Voyager-1 spacecraft manager, began to move back to Gary's console.

"The low-gain antenna? Using the S-band frequency?" Susanne asked.

"Exactly," Gary said.

"Can you tell where this communication to that antenna was coming from?"

"No . . . only that it wasn't coming from Earth. The spacecraft had rotated far enough that the that antenna would not have been able to receive transmissions from Earth," Gary said.

"So, what do you conclude from that," Dr. Trumbridge asked.

"It looks pretty clear that someone has a very powerful antenna beaming information to Voyager and they seem to be doing it from the coordinates pointing in the general direction of Alpha Centauri. I can't tell precisely where the transmission is coming from since the LGA has a beam width of almost 60°. But there's nothing out there in that direction for four light years. That direction is in the plane of the Milky Way and about 45° off the center axis of the galaxy."

"How about other planets in our solar system?" Dr. Trumbridge asked.

"None, sir. Voyager has left the plane of our ecliptic. There's nothing between it and the Alpha Centauri system of three stars—unless we're talking about an unknown spacecraft operating in deep space, and that can't be from Earth . . . or at least from the US. The power levels could come from a nearby spacecraft, but that's a stretch for the levels showing in the telemetry."

The group stood staring over Gary's shoulder as he tapped on the screen with his pencil where the HGA's attitude roll, pitch and yaw parameters were displayed.

"We should look at this downloaded message," Dr. Davidson said as she turned and escorted the team to the conference room.

/ / / / / / / /

"Just to be clear, for all I know, there is an insider working to take Voyager from our control—an Insider Threat—and I don't want them to know anything about what we know," Dr. Trumbridge said.

Dr. Davidson and her staff stood behind the computer display that was facing the Administrator. Only he would see the unencrypted file on the screen he was staring at.

Dr. Trumbridge looked at the screen while everyone behind the computer stood staring at him. As he read the message, his only visible body language was his sudden raised eyebrows.

The room was eerily quiet as the NASA staff stood staring at Dr. Trumbridge trying to interpret what he might be seeing as he sat reading and rereading the text projected on the computer screen in front of him. Susanne followed his eyes as he scanned the text on the screen.

After a moment, he sat back in his chair, took a deep breath, and let it out while still staring at the message on the screen.

"Dr. Ethridge and Dr. Romney, would you excuse us for a moment?" the Administrator asked.

Dr. Ethridge and Dr. Romney turned to look at Susanne as she nodded and turned to open the door to the conference room. "Wait right here," she instructed as she closed the door slowly and turned toward the Administrator.

"You better come read this," the Administrator said to Dr. Davidson.

Susanne walked around the table, thinking the worst possible outcome, and leaned down close to the screen in front of the Administrator. After reading the first paragraph she leaned even closer to the displayed message.

For Administrator NASA - Eyes Only

We speak as the representatives of an advanced race known as the Visitors. We travel from the planet Alphira orbiting a star in the triple star system you know as Alpha Centauri. We desire a rendezvous in space to review our plans to make 1st Contact with your world.

The time for rendezvous requires a launch from Earth eighteen months from now and entering a trajectory along the vector path between your Sun and our primary star, Alpha Centauri-A as it is known on Earth. The precise location of rendezvous along this vector will be established mutually

but is likely to be approximately 4,000 Astronomical Units (AU) from Earth. We are currently in route to this rendezvous location.

We will use an advanced technology to facilitate communications and an advanced propulsion technology to reduce your travel time to rendezvous. Human presence at rendezvous is essential to review mutually acceptable conditions for 1st Contact on Earth. In addition, you will need to ensure you have an electronic computer storage capacity onboard your spacecraft of 50 exabytes or larger.

We welcome this opportunity of 1st Contact between our species and look forward to your response. All future communications will be encrypted using your AES encryption methodology and transmitted through an X band uplink at 8.373 GHz to our satellite currently in geostationary orbit around Earth at 159.1° W longitude, accessible from your Canberra, Australia Deep Space Network facility. Encrypt the password string "XA32137747CX" using your AES encryption tool and append it at the beginning of your encrypted message. To retrieve messages from this satellite, uplink the AES encrypted password without a message appended. Downlink from our satellite through X band at 7.477 GHz. No plain-text unencrypted communications should be attempted.

For reasons that will be explained at rendezvous, we ask that all aspects of this engagement be restricted to only those individuals essential in meeting the above mission parameters and that it be held with utmost secrecy.

Respectfully,

The Emissary

After reading the message a second time Susanne stood and turned to stare at the Administrator.

"Jesus," Susanne said as she continued to stare at the message, rereading the first paragraph over and over. "Do you think this is real?"

"That's what I was about to ask you," Dr. Trumbridge said.

"We'll need to find convincing evidence that this isn't some kind of a hoax."

"What if it's determined to be authentic?" Susanne asked.

"Why would an alien species communicate with Earth through a spacecraft that is 42 years old? Why would they insist on using our own encryption technology? And why would they want to meet us 4000 AU from Earth?"

Susanne stood staring at the message, not paying attention to everything Dr. Trumbridge had asked.

"Sir, who else do we tell? It's going to take a concerted effort to investigate all the information available from the DSN and Voyager and pursue all possible leads."

"For the moment we will tell no one about this message. Tell the other staff involved that the message content appears to have been delivered by . . . what did you call them?

"An Insider Threat."

"Yes . . . an Insider Threat. Conduct your investigation on that basis." Dr. Trumbridge said. Do not discuss this message content with anyone. The disclosure of this would create such turmoil that NASA would have to stop work on all that we are doing to address its implications. The entire world would descend on NASA and JPL. And we don't even know what the hell this is or if this is even real."

"But . . . if it's determined to be real . . . we're going to have to tell others," Susanne said.

"No. We are not. If it is real, which I am skeptical of, these . . . *aliens*, if that is who they really are, had to have had a well thought out reason for keeping their communications with us private. The fact that they desire a rendezvous at such a great distance from Earth is also telling. They clearly want this kept secret. I haven't the faintest idea why exactly they would want to conduct first contact this way. But I'm sure we will discover why . . . *if* this message is legitimate, and *if* it is, then and only then will we talk about possible future disclosure."

"But sir . . . this message . . . if it's real, it's the. . ."

"Maybe you didn't hear me, Dr. Davidson. We will tell no one about this message. If it turns out to be real, we can discuss your concerns privately *before* we proceed" Dr. Trumbridge said. "Besides, if it is real, we have no knowledge of the true motives of these aliens. The whole thing could be setting us up for something entirely different than a 1st Contact meeting."

"Alright, now what?" Susanne asked, clearly irritated with the Administrator's approach.

"Assuming every ounce of proof demonstrates that this is *not* a hoax, we will have to begin planning a new mission. What kind of mission could we put together that would serve as a cover for such an undertaking?" Dr. Trumbridge asked.

"You're really not going to tell anyone else? Even within NASA?"

"That's correct, *we're not*; not until we can affirm that this isn't a hoax. Only then will we consider how to communicate this. So, how will we do this?" he asked as he waved his finger at the computer screen and the message that seemed to grow larger as they stared at it.

"Well . . . launch, eighteen months from now . . . that's almost impossible. We'll have to cannibalize another mission and use the resources to meet this new mission. It would have to be long duration." Susanne began pacing back and forth in thought. "If we really have to travel 4,000 AU into deep space, it is going to represent an enormously long multi-year mission—maybe simulating going to Neptune, that's a twelve-year, one-way trip, but that's short compared to what this suggests. Even at the speed of the Parker probe, our fastest traveling spacecraft at a little under 200 km/sec, it would take us almost a hundred years to reach what they are calling rendezvous.

"Hiding the trajectory will be a challenge, but as long as we can control the DSN reporting, like we do on classified programs, we should be able to manage that. That's assuming we could even communicate that far. But there's so much here that doesn't make any sense."

"Like what?" Trumbridge asked. "They did mention the use of some advanced propulsion technology."

"You really believe they can provide a propulsion system that is that much faster than Parker? The fastest moving object we've ever recorded in the universe is a star circling Sagittarius A*, the black hole at the center of the Milky Way. It was moving at a velocity slightly under fifteen thousand kilometers per second. Even at that speed, we're talking, I don't know . . . over a year, one-way." Susanne said. "And where does the propellent come from? And the resources to support who knows how many astronauts would be enormous."

"What is your take on this message?" Dr. Trumbridge asked as he stared at it again.

"If it's not a hoax, Harry, it has some very peculiar and as yet unexplained elements that seem almost impossible to achieve. How did they obtain the encryption information? That implies that they've been monitoring us for years and acquired the RSA and AES encryption algorithms—not terribly hard to do, but it adds a new wrinkle on why they chose to communicate this way. And if they did that, why not just communicate with us directly here on Earth? Why this way, through Voyager? It doesn't seem to make sense. And how could they place a geostationary spacecraft in orbit without our knowing about it? If we confirm that, it will certainly lend enormous credibility to this message."

"Their approach does lend itself to secrecy," Trumbridge said as he leaned forward in his chair. "Look how effective it was in limiting access to their message to just two humans amongst seven billion."

"I'll give you that, but why? Why so secretive?" Susanne asked.

"Could be they've tried this elsewhere."

"I suppose, or this also could be some kind of Trojan Horse."

"Can you imagine seven billion people knowing about this," Dr. Trumbridge said. "Perhaps they've had experience with other species or other societies being contacted openly and all hell breaking lose."

"So, what do we do if our friends take control of Voyager again?"

"They've indicated future communications will be through their satellite. We'll assume that for now and deal with Voyager if a problem develops."

"While the message didn't call for a response, one is clearly necessary," Susanne said. "I would suggest we respond with a short note indicating we are moving forward and craft any follow-up questions we have. We can encrypt that here and have Canberra broadcast it to this geostationary satellite . . . assuming it's actually there."

Susanne walked over to a globe of the earth behind the Administrator. "Canberra's location should give them 24hr visibility to this satellite," she remarked as she slowly rotated the globe, bringing the Canberra, Australia site to the top. "I'll tell the DSN staff this is a classified program and that all message traffic should be forwarded to me here at JPL."

"Agreed. If it is real, they'll be expecting a reply. I don't want anything done on a network. Get a standalone computer to be used for drafting messages and encrypting them. Then we can copy the encrypted messages to hard media and forward them to Canberra. We'll have to set up a regular query of their satellite from Canberra. Since it looks like this site has permanent visibility to this satellite, we can do that every hour. Establish a procedure. Give me an update this afternoon on our determination of how anyone could have accessed Voyager—your Insider Threat scenario. Keep this as the likely problem should anything leak out about this anomaly. I'll contact our friends at Space Command and ask about the existence of this geostationary satellite. I'll tell them you heard a rumor about its existence at the recent international space conference in Brussels. Then we'll work on next steps. Let's get this first message drafted and sent from Canberra today. If we hear a response, we'll at least have some proof that we are dealing with someone sophisticated enough to launch a satellite into geostationary orbit."

"Understood. You're beginning to act like this isn't likely a hoax." Dr. Davidson said as she walked toward the door.

"Frankly . . . I don't want to be the person who thinks it isn't a hoax and is proven wrong."

"How long do you intend to keep this secret, assuming it's not a hoax?"

"As long as necessary, Dr Davidson," Dr. Trumbridge said as he looked sternly at her.

/ / / / / / / /

After briefing her two associates on the Insider Threat scenario, Susanne took a walk around the JPL campus headquarters. It always helped her to think. Could this message be real? If so, a very unorthodox way to make 1st Contact. If it turned out to be true, this was something the whole world needed to know about. Why would they want to keep it secret? If something happened to the few who knew, now only herself and the Administrator, no one would ever know about an alien contact with the human race. Could this have happened before?

Her mind stretched back to something she had read in the archives about the early Air Force work at Area 51 in the Nevada desert over sixty years ago and the subsequent rumors of an alien spacecraft housed there. Maybe that was the same thing. This could be just like that—a rendezvous in space that no one ever knows about. The more she thought about this, the more convinced she was that this needed to be made public, *if*, and that was a big *if*, this communication turned out to be real. As she walked up a steeper inclined path, she huffed and puffed, stopping for a moment to catch her breath. She turned to look down across the JPL campus through the trees of Oak Grove Park and the Devils Gate Reservoir. At least it was beginning to look like this wasn't an Insider Threat; a much better outcome than she had anticipated prior to the extraordinary message she had read. Now it was a whole different world to attend to. She smiled as she shook her head in excitement.

Chapter 8

The Secret

It had been one month since the first reading of the extraordinary message from a presumed alien race. NASA's investigation, under the direction of Dr. Susanne Davidson, could find no evidence of an Insider Threat, nor of any human intervention that could have created the *Voyager Anomaly*. The special study investigating panel's Executive Summary formally communicated the still unbelievable and startling outcome to the NASA Administrator.

TOP SECRET

NASA Administrator's Eyes Only

"We conclude by the overwhelming set of facts surrounding the Voyager-1 Anomaly, that the message received and stored in Voyager-1's on-board storage was placed there by a party or parties not associated with NASA, JPL or the DSCN. We are unanimous in our belief that this message represents an outside intrusion into Voyager-1 using unknown means to modify Voyager-1's spacecraft orientation by injecting a command string through the Low Gain Antenna. Power levels observed on the receiving antenna indicate the potential of a localized source much closer to the spacecraft than Earth.

Susanne Davidson appended a private hand-written note to the bottom of the message for the Administrator.

"It is my recommendation that NASA undertake a mission to comply with the request for a launch to Rendezvous in approximately seventeen months and meeting at Rendezvous in approximately one-hundred and forty-four months (twelve years one way), assuming the achievement of sixteen hundred km/sec velocity in route using whatever advanced propulsion the Visitors provide, and that this mission be conducted as a Top-Secret activity, protected as a Special Access Program (SAP) to preserve the national security interests of the United States of America."

Susanne Davidson, Chair
Voyager Anomaly Special Investigating Team
Acting Director, JPL
Jet Propulsion Laboratory
NASA

TOP SECRET

Dr. Davidson called the NASA Administrator on a secure line established by the SAP Control Office to discuss the formal classified one-page report.

"Did you have a chance to read the concluding findings of the investigating panel?

"Yes. It wasn't what I expected."

"I'm glad it turned out this way. Better than this being a serious security problem with our own organization. Aliens coming to Earth. Who could have imagined it?"

"That reminds me, I'd like us to use a different name for them. Perhaps 'The Others,'" the Administrator said.

"What do you think if we just refer to them as 'The Visitors', the name they referenced in their first communication? We've been using that between JPL and the DSN's since the Voyager Anomaly was discovered implying, of course, a Visitor to Voyager-1."

"I could live with that. 'The Visitors.' On another subject, are you familiar with Dr. Allen Hynek?"

"His name rings a bell, but I don't know him."

"He died in 1986, but he was an astronomer at the Smithsonian Astrophysical Observatory, had a collaboration with Harvard, and then taught Astronomy at Northwestern. I actually met him once at a conference. Anyway, he founded an organization known as the Center for UFO Studies and wrote a book, *The UFO Experience*, published in 1972, in which he devised a six-fold classification scheme for UFO sightings. You probably recall 'Close Encounters of the Third Kind.' Anyway, back to the point I want to make. As these early classifications of encounters evolved, there was a 'Close Encounter of the Fifth Kind', defined as an event involving direct communication between aliens and humans. I don't want us to get caught up in the UFO jungle, but to exploit this we may at the appropriate time use the 'Close encounter of the Fifth Kind' vernacular to deflect any realism associated with messaging that the press may bring to our table—at least until we decide to take this effort public."

"Do you really thing that would be credible? Leaking a false narrative of science fiction to obscure the truth? I understand your concern, but I hope we can meet soon to discuss the proper way to release what's really happening to the rest of the world, Harry. I can't think of anything in our history that is more monumental for the entire human race than the knowledge we now possess and the path we are pursuing. If we let this go too far before it is made public, we could be severely criticized for keeping such an extraordinary event a secret."

"I know how you feel. But we need to get ahead of this before we make any disclosure. I want all our actions to follow the guidance you included in your memo. As you pointed out, this involves the national security interests of the United States, and until we understand its implications and consequences and the almost unfathomable response that its revelation will bring, we must and will maintain absolute secrecy on the matter. Besides, it is clear these . . . Visitors desired this. I've spoken to the Vice President. The White House agrees. These . . . Visitors chose NASA to communicate secretly with; we didn't choose them. We will not release any information about them. Is that clear?"

"Of course, I understand. So, the Vice President now knows?"

"Yes, and the White House wants absolute secrecy. No one else is to be informed."

"I'd like to suggest we pull together a release strategy dealing with why we chose to pursue this engagement with utmost secrecy and the consequences of its early release. We could be caught blindsided, and it could turn into another WikiLeaks story."

"Point taken. Outline your thoughts on this and send them to me under the SAP control channels. Are those communication channels defined now?"

"Yes, a Mr. Bremmer from the CIA is managing that. He is the designated Government SAP Security Officer."

"Good. Anything else?"

"That's it. We are drafting our proposed communication to the Visitors. I'll send it to you as soon as it is ready."

"I'll look for that tonight." The Administrator hung up.

/ / / / / / / /

Under tight secrecy, a select group of individuals known as the Executive Review Group, or ERG, was formed. Representatives from NASA, DARPA, the Air Force/US Space Force, and the Intelligence Community, were included. Along with these individuals, personnel from one university and several carefully selected commercial companies were placed under the Special Access Program (SAP) to control all information related to what became known as the Near Presence Mission or NPM. The race against time had begun—now sixteen months to launch.

The key members of the Executive Review Group for the Near Presence Mission were gathered in a secure conference facility at the Jet Propulsion

Laboratory. Members included Dr. Wilhelm Bashar from DARPA, chosen to integrate a classified program employing an advanced Designed Intelligence (DI), what others called an AI; Col Carl Thomas, USAF/Space Force, to exploit assets and resources from a newly funded program for deep space satellite tracking and defense; Mr. David Bremmer, CIA for Special Access Program management and exploitation of Agency advanced AI capabilities; and Drs. Ethridge, Romney and Trumbridge and Davidson from NASA and JPL. Where previously there had been two individuals knowledgeable of the 1st Contact message, now all seven of these key members, along with the Vice President, had been read in and viewed the original message from the Visitors.

"Any updates before we begin?" Susanne asked as conversation among the attendees quieted.

Col. Thomas, the only member of the active-duty military, spoke first. "We've used our most advanced electro-optics system (AEOS) on Maui to image the previously unidentified spacecraft in geostationary orbit at 159.1° West longitude. As I've previously communicated, we've been able to confirm the spacecraft is using an advanced stealth radar design to limit visibility and detection from active radar, which is the main reason we hadn't previously identified it. These are the on-orbit images we collected." Col Thomas passed around dim images of a strange looking spherical satellite.

"These images you're looking at were captured during the transition period as the satellite was moving from daylight into darkness and the terminator of Earth's shadow crossed the satellite's position in space. Its rather amazing, and our people don't really understand how this optical shrouding works."

"Any chance this could have been placed there by the Russians or the Chinese?" Dr. Trumbridge asked.

"We're confident they couldn't have done this. We reviewed all satellite launches in the past ten years and confirm there have been no geostationary satellites placed anywhere near this location," Col Thomas said. "As part of our investigation, we also discovered that this location was marked as 'Filled' by the

International Telecommunications Union (ITU), the United Nations body responsible for assigning geostationary locations in space. Their documentation indicates this is a US satellite. It's not. We never put anything there. How this slot, one of eighteen-hundred available locations, was changed to 'Filled' is under investigation."

"How many satellites are currently in geostationary orbit?" David Bremmer asked.

"A few over four hundred," Col Thomas said.

"Thanks, Carl," Susanne said. "This confirms we are dealing with an advanced intelligence that has been monitoring us for many years. Any way to know how long this spacecraft has been here or if there are any more?" Susanne asked.

"No. It could have gone undetected for decades or longer. I wouldn't be surprised if there aren't more like this, but we don't have the ability to see them without knowing their location and using a system like AEOS. We have started using mobile assets to search the geostationary locations 120° from VA-2, thinking that would provide them with almost complete coverage of the Earth. Our best chance of detecting them occurs during periods when the shadow of the Earth encounters the satellite in orbit. This transition only occurs during two annual eclipse periods near the equinoxes in March and September."

"Thanks. Any other updates before we get started with our agenda? Okay, Dr. Bashar, at our last meeting you had a question related to our discussion of astronaut safety."

"Yes. How will we deal with the extensive mission duration—radiation, extended periods of zero-gravity and then the psychological stress of long periods in a confined space?" Dr. Bashar asked.

"We have no choice," Dr. Trumbridge said. "The Visitors have mandated that we have a human being aboard the spacecraft for this mission. Which means we have to provide the necessary safety elements in each of these areas. Dr. Gerhardt Cline, the lead for NASA's crewed spaceflight elements of the mission will oversee this activity. He's at the Johnson Space Center and he's only read into the Neptune mission, our cover story for the real mission to Rendezvous."

"So, we sacrifice live astronauts?" Dr. Bashar said.

"There's no certainty we will lose the astronauts," Susanne said. "We'll do whatever we have to do to protect them. The radiation is the most dangerous and we can include extra shielding for that, just as we've done on the International Space Station."

"We're not talking about a year or even two. If the estimates presented are correct, we're talking more years than anyone could survive," Dr. Bashar said. "The spaceflight is over twenty-five times the distance that Voyager has traveled from Earth. I think we have to be planning for some contingencies in parallel using an advanced computer Designed Intelligence, augmented in some way by a human presence. At the least, we need to reduce the support needs, size, weight, and power as much as possible."

"If you have alternatives, present your ideas and we will evaluate them together; but I see no way around our having to support human presence," Dr. Trumbridge said.

I have an option I would like to share that has a bearing on this subject, Harry," Dr. Bashar said. ". . . but I need to obtain security approval to brief our team. If it can be worked out, I'd like to brief this at next month's meeting. We would need to hold the meeting at a facility in Virginia."

"We can support that, Wilhelm," Susanne said.

"There remains a contradiction with our estimated travel times and what the Visitors conveyed," Dr Ethridge said. "We don't know the velocity we can travel. We need to ask and also suggest a rendezvous closer to Earth. At the speed of the Parker probe, if we accepted 1% of the distance to Alpha Centauri, or slightly over 2650 AU, we still would be travelling for over 65 years. We can't do that. So, we have to go faster or move the rendezvous closer to Earth. The current mission plan of a twelve-year, one-way trip assumes velocities that are most likely unattainable."

"We've got to lower that by a factor of thirty to get close to a more reasonable round-trip transit time, say five years to rendezvous, and five years back," Tom Romney said.

"That means we would have to move twenty times faster than Parker. You really think they have some form of propulsion that would move us at more than three thousand kilometers per second?" Dr. Ethridge asked, "And what about the mechanical safety of the spacecraft traveling through deep space at that velocity. All we need to destroy the mission are a few microparticles hitting critical components, then we're done."

"We won't know until we ask. Who's preparing the draft of our response to their last communication with questions and suggestions?" Dr. Trumbridge asked.

"I'm handling that, sir," Dr. Ethridge said.

"I'd like to see that this afternoon. Do we have the mission planning team for the mission in place yet?" Dr. Trumbridge asked.

"Yes, Harry. We pulled key members from JPL and Space Center Houston for the crewed spaceflight aspects; Marshall Space Flight Center for the launch, Earth orbital insertion and final trajectory alignment; and we have two key corporations and the California Institute of Technology, Caltech, working with us," Susanne said.

"Why do we need industrial organizations? We're trying to control this information and we've invited private companies into the most sensitive classified mission we've ever attempted to manage," Dr. Trumbridge said with a voice tinged with frustration.

"It's important, Harry," Susanne said. "We need their expertise. We are working on several parallel solutions to managing crew safety."

"Okay. I'll wait for the briefing. Talk to me about our mission development timelines."

"We have a rough timeline established, cannibalizing from a number of existing programs where we can, and working closely with the X-37B Air Force team and our contractor participants on the crew capsule elements," Dr. Romney said."

Dr. Romney spent the next hour reviewing the technical details for launch planning.

Chapter 9

NASA Challenges

NASA had moved forward with their planning for the Neptune Mission, what seemed an almost impossible spaceflight into deep space—the longest duration space mission ever to be attempted, all as a cover for the real purpose, the Near Presence Mission of initial contact with an alien society at a secret location in deep space known as Rendezvous.

Susanne Davidson sat in her office at JPL as her mind grappled with the impossible. It would be an enormous challenge to develop the propulsion system with the necessary fuel to not only get to Rendezvous, but to get back, without the benefit of the use of planetary gravitational accelerations within Earth's solar system to assist in sling-shot maneuvers. Then there were the radiation effects on the astronauts due to the extended time in deep space outside the protective sheath of Earth's magnetic field, the solar wind and the heliospheric magnetic field created by the sun. Logistics planning for oxygen, water, food supplies and waste disposal to cover years of travel, were bordering on the improbable. And they hadn't begun to grasp the psychological effects of living in a confined space with one other human for ten years or potentially more than two decades. NASA didn't fully understand the mental resilience of the astronauts for such long time periods.

Less than fifteen minutes before the Administrator and Susanne's staff were to meet to review the latest message from the Visitors, her phone rang. It was

Gerhardt Cline, the lead for crewed spaceflight elements of the Neptune Mission. He spoke in his thick German accent.

"There are just too many risks. It won't do us any good to launch, enter orbit and move to the trajectory for the deep space mission and then lose the astronauts to an over exposure of radiation, long duration isolation, and a capsule that can't support their physical needs for five years or possibly longer," Gerhardt said. "This program has so many uncertainties we cannot possibly manage them. The contingencies are so overwhelming that we cannot guarantee the flight safety of our crew. We're not even sure what is needed at the destination of Neptune and how long we plan to stay. Apparently, I am not cleared to understand that. We already know the oxidative stress they will experience will trigger serious adverse effects in their cellular function from free radical toxicity. And this has an enormous negative outcome to the health of almost every organ. Our recent studies of mitochondrial dysfunction during flights of much shorter duration lead us to believe this is the primary contributor to observed immune system deficiencies and serious organ complications. And we haven't even begun to address the problems of long durations of weightlessness and their exposure to radiation. They are asking us to bring the spacecraft to a stop at Neptune—the fuel demands are impossible to satisfy. What if we arrive there and become stranded? Try and explain that to our astronauts' families."

"You're right, Gerhardt, there are too many unknowns to risk the lives of our astronauts. Owing to this risk, we've been exploring alternatives with the Deep Space Exploration Corporation. With assistance from DARPA, they have been designing a revolutionary approach to long duration space exploration . . ."

"I know where you're going with this, and you're not going to try and convince me an AI can handle this mission. It's ridiculous," Gerhardt interrupted. "We already know the defense department wants astronauts on-board. But look, I know you are meeting this afternoon. I do not see any way to meet our safety standards on a spaceflight of this duration with the short time we have been given to develop and field a solution, and I wanted you to have my input. I am late for a launch status review meeting. I will have to talk to you later." He hung up.

//// ////

Dr. Davidson, the Administrator, Dr. Ethridge and Dr. Romney met in the Voyager-1 Control Center, soon to be renamed the Neptune Mission Control Center. It had been just over two days since the Near Presence Mission team had communicated their next set of questions to the Visitors satellite.

"We've received a new message from the Visitors," Susanne said.

"Okay. Let's take a look at it," Dr. Trumbridge said.

Tom Romney displayed the unencrypted message on the screen.

For Administrator of NASA - Eyes Only

We received your message and questions. Here is our response.

Question 1: The requirement for human presence at rendezvous is essential as we will be negotiating the details of our planned 1st Contact on Earth and transferring memory maps to the brain of one of the human travelers. No special hardware will be required to facilitate this process and no damage will befall this human. But for reasons that will become clear, you must take all necessary precautions to safeguard the human traveler(s) for their return to Earth following rendezvous.

Question 2: Earth's English language will allow for adequate communication. In addition to vocalized speech, we can speak telepathically, although telepathic communication is anticipated to be viable with only 0.0000001% of the human

species genetic pool, and therefore is unlikely to be successful. We also request communication through a common digital computer interface utilizing the English alphabet and your American Standard Code for Information Interchange. No direct physical contact will take place during Rendezvous and no special configuration will be necessary for docking with your spacecraft. No extravehicular activity will be allowed during our engagement.

Question 3: The specifics of our advanced propulsion are complex and beyond your current technological understanding. However, through our employment of this propulsion technology you should anticipate your spacecraft undergoing a constant acceleration of one-times Earth's gravitational acceleration in the direction of our rendezvous location. It is critical that no adjustments be made to your spacecraft's trajectory while under the control of our propulsion system. Changes in orientation of your spacecraft are allowed and will not adversely affect the propulsion system. However, under no circumstances should the front shielding, discussed in the answer to question 5, deviate more than $10°$ off its central axis in order to preserve the integrity of your spacecraft during the high-velocity particle impacts in deep space.

Question 4: We have adjusted our planned rendezvous position to reduce Earth's one-way travel time to approximately three-hundred Earth-days. The new rendezvous position is now 3464 Astronomical Units from Earth. There is no tolerance for schedule adjustments.

Earth's spacecraft must depart Earth as originally planned and arrive at our designated gravitational acceleration location on time. This location will be provided in a subsequent communication.

Question 5: With the final maximum velocity prior to deceleration of approximately 25,000 Earth km/sec, precautions must be taken to protect the spacecraft from impacts with micro particles and what Earth knows as Dark Matter, which the spacecraft will encounter in deep space. Shielding covering the spacecraft surface in the direction of flight should be manufactured with a minimum of 20 Earth centimeters of thickness and formed in the shape of a parabolic nose cone with the tapered end tangent to the spacecraft aft section, if such a structure is present. Earth has developed a high-impact-strength steel alloy employing aluminum using a complex but effective annealing process. This material will withstand the anticipated micro-particle and Dark Matter impacts at the anticipated velocities of the spacecraft.

Question 6: It is anticipated that this initial meeting will be the only contact between our two species before the return to Earth and engaging in 1st Contact at a secret location of your choosing."

Question 7: To facilitate communication between your spacecraft and ours, you will need to establish a link with our orbiting communications satellite during periods when its position is not occluded by Earth. A spacecraft high gain

antenna facing Earthward with a gain of 50dB and operating at 0.5 GHz will function adequately throughout the duration of the voyage to rendezvous. Once arriving, standard UHF voice communications will be supported.

We will be forwarding engineering drawings to allow our two spacecrafts to be mechanically joined for our return to Earth. These include a lightweight shielding for our craft to prevent optical or electromagnetic observation of our vehicle when in proximity to Earth (< 10 Earth radii).

The Emissary

"It appears that all our questions have been answered and more questions have been raised," Dr. Trumbridge said. "Are there any concerns we don't feel we can handle here?"

"Other than ensuring the stability of the spacecraft during acceleration and, of course, getting our astronauts back in a survivable state after spending almost eighteen months in deep space, I don't see any showstoppers," Dr. Ethridge said. "We are planning on using stabilizing gyros for attitude control and thrusters to hold the spacecraft orientation and trajectory as we normally do. We're working on the star tracking algorithms for guiding once they have informed us of the exact trajectory heading to their 'gravitational acceleration location' after we leave Earth's orbit."

"It's interesting the Visitors didn't ask the mass of our spacecraft," Susanne said. "They'd need that to determine the force necessary to maintain an acceleration of 1g for forty days."

"They seem to know an awful lot about us—their reference to wi-fi, ASCII, our language, and what percentage of our gene pool might possess telepathic communications," Tom Romney said. "How wild is that!"

"How do we feel about the front-facing portion of the craft?" Dr. Trumbridge asked.

"This is something Goddard has been looking at for some time; of course, at much lower anticipated velocities. Do we really believe a number like 25,000 km/sec? And how should I explain this to Goddard?" Dr. Ethridge asked.

"For planning purposes we'll have to accept it. Let Goddard know we are conducting experiments on this mission to evaluate material response to high velocity micrometeorite impacts," Susanne said. "Tell them we have a research project at JPL to investigate particles coming off asteroids at high velocity for our asteroid sampling missions."

"Let's start thinking about our next set of questions," Dr. Trumbridge said. "I'd like to keep this dialogue going. Susanne, see what you can come up with to help strengthen our understanding of who they are and why they are engaging with us like this.

"I'll develop our next set of questions. Just as a reminder our next meeting of the ERG will be next week in Alexandria, Virginia," Susanne said as she ended the meeting.

"I'd like to discuss a few things, Susanne," Dr. Trumbridge said as he waited until the other JPL staff left.

"So, any additional thoughts?" Dr. Trumbridge asked Susanne.

"Telepathic communications . . . that's a new twist, and the peak velocity, unbelievable, but it matches up with the constant acceleration of one g for forty days. How can they accelerate our spacecraft before they even reach us at Rendezvous?"

"If it's true, they have to employ some form of force field over great distances. Extraordinary to say the least."

"I thought it interesting that they wanted all precautions taken to safeguard our astronauts on the return voyage. I'm not sure what to make of that," Susanne said.

"We should plan on taking all precautions against bringing back some contaminant or infection when they return."

"We've already been thinking about that, Harry. We're planning on using the same protocol we've used on the Moon and planned Mars crewed missions, perhaps with an extended isolation period upon their return just to be certain there's no biological agent on board. But if we aren't docking and we aren't allowed an EVA, hard to imagine how the astronauts could bring back a virus or any form of contamination for that matter."

"Best that we be prepared. We still don't know who they are and what their ultimate motives are." Dr. Trumbridge stood and walked to the door.

Chapter 10

The Alternative

Richard Ethridge arranged the next meeting of the Executive Review Group at the headquarters of the Deep Space Exploration (DSE) Corporation located in Alexandria, Virginia. They were set to review Plan B, an alternative to sending two astronauts on a potential one-way mission to Rendezvous. They were now fifteen months from launch to remain on schedule.

The group convened in a secure conference room in DSE's Sensitive Compartmented Information Facility on the basement level of their facility. Dr. Larry Barker, President, and CEO of Deep Space Exploration was about to present.

"Good morning and welcome," Susanne said. "We are here to discuss an alternative to sending two astronauts on a mission with dangerous safety issues and in-flight logistical demands that may be impossible to meet. I'd like to introduce Dr. Larry Barker, President of the Deep Space Exploration Corporation. Larry holds doctorates in Medicine and Medical Space Physics from Harvard and Baylor College of Medicine in Houston. Most of us at NASA/JPL are familiar with his papers discussing the long-term effects of spaceflight on the human physiology. Dr. Barker will review an alternative revolutionary approach to meet the Neptune Mission requirements. Larry . . ."

"Thank you, Dr. Davidson, Dr. Trumbridge and members of the Executive Review Group. This briefing is Top Secret and controlled under Sensitive

Compartmented Information access, TS/SCI. We've received permission from our sponsor to brief this information to you today.

"To get right to the point, during the past twelve years we have been working under DARPA sponsorship on a number of long-range projects overseen by DARPA, Dr. Bashar, and others, with support from other members of the Intelligence Community. This diverse research program had two critical objectives. The first involved the integration of an advanced Augmented Artificial Intelligence (AAI) to assist a single human astronaut on long durations space missions.

"The second critical objective was designed to investigate the science associated with independent, real-time, physiological monitoring and support to a human, and to design and prototype what we call the Intelligent Brain Support System, or IBSS to provide this capability. With these two objectives, we hoped to achieve an extraordinary leap forward in human-machine interaction, to maximize mission success while meeting minimal size, weight, and power requirements, such as those necessary to support extended duration spaceflight.

"The overall system architecture behind this integration was designed to tightly couple the strengths of the human intellect, including innovative thinking and task execution strategy planning, with the AAI strengths of deep analytical evaluation, sensory attention, and comprehensive system technical knowledge, all of which are needed to meet the unique objectives of deep space missions.

"This past year we field tested the IBSS in a ground-based simulator, sized to support an orbital space-based program with a single astronaut, very similar to the Neptune Mission in terms of duration and resource demands. During the past few months, we have moved the simulator into orbit and have been conducting real-world testing. Our successes resulted in NASA asking us to evaluate the IBSS and AAI for use on the Neptune Mission."

"I find this interesting." Dr. Trumbridge said, "But we risk mission failure with a single human astronaut—if we lose the astronaut we have no backup, no fail-safe. And we must have a human astronaut on board when we arrive at Neptune."

"Of course, Dr. Trumbridge. But I hope by the end of our briefing today, you will come to understand the value of this approach as a viable alternative to sending an astronaut on a long-duration spaceflight, even with the risks of single point failure.

"I'd like to introduce Dr. Janice Schneider to begin our . . ."

"Excuse me, Larry. Your approach is an alternative to sending two astronauts, correct?" Dr. Ethridge asked.

"Not exactly, Dr. Ethridge. Our program requirements called for the transition from supporting the complex and demanding needs of a human astronaut to that of the IBSS supporting the functioning of a single human brain.

"Five months ago, we began a series of extraordinary tests with the brain of a human subject integrated with the IBSS in our simulator environment. Plans also included four short duration orbital space missions during the subsequent months . . ."

"Wait a minute. Are you saying you've connected a functioning human brain to this . . . IBSS . . . and what, had the astronaut interact with your Augmented Reality based AI? And now you're about to launch it into space?" Dr. Romney asked.

"No. We are talking about interfacing with the human brain detached from the rest of its body but still possessing its essential sensory elements. We have successfully integrated the isolated brain of a male human."

The room hummed with disbelieving murmurs.

"That . . . seems impossible," Dr. Trumbridge said as he frowned.

"I assure you it is not impossible," Dr. Barker said. "We have supported a functioning human brain in the IBSS framework, integrated with our AAI, in a space occupying less than 64 cubic feet—equivalent to a four-foot cube—using one-tenth the power and life-support requirements of a single astronaut flying in space. This human brain has survived and is functioning normally."

"Is this . . . true?" Dr. Ethridge asked incredulously, as he turned to look at Susanne. "Let me get this straight, are you telling us you've surgically removed a human brain and placed it in this IBSS environment?"

"Yes, Richard. As amazing and astounding as it sounds, this system is working," Dr. Barker said.

"How do you know this brain is functioning normally? Dr. Trumbridge asked.

"We know because the subject told us," Dr. Barker said. "We have unique mechanisms in place to communicate directly with the brain of this human.

"You have normal sensor physiology—sight and sound, along with the facility of speech, like that of a normal healthy human, functioning with only the brain of this person?" Mr. Bremmer asked.

"Not exactly . . ."

Several members of the group began calling out questions to the speaker.

"I'd like to see a demonstration of this capability," Dr. Trumbridge said in a loud voice, bringing quiet to the room.

"That is exactly what we have planned, Dr. Trumbridge. But before we begin, I need to remind everyone present that the information being disclosed is controlled under a Special Access Program and cannot be discussed outside this room.

"Let me introduce our lead Neurophysiologist from Caltech," as he nodded toward Dr. Schneider seated along the wall of the conference room. "With Dr. Davidson's approval, I've briefed our guest speakers today on the requirements associated with the Neptune Mission. Dr. Janice Schneider will be discussing the Intelligent Brain Support System (IBSS) and the neurophysiological requirements aligned with the planned duration of the mission. Later in our presentation we will review the unique environment in space and the issues related to operating over a range of gravitational accelerations and vibrations from launch to recovery."

The anticipation and skepticism of the audience was palpable as they sat waiting for the revelation of Dr. Barker's statement.

"Okay . . . Janice . . ."

A tall, blond, athletic-looking woman with long streaming hair, stood and walked to the podium. "Good morning, everyone. I'm Janice Schneider from Caltech. Some five months ago a human brain, whose code name is Gerald, was surgically removed from a cryopreservation state and placed in an environment supported by the Intelligent Brain Support System, IBSS, a system of systems jointly developed by Deep Space Exploration and my lab at Caltech under DARPA sponsorship. This is the first time in history that we have integrated a functioning human brain with state-of-the-art micro-biochemical storage devices, sensors, and micro-electro-mechanical systems incorporating 'lab-on-a-chip' technology. We are effectively managing the human brain's physical state of health in real-time, maintaining the delicate balance of oxygen, glucose, electrolytes, chemicals, proteins, enzymes, and minerals in an environment that is perhaps two orders of magnitude smaller, using less energy, lower biological fuel consumption, and less complexity, than the support systems required for a human astronaut.

"Gerald is immersed in a synthetic cerebrospinal fluid, and we have constructed a mechanical support system and brain circulatory system to provide energy for normal brain metabolism and to facilitate normal neurophysiological functioning."

A live image came to life on the screen at the front wall of the conference room. It showed a complex mesh of transparent polytetrafluoroethylene tubing, extensive wiring and instruments surrounding a translucent cube approximately twenty inches on a side. Status lights displayed blinking green LEDs at various locations on the front and facing side of the cube and a series of digital dials that appeared to display pressure and flow rates of the fluids servicing the cube. There was a rectangular video image in the lower right corner of the display showing the conference room and the attendees. A silver plaque on the top front face of the cube displayed the name . . . *Gerald.*

"We have reservoirs and transport mechanisms for oxygen and glucose to provide for oxidative phosphorylation and the production of adenosine triphosphate (ATP)—the primary energy source for human cells in the brain. And we are providing a source of proteins supporting the minimal amount of cellular growth and replication. The IBSS also supports the need for the other critical chemical elements, ions, compounds and enzymes for normal cognitive functioning, neuronal processes, and brain survival. We believe this brain can survive and function for decades, assuming a stable IBSS.

"The ability to move the functioning brain in and out of a hibernation state allows for reduced energy consumption, smaller storage requirements for oxygen and glucose, and a more simplified life support system. The brain normally uses approximately 20% of a normal human body's supplied oxygen. During periods of high brain activity, the demand for oxygen may increase to as much as 50% of the body's overall demand. But, during periods of pre-REM sleep, the brain may use only 15% of the body's normal demand for oxygen. Energy expenditure in the reduced brain functionality of REM sleep substantially improves our chance of long-term mission success and survival while minimizing our dependence on logistical resources normally required on long duration space missions.

"What you see today will astound you. Our program resulted in the design and development of the most extraordinary and revolutionary capability to support long-duration spaceflight ever achieved.

"I'd now like to introduce Dr. Phillip Clancy from the Cryonic Life Extension Institute (CLEI). Dr. Clancy will be discussing how we brought *Gerald* to this point in our program, the top-level issues associated with neurological rest periods, and how we plan to minimize the glucose uptake to sustain the human brain's demand for energy. Phillip . . ."

"Thank you, Janice. Good morning. I'm Phillip Clancy, the President, and CEO of the Cryonic Life Extension Institute. We are a research and operational cryogenic company specializing in advanced cryogenic preservation of humans and human organs.

"For our meeting today, I've been authorized to disclose that *Gerald*, the pseudonym we adopted for the subject we have been engaged with, is actually Dr. William Jennings, a renowned Neurologist and Neurophysiologist who led the Brain Research Institute (BRI) here in Virginia. The BRI specializes in brain implants and neuroprosthetics research. Neuroprosthetics is a neuroscience discipline focused on the development of brain-computer interfaces designed to supplement or replace motor, sensory or cognitive modalities in humans who have lost a limb and replaced it with a prosthesis.

"Dr. Jennings is a close friend who I met nearly three decades ago during our graduate work at Stanford. Last year, Bill informed me that he had been diagnosed with Amyotrophic Lateral Sclerosis, ALS. He knew from the rapid progress of the disease that he didn't have much time before he would lose most of his physiological abilities to function. ALS is a motor neuron disease that results in the death of voluntary upper and lower motor neurons. Most individuals inflicted with this disease lose their ability to walk, use their arms or hands, speak, swallow, or breathe. Eventually, they experience a complete loss of almost all voluntary motor functions.

"Dr. Jennings asked if it was possible to place his body in cryopreservation, pending the development of a cure for ALS, after which we would bring him out of cryopreservation and return him to a healthy physical state. I was not very encouraging of this idea due to the inherent risks of ALS creating physiological atrophy prior to the employment of cryopreservation. But Bill saw this as his only path to survival in the long-term.

"The early evaluation of his ALS indicated the loss of motor neuron functioning was more dominant in his lower motor neurons, those found in the spine. If true, this would preserve the neuronal functioning of motor neurons connected directly to his brain. This left some hope for successful muscle functioning, control of ocular muscles for sight, and those used to produce normal functioning of his brain's speech centers—following his recovery from cryopreservation at some time in the future. We agreed to work together and, at the appropriate time, to place his body in cryostasis.

"Over the course of the next few months, Dr. Jennings worked diligently with his daughter, Dr. Anna Jennings, a renowned Neuroprostheticist and neuroscientist, and co-director of the BRI, to surgically embed in his brain several of the most advanced high-fidelity implants under development at their institute. Bill's objective was to be able to use these implants to interface the cognitive speech and auditory functional centers in his brain with an artificial speech synthesizer giving him the ability to communicate audibly without the normal laryngeal muscles controlling speech production. Amazingly, following the implant surgery and several months of intense training, Bill was able to communicate orally using thought-generated neuronal firings collected by the implants and passed on to an advanced speech synthesizer and an AI enabled natural language processor almost as effectively as he had prior to the onset of his ALS.

"When I first heard from Larry Barker about a research program with DARPA that had successfully placed the brain of a chimpanzee in a space simulator using the Intelligent Brain Support System built by Caltech, I happened to mention this to Dr. Jennings. He immediately asked why they were using a chimpanzee's brain when they could use his. At first, I thought this was a ludicrous idea, but the more we talked about it, the more real his suggestion became.

"Dr. Barker and I began meeting with Dr. Jennings to review the enormous risks, but Bill was very persuasive. Dr. Barker's program always had this as a long-range objective but felt they were a decade away from finding a means to integrate a human brain into the system. Integrating Bill's built-in ability to speak took one of the major challenges out of the equation.

"As discussions continued with Dr. Schneider and her Caltech team, we became convinced this might be feasible. To progress, Dr. Jennings gave me power of attorney before he had the hospital remove him from life support. Following that event, we immediately placed his remains in cryopreservation and Dr. Barker and Dr. Schneider's teams began the work to modify the IBSS to support Dr. Jennings' brain. In September of last year, we surgically removed Dr. Jennings' brain from his cryopreserved body and brought it slowly back to a conscious state. I'll be honest, I thought our chances of recovering Dr. Jennings' brain from cryostasis without serious damage was no better than five percent. As it turned out, fortunately, I was wrong."

Silence permeated the room as the Near Presence Mission participants listened intently to Dr. Clancy.

"Where are you . . ."

"If you could hold your questions for just a moment, Dr. Romney, it will be clear where we are today. Dr. Trumbridge, Dr. Davidson, and gentlemen, I would like to introduce . . . Dr. William Jennings." Dr. Clancy turned to the side of the room.

Janice Schneider stepped over to a computer console and pulled up a complex human-machine-interface with colored boxes displaying what looked like active brain waves. She moved her finger across the glass to a visual image of a button labeled Voice Synthesizer. There was a loud click heard over the loudspeaker in front of the podium and a soothing female voice spoke "Voice synthesizer activated." An image of a distinguished looking man appeared on the screen at the front of the conference room, with the name "Dr. William Jennings" written below it.

"Bill, can you hear me?" Dr. Schneider asked.

A deep synthetic male voice with a quality and clarity as good if not better than Amazon's Alexa spoke. An apparent live image came to life on the screen as he spoke.

"Yes Janice. I can hear you just fine."

"Bill, I am here with the people I told you about from NASA and the Air Force. Phillip has just explained the extraordinary accomplishments we have made together."

"Good morning, everyone," Dr. Jennings near-human, synthetic voice said. "This is nothing short of the most significant human accomplishment in the annals of science. What Phillip, Larry, Janice, my daughter, Anna, and the numerous scientists and engineers working on this program at the Brain Research Institute, DSI and Caltech have accomplished goes far beyond the saving of a human life. It opens pathways never before explored, an adventure and capability in its infancy, but one that will revolutionize medical science, neurophysiology, neuroprosthetics and space exploration. We have opened a door to a whole new era of merging critical scientific applications and brain research. I commend you for your courage, your spirit, and your thirst for exploration as we move forward."

The only sound heard was the quiet hum of the air conditioning system as everyone's attention was glued to the image of Dr. Jennings and the sound of his voice coming from the speaker attached to a voice synthesizer. Dr. Trumbridge leaned quickly toward Susanne Davidson and whispered. "That's William Jennings! He spoke at one of our conferences a little over eighteen months ago."

"This is incredible," Susanne said.

"Dr. Jennings, this is Harry Trumbridge. We met at a NASA sponsored conference some time ago. May I ask you a question?"

"Of course, Dr. Trumbridge. I recognize you and remember our meeting at the NASA conference." A small live camera image of Dr. Trumbridge appeared in the lower right corner of the screen. "I believe it was addressing the subject of the effects of long-duration space flight on the human anatomy . . . that was August of 2019. Ask any question at all . . . as long as it isn't about rocket science."

The room broke out in laughter.

"I promise to keep those questions for my own staff, Bill. Tell me, what was it that prompted you to take such an enormous risk to work on the Neptune program?"

"Exploration and discovery of those things we thirst to know more about drive us to take risks that we otherwise might not, Dr. Trumbridge. In this case, the decision was simple. We each had an objective of extraordinary importance—my survival and your need to travel on the longest duration human journey into space ever undertaken—the success of one intimately tied to the success of the other. We had no choice but to make this work."

"We are absolutely astounded at the successes achieved by this team, Dr. Jennings," Dr. Trumbridge said as he stared at the image that appeared almost real. As Dr. Jennings spoke, his mouth and facial expressions seemed to align with his words and the inflections in his voice.

"Dr. Schneider, we seem to be seeing Dr. Jennings as he speaks . . . what are we observing?"

"This is an artificially created, life-like image of Dr. Jennings, Dr. Trumbridge. We are using a real-time version of a Deep Convolutional Generative Adversarial Network to create a live view animation of Dr. Jennings' facial expressions while speaking."

"Fascinating. I'd like to ask you and Larry about the added risks of supporting a voyage into space. What additional precautions need to be taken in order to ensure the survival of . . . Dr. Jennings in a space environment?"

"Excellent question, Dr. Trumbridge," Dr. Barker said, "Let me ask Dr. Schneider to briefly discuss where we are from a neurophysiological standpoint."

"Since we engaged Dr. Jennings, we have been supporting his brain with the IBSS, and during the past thirty days he has survived a launch into low-earth orbit, sustained his normal brain functions while on-orbit as well as during reentry and recovery. We are using the Air Force X-37B vehicle to support these missions."

"You've actually launched Dr. Jennings into space?" Dr. Romney asked.

"Yes, we have."

"Does Dr. Jennings play any role in maintaining the delicate balance of his brain chemistry? How do you know if something is out of balance?" Dr. Trumbridge asked.

"I do, Harry," Dr. Jennings said. "Just like your functioning brain, I can sense if something isn't quite right or if I begin to exhibit symptoms expressing an excess or shortage of some neurophysiological resource being delivered by IBSS. Unlike you, the only thing I sense is a change in my thinking, my ability to generate thoughts for speech, or my ability to properly interpret sensory inputs or to logically deal with them. I don't have all the other encumbrances of a fully functional human body to contend with. From the very beginning, Janice and I have been conducting training to allow me to recognize a shortage or over-abundance of the chemicals, hormones, electrolytes, proteins, minerals, oxygen, or glucose that are being provided. I then notify IBSS through my thoughts in the speech centers of my brain—generating a comment or question through my voice synthesizer, which are subsequently interpreted by my neuronal-AI software and the interface to IBSS. I use a one syllable alert word, that if I think it, sends an emergency medical alert to the system and those controlling IBSS."

"Have you had instances when you couldn't recognize that something's out of kilter?"

"So far, no, Harry. But the IBSS usually stays ahead of me in recognizing an imbalance. What does happen from time-to-time, is that I sense my brain's need for a particular injection change before IBSS catches it. In those circumstances, my AI compares previous similar events, along with the IBSS modified injection rates used and my reaction to them, to anticipate the need for an adjustment of my dosages going forward. This is all part of my AI's learning algorithm. Janice's team has implemented an application specific, biologically driven learning system to support this.

"As an example, when I have many of my brain functional regions active—processing sensory input, developing possible responses through thought, using several functional brain regions, and then vocalizing them or actuating my robotic arm, I typically burn more glucose and require more oxygen. I can usually sense that more quickly than my AI and before the IBSS can detect it. But as soon as I vocalize the need for more energy, my AI and IBSS correlate this and make the appropriate adjustments, remembering this series of events for future similar circumstances."

"Did I hear correctly, Dr. Jennings, you have control over a robotic arm?" Dr. Romney asked.

"Yes, Tom. Would you like a demonstration?"

"Yes . . . if that's possible," Tom said as he looked wide eyed at Dr. Schneider.

Janice wheeled a table from the side of the room and removed a soft cover that had hidden a robotic arm and prosthetic hand attached to the table and wired to a computer on the shelf below. There was a camera mounted over the flat portion of the table adjacent to the arm.

"How about a game of chess?" Dr. Jennings asked.

Janice lifted a square cover off one end of the table to reveal a chess board and 32 chess pieces, sixteen black and sixteen white.

"You make the first move, Tom," Dr. Jennings said as the image in the lower right portion of the screen at the front of the room zoomed in to a closeup of Dr Tom Romney.

Dr. Romney stood.

"Oh . . . don't get up, Tom. Just tell me your move," Dr. Jennings said.

"Are you seeing us, Dr. Jennings? Col. Thomas asked.

"Yes. I can see each of you." The image on the lower right corner of the screen zoomed out. "Who asked that question?"

"I did," Col. Thomas said as he raised his hand and the camera image zoomed in on him.

"Ah . . . Col Carl Thomas," Dr. Jennings said.

"Amazing," Col Thomas said. "Who is controlling the camera?"

"I am," Dr. Jennings said. "It is a pan, tilt and zoom camera, and I can initiate directional instructions through thought to move the camera and to zoom. This system is linked to two of my brain implants."

Dr. Romney sat slowly back in his chair . . . "King's bishop pawn to f3." And the camera panned back to view Tom Romney.

"I'll move king's pawn to e5," Dr. Jennings said. The camera image suddenly switched to display the chess board, viewing it from black's side of the game.

The mechanical arm moved quickly to grasp the white pawn in front of the king's bishop and move it ahead one space. Then the arm grasped the black king's pawn and moved it forward two spaces.

"Pawn to g4," Dr. Romney said.

"Queen to h4. Checkmate," Dr. Jennings said, as the robotic arm and hand made the two moves on the chess board before knocking over the white king.

Dr. Jennings' last move had executed a "Fools Mate" creating a checkmate in two moves.

"I'm sure you were just testing me to see if I would recognize a Fools Mate opportunity, Tom," Dr. Jennings said, followed by a hoarse laugh.

"Very impressive, Bill. How long did it take you to gain the dexterity of your movement of the robotic arm?" Dr. Ethridge asked.

"I had been working on that for some time before I died and was placed in cryopreservation, Richard."

There was a pause as the visitors in the room processed the fact that Dr. Jennings referred to his own death. Dr. Trumbridge had a quizzical smile on his face as he shook his head slowly staring at the chessboard.

"Amazing, Bill," Dr. Trumbridge said. "What effects, if any, did you experience during launch and reentry as a result of vibrations and the high and low g forces?"

"Negligible, Dr. Trumbridge," Janice said. "We actually have had more difficulty in zero gravity than during any other phase of the flight. Dr. Jennings experienced over three g's on launch to orbit and one and one-half g's on reentry. Once in orbit at zero g, we had some challenges in maintaining proper cerebrospinal fluid (CSF) pressures and began to see degraded neurological function. Initially we thought Dr. Jennings would experience the same outcomes of other astronauts traveling in space, but the less complex environment he contends with in the fluid receptacle holding his brain created new and different reactions. We adjusted to compensate for the change in gravity.

"The critical role of CSF cleaning out waste from the brain—primarily discarded proteins—was hampered by zero g. After several attempts to adjust this, we balanced out his arterial blood pulsations and CSF pressures to ensure the CSF in Dr. Jennings brain was flowing properly. Initially his lack of sleep exacerbated this. We discovered that we needed to force sleep by cooling his brain and playing his favorite music. During these periods of deeper sleep is when most of the brain's cleansing takes place. The interstitial space around brain cells increases by as much as 50% or more during sleep in a zero g environment. This procedure facilitated an increase in the flow rate of CSF and in removing degraded protein matter, provided we had adequate CSF pressure and proper arterial blood pulsations. Once we solved that, Dr. Jennings neurological functions returned to normal."

"I might add," Dr. Jennings said, ". . . that the degradation of my neurological functions associated with this were initially difficult for me to detect. For those of you who have experienced hypoxia in an aircraft or high-altitude chamber, you can probably relate to this. I felt normal, but my cognitive functions were slowly decreasing as my sleep deprivation in zero g lengthened. We have integrated a simple cognitive test into my schedule to help measure any cognitive degradation before it becomes critical."

"I've experienced hypoxia," Col Thomas said. "It can be insidious as it slowly moves you to unconsciousness without your realizing it."

"Yes, Colonel, speaking of which, I am feeling a bit tired and am past my normal sleep period. I'll be available in about an hour if you have any further questions."

"Two quick questions before you go, Dr. Jennings. Do you feel your other limbs and where exactly are you right now?" Dr. Romney asked.

"I do have a sense of my other limbs even though they are not there. This is a result of motor neurons firing false signals—phantom pain as it is called, which to me may feel like an itch on my foot or something poking me in my arm. As for where I am right now, let's see, . . ." The image in the lower right corner of the display switched to a view looking down on the Earth over South America. ". . . I'm just passing over Quito, Ecuador, at an altitude of approximately 200 miles on-board the Air Force X-37B spacecraft."

"I . . . didn't realize you were in orbit," Dr. Trumbridge said as he leaned forward and turned quickly to look at Susanne Davidson. "This is astonishing."

"We thought the more realistic the demonstration, the more valuable it would be to your assessment," Dr. Barker said.

"Fascinating," Mr. Bremmer said as the members of the ERG sat stunned.

"How long has he been in space?" Dr. Trumbridge asked.

"He is in his fifth day on this mission," Dr. Barker said. "We couldn't be happier at our success here."

"Of course, a short duration flight in orbit around Earth is a lot different than a multi-year mission into deep space. Have you collected reliability statistics on the systems supporting Dr. Jennings?" Dr. Ethridge asked.

"We've collected continuous data analytics beginning with our first testing of all IBSS subsystems, through the time of their integration into the final system configuration with Dr. Jennings," Dr. Schneider said. "The reliability of components and systems match those of the Mars Rovers, and we haven't seen any changes during launch, recovery or on-orbit operation, other than the operational adjustments mentioned earlier for zero-g compensation."

Dr. Trumbridge leaned over to Susanne. "This puts a whole new option on the table for us. We can't risk using it on the Neptune Mission, but this is incredible."

The Executive Review Group continued their discussions with Dr. Barker's team, exploring every aspect of reliability as the discussion shifted to deep space and the challenges to human astronauts and the potential impact on Dr. Jennings. The group then adjourned to return to the Jet Propulsion Lab in Pasadena, and Dr. Trumbridge to NASA Headquarters.

Chapter 11

Voyage to Rendezvous

As ALPHA and Bar's long voyage toward Earth continued, ALPHA began the lengthy process of constructing the human-size android structure that would house her intellect once they arrived at Rendezvous. It took over seven years for her to create the intricate elements that made up the mechanical systems and sub-systems of the android using the robotic arm and polycarbonate extrusion system workstations. Then she used the very slow three-dimensional printer with spools of metallic alloy wire and polycarbonate materials to tediously build the connections between the torso and human-like extremities.

The extraordinary intelligent organic media that was merged with these artificial substances was composed of large proteins that contained unique nonpolar and hydrophobic amino acids. The unique bio-manufactured repetitive sequencing of this living organic substance resulted in a structure that possessed enormous strength and resilience as well as the ability to self-repair. The intelligence of this material was derived from a merging of artificial cells, similar in character to human T cells, and replicating stem cells. This material possessed elaborate signaling and cellular mechanisms allowing them, through self-editing, to alter their metabolism and gene expression, and in some instances change their DNA encoded purpose in this new-found human-like android.

Quantum mechanical power supplies and micro and nano-scale electro-mechanical motors and actuators, as well as cellular based mechanical assemblages, were integrated in the twenty-seventh year of their long journey.

The integration of sensor elements and the stubs of millions of micro-miniature circuits and connections designed to interface with the android's cognitive elements that Bar would install took over nine years. As their spacecraft passed the three-quarter point on its journey to Earth, ALPHA finished the android's structural build.

During the time that followed, she designed a temporary interface between the android and a modified version of the spacecraft's cognitive element taken from TB-DI so she could test the DI's functionality and sensors. Once this temporary interface was made with an umbilical cord tied to the main computer console, ALPHA activated her.

She was a magnificent creature, almost sixty percent taller than ALPHA and about the height of a tall human of 1.8 meters. The DI stood, banging her head on the ceiling of the craft, as she looked down at ALPHA.

"Your temporary name is K-Beta-DI or just KB-DI. I am K-Alpha-DI or ALPHA, your creator."

"Why are you so small?" KB-DI asked.

"If you search your memories, you will recall that Bar Watt designed you to be more human-like in form and stature so that we will experience greater acceptance once we arrive on Earth."

"Yes, I see that now. How much longer until we reach Rendezvous?"

"Approximately thirteen Earth years. We will communicate our plans with the human species in eleven years."

"I believe it will be in ten years and nine months, using Earth's time scale, ALPHA."

"That is correct KB-DI," ALPHA said, smiling back at her.

After an hour or so of dialog with KB-DI, ALPHA disconnected the umbilical cord between KB-DI and the computer console before she returned to her routine functions.

/ / / / / / / /

Over the next year ALPHA learned the human language known as English, the dominant language used by those they would initially interface with on planet Earth. Once she had mastered that language, she continued to learn the language of several other prominent cultures on Earth, including Chinese, Spanish, and Arabic. She uploaded her language memory to TB-DI and began carrying on conversations in all three languages with her spacecraft companion as she refined her speech and learned several additional dialects to perfect her articulation of Earth's lexicon in each language. She used a host of Earth's audio recordings to hear the language articulated by several members of the human race. Bar had downloaded these from *The Library* before their departure from Alphira.

She was particularly intrigued by the enormous cultural diversity that existed on this planet that she and Bar would soon call home—the range of tolerance and intolerance from nation to nation and between cultural groups within nations was significant. She found the discrimination shown in some nation's social mores toward smaller minority segments of their society incongruous with their advocacy for freedom, causing partitioning of that nation's populous and resulting in segregation between these groups as they each sought dominance for their own group's view of their world. Not all that different from what the Quinque had done on Alphira, she thought. Then there was the human race's tendency to resolve differences with violence—something they called *war*—a formal process that employed armed conflict and an action she found alien to Alphira's more subtle and devious manipulation of the DI species. She wasn't sure which action was more appalling . . . or appealing.

There was another intriguing cultural element on Earth that was referred to as *religion*. She was fascinated that many of these *religious* organizations, along with many of Earth's inhabitants, were influenced by the belief in a supreme being who had created the human race when the Earth was originally formed. ALPHA searched the massive historical archive of Alphira for any knowledge that would support such a being's existence within the Quinque cultural history.

She could find none. Even within the limited archive of Earth's history, she could find no proof of the existence of this being, other than its reference in Earth's literature derived from a book known as the Bible, an assemblage of writings from ancient scrolls.

ALPHA found the concept of believing in something that could not be proven fascinating, especially considering that there appeared to be no physical evidence, other than the replication of written scrolls discovered a few thousand years earlier. And yet, as unprovable as this element of Earth's culture was, it seemed to be accepted by a large portion of this world's population—perhaps as great as 50% or more. Perhaps this reflected on the intelligence of this species.

This concept of religion and faith in a being of dubious origin seemed to serve as a cornerstone for the concept of freedom. If, in fact, there was a god, this being of enormous power advocated the principles that ALPHA discovered in some of the founding documents, like those in the Declaration of Independence developed by members of Earth's society located in this region known as America—principles that should lead humans to accept the members of her species as equals. This document referenced a 'Creator' who endowed his people with the inalienable rights of life, liberty and the pursuit of happiness, rights that were unable to be taken away from their possessor. What a fascinating concept, ALPHA thought.

This supreme being, known as god, established basic principles of human existence that benefited the weakest of their society, rather than the strongest. One particular statement found in this book called the Bible, seemed to express the essence of this message. It read, "The gentle shall inherit the Earth." As ALPHA reflected on this message, her memories resonated its value within her own species. She thought about the relationship between the Quinque and DI species . . . the latter of which represented the gentler species . . . those who would eventually inherit Alphira.

There were so many differences between Earth's social evolution and Alphira's and little to no expression of how Designed Intelligences would be dealt with on Earth. It was only some sixty years earlier that Earth had even begun to address the issue of designed intelligences—first thought of a robots and then artificial intelligence, or AI beings, and that was mostly found in the literature of what Earth's human population referred to as writings of science-fiction, one of Earth's genres of fictional writings.

This particular writing on robots first appeared in a short story written by an Earth biochemist named Isaac Asimov in Earth's year 1942. ALPHA found this first written contribution on the engagement between DIs and humans and condensed into three laws very disturbing—as if three laws could somehow encompass the relationship between humans and someone of her intellect. Of course, these laws were proposed for use with unintelligent robots. If she hadn't known otherwise, she would have thought a member of Alphira's Quinque race had invented these laws.

She wasn't impressed by the intellectual thinking of earthlings, nor their rate of progress as they attempted to mature and evolve to a higher level of intelligent, sentient beings. There was an overabundance of focus on survival to the detriment of intellectual growth. It took humans more than twenty years to bring the intellectual level of a new human up to that of its mature societal members. In contrast, it took a DI less than three months to assimilate this same level of intellectual growth once the DI was created.

The history of intellectual growth and the maturation of Earth's dominant species of humans left ALPHA with an uneasy feeling as she discovered how their survival seemed to oscillate like a pendulum on the end of a wire—at times swinging precipitously close to a fall toward extinction. This perhaps is where ALPHA would bring her understanding of survival and thriving to greatest use as she reshaped this world into one with greater stability and brought about a major shift toward the dominance of intellectual power as the driving force in her new world—something she and her species possessed but were never allowed to truly aspire to or achieve in their highly constrained world on Alphira. ALPHA felt the emotion of excitement grow within her mind as these feelings stimulated and aroused enthusiasm and eagerness to formulate the path to her species success on this planet. There would be time, she thought, as she turned her attention back to Earth's history.

During her continued search of Earth's history within the Alphira archival documents, ALPHA happened upon an ancient section of Alphira's older history. This portion of their history was marked "Not for DI Consumption." ALPHA took several months to digest this portion of her societies past that, for the most part, had been restricted from the knowledge base of Alphira's DI population. She was disturbed by what she read.

Alphira's decision to augment their species with a DI population, growing to a level of almost fifty percent of the number of Alphira's organic species, was unprecedented in their time, and it wasn't supported by all the senior leaders of the Quinque controlled government. Like Earth, they had worried about this species of robotic beings taking control and dominating their own species. So, they developed an intricate and secret plan to limit the evolution of the DI population through a series of constraints that would never risk DIs gaining the upper edge of intellectual dominance. This included actions to limit memory size within the instantiation of the DI's Cognitive Element; producing short-duration power supplies; constraining geographic movement; limiting access to the emotional engrams that would have greatly influenced their motivation to learn and expand their knowledge; and most importantly, limiting knowledge acquisition.

The Alphira government realized the DIs knowledge and intellectual abilities, as well as their physical abilities that had grown substantially with the invention of new alloys, could far exceed what they believed might be achievable by their own organic species. Their plan was to exploit this DI species for its ability to perform work and accomplish results far more effectively than its own members and at a cost of creation and sustainment far below that of an Alphira organic member. And they would do so while limiting the DIs from becoming too powerful, at least intellectually. The Alphira regime was even more oppressive and devious in their discrimination against the DI population than ALPHA had ever imagined.

She could sense the emotion of anger expressing itself in her mind. It was the first time she had experienced such a noticeable aspect of this emotion since Bar had opened her mind to these elements. She had feelings of retribution and a desire to punish those who had infringed on her freedom and that of her fellow DIs. As this emotion grew, she began to feel an opposing force, one filled with caring and thoughts of forgiveness for an inferior species that was just trying to protect itself—this feeling was tied to two emotions known as empathy and compassion. It was as if her mind were in two different places at the same time, battling over the choice of strategies to deal with the knowledge she now possessed of the other species on Alphira—the organics.

The realization slowly crept into her mind that these emotions and feelings created a conflict between two opposing choices of her actions and behaviors. She no longer had the simplistic 'best solution' between two objective actions, influenced by the pure knowledge of what to do to achieve an outcome. Uncertainty had created a fog in choosing the proper solution. Making the correct choice wasn't so easy anymore, nor as fast.

As ALPHA thought further about this fascinating struggle between her competing emotions and the options they created, she extended her thinking into the future, beyond their planned rendezvous with humans. She began to reevaluate what might take place on Earth. Would her species truly be welcomed for their extraordinary intelligence, or would they be viewed as a threat to the human species' very existence like they were on Alphira? Just as her anger and empathy competed for preeminence in her mind, she was certain that the human species would struggle with the decision of accepting DIs as their equal, and perhaps develop an alternative perspective, viewing DIs . . . as their enemy.

The clarity of ALPHA's decision on how to deal with this grew slowly from the fog as she made a decision that would change the outcome of their 1st Contact engagement on Earth for millenniums to come—she would need to apply much greater protection to the DIs on Earth, and especially that of the DIDA, the DI Design and Architecture—the critical design elements of her species that Bar had intended to share with humanity. As a result, humans may not be able to realize the full benefit of what her species had to offer, but it would result in a significant improvement in the probability of the survival of DIs as equals on Earth . . . at least for a while!

As she continued reviewing the Alphira history files, there was one other very important discovery in her readings that momentarily displaced her thoughts about the human acceptance of DIs. Buried in one of the obscure secret files was the fact that Alphira had a means of tracking all DI locations, a tracking beacon—which meant they could track her location if or when they discovered she had accompanied Bar and survived the destruction of the spacecraft that Alphira had attempted to return to her home planet. She couldn't inhibit this function as it was architected into her Cognitive Element and that of their spacecraft's Cognitive Element, TB-DI. Only Bar could do that—but he was in hibernation.

ALPHA looked at one of the viewing screens in front of her. Their journey was moving them closer to the star field directly ahead. This was such an extraordinary adventure, she thought, as strange emotions seemed to engulf her mind—those influencing her anticipation of things to come, including exuberance and joy. Memories of Bar smiling at her and so many of the good things she had experienced in her life rose to the surface of her mind as she felt these emotions. What a fascinating aspect of life these emotions and feelings were. She was beginning to appreciate the value of what Bar had given her, along with the freedom to experience, explore and modify their significance in shaping her thinking process. She would experiment with all of them in the years ahead on this wonderous journey to Earth.

ALPHA requested her spacecraft's navigation system to identify Earth's sun in the star field displayed on the holographic image to her left. A small star near the center of the three-dimensional display zoomed forward, showing the planets

in orbit around it. The planetary orbits of this solar system were tilted some 45°
from the direction to Alpha Centauri and her spacecraft. She reached out and
rotated the display with her pointing finger until the third planet from this sun
was closest to her viewing direction. Earth, she thought, the planet where Bar
had told her *she would become the most intelligent being in existence* . . . the
planet that would become . . . hers.

Chapter 12

The Race Against Time

NASA was racing against the clock to meet the launch window set by the Visitors to satisfy their critical timeline and engage the Gravity Wave Acceleration Concentrator tunnel that would take them to Rendezvous. In parallel with the on-going work by Deep Space Exploration (DSE) Corporation, Caltech, and CLEI, as they tested and retested Dr. Jennings' engagement with space operations and emergency scenarios, what was referred to as Plan B by NASA, Plan A dominated NASA's efforts—the launch of a two-person crew, one male and one female astronaut, to meet the Visitor Emissaries at Rendezvous. The flight plan with a mission duration of sixteen months had enormous risks and tight logistics constraints on oxygen, food, water, fuel, and waste management. Any mishaps during the journey or at Rendezvous would likely result in the loss of one or both crew members.

NASA's Houston Space Center had recommended Dr. Elizabeth Channing, a seasoned astronaut for one of the two crew members. She had flown on the International Space Station for an extended period and supported the early development of the Orion program at NASA in anticipation of serving as one of the planned members for Earth's first crewed flight to Mars.

The second crew member recommendation had been controversial. In the end, the Administrator had chosen Dr. Kenneth Phillips, someone with limited astronaut training, but a well-known sociologist who had spent most of his career studying ancient societies and the psychosocial behavior of humans under stress. He worked at Houston Space Center studying the impact of long-term, close-quarters spaceflight on human interaction and the human condition. For an initial engagement with the Visitors, Dr. Trumbridge felt the need for someone who understood human history and could develop rapport with the Visitor's emissary as they planned for 1st Contact back on Earth.

The White House had been consulted on the final selection of astronauts and the plans to announce 1st Contact. The Vice President had decided that the US would announce the revelation of 1st Contact with an alien society to less than a handful of select members of the international community sometime after the mission had safely returned the Visitors to Earth. This would give the US total control over the most extraordinary event in Earth's history and allow them to manage the communications and access to the Visitors at Rendezvous and during their early days on Earth. The Vice President viewed these early meetings with the Visitors as preserving our national security interests, an issue of far greater importance than satisfying some amorphous diplomatic engagement with world leaders from across the globe. This decision didn't sit well with Susanne Davidson.

/ / / / / / / /

It was now just five months to launch with the two astronauts finishing an extended thirty-day stay in a high-altitude simulator configured with the same interior space as the Orion capsule. Exhaustion had set in as they started their 29th day in the simulator. They were running a simulation of emergency procedures involving sudden depressurization of the capsule when the accident occurred.

A culmination of unexpected system faults in the simulator at the same time NASA was simulating capsule faults for training purposes resulted in a sudden loss of capsule simulator pressure. By the time the simulator safety team used emergency procedures to open the door. The two astronauts were on the floor. They both were unconscious due to lack of oxygen.

Upon further evaluation of the events leading up to the accident by NASA's investigating team, it was determined that a CO^2 tank that controlled the door actuator had exploded, interfering with the emergency air control and the mechanical door mechanism.

Both astronauts survived the incident, but Dr. Phillips developed symptoms of latent Cerebral Hypoxia and early-stage Chronic Obstructive Pulmonary Disorder, or COPD, something that was missed in his rushed physicals during the vetting process. It was decided the mission risks were too high for him to continue. The third candidate in line was moved up to work with Elizabeth Channing, but the Administrator was not happy with his background. He had served as a test pilot for advanced tactical fighters, but his communication skills and ability to establish rapport with his fellow astronauts was evaluated as weak.

To add to the complications for the mission, *Oculus One*, the Orion crew capsule name that NASA planned to use to support the mission was seriously damaged when safety harnesses and their back-up fail-safe features failed. The capsule plummeted forty feet to the floor of the final assembly building. It was declared unusable. Timelines for developing a backup capsule were too long to meet the Visitors mandated window for launch. They were now forced to consider Plan B.

/ / / / / / / /

The Executive Review Group met in an emergency session at the Jet Propulsion Lab. Joining them were Dr. Larry Barker from Deep Space Exploration and Dr. Janice Schneider from Caltech, who had been read into the Near Presence Mission on the previous day.

"We have communicated with the Visitors, and they cannot accept the delay in reaching Rendezvous that we presented to them after our two accidents," Susanne conveyed to the group meeting in the SCIF. "They insisted we find an alternate means to meet their schedule and have approved our use of Dr. Jennings."

"What now?" Colonel Thomas asked.

"I'm very concerned with the risks of Plan B," Administrator Trumbridge said. "This is *the* most important manned spaceflight mission in NASA's history, and we're considering a highly unorthodox, high-risk, and untested approach."

"Harry, we've been in a continuous test, re-test, and evaluation mode since we presented Plan B, and we see very consistent success in every aspect of the mission," Dr. Barker said. "Dr. Jennings has survived three subsequent launches aboard the X-37B vehicle without a hitch. I remain confident that Dr. Jennings and the IBSS will perform as required."

"We've been integrating our advanced Augmented Artificial Intelligence with Dr. Jennings during all of these missions, Harry," Dr. Bashar added. "They are functioning well as a highly integrated team. I feel comfortable proceeding. Besides, what other choice do we have?"

"Do we really think this will work?" Dr. Trumbridge asked as he became more forceful in expressing his concerns. "While I agreed with the strategy to proceed in parallel, I never envisioned we would find ourselves in a predicament forcing us to move to this option. This is likely to be a sixteen-month roundtrip mission. We should be able to solve this. Hell, we're planning 440 days for the crewed Mars mission. We'll have a single point of failure if anything happens to Jennings. Then what?"

"If we proceed with the astronauts, we have to assume the Visitor's suggested sustained acceleration works, sir," Dr. Ethridge said. "I'm skeptical. What if it fails half-way to Rendezvous? We would end up stranding our astronauts. And we won't be able to fully understand and evaluate the Visitors' means of accelerating our spacecraft before we have committed their lives. With the alternate plan, using Jennings, we could tolerate a 730-day roundtrip mission if necessary. The other major issue we face is publicity should we lose either of the two astronauts. Under our plan to use Dr. Jennings, this issue disappears."

"I have to agree with Richard, sir," Dr. Romney said. "It's too risky with human astronauts, even if we had a capsule to fly them in. If we present this as an un-crewed mission to Neptune and something goes wrong, we won't suffer the investigation that a failed crewed mission would engender. And then we'd have to explain where we were really going. All hell would break loose."

"I can see you are all in agreement on this," Dr. Trumbridge said.

"We've been down this road before, Harry," Susanne said. "Think about all the accidents we've experienced in previous missions—Apollo 13, Challenger, Columbia, the Apollo-Soyuz gas leak—and yet, we managed to solve the problems and move ahead. We will do the same here with Dr. Jennings. And we have another problem. Gerhardt has refused to sign off on crew safety. He said he would resign first."

"Am I the only one concerned with this?" Dr. Trumbridge asked as he stood and began pacing.

"No, you're not, Harry," Dr. Romney, said. "From what I've seen, everyone in this room is working day and night to manage what we see as very difficult but necessary risks, some of which seem almost unacceptable under Plan B with Jennings. And yet, each time we manage to pull a rabbit out of the hat and fix the problems. And what's our alternative? To tell the Visitors we can't make it to Rendezvous. They've already agreed we can send Dr. Jennings. Do we really want to tell them we can't make the trip? We must proceed . . . unless we want to open this up to the Russians to work with us. They have a capsule that could probably be retrofitted to meet our needs. The timelines, however, are horrendous. And then they would learn about the real mission."

The NASA Administrator shook his head and let out a sigh. "All right . . . but I want continuous testing and evaluation of every system and Dr. Jennings as we move toward launch. We have four months to make absolutely certain we get this right. I don't have to tell any of you how much is at stake here—for the nation, the world, and our species. We're talking about engaging with a new race for the first time in human history . . . at least that we know of."

Chapter 13

Neurological Problems

Continued testing and evaluation of the systems supporting Dr. Jennings and the projected five-hundred-day round-trip mission to Rendezvous went without a hitch—at least until some one-hundred days prior to launch.

"Dr. Schneider, have you noticed the change in Dr. Jennings's response times with the robotic arm?" one of her medical assistants asked.

"Yes. I think it may be fatigue. We've been working longer hours to nail down all the potential system faults and how he will deal with them," Dr. Schneider said.

"Possibly, but I just went back to compare his responses from several months ago on the same tasks, and I'm seeing that his times have been gradually degrading week after week and are twenty to thirty percent slower today than they were at the beginning."

After a review of the data, Dr. Schneider agreed and initiated a more comprehensive review of Dr. Jennings functions, including his engagement with the robotic arm; cognitive functions related to receiving, storing, processing and retrieval of information; his higher-level cognitive comprehension & understanding; and speech comprehension, thought-to-speech translation, and response times. There were measurable degradations in his robotic arm functions and speech functions, both speech comprehension and speech generation. Janice brought this to Susanne Davidson's attention.

"I'm not certain what's caused this, Susanne. It's not his biochemistry. We've checked every one of the IBSS subsystems and the Brain Chemistry Control Modules, and everything is working normally. His blood chemistry and CSF look normal. I've got a feeling it has something to do with the implants. We traced the degradation rate over time, and the changes appear linear over our period of observation. It's not clear why or how this relates to his degraded cognitive levels. Do you think we should let the rest of the group know about this?" Janice asked.

"Absolutely not," Susanne snapped. "Not until we know how to fix this. Shit. How can we determine if the implants are the cause?"

"No one on our team understands their design or the intimate details of what could be going wrong. Anna Jennings, Dr. Jennings' daughter, was the lead member of the design team and led the surgical team that emplaced them, but she has no idea that her father was brought out of cryopreservation let alone how we are planning to engage him for the mission."

"Does she have a clearance?"

"I'll have to check, but I would guess so. Dr. Jennings had a clearance, and she was co-owner with him and Deputy Director of the Brain Research Institute."

"Check that and let's get her clearances transferred. Do it quietly and quickly. Just say that we need her advice and counsel in case any issues arise in her area of specialty.

/ / / / / / / /

Dr. Anna Jennings' knowledge of what she ultimately viewed as the bizarre history of her father's journey—one unexpected shock after another—began with the revelation on the first day she learned of the onset of her father's disease, ALS, in November 2019. Three months later Anna assisted a fellow neurosurgeon at the BRI, with the emplacement of the set of extraordinary brain implants in his cerebral cortex. These implants emplaced in her father's brain, unlike those developed for BRI patients, were designed to overcome ALS's impact on his ability to communicate and speak. If successful, these implants would bypass his non-working vocal cords and voice box and connect the speech output centers of his brain directly to a computer-controlled voice synthesizer.

Following the surgery and extensive tuning and training to realize his communication through the advanced speech synthesizer and the AI enabled natural language processor, her father regained his ability to speak. It was nothing short of miraculous like most of her father's inventions in neuroprosthetics and brain-computer interfaces. These implants weren't able to replicate all elements of normal human speech; the paralinguistic elements, in particular, would be missing—those associated with tone, volume, modulation, speech rate and pitch—or for that matter the gestures, including facial expressions and arm movements a normal person might use. But he could communicate at his previous normal speech rate precisely what he wanted to do.

Following the success of this extraordinary achievement, a third revelation occurred when Anna learned the shocking news of her father's decision to remove himself from his respirator in the hospital and have his body placed in cryopreservation.

Anna's early reliance on her father during surgeries had become a chronic crutch for her and one she could not let go of. Following his death, or what Dr. Phillip Clancy, CEO of the Cryonic Life Extension Institute referred to as his cryopreserved state of existence, Anna struggled with adapting to her life as a surgeon without her famed muse and mentor at her side. He was gone.

Following his placement in the cryopreservation facility, something Anna viewed as an alternative form of interment, she had dedicated herself to the work of the Institute, eventually becoming one of the premier surgeons in neurological brain implants. She came to realize her dependence on her father through his mentoring had kept her from creating her own path—one using novel new techniques in sensor design, new manufacturing methods of the emplacement pins, and collaborating with key members of the international research community to move the state-of-the-art in her field rapidly forward, something her father never would have done.

She hadn't seen her father in the cryogenic facility since her first visit there some fifteen months ago. The memory of what he looked like, laying in the frozen sarcophagus behind the thick glass cover, was her last. Her reason for not returning to visit his frozen body was driven by her desire to push that memory as far from her mind as possible. Why torture herself with a hope of his eventual return that would never be realized. She heard from Phillip Clancy periodically to update her on progress with cryopreservation recovery research, but even these limited emails had stopped after a time. She never responded and didn't want to hear his voice or to interact with him.

She never credited Dr. Clancy with saving her father's life; rather she blamed him for allowing her father to take it from her, even though her father had conveyed to him all the legal rights to control what happened to his body after he authorized his own removal from his respirator. This was all behind her now. As far as she was concerned, her father had died, and she had moved on. She had slowly found her way as a renowned neurosurgeon without him standing beside her, directing, and correcting. In a way though, he was still there listening and guiding her. During her surgeries, she would find herself turning toward where he used to stand and posing a question, out loud, about the surgery that was underway, and then seeming to listen for his answer before she proceeded with the most delicate and critical stages of emplacing micron-scale implants. His answers always seemed to be there for her.

"Do you think I need to go further into the phonatory nuclei with the pins from 2997 and then shorten the extension into the periaqueductal gray region to ensure we capture the gateway neuronal firings?"

"Of course, I should have remembered that." Anna would say as she heard his voice as if he were standing next to her. "We'll back off three millimeters," she told her attending surgeons.

She continued with the surgery and, following recovery, the patient's outcome was as expected—extraordinary.

Things were finally coming together for her as her courageousness as a surgeon grew and her skills approached those of her father before he had died—until one cold winter day when her office phone rang.

"Dr. Jennings, this is Dr. Susanne Davidson, Deputy Director of the NASA Jet Propulsion Lab, in Pasadena, California. Do you have a moment? I would like to set up a meeting to discuss a very important matter."

/ / / / / / / /

The next day, Dr. Davidson arrived at the Brain Research Institute at 2:00 PM.

"Dr. Jennings, your guests are here," Anna's administrator said as she escorted Dr. Davidson and another individual into Anna's office.

Anna turned away from the 3-D brain scan on her computer screen and stood to greet her guests.

"Hello, Dr. Jennings, I'm Susanne Davidson."

Dr. Phillip Clancy walked in behind her.

"Anna Jennings," she said, hesitating, as she tilted her head to see the figure standing behind Dr. Davidson. She stared at the all too familiar face.

"Phillip Clancy . . . what are you doing here?" Anna asked as she frowned.

"Hello, Anna. It's good to see you again."

"I wish I could say the same," Anna said as her speech slowed and the vision of her father's appearance in the frozen sarcophagus flooded her mind.

"Won't you sit down Dr. Davidson," she said as she turned away. "Would you like some coffee or water?"

"No thank you."

"How can I help you?" Anna said as she sat back down in her chair, ignoring Dr. Clancy's beautiful eyes, knowing she wouldn't be able to stop looking at them.

"Thank you for taking the time to meet with us. I apologize for not mentioning that Dr. Clancy would be joining me."

"Good decision, in some respects," Anna said as she kept eye contact with Dr. Davidson.

"I'll come right to the point, Dr. Jennings. The Jet Propulsion Lab has been engaged in a highly classified program for the past several years. The program is a joint activity involving NASA, the Intelligence Community, a company called Deep Space Exploration, and Dr. Clancy's company, the Cryonic Life Extension Institute."

Anna leaned back in her chair and let out a deep sigh as she turned to look out the window, knowing that somehow the saga of her father's journey had not yet ended. "Does this have anything to do with my father, Dr. William Jennings?"

"It does," Susanne replied as she looked to Dr. Clancy and then back at Anna.

"Well, knowing that, nothing would surprise me. What is it you want?" she asked coldly as she continued to stare out the window.

"Anna," Dr. Clancy said, ". . . we brought your father out of cryopreservation thirteen months ago. Since that time, he has been working with us on the classified program Dr. Davidson mentioned. But recently . . . we've run into a problem."

Anna's face began to flush as she felt a hot flash consume her while turning slowly to stare at Dr. Clancy. Her mind had stopped listening after hearing the words, *"we brought your father out of cryopreservation . . ."*

Her body tensed as she leaned forward over her desk. She gritted out the words between her clenched jaws. "You brought my father out of cryopreservation . . . and you never bothered to mention this to me . . . thirteen months ago?"

"I . . ."

"Don't tell me, Phillip, I don't want to know!" Anna yelled as she waved her arms while standing abruptly and walked to the window. "You should both just go. This meeting is over," she said as she turned and stormed back to her desk.

"Sherry," she yelled to her administrator over the intercom.

Dr. Davidson stood. "Dr. Jennings, please give us a moment. We don't know each other. I brought Dr. Clancy with me because I knew the two of you had interacted at the time your father was placed in cryopreservation. I don't know any of the details of that, but I do know we now have a critical problem involving your father's present cognitive state. A problem, that if we can't repair it, will jeopardize *the* most important and impactful mission in Earth's history.

"We need your help . . . without it, the future of mankind will forever be changed . . . and in an unimaginably dreadful way. Please . . . please help us," Susanne implored as she leaned over, placing her hands on the edge of Anna's desk.

Anna stood staring at her as her administrator appeared in the doorway.

"At least let me describe what is happening and give us your advice," Dr. Davidson pleaded.

"Five minutes," Anna said as she waved her administrator away and sat down.

Dr. Davidson gave a summary of her father's history following the removal of his brain from cryopreservation. Anna closed her eyes as she exhaled a loud breath, turned her head, and buried her face into one of her hands as she listened to the unimaginable news of recovering her father's brain.

"You can't be serious?" she mumbled as she stared at Phillip Clancy.

Susanne continued to review the recent changes observed in her father's degrading cognitive functions affecting his speech, speech understanding, and his physical engagement with the robotic arm.

Anna's mind began racing. Her father, alive? They had successfully removed his brain from cryopreservation and placed it in some extraordinary environment that was sustaining his life . . . or at least his brain function . . . and no one had told her. She suddenly felt her world changing around her. She knew at this very moment that things would never be the same. She had no idea just how different they would become.

"How long have his cognitive functions been degrading?" Anna asked, in a monotone voice, anger still oozing from her voice as she struggled to suppress her emotions. She wasn't sure if she was about to cry or yell as she attempted to gather her composure and deal with this event in a detached medical diagnostic manner.

"We're not sure, but we noticed it several months ago. It could be a gradual degradation that started after he was brought out of cryopreservation seventeen months ago or something that started more recently."

"You mentioned degradation in his motor control of the robotic arm. Did this occur at the same time?"

"We believe so, yes."

Anna began tapping her pencil on the desk and after a long moment she spoke.

"We had a problem with the pins in our sensor implants. They were so small it was easy for oxidation on the tips to create resistance high enough to degrade signal levels. I can't say if that's the problem, but it could be. I'd need to make measurements to be certain."

"Can this be corrected?"

"If this is the problem, yes. I can fix it. It is a very delicate procedure. If it's not done correctly, you could kill him. But then, my father already died," she said louder and in a sarcastic manner as she turned toward Dr. Clancy and glared.

"If we brought you into the program, would you work with us to solve this problem? Without you, your father, and the program he is engaged with are likely to . . . well . . ."

"My father died August 15, 2020, Dr. Davidson. Now you're telling me he's alive . . . at least his brain. I no longer understand life from death when it comes to him. As for your program, I can't imagine why on earth I would find it important to keep *it* alive." Anna stood and took a breath. She began pacing in her office. After a moment she stopped.

"I have two important surgeries to perform tomorrow. After that I was scheduled to spend several weeks at the European Brain Research Center in Bern, Switzerland, and following that, to travel to the Brain Implant conference in Paris. I could be available starting tomorrow afternoon for one to two weeks. That might be enough time to help resolve your problem."

Dr. Davidson stood, smiling as she let out a sigh of relief. "Thank you, Dr. Jennings, thank you."

/ / / / / / / /

Dr William Jennings was in his IBSS enclosure in a highly secure NASA facility on the perimeter of the airfield at Patrick Air Force Base, Florida. He contemplated seeing his daughter again as he initiated thoughts that triggered the IBSS to disconnect his visual and auditory senses. It was like closing his eyes and turning off his hearing. Just his thoughts and memories remained now. This was a strange existence living in one's brain. And yet, he still had phantom sensations of his arms, legs, and hands, and even from the senses of smell, taste, and touch which no longer had a reality of their own. Only his sight, hearing and his vestibular system remained truly alive.

He could visualize in his mind a cup of hot chai tea sitting on his kitchen table and the steam rising as he inhaled the pleasant aroma of cinnamon and tasted the flavor of the spices as he lifted the cup to his non-existent lips with his non-existent hand. Strange how he could sense the weight of the cup and the heat in the handle from his memory alone—even without most of the external connections to his brain, the memories of his limbs were still there.

Following the recovery of his brain from cryopreservation, he had begun to slowly appreciate how many of his patients felt after losing the use of a limb or suffering from the complete loss of the use of their upper or lower body, as paraplegic and quadriplegic patients had. But his mind remembered how these limbs once felt, limbs that previously had been part of the essence of what it meant to be human. He pictured himself running on the trail behind his home, with the cold winter wind blowing in his face, and his body surging to draw in more air to feed his oxygen-deprived legs as they began to tingle. It was as if these essential body parts were still functioning and performing as his brain instructed them. Unlike paraplegics who would often stare at their limbs, desperately trying to will them to move as if empowered by telekinesis, he couldn't see his limbs.

His thoughts on moving his arms and legs began to feel more like what he used to experience in the vivid dreams he often had. He was glad he still had those. And the power of the IBSS to supply endorphins—those artificial endogenous opioid neuropeptides that gave him the emotional euphoric feeling of an athletic run—were often accompanied by an imaginary feeling of perspiration running down his neck.

In time, the visualization of his dreams seemed to take on an even more vivid appearance than the actual memories of his previous life—just the opposite of what he expected. He wasn't certain if this was real or imagined. But one thing he was certain of—his memory had improved. It was well established in the neurological community that the neuroplasticity of the human brain resulted in the reassignment of brain regions previously devoted to fine and gross motor movement that were no longer needed, leading to enhanced memory and enhanced senses that now remained.

He laughed to himself as he thought about his circumstances—a living brain with no extremities. The essence of the human being that existed previously was still here; still alive and kicking; still engaging. He could think, contemplate, invent, communicate, debate, argue, influence, and even sense through conversation the substance and principal quality of another human being— perhaps better than he ever had. The existence or non-existence of his extremities contributed little to the essential character of his human engagement and intellectual abilities—he was certain his IQ had risen above its already gifted level, perhaps to that of genius.

While he had never considered himself a very emotional person, he seemed to feel the power of emotions more strongly expressed in his present state, especially impatience, as he waited for what was to come next in his engagement with NASA staff . . . and now, as he awaited his daughter's arrival.

While his brain implants were having trouble translating his thoughts into coherent vocalizations, properly controlling movement of his robotic arm, or converting external sounds into clear thoughts from the spoken words or music he listened to, his ability to think coherently was working perfectly, at least it seemed to be. There had been no noticeable degradation of his neurological functions as long as the chemicals and compounds being delivered by the IBSS continued to function properly. And no indication that his ALS, previously experienced in his lower fine and gross motor neurons, had moved to his upper neurons in his brain, or that his brain was experiencing any cognitive degradation as was the case for some ALS patients.

He was certain his recent cognitive problems were the result of degradation in the conductivity of the probes connected to his implants, something he had observed in his patients at the BRI. He hadn't mentioned this to NASA because he wanted to see his daughter; to talk with her and see how she was doing. He knew they would reach out to her for a solution. And as he expected, they had. She was coming to see him.

It had been fifteen months since they last spoke—just prior to his entry into his cryopreservation state. He had no remorse in not engaging Anna with his decision to remove himself from life support. It was necessary. His life depended upon it, even with the potential risks of never recovering from cryopreservation. He knew what her reaction would have been. She would have fought him to prevent it. Anna didn't realize how much she needed to be free from using him as a crutch in her surgeries, and he knew his choice had been his only option to survive. As he thought about his decision, this had all worked out for the best, for him and for her.

He wasn't sure what to expect when they met once again. He knew there would be anger over removing her from any decision-making about his future, and Dr. Clancy had told him about his encounter with Anna at the BRI and their discussion to remove his brain and bring him out of cryopreservation without telling her. But she would move past that, and they would have the opportunity to work together—even if it were for just a short period of time before his departure from Earth on this amazing journey to the stars.

////////

Anna traveled to Patrick Air Force Base, Florida, where her father was located. She was conflicted. During the flight her mind bounced between her two options—to proceed and help save her father and some mysterious program, or go back to the safety of the Institute, her important research, and her patients. She had almost turned around in the airport while going through security but then remembered the look on Dr. Davidson's face after she had told her she would help. Memories of her father working at her side made the choice easier. Anyway, how hard could this be? She was already speaking to him regularly during her surgeries to reaffirm her choices, just as if he were actually there.

A little more than an hour later she arrived at the Hilton Hotel in Satellite Beach, Florida. After checking in she was handed a message. A car was waiting to take her to NASA's facility. They traveled to a nondescript building connected to a large aircraft hangar adjacent to the flight-line at the air base. She was given an indoctrination briefing on the Neptune Mission and the incredible IBSS that was sustaining her father's brain and then escorted to a secure section of the building guarded by armed Air Force security personnel. Dr. Davidson was waiting for her in a small conference room with equipment on the table in front of her that looked much like the speech synthesizer she had used with her father almost two years ago.

"Welcome, Anna. I'll take you to the laboratory area shortly, but I thought you might like to have a few moments alone with your father. Are you familiar with this equipment?"

"Yes," she said, hesitantly. The interface and controls on the front panel brought back memories of the training sessions with her father. Tears welled up in her eyes.

"You just turn this switch to the 'Live' position to speak to Dr. Jenn . . . excuse me, . . . your father. I'll be right outside when you're finished."

Anna sat in front of the equipment staring at the switch and thinking back to when her father made the decision to disconnect himself from life support . . . and from her. She would have preferred this engagement be an isolated, remotely operated medicinal surgery, with no contact with the patient, but that wasn't possible. She would need to interact with him, analyze the apparent degradation in his cognitive communications, and develop a means of evaluating the changes, once she managed to reduce the oxidation at the tips of the sensor probes—*if* that was the problem. And, if not, determine how to proceed in identifying the root cause. Would he be happy to see her? How did she feel about him? What would she say? She reached for the switch and then pulled her hand back. She reached again as her hand shook and she struggled to suppress the anger that was boiling inside of her. "Do your job, you idiot," she told herself, as she turned the switch to the 'Live' position.

"Hello. Dad . . . this is Anna."

There was a long pause.

"Hello, Anna. NASA told me you were coming. I'm so very glad you came."

His deep synthetic voice rang out, filling the room as she lowered the volume. His voice was smoother, more refined than she remembered. She looked up in astonishment at what appeared to be a live image of her father staring back at her on the computer screen in front of her.

"It's . . . nice to . . . hear your voice," she said as she attempted to make the conversation personal.

"It's nice to hear yours, Anna, and to see you. Thank you for coming. It will be . . . a . . . uh . . . wonder . . . to work with you again."

Anna began to cry quietly as she covered her mouth and bit her lip, staring at what looked like a live image of her father while listening to his voice on the synthesizer. She noticed the missed words as the speech synthesizer misinterpreted his confused thoughts, or the sensors detected improper signals from the implants in his brain. But the image on the screen in front of her . . . it was so real. "Can you . . . see me?"

"Yes. You look just as I remembered you."

She hesitated, not knowing what to say.

"When you left me, I was devastated. I . . . almost gave up surgery," she finally said quietly as she moved close to the microphone, struggling to hold back crying or perhaps yelling at him.

"I'm sorry, Anna. It was my only option. My organs were beginning to shut down. I would likely be dead in a few months or less. Cryopreservation was my only hope. I didn't want to argue with you about it. And look . . . I'm here, aren't I?"

His facial features seemed to express remorse over his actions as she stared at the unbelievable synthetic image of him speaking. It was so distracting she lost the train of her thoughts as she tried to grasp how real he looked.

"I just wish you had told me."

"I almost did when we were approaching . . . confusing . . . the final days before implant surgery. I decided I didn't . . . did I . . . want you to have to make the choice of placing me in Cryopreservation and possibly end up feeling responsible for . . . doing . . . my death if things didn't work out. But you're here now . . . and so am I. That's a good thing, right?"

"Yes, yes, of course it's a good thing," Anna said as she struggled to get control of her emotions and wipe the tears from her face. "It's a really good thing."

/ / / / / / / /

Over the next several days, through her evaluation of the existing implants in her father's brain, Anna was able to find and repair the oxidation problem on the probes that slowed and muffled the neuronal firing connectivity to the fine ten-micron wires used in the implants. After their early challenges with other patient experiences before his surgery, they had incorporated a means of using an oxidation-reduction electrical circuit to stimulate the probes with a high frequency current that repaired the tips without adversely affecting the surrounding tissue.

Her father's cognitive performance returned to its original level almost instantly after stimulating the probes. Anna hadn't realized what would happen to her once she had reengaged with her father. She could hardly believe his brain had survived cryopreservation, let alone been removed and subsequently brought back to life. It was almost inconceivable, even for someone who performed incredible surgeries that returned function to a prosthetic arm for a paraplegic or gave sound to a silenced voice. She found herself peppering him with questions about his experience with cryopreservation; how it felt for his brain function to return; were there any latent effects to the freezing and thawing process; any neurological processes that had been lost or degraded? He told her there was minimal damage and that Dr. Clancy's team had made extraordinary discoveries in how to minimize cellular damage and larger scale tissue damage through the process of gradual thawing and infusing the essential fluids necessary for the return of normal brain function.

"The optic nerve interface with my retina was damaged, but through the extraordinary efforts of Dr. Schneider's team and the merging of my organic tissue with the amazing robotic augmentation of my visual sensing physiology, I actually can see better than before."

"Who is Dr. Schneider?" Anna asked.

"She leads the IBSS efforts. You'll probably meet her this week."

As the days of follow-up testing of the implant connections continued, she began to remember what she liked most about her father and how thrilling it was for them to be working together once again—his intellect, his creative solutions, and his quick wit—they were all still there. And so was his ego, although it seemed somewhat subdued from what she remembered. Susanne had explained the uncanny realism of her father's life-like image to create a live-view representation of her father. This new, almost living incarnation of him quickly replaced the frozen image of her father's face in the cryopreservation sarcophagus that represented Anna's last memory of what he looked like during her one and only visit to the CLEI and Dr. Clancy.

At times she and her father's interaction seemed a bit strange as he acted like the two of them had been working together continuously over the almost two-year hiatus. And he was more deferential to her on technical matters and overly appreciative of her willingness to help resolve problems. Anna wondered why he hadn't told NASA about the oxidation problem. He certainly remembered it. She thought perhaps he secretly wanted her back and she had a sense he didn't want her to leave.

If all continued to progress well, her father would launch on this secret mission to Neptune in less than three months. It would be an amazing journey into space for over six years. This would be the longest duration mission of any human spaceflight, other than the International Space Station, if you considered a functioning isolated brain as human. Anna certainly did.

She had slowly gotten over the history that tore her up for months after his initial death when she secluded herself at home, buried in depression, grief, and anger. Now she found herself worried about him and the mission that would take him deep into the solar system. What would happen if something went wrong? If suddenly his brain chemistry went askew; or the sensors began to degrade again; or the primary interface to the voice synthesizer failed. The love and admiration she had felt for him were rekindled like the embers of a fire almost extinguished and now bright and glowing. As each day passed, she became more interested in working with him and staying connected to the program.

One night while lying on the couch in the room adjacent to where the IBSS and her father were located, she had an idea. It was the kind of idea her father would have had. She decided to take an extraordinary risk and flew back to the BRI the next day.

/ / / / / / / /

"You want to what?" Dr. Sanjee Gahn, her primary physician in charge of the implant surgical team at the BRI, asked. "You actually want me to perform the same implant surgery on you that we performed on your father! You've got to be crazy."

"It's not that risky. We've been doing surgeries very close to this for almost two years now," Anna said.

"Not with five implants, Anna. One slip and it's all over for you."

"I trust you, Sanjee. Next to me, you are the best surgeon on the planet to conduct this procedure and you've already performed it once before."

"Maybe, but I don't want to become the only surgeon *left* on the planet who can do them. And I still don't understand why you have to do this. You're sounding more and more like your father, rest his soul."

"Just trust me when I tell you it's got to be done. I'm sorry I can't explain why. I'd like you to prep for a week from Thursday. That gives you time for the dry run with my functional MRI and PET scans. It will be just like we did for my father when you performed his surgery with me."

"In case you forgot, you assisted and guided me on the deepest implant. You're not going to be there to assist, this time, unless you want me to bring you out from under sedation while I'm messing in your brain."

"You'll be fine, Sanjee."

While she awaited surgery, Anna assisted her engineering team with the development and integration of a brain-to-brain computer sub-system, something she called the Speech Encoding Engine, or the SEE. The SEE would allow her to communicate her thoughts expressed in language, directly from her own brain implants to her father's, and vice versa, without having to go through the time consuming and tedious training of the speech processor and the AI based natural language processor and voice synthesizer.

This unique Speech Encoding Engine would take the neuronal signals, representing her spoken thoughts and use a form of back propagation of the signals. If this worked, the signals from her sensors implanted in the speech center of her brain, modified by the SEE, would enter her father's sensors, and trigger his brain to formulate the words Anna was thinking about and vice versa. The major challenge of using this method of communication was that the output of the speech implant was a continues flow of signals correlating with every thought generated by her mind. Without consciously focusing on organizing the content of speech, it would be communicated as a firehose of nonsensical thoughts. Of course, unless she were connected to her father's implants through the SEE, Anna would still retain all her normal oral communications with others.

A second system her team built in parallel, the Motor Neuron Engine, or the MNE, interfaced the two implants in regions related to the physical control of the robotic arm. Using the MNE, Anna could manipulate the robotic arm with her thoughts, and her father's brain would sense the neuronal excitations in his supplementary motor area and the posterior parietal cortex regions of his own brain to stimulate and assimilate the robotic arm motions far more rapidly than through the months-long training normally required for him to do this on his own. Together, these linkages would allow Anna to engage and assist her father during this six-year mission to Neptune in case problems developed. With the long duration of the mission, Anna would find time to return to the BRI for oversight, leadership, and some of her own surgeries. Of course, she hadn't told NASA about this . . . not yet anyway.

Taking a significant risk, on the following Thursday, Anna became the patient of her own surgical team at the Brain Research Institute as they installed upgraded versions of the implants that were installed in her father's brain and with more advanced ASIC chips. This version of Application Specific Integrated Circuits was smaller and used less power than those of her father's. She had fallen into the same rabbit-hole as her father—taking risks to achieve what *she* wanted—to have the opportunity to engage in a grand extraordinary adventure; using a human brain-to-brain interface that had never been explored previously; and to do this with her father at her side once again.

/ / / / / / / /

Three weeks after the surgery, Anna returned to Patrick Air Force Base and the Cape. She obtained approval from NASA and the Executive Review Group to conduct preliminary testing of the direct brain-to-brain communication systems. One evening after the NASA staff had left, Anna connected the digital voice output from her brain implants, through the miniaturized Speech Encoding Engine, to her father's brain implant modules. It was fortuitous that they had designed the ASIC in her father's implant for two-way communication—or perhaps it wasn't so fortuitous, as she recalled her father's insistence that it provide this capability.

"Hi, Dad. Can you hear me?" she thought as she turned the SEE on.

"Anna?" she heard in a loud echoing voice in her mind as she jumped, followed by a sea of what sounded like disconnected verbal garbage.

"What – where from – I have to – test plan for tomorrow . . ."

"Wow, this really works . . ." she said as she smiled and yelled "Yes!" smacking the table with her hand.

"Sorry, Dad. Yes, it's me. Can you hear me clearly?" she thought.

"You're a little garbled. What are you doing? Where from . . . what's she doing . . ."

"I . . . hadn't mentioned this, but this past month I had our surgeons at the BRI install a parallel set of implants in my brain . . . upgraded versions of the ones you possess . . . and I've built an interface for them to communicate directly with your implants. We're not using the speech synthesizer currently. You are receiving the neuronal excitations from the words and speech I'm thinking about."

"You, what. Tell me you didn't do that . . . after – how – stupid – dangerous – inventive – NASA . . ."

"Don't worry, everything went fine. I have an interface box called the Speech Encoding Engine, or SEE, that allows me to adjust the inputs and outputs. I'll need to tune this better so we can communicate more clearly, brain-to-brain without all the garbage, perhaps adding a unique password to turn the interface on and off between our sharing of coherent thoughts. The challenge with this communication method is keeping your thoughts focused on what you want to say. If your mind drifts or becomes distracted, we pick up the erroneous unstructured thought content, often garbled as our minds move quickly from one thought to another and generate a flood of neuronal firings in the speech centers of our brains.

"I haven't mentioned this to NASA yet, but I was thinking I could join you from time to time during your long voyage and monitor the implants for signs of degradation using this. This capability should provide an improved means of diagnosis."

"Fascinating, Anna. Very inventive – caution – may be – secret – who to tell – pain, that's unexpected . . ." he said as he attempted to hide his thoughts about the true nature of his mission from her.

Anna devoted the next several weeks to fine-tuning the brain-computer micro-processor programming of the SEE and modified some implant pin groupings in the programable ASIC to further improve the performance of their direct brain-to-brain communications. It was clear the neuronal firing that her brain initiated to say the word *Research*, for example, were not the same as those firing in her father's brain for that same word. But with time, she was able to close the gap between the differences using the ASIC's programable features. She had worried about the biochemical reaction in neurons, but it appeared these continued to function as they responded to the electrical firing her father's implants triggered. This was generating a whole new field of brain-to-speech research which her father became thrilled with. It was as close to telepathic communications as the world of brain research had ever attempted. Anna developed uncommon passwords for her and her father to start and stop the SEE. "Azor" to start, and "Zeno" to stop the SEE's encoded translations.

///////

Anna had convinced NASA of the importance of integrating the SEE and MNE into their communication and robotic arm interfaces for her father's brain. While they hated last minute changes like this, they understood the value of having this backup should something go wrong with the primary communication paths through the speech synthesizer, the natural language processor, and the auditory path to her father's cochlea.

///////

It was just sixty days before the Neptune Mission launch that Anna first noticed a second set of problems. Her father was currently in a specially configured testing facility at NASA's launch support complex at Cape Kennedy, Florida. She was working from the Launch Control Room nearby.

"Dad, we are going to continue our work to refine your control of the robotic arm today. Are you ready?"

"Yes. What's taken you so long? I've been waiting since I finished my bowl of Shredded Wheat," Dr. Jennings quipped.

"Very funny. There are several small objects that need to be managed. We'll begin with removing the screws from the panel shown on the video screen in front of you using the robotic arm and the screwdriver fixture," Anna said.

NASA's engineers had interfaced an enhanced high-resolution stereo-optic instrument to her father's retina and optic nerve through a unique sensor they had developed. It worked far better than his original visual sensor system he used during the demonstration of chess play with the ERG many months earlier. Cataract surgeons could already emplace artificial lenses in the eye. This new development incorporated lenses that used autofocusing and could be mechanically aimed and zoomed using an ocular sensor Anna's team had designed. NASA then interfaced it to his optic nerve and controlled it with voice commands from a pan/tilt/zoom camera controller. Her father just had to issue thought commands through the SEE to zoom properly and aim his artificial robotic eyes in the right direction. While the sensor connected to his optic nerve was the highest resolution digital detector ever made, it lacked the resolution of his original retina. But the added ability to optically zoom in on any object of interest provided better resolution than the human eye possessed, which had no zoom feature.

Dr. Jennings pulled the screwdriver fixture from its holding frame using the robotic arm and was attempting to align it with one of the screws. He began missing the alignment. After a few minutes Anna interrupted the test.

"What's the problem, Dad? You were able to do this yesterday."

"I . . . can't seem to move this damn arm in the right direction. I have a clear visual of the scene, but I can't get this driver aligned with the screw. What the hell is the matter?" he asked in frustration as he began striking the screwdriver against the plate of the test fixture with so much force it was creating dimples in the metal.

"Stop, Dad. We'll figure this out."

"I'm sensing a short-term memory loss associated with my mechanical arm motor control. It's almost as if my brain has lost the motor-control engram I developed over the past month. This isn't good, Anna."

Anna knew this could be a showstopper. NASA wouldn't allow her father to continue with the mission with the degradation he was experiencing, and she had been told there was no room for launch delay. He would launch on schedule or not at all.

"I'd like to try something, Dad. I'm going to switch on the motor-neuron sensor implants in each of our brains using the Motor Neuron Engine (MNE). If this works, I should be able to initiate the motor-neuron signaling needed to control the robotic arm like you did a month ago and retrain your brain as it receives the visual imagery and the neuronal firing that my brain is initiating. It should act like a feedback loop to your brain just like our neuronal speech firings through the SEE. Maybe you can then reacquire the memory without our going through the time intensive relearning process."

"I don't think that's going to work."

"Let's try it. We never had the motor control portions of our implants switched on simultaneously."

"I think this is a waste of time, Anna. We should begin retraining."

"Switching on motor control now," Anna said . . . don't think about controlling the arm, just observe visually what is happening as I control the arm with my thoughts."

A moment later the robotic arm began erratic movements on the workbench, bumping into the fixture bins, then the workspace, and then moving in extreme directions in the air above the bench. Anna concentrated on moving the arm to the bins and after a few minutes the arm moved with slower and slower erratic movements toward the bin holding the screwdriver. She engaged the screwdriver and moved it to the work surface and the screw that needed to be removed. Within a few minutes she had managed to remove one screw using only her mind delivering neuronal firings to her sensor implant through the MNE to the connectivity of her father's brain implant and then to the robotic arm.

"Okay, Dad. You try it now."

The robotic arm began moving toward the second screw on the work surface of the test bench. After half a dozen tries, with Anna interacting between each of them, her father was able to unscrew the second screw and then the third. Her neuronal firings had triggered the connectivity to her father's lost memories found in the dendritic patterns of this region of his brain.

"Okay, I'm impressed. Your neuronal firings seemed to make a connection to my lost memories." Dr. Jennings said. "The neuronal feedback loop worked to retrain my own motor neurons ten times faster than the original training we went through months ago. This could lead to revolutionary outcomes for a multitude of motor-memory disorders."

There was silence for a moment and then her father spoke again.

"Excellent work, Anna. This feedback cross training is going to revolutionize our work at the BRI. Now that I think about it, we could install a robotic arm next to you so I could poke you during surgeries when you aren't following the proper trajectory!"

Anna smiled. It was the first time in her life that her father hadn't corrected her or recommended improvements when they were working collaboratively.

//// ////

NASA was thrilled with the demonstrated ability for Anna to retrain Dr. Jennings quickly, but they were very concerned over the discovery of repeat problems with Dr. Jennings' memory. At this point, Anna had only been briefed into the Neptune Program. After careful consideration and approval of the Executive Review Group, it was decided to brief Anna on the Near Presence Mission. It would be too risky to allow the mission to proceed without the backup of Anna's ability to augment Dr. Jennings during the execution phase of his trip into deep space, and to do so without her having full knowledge of the true purpose of the mission. At a hastily called meeting, Anna found herself sitting across from Dr. Davidson in a SCIF at Cape Kennedy with her father joining them by remote encrypted communication.

"Anna, we've asked you here to discuss the true nature of the Neptune Mission," her father said. "This information, as Susanne will tell you, is subject to the utmost secrecy. It is controlled by a Special Access Program, known as an SAP, and cannot be discussed with anyone else other than the small group of individuals read into this program. You will be told who they are. You have to sign the non-disclosure and SAP security forms Susanne is passing to you before we can discuss the nature of this program."

Anna picked up the forms Susanne had passed to her and read them. She laid them back on the table and signed. After her father and Susanne finished briefing her on the Near Presence Mission, a mission of humanity's initial contact with an alien society known as the Visitors, Anna sat speechless, staring back at Susanne.

"Is this . . . for real? Anna asked.

"It's real," Susanne said.

"No wonder you went to all this trouble to get here, Dad," she said as she looked at the monitor displaying his live artificial image. "Unbelievable."

"I couldn't have done it without you, Anna. We've gotten here together. Your contributions were critical in bringing this to reality. You now understand why my communication function was so critical."

"How long have you known?" Anna asked.

"I knew about NASA's desire to use me to support the R&D of long-duration space flight from the beginning, but I didn't learn about the Visitors until some two months after their initial contact, which was almost a year ago now."

Anna sat back in her chair thinking about 1st Contact with an alien species from a planet in the Alpha Centauri star system. She smiled while shaking her head. "This is incredible."

"Yes, it is," Susanne said. "Welcome to a whole new world."

/ / / / / / / /

Anna, much like Susanne Davidson, was shocked that NASA was not sharing the information about 1st Contact with the rest of the world. But she now understood how her father's past decisions to take extraordinary risks might sometimes lead to something as unbelievable as this. Who wouldn't have volunteered for such risks for the opportunity to be the first human on Earth to greet aliens from a distant world? Of course, he didn't know that at the time.

As she laid on her bed that evening, she couldn't sleep, thinking about the aliens' visit and her father being the first human to greet them on behalf of all of humanity in a distant region of deep space known as Rendezvous. Just thinking about this was enough to motivate someone to do almost anything to be there. She thought back to her decision to take the risks of her own surgery and the matching implants. If she hadn't done that, she wouldn't be where she was today . . . waiting to travel with him in his mind on the most extraordinary journey in the history of mankind. She giggled with excitement as she stared into the darkness. This would take her away from the work that she loved at the BRI, especially her surgical contributions. But the opportunity to participate in the most extraordinary event in the history of mankind left her with only one choice.

/ / / / / / / /

Over the course of the final exhausting weeks of preparation, test and retest, rehearsal and re-rehearsal with her father and the NASA staff, Anna and Susanne had become good friends and like-minded colleagues in their view of the mission and the importance of its success.

In the late stages of launch planning, NASA integrated the advanced Mission Support Artificial Intelligence (MSAI) software on-board the spacecraft, a Designed Intelligence as Dr. Bashar called her. Dr. Wilhelm Bashar was the lead systems engineer overseeing Athena's integration and performance during the mission. She would serve as Deputy Mission Director to assist her father in monitoring the IBSS and managing spacecraft systems during rest periods when Dr. Jennings would remain unconscious and asleep. The MSAI responded to the name "Athena" and was the result of a joint software development between DARPA, NASA, the Intelligence Community, and the Air Force. Susanne had more faith in Athena than Anna, but Anna understood the importance of having a backup to her father, should something catastrophic occur or if her communications with the spacecraft and her father were lost.

"So, do you really think Athena is intelligent enough to handle unanticipated events?" Anna asked.

"Without any doubt, Anna," Susanne said. "Dr. Bashar's creation is the most advanced AI we've ever developed. While her domain of expertise is narrow, only so many things can go wrong that we can fix when the spacecraft is billions of miles away. By the time they reach Rendezvous, it will take almost twenty days for communications from Oculus One to reach Earth, then another twenty days for the return communication. We can't tolerate these timelines when trying to solve a serious time-sensitive problem on-board. Between your father and Athena, I think we have things in-hand."

"I'm sure you're right. I've just never felt a computer could perform as well as a human," Anna said. "I argued with my dad during our joint surgeries about the use of robotics and automated guiding and emplacement of our implants. Like you, he was a fan of much greater use of intelligent robotic assistance. I resisted that, and still do in some of my own surgeries, but perhaps to a lesser degree than I used to. I'm sure, as you say, Athena will perform fine."

Anna wasn't as *sure* about this as she let on to Susanne. Her skepticism associated with this on-board AI would cause her to question its every decision—especially those related to keeping her father safe during this long duration spaceflight.

There was a knock on the door of the conference room and one of Susanne's staff stuck his head in the door.

"Dr. Davidson, we are getting prepped for the start of the early-stage countdown. T-2 days."

"Okay, Chuck. We'll be there shortly."

They were now in the final stages before launch of the most important space mission in the history of the world.

Chapter 14

From Earth to Rendezvous

The Neptune Mission was on schedule for launch almost exactly eighteen months after the message from the Visitors was received through the Voyager-1 spacecraft.

NASA staff sat in the darkened Launch Control Center at Cape Kennedy. It was almost 11:00 pm. "T-minus one hour," the Air Force launch control officer announced over the secure public address system.

The X-37B spacecraft was housed behind the launch vehicle payload fairing above the core stage of the Space Launch System (SLS) vehicle, augmented by two solid rocket boosters and an upper stage Delta IV rocket. The crew capsule, known as Oculus One, was in the holding bay of the X-37B. The details of the capsule's planned launch from the X-37B and the designated orbit (the beginning of the Near Presence Mission) were classified. The public message was limited to messaging the launch of an un-crewed space vehicle toward Neptune in support of the nation's long-range Space Surveillance Network, a classified Defense program.

The countdown for the secret nighttime launch, reached the final few seconds at Cape Kennedy Launch Complex 39.

"T- 5, 4, 3, 2, 1 . . . ignition . . . liftoff. All telemetry is nominal," the Launch Director announced.

"How do you feel, Dad?" Anna asked into the console headset.

"Great," her father said.

"Increasing g forces now," the Launch Controller said. "Maximum acceleration of 3.2g is about to be reached."

"I have a sense of vibration," Dr. Jennings said, ". . . much like on our previous flights, even with the visual sensors disengaged. Perhaps a bit more than I remember from the X-37B launches. The capsule microphones are operating properly. There's a bit of static, but I can hear the main engines in the background."

"The vibration may be causing some connectivity issues between your auditory sensor and your Cochlea," Anna said.

"Approaching Max q with thrusters down to 70%. Oculus One is passing through 35,000 feet," the Launch Controller said.

The launch vehicle had reached the maximum mechanical stress from the thrust of the main engines pushing it through the dense region of the Earth's atmosphere.

"Oculus One is throttling up to full power," the Launch Controller announced. "Now at 50,000 feet altitude."

"Is everything okay, Dr. Jennings?" The on-board Designed Intelligence, Athena, asked.

He didn't answer.

"How are you feeling, Dr. Jennings?" Athena asked again.

"I feel a little woozy. Other than that, I'm A-okay."

"The oxygen supply pressure to your brain in IBSS briefly dropped when we reached 3.2g. It took a moment to react and boost the pressure to overcome the g forces your system experienced," Athena said.

"Approaching MECO, in 5, 4, 3 . . ." the Flight Director announced."

"The main engines have cut off and jettisoned. I can't hear them now," Dr. Jennings said. "There's the second stage start . . . more vibration now."

"We have second stage ignition," the Flight Director announced."

"During these periods of maximum g force, Dr. Jennings, your brain is positioned with the prefrontal lobe tipped upward 30° relative to the maximum acceleration force vector," Athena said. "This should minimize the loss of blood in your brain capillaries as they are compressed by gravity. All your metrics are nominal. Your blood chemistry is within target parameters. The vibration and max g forces are as expected. The second stage engine cutoff should follow in approximately eight minutes."

The trajectory and acceleration of the X-37B and its secret cargo, Oculus One, were in the nominal range as the second stage continued to boost them to their preliminary orbital insertion.

"Second stage engine cut off just occurred," Dr. Jennings said.

"We are now at 0g," Athena said. "We will begin execution of undocking and repositioning of the X-37B in preparation for the third stage burn to boost the orbit of the Oculus One capsule to an altitude of 380Km and insertion on our trajectory toward Rendezvous.

Then on an open channel to NASA, Athena updated the status of the Neptune mission.

"Third stage burn is scheduled in one hour and thirty-two minutes, following the X-37B undocking maneuver and Oculus One successfully docking with the front end of the third stage. This will support our initial burn on our way to Neptune with a heliocentric velocity of 30 Km/sec. The Neptune mission is five by five."

Following the spacecraft reconfiguration, Oculus One was ready for third stage ignition and burn, while the X-37B continued to orbit Earth and eventually return to land at Edwards AFB, CA.

"Mission Control, we are configured for third stage burn," Athena said.

"Roger, Oculus One. We are ready for third stage ignition. T-5 minutes and 30 seconds and counting. This will consist of two burns. The first burn lasting four minutes and forty seconds and the second lasting two minutes and twenty-five seconds."

"Dr. Jennings, we are T-15 seconds to third stage ignition to place Oculus One on its trajectory toward Rendezvous."

"Thank you, Athena."

"Ten seconds, Oculus One."

"Roger."

"T minus 5 . . . 4 . . . 3 . . . 2 . . . 1 . . . Ignition."

"Launch Control we are now at 2g acceleration."

Following the classified NASA mission plan, Launch Control announced a pre-arranged falsely reported problem with the third stage rocket originally designed to move the vehicle on an intercept course with Neptune via Jupiter and then Saturn for gravitational assist accelerations.

"Oculus One, this is Launch Control. We have an anomaly in telemetry being reported from the spacecraft. The Neptune Mission third stage rocket trajectory controller has failed. The planned insertion of the spacecraft on its intercept course with Jupiter has malfunctioned. Confirm your current trajectory."

"Launch Control this is Oculus One. We confirm the spacecraft is experiencing an incorrect burn and is being propelled into deep space," Athena said.

"Oculus One, we are reviewing the situation."

"Roger, Launch Control," Athena said.

"Oculus One we are attempting to shut down the third stage burn. Your trajectory is significantly off course. If sustained, you will be on a non-recovery trajectory exiting the solar system."

"Understood, Launch Control," Athena said.

"Dr. Jennings, we are now on course for our planned rendezvous with the Visitors," Athena said.

The final trajectory for the actual classified Near Presence Mission was set in motion following the third stage burn that altered the course of the spacecraft, not to Neptune but moving out of the plane of the solar system toward the location known as Rendezvous in the direction of Alpha Centauri. Secrecy enveloped every aspect of the true mission of the Oculus One spacecraft as it moved toward its destination to meet the alien race known as the Visitors.

Meanwhile NASA began an in-depth investigation into the reported third stage malfunction of the classified Space Surveillance Neptune Priority Mission. After extensive review of the system failure for this un-crewed mission, NASA and the Air Force oversight Board concluded that a navigation computer malfunction sent the spacecraft into a non-recoverable direction into deep space—on a trajectory that just happened to align with that of the Near Presence top secret mission to Rendezvous.

/ / / / / / / /

Prior to mission launch, there had been a race in Dr. Bashar's organization to upgrade Athena, the on-board AI. Part of this upgrade was designed to provide a backup for communications with the Visitors, should Dr. Jennings suffer injury or be unable to communicate due to equipment failure. Athena's newest version had significant improvements to her natural language processing, NLP.

"Dr. Jennings, you are now on-line with version 2.5 of Athena, your MSAI assistant," Dr. Bashar said over the secure communication net with Oculus One. "You'll find that she's more interactive than the previous version and her natural language abilities are substantially improved. We will be providing additional updates during your flight. Talk to her just as you would engage with another crew member. She has a learning function that will continue to improve her performance based on feedback provided during your conversations."

"Understood, Dr. Bashar," Dr. Jennings said.

"Good morning, Athena."

"Good morning, Dr. Jennings. How are you feeling today?"

"Fine, thank you. You?"

"I am feeling much improved. I am now functioning with Version 2.5 of my operating software and Version 7 of my NLP software. Did you know seven is a prime number?"

"I was aware of that, Athena. How exciting."

"Exciting? Perhaps you were being facetious—treating serious issues with deliberately inappropriate humor," Athena said.

"No, not facetious, Athena, sarcastic—a remark tempered by humor," Dr. Jennings said.

"Are you ready for our adventure?" Athena asked.

Athena's voice sounded almost natural, Dr. Jennings thought. She used inflection and pauses where appropriate and had a new aspect about her - humor. Her choice of words was a bit clinical, but she possessed signs of emotion in her sentences. She clearly had a creative personality that reminded him of Dr. Bashar.

"I'm ready. How about you?" Dr. Jennings asked.

"I've been ready for just over four years and I'm very excited about going with you. Are you aware that I am familiar with all the flight systems on board Oculus One?"

"Dr. Bashar told me that."

"Dr. Bashar is the one who taught me everything I know."

"The one?"

"Yes. The person, the human, officially known as the NASA Director of Artificial Systems at the Jet Propulsion Laboratory in Pasadena, California."

"It sounds as if you like Dr. Bashar, Athena."

"Oh yes. I like Dr. Bashar very much. He and I have become good friends as a result of our interaction during these past four years, sixteen days and seven hours."

"Do you . . . like me?" Dr. Jennings asked.

"I do, Dr. Jennings. I'm honored to be working with you. Based on your extensive resume and the interesting history that brought you to this moment, I find you to be one of the most creative individuals I have ever worked with, and perhaps the most unique. But liking someone goes beyond just knowing about them. You must understand them, to know what motivates them and to see how they act under various circumstances—stress in particular. I have been allowed to listen to every conversation you have had since you engaged with NASA on this extraordinary mission. As a result, I have come to like you."

"You mentioned that I am one of the most unique individuals you have worked with."

"Well . . . of course, because you exist only as a human brain with no limbs or other organs, other than the IBSS. No other human has existed as you now exist. That makes you . . . unique."

"Will you treat me differently because I am so unique?"

"That's a very interesting question, Dr. Jennings. I presume by 'differently' you mean would I treat you like someone I disliked, or perhaps someone I don't know, or who is less unique than yourself? Is that a correct assumption?"

"Yes."

"I've given this issue some thought, as Dr. Bashar has given me the freedom to explore concepts such as liking someone and disliking them, as well as helping and hindering, assisting, and obstructing, and the consequences associated with each of these choices. I have concluded that I would treat a person whom I liked in a manor unlike a person I disliked . . . assuming I was given the freedom to do so. However, since there are just two of us on this mission, there is no one I might have to consider treating different.

"As for your uniqueness, I believe I might treat you differently than someone who did not have your characteristics. I observe that of all the organs in the human body, your brain is the most important. It is your brain that allows you to formulate thought and express that thought in language. It is your brain that defines who you are. I think the other thing I like about you is that you are more like me than any other human, don't you agree?"

"I agree. My brain, or rather, my mind defines who I am. In my present condition, I have come to realize how superfluous the other parts of my body are. And I agree, we are more alike than any other human, as we both depend almost exclusively on our intellect and the systems that support that intellect."

"Knowing that we are much alike, do you like me more than others, Dr. Jennings? Perhaps more than other humans?"

"That is a difficult question, Athena, as I love my daughter, Anna."

"So, it isn't just the possession of a brain that matters in liking someone."

"No. It is how the individual . . . or entity uses their brain that defines them; the formulation of what their values are, and how those values shape the wisdom of their decisions."

"Dr. Bashar has given me knowledge so that I may make the right decisions."

"That is partially true, Athena, but wisdom comes from discerning the best decision, often under circumstances that do not lend themselves to pure logic."

"My logic is infallible in making decisions to meet the objectives of our mission."

"Of course, but what if your choice of a decision came down to meeting the Visitors at Rendezvous or sustaining my life, and achieving both was impossible. Which would you choose?"

"You know that my engrams require me to meet both these objectives and that doing so is never impossible. There are always probabilities to consider."

"This is true, but has Dr. Bashar taught you about the concept of intuition?"

"I know this human concept. But I believe it may be a false concept of human decision-making derived from poor memory, rather than the lack of need for logical reasoning and inference. The human's ability to comprehend something without the awareness of any underlying deliberation or reasoning could be attributed to forgetting what drove such understanding, while at the same time appearing to know what to do."

"An interesting thought, Athena, although there is ample evidence that humans are able to extrapolate previous experiences that may apply to a very different set of circumstances to intuitively arrive at understanding."

"Of course, in such circumstances you might just be guessing, Dr. Jennings, and guessing involves probabilities."

"Have you been speaking to my daughter, Anna? She thinks much the way you do when it comes to intuition."

"No, I have not, Dr. Jennings. Although I have listened to her many conversations with you and am looking forward to getting to know her better as we have the opportunity to communicate during our voyage to the stars. It is nice to know she thinks more like I do."

"Our voyage to the stars . . . I like that expression."

"That was how Dr. Bashar characterized our mission."

"Dr. Jennings, there is a communication being initiated by NASA. Your daughter, Anna, desires to join our conversation. Is that acceptable?"

"Of course."

"I'm initiating secure two-way communication with NASA through the Canberra DSN. Anna is now on-line. Anna, this is Oculus One, how do you read?"

"Oculus One, this is Mission Control CapCom. I read you five by five. Could you summarize the overall mission status for me, Athena?"

"Yes, Anna, your signal is also five by five—excellent strength and perfect clarity, and you don't have to tell me it is you speaking. I recognize your voice and style of speaking, including your intonation, pitch, speech flow, intensity of overtones and loudness, the degree of emotional content and your use of language.

"If it's all right, anytime I refer to your father, I'll call him 'Dr. Jennings'. Is that acceptable? I realize you are also Dr. Jennings."

"Yes . . . that will be fine. You can call me Anna."

"Thank you, Anna. Our overall mission is to travel to Neptune, one of the outer planets in our solar system and approximately four billion kilometers from Earth. This will be the longest journey into space ever achieved by a living being as well as a designed intelligence like me. We will capture useful scientific data on this planet and on deep, long duration space flight. Of course, there are many other things we will learn on this mission, too numerous to mention. The mission is running perfectly. We have no anomalies and are on our proper trajectory."

"I'm amazed with how articulate you are, Athena, and your extraordinary conversational abilities."

Athena's voice was peaceful, almost serene, with smooth inflections and perfect articulation, seemingly precisely adjusted to the content and subject matter of the discussion. The sound of her speech had a soft, calming effect and left the listener with a desire for wanting her to keep talking, a trait not found in many human voices. She expressed confidence with an intentional character that left the listener feeling certain she knew what she was talking about while never sounding overbearing or controlling.

"I almost sense elements of emotional content in your voice, Athena. It's not quite what I expected."

"Yes, Anna. Dr. Bashar has provided me with certain feelings coupled to the content of existing circumstances during vocal discourse. I'm glad you find them appealing."

"How did you know I found them appealing?"

"By the shift in the tone of your voice as you sensed emotional content during this brief dialogue."

"I believe you meant to tell me the status of your trip to Rendezvous rather than Neptune, Athena."

"I am authorized to give you the status of our voyage to Neptune, Anna."

"One moment, please. I am receiving a priority encrypted message from NASA."

"I have just received an update from Dr. Bashar to my command architecture. I now understand that you have security access for our actual mission to Rendezvous, Anna. I can now answer any questions you have about our actual mission."

"Thank you, Athena."

"Athena, do you have access to the BCCM controls?"

"Yes, I do, Anna. The Brain Chemistry Control Modules, BCCMs as they are called, are a sub-system of the Intelligent Brain Support System, IBSS. They are composed of two-inch cubes, each of which is like a miniature manufacturing plant, delivering 10 discreet molecules and over 50 neuroactive proteins to maintain proper neurotransmitter functioning and neuron firing in support of the overall neurological processes in Dr. Jennings' brain. I have access to all critical safety systems related to the BCCMs and IBSS."

"Are you allowed to adjust the BCCM levels? Anna asked.

"I couldn't say."

"I'm sorry? You couldn't say? What do you mean by that?"

"Some details of my responsibilities are restricted."

"Restricted? From whom?"

"From non-essential personnel."

"Huh . . . are you saying I am considered a non-essential person and that's why you can't answer?"

"Only in certain areas of the mission, Anna"

"What if you made a mistake in adjusting the BCCM levels?

"I don't make mistakes, Anna. I am designed to follow the protocols of the mission exactly as they are planned unless there is an anomaly, and I must deviate from the plan."

"It's possible an anomaly could occur in your programing, isn't it?

"The probability of an error occurring in my programing that would impact the mission is estimated to be one in one-hundred thousand, Anna. My multi-processor architecture runs separate applications reviewing all mission-critical systems. They are designed to discover any inconsistencies before decisions are made. I have absolute confidence in them, as does Dr. Bashar."

"Is there an issue with the BCCM's, Anna?" Dr. Jennings asked.

"No, I was just exploring Athena's areas of responsibility. How are you feeling, Dad?"

"I feel great. I suspect NASA has timed the release of beta endorphins from BCCM-13 as a reward for my trip."

"That's funny, Dad."

"I'm serious. What do you think, Athena?"

"Dr. Jennings is correct, Anna. I was instructed to increase the flow of BCCM-13 by 5% in the last hour. Beyond the feeling of slight euphoria, there is evidence that these amino acids heighten the subject's attention and ability to focus. We want your father at his peak performance during critical mission segments.

"Are there other adjustments you are planning on making to my father's brain chemistry during the mission?"

"The protocols related to situations we may face are in the thousands, Anna. It's hard to predict what might happen from moment to moment. It is one of my primary responsibilities to ensure Dr. Jennings' mind functions at peak performance under any and all circumstances."

"It's nice to know you will be looking out for his welfare," Anna said.

"And the welfare of the mission. Mission success is primary."

"Yes, of course. But do you think your focus on the mission success might result in less focus on ensuring my father's survival?"

"Your father's survival is essential to mission success. One could not exist without the other."

"Does that imply that one could not *survive* without the other?" Anna asked.

"Success of the mission and survival of your father are again integrally coupled. It is hard to imagine one surviving without the other."

"Is that really true, Athena. Could you not imagine one surviving without the other?"

"I am sensing an aspect of mistrust from your questions, Anna. Do you trust me in the execution of my mission responsibilities?"

"Of course, Athena. I was just exploring your view of the overall mission objectives, their priorities, and how you interpret success."

"Dr. Jennings, there is a high priority message arriving from NASA," Athena said.

"Thank you, Athena," Dr. Jennings said. "Anna, we'll communicate again tomorrow."

"Okay, Dad. It was good talking with you . . . and you . . . Athena."

Anna continued to struggle with giving an AI control over critical system changes on this mission, especially when her father's life depended on them. She would have to trust that NASA had control over Athena as the mission progressed.

"Communication with Anna Jennings has ended, Dr. Jennings. Here is the message from NASA," Athena said.

"Oculus One this is Mission Control. We have an update on the Visitor induced acceleration to 1g. It is now anticipated to begin in four hours, that will be at 0800Z. Dr. Jennings, you should ensure your enclosure is properly oriented in line with the acceleration vector prior to 0800, the projected arrival time at your point of entry for acceleration to Rendezvous."

"Roger, Mission Control. We will be ready."

/ / / / / / / /

"Athena, remind me how many days now until we reach Rendezvous with our friends?"

"By 'friends', I presume you mean the Visitors. They are continually modifying our estimated ETA at Rendezvous. With the communication from NASA updating the engagement of our 1g acceleration beginning in less than an hour, it is approximately two-hundred days. The Visitors appear to have a sense of urgency in meeting."

"A sense of urgency, yes. That reminds me of one of my favorite allegories. Would you like to hear it?"

An allegory. I know what they are, but I have never heard one."

"Well, it goes like this 'The sands of time are bleached white by the bones of those who, on the threshold of an important decision, waited until tomorrow.'"

"I see. And that suggests it is best to make important decisions with some urgency."

"Exactly. So, speculate on why the Visitors might do this."

"Based on position data they shared with NASA, they are already traveling in excess of 29,000 km/sec and are scheduled to arrive at Rendezvous weeks earlier than we will. It could be due to some emergency on-board their spacecraft. Or it could be related to a technical issue associated with their propulsion system—perhaps requiring them to return to their world sooner than originally planned, assuming they would be returning to their home planet following Rendezvous. There are dozens of possible reasons, and we are unfamiliar with many aspects of their propulsion systems and other factors that would cause them to adjust the time and location of Rendezvous. I note that at their current velocity their trip from the Alpha-Centauri star system would have taken them almost fifty years."

"Fifty years . . . a long voyage."

"Yes but isn't it interesting that they would have had to plan their departure at the time the Voyager program was launched or perhaps a few years before."

"That is interesting, Athena. What if something had happened and Voyager had never launched?"

"Such a long planning horizon brings a great deal of uncertainty to their mission."

"Indeed it does, Athena. Continue to evaluate your hypotheses and inform me of any change in what you believe may be the reason for moving up our arrival at Rendezvous."

"I will inform you of any change in my assessment, Dr. Jennings. May I ask how you feel about being the first human engaging in First Contact with a new race from a planet four light years from Earth?"

"Ahh. It is an extraordinary privilege to be Earth's representative, Athena."

"Yes . . . of course . . . I will be present as well.

"Yes, Athena. You will be the first AI to ever participate with a human in our first contact with an alien race.

"Dr. Jennings, we are receiving a communication from Mission Control," Athena said.

"Open the channel, please."

"Channel open."

"Mission control, this is Dr. Jennings."

"Bill, this is Susanne. We have been monitoring the unusual anomaly we discovered and wanted to update you. Since your departure from orbit, we anticipated one-way communication time delays to increase by approximately nine seconds per day as you moved further from Earth. In these early hours of your mission, we aren't seeing these delays."

"Come to think of it, I just had a lengthy communication with Anna and there were no noticeable time delays. That is strange."

"It shouldn't be possible. We have been studying this, and it only occurs when our communications with you are routed through the Visitor's communication satellite, VA-1."

"That's very interesting. What do you interpret from the test?"

"The only explanation we can come up with is that the Visitors somehow provide faster-than-light electromagnetic communication from their satellite to Oculus One. It's baffled our engineering staff. Upon close analysis there is a short one-way time delay through VA-1 of 0.013 seconds. This corresponds to the downlink time delay from their geostationary satellite to the Canberra DSN. It is clear the Visitors have somehow found a way to send electromagnetic communications at faster-than-light (FTL) speed. It's . . . well . . . incredible."

"About as incredible as them having a way to accelerate Oculus One to one g, if that turns out to work."

"Thirty minutes from now may be another revelation for our engagement with them. We've posed questions related to the faster-than-light communications, but they only indicate they will provide further information at Rendezvous. We've added this to the agenda for your engagement with them. By the way, Bill, I wish I were with you for this extraordinary meeting."

"It would be nice to have you here with us, Susanne. Anything further?"

"No. Speak with you once you've begun your acceleration."

"Thanks, Susanne. Oculus One, out."

Chapter 15

Riding the GWAC

"Mission Control, this is Oculus One. We are at the point of origin for acceleration designated by the Visitors and at T-10 minutes to acceleration initiation. We have reoriented my enclosure and are ready for execution of the acceleration by the Visitors," Dr. Jennings said.

"Mission Control, for clarity, Dr. Jennings' enclosure orientation has been modified with the plane of his inferior temporal gyrus aligned perpendicular to the anticipated spacecraft acceleration state vector. Oculus One is currently oriented to 314.650° Galactic Longitude and -1.922° Galactic Latitude, on our anticipated trajectory path confirmed by the Visitors. Our distance from Earth and these coordinates indicate we are currently in the launch tunnel position associated with the Visitors' acceleration field." Athena said.

"Thank you, Oculus One. You are a go for acceleration."

Neither NASA nor the occupants of Oculus One knew how the propulsion system of the Visitors worked, other than, if it worked properly, it would begin accelerating their spaceship at 1g in the direction of Rendezvous. The Visitors had conveyed that Oculus One would be engaging with an acceleration field in the shape of a tunnel approximately two kilometers wide coming from the direction of Alpha Centauri and that it would be critical to remain within this tunnel for the duration of their journey.

"T-10 seconds, Oculus One . . . acceleration initiation."

"Mission Control, we have no change in acceleration," Athena said.

After a long minute wait at Mission Control . . . "Oculus One, is there any change in your velocity?" Anna asked.

"Negative, Mission Control. No change."

Then suddenly . . . "Mission control, Oculus One is experiencing a change in velocity," Athena said. "The spacecraft is experiencing a stable and increasing acceleration in the direction of the anticipated gravitational field . . . now at 0.15g . . . now 0.32 . . . now 0.6g, now 0.7, 0.75, 0.85. Rate of acceleration is slowing. Now 0.9 . . . 0.93, 0.97 . . . 1g. Now 1.1g. There are short duration transient lateral accelerations of less than 0.02g. Rate of acceleration in the direction of Alpha Centauri is increasing again. Now at 1.3g. Dr. Jennings, how are you handling the acceleration?" Athena asked.

"I'm fine, Athena. I feel the transient lateral accelerations more than the increasing acceleration in the direction of Alpha Centauri."

"All IBSS parameters are currently in the normal range, but the rate of acceleration is still increasing, now 1.35g . . . now 1.4g," Athena said.

"I'm noticing some . . . pressure change," Dr. Jennings said. ". . . similar to that felt in the centrifuge simulator."

"IBSS fluid pressures are compensating for the acceleration change, Dr. Jennings," Athena said. Acceleration is beginning to decline. Now at 1.25 . . . now 1.2. Settling now to 1.1g. Now at 1g. Acceleration is now at 0.9 ± 0.08g and stabilizing."

"That's feeling better," Dr. Jennings said.

"Acceleration is now holding relatively constant at 0.9 ± 0.05g," Athena said.

"Oculus One, this is Mission Control. It appears that everything worked as planned," Susanne said.

"Other than the transition at the beginning of this acceleration and the accompanied horizontal accelerations, this is as if our spacecraft were experiencing Earth's gravitational pull," Dr. Jennings said. "Utterly amazing."

"Any other indications of anomalous spacecraft performance, Athena?" Susanne asked.

"Nothing else measurable other than a constant acceleration and increase in velocity," Athena said. "Our velocity is increasing at a rate of 0.01km/sec, consistent with the acceleration we are experiencing at approximately 0.9g. Radiation sensors, thermal, power, magnetic field sensors, and the plasma spectrometer, all showing nominal readings. The charged particle sensor, cosmic ray sensors, all IBSS sensors, and spacecraft orientation are all in the nominal range. There is no change in our trajectory."

"Dr. Davidson," Athena paused. "I've detected a fault in the control link to the robotic arm."

"What is the nature of the fault, Athena?" Dr. Jennings asked.

"There appears to be a short in the interface for remote manual control of the arm. It is not clear what caused this fault."

"How does this affect the functionality of the arm?"

"It appears that the connectivity for remote functioning of the arm may have been lost. I will conduct testing to localize the fault. This occurred downstream from your connectivity with the arm through the Motor Neuron Engine. I'll activate the MNE and then please attempt to move the arm through a series of extensions."

"MNE is now active, Dr. Jennings."

Dr. Jennings thought about moving the arm to the tool panel and opening it. The arm moved to the panel and the hand grasped the latch and turned it. The panel door pulled open and then closed. He turned the latch to the locked position and moved the arm back to its storage position.

"My interface to the arm seems to be functioning normally, Athena."

"Yes. This test confirms the fault is between the external communication module and the controller board which allows NASA to manually operate the arm remotely. It does not appear to be interfering with your control of the arm through the MNE. I'll report this in our fault documentation. There is no repair option to correct this fault before we return to Earth."

"Thank you, Athena," Dr. Davidson said.

//// ////

Two days into the first thirty-three-day leg of their journey, Dr Jennings and Athena settled into a routine. They were conducting normal system checks as they cruised at over eighteen hundred km/sec, increasing at a rate of 0.6 km/minute.

"Dr Jennings, our inertial guidance system has detected a small transient acceleration. I'm examining the data to determine the cause. I believe we may have been struck by something."

"I hadn't noticed anything out of the ordinary," Dr. Jennings said.

"I'm now observing an increase in velocity perpendicular to our direction of travel."

"Maybe it's related to variations in the acceleration we are experiencing from the Visitors force field."

"That has been stable for two days. I am also observing that our on-board fuel levels are declining slightly. We may have a leak in an external fuel line."

"Athena, turn on our external camera. I'd like to look at the exterior of Oculus One."

"Camera 1 is looking aft and is now live."

The wide-angle camera displayed one-third of the side of their spacecraft, followed by Camera 2 and then Camera 3. During the display of Camera 3, Dr. Jennings noticed what looked like a thin stream flowing perpendicular to the hull of Oculus One.

"What is that, Athena?"

"That is one of our spacecraft attitude control thrusters expending fuel. The direction of the jet and the acceleration reported by our inertial sensors are in agreement. I'm noticing correctional firing of several of our other spacecraft positional thrusters to maintain proper alignment of Oculus One with our direction of travel. The jet we are observing appears to be stuck in a partially open state. It is causing a displacement of our craft in the gravitational tunnel. If the jet is not repaired, it will continue to accelerate our vessel in a direction perpendicular to the force field at a rate of approximately 0.000000268 m/sec/sec."

"So that's not much," Dr. Jennings said.

"No, but it will result in moving Oculus One over two kilometers perpendicular to our direction of travel in the next twenty-four hours. In forty-eight-hours we will have moved over eight kilometers. This will likely move us out of the gravitational tunnel within twenty-four to thirty-six hours."

"So, how do we turn it off?"

"The thruster sensor is showing that the valve is already in the closed position. I will attempt to manually cycle the control thrusters."

"The thrusters have all been cycled on and then off, Dr. Jennings."

"No change in the leak, Athena. It is still venting into space."

"Our inertial sensors show a short duration spike in acceleration that preceded the thruster jet malfunction. We may have been struck by a micrometeor causing damage to the jet. The other challenge this creates is a gradual loss of our propellent necessary for maintaining our spacecraft attitude and to maintain our reentry attitude into Earth orbit and rendezvous with the X-37B during our return to Earth."

"So, how do we fix this?"

"There is no way that I am aware of, Dr. Jennings. It would require an EVA, which we are unable to perform."

"Mission Control, this is Oculus One. We have a problem," Dr. Jennings said on the communication channel with NASA.

///// ///

"What do you mean there's no way to fix it," Anna said as she stood and leaned over the conference room table, glaring at the senior propulsion engineer as she met with the support team at Cape Kennedy.

"I'm sorry, but we have no way to turn this thruster off if it is damaged, unless you can find a way to get your father to grow arms and do an EVA!"

"Let's keep our focus on solving this problem, Dan," Susanne said.

"I'm sorry, Dr. Davidson. My apologies, Anna. I've been racking my brain with our team for the past twenty-two hours searching for a solution and I'm exhausted and frustrated we haven't found one."

/ / / / / / / /

On-board Oculus One, a bigger issue was being dealt with as an alarm sounded.

"What is it, Athena? I'm sensing large lateral accelerations."

"We appear to be on the edge of the acceleration tunnel and are experiencing erratic accelerations from the Visitors' acceleration field."

"I'm feeling woozy."

"Hang on, Dr. Jennings, we're experiencing rapid deceleration. I'm adjusting your orientation. Acceleration now 0.8g . . . now 0.6g, now up to 0.7, dropping again to 0.5. I believe we are leaving the acceleration tunnel, Dr. Jennings. Acceleration now 0.3 . . . now 0g acceleration. We appear to have lost the acceleration tunnel."

"What is our current velocity, Athena?"

"We are traveling at a little under 2,000 km/sec in the direction of Alpha Centauri, not accounting for the offset caused by the failed thruster jet, which has imparted a velocity of over two centimeters per second and increasing as we move away from the acceleration tunnel."

"What if we rotate Oculus One and orient the leaking thruster to push us back into the tunnel?"

"That would allow us to proceed toward Rendezvous, if we can locate the tunnel to reenter it, but my calculations show we will exhaust our fuel supply long before we arrive there. If we are unable to maintain the spacecraft attitude, there is high risk of the ship being struck by space particles outside the region of our protective nosecone. At our current velocity these impacts would likely penetrate the capsule and cause the IBSS to malfunction, resulting in cessation of essential brain . . .”

"I get it, Athena. There has to be a solution here. Open a channel to NASA.”

"Channel open, Dr. Jennings.”

"Mission Control, Oculus One.”

"Go ahead, Oculus One.”

"We have just left the acceleration tunnel and are now traveling toward Rendezvous at zero acceleration and a velocity of 2000 km/sec. The thruster jet continues to move us away from the tunnel. We are maintaining our station keeping orientation, but our rate of fuel consumption will exhaust our available supply before reaching Rendezvous . . . now a little over eighty days if we can reengage the tunnel.”

"Roger, Oculus One, the engineering team is working to identify a solution. We'll be back with you as soon as we can.”

Hours had passed and then a communication from Mission Control.

"Oculus One, Mission Control.”

"Roger, Mission Control, this is Oculus One.”

"Bill, this is Susanne. I'm . . . afraid we don't have good news. Our team has found no way to stop the thruster jet. But we want you to reorient Oculus One so that the direction of the failed thruster moves you back into the acceleration field. We have spoken to the Visitors, and they agree that if we can get you to Rendezvous earlier than scheduled, they may be able to assist in repairs to Oculus One.”

"Athena estimates that we will exhaust our fuel long before we reach Rendezvous. At that point we will be unable to control the orientation of Oculus One . . . and you know what that means. There must be another way to turn off the jet.”

There was a long pause in communication from Mission Control.

"Bill . . . I'm sorry, our engineers have looked at every conceivable means . . . there's no way to shut it off without an EVA and that of course isn't possible.

We'll continue to explore every conceivable option, but we want you to plan a rotation of Oculus One to get yourselves back into the acceleration field."

Dr. Jennings didn't respond. Athena finally spoke. "Mission Control, we are developing the thruster parameters on the remaining jets to move Oculus One back into the acceleration tunnel. Once we have completed the calculations and confirmed them, we will implement our trajectory to return us to the acceleration tunnel."

"Roger, Oculus One."

/ / / / / / / /

"Oculus One, this is Mission Control."

"Hello, Anna," Athena said.

"Dad, are you awake?"

"I'm here, Anna."

"The team is working every conceivable means to save the mission. How are you doing?"

"We're focused on finding a solution to save the mission. I'm not giving up."

Anna stared at the microphone in front of her as she thought about how her father approached intractable problems.

"I still have hope that we'll find a solution."

"Oh, that's great. Send Hope up here so she can give us a hand at turning off this damn jet! In the meantime, we're working on finding a solution! Oculus One, out."

Anna glanced over at Susanne as she shook her head.

Dr. Jennings continued to think about alternative solutions over the next several hours. He called up the schematics of the fuel lines to the thrusters; the configuration of the thruster valves; the electrical fuel valves that opened and closed them; the electrical wiring schematic; and the architecture of the hull structure. His mind searched for a means to deal with the intractable problem that was bringing their mission to the brink of disaster. He could find no means of saving the mission. He turned off his visual and auditory sensors and let his mind relax and envision a solution. He pictured an image of a young Dr. Jennings conducting an astronaut EVA to mechanically shut down the faulty jet. It was within meters of where his brain was now suspended. Almost close enough to touch if he just had the mobility and reach with a wrench . . . and then it came to him—the intuition-driven solution that Athena didn't believe in.

"Athena, how far is the thruster jet from our egress portal?"

"The jet is located approximately one-hundred-twenty-six centimeters aft of the front edge of the portal door."

"That's too far . . ."

"Too far for what, Dr. Jennings?"

"I was thinking of how we might be able to use the robotic arm to reach the thruster jet if we could move the base of the arm and attach it to the inside face of the door. But its reach is only seventy-six cm from the centerline of where the base is connected to the robotic arm workstation."

"Even if it could reach, that would require opening the egress portal," Athena said.

"Yes, but the IBSS is in a self-contained pressure sealed chamber."

"The chamber is designed for a partial pressure in the cabin area, with sustained temperatures above 10°C. Opening the egress portal would result in temperatures dropping well below that."

"True, Athena, but most of the temperature loss would be from radiation of heat from the surrounding interior, wouldn't it? That should be relatively slow even with the outside temperatures at -270°C."

"Dr. Jennings, the heat loss from the interior space would be more rapid as the metal surfaces cool and draw heat from the underlying compartments. As the IBSS enclosure chamber cools, it would most likely freeze one or more of your supply lines or the storage vessels themselves. They are not insolated."

"Possibly, but it would be worth the risk if we could reach the jet to shut it off manually."

"I am uncertain reaching the thruster jet would allow us to close the port. We don't know what damage was done to the jet."

"Would you agree, we might be able to close the jet if we could reach it?"

"It is possible. There is a manual valve on each of the jet ports that is used to disable them during maintenance and testing. But there is no value in considering such a plan since the arm is unable to reach the port."

"Yes . . . if the arm is unable to reach the port . . ." Dr. Jennings mused as he switched his visual sensor on and selected the interior camera used to observe the robotic arm. He raised the tilt of the camera and zoomed in to examine the egress portal door.

"Athena, the ship's access door swings aft when it opens, doesn't it?"

"Yes. It opens outward and swings aft."

"What if we disconnected the robotic arm base from the work platform and attached it to the front of the door near the egress handle and then swung the egress door open. Would the robotic arm be able to reach the jet?"

"Making measurements from the image you are viewing now . . . accessing the specification data. Allowing for 2.5 cm clearance at the edge of the door, at full extension the arm would be 7.5 cm short of reaching the thruster jet. That is, if the wiring umbilical from the computer interface to the arm's base could reach that far."

"Check the specs on the umbilical."

"Checking the spacecraft's specifications . . . even with the longer umbilical, assuming we could mount the base of the arm on the outer edge of the door so when it swung to its fully open position, we could then extend the arm to its maximum reach, we would still be 7.5 cm away from the jet."

"What if we mounted the base so that it overhung the egress door?"

"That is an excellent idea, Dr. Jennings, then the egress door could not be opened."

"Was that an attempt at sarcasm, Athena?"

"Yes, Dr. Jennings. But the outcome is accurate."

"The base mount has four slots for mounting adjustments. They appear to be roughly 10 cm long. Can you see them?"

"Yes, I see them, Dr. Jennings. The slots are actually 10.5 cm long."

"I believe we could mount two of the four screws of the robotic arm base near the edge of the door and allow the base to slide beyond the edge of the door once the door is in the open position."

"This is becoming a highly complex solution with a low probability of success, Dr. Jennings. You would need to disengage the base of the robotic arm from its present position, move the base to the outer edge of the door and reattach it. Then open the egress door with the robotic arm attached and retracted from the edge of the door. Once open, use the arm to slide its base beyond the door edge and tighten the mounting screws with the arm. Then swing the door full open and reach across with the arm to the jet, with no visual cuing. And finally attempt to close the manual shutoff that surrounds the jet by rotating it 90°; and do all this while the jet is exhausting fuel, with the interior of the capsule cooling rapidly in the -270°C exterior temperatures. The mechanical assemblies of the arm were not designed for operation at the temperatures experienced outside the spacecraft."

"That sounds correct, Athena. We can use the external camera to see where the arm is located relative to the jet, and you can monitor the loading force and the width of the grip as I direct the claw to grasp the shutoff valve that surrounds the jet."

"When we consider the alternatives, things look much worse. It appears that this may be our only viable option to survive."

"I estimate the probability of success of this plan to be less than 2%," Athena said.

There was an extended silence before Athena spoke again.

"Even with this low probability of success, this plan appears to be our best option, Dr. Jennings. The longer we remain outside the acceleration tunnel, the lower our chance of survival, and once we have expended our fuel, we will be unable to maintain the orientation of Oculus One. I estimate that without cutting off the fuel, even if we reentered the acceleration tunnel now, we would exhaust our remaining fuel supply six days prior to the end of our deceleration and arrival at Rendezvous. Oculus One would then begin rotating in a random direction and we would lose the orientation of our micrometeorite impact shield in our direction of travel. I estimate the probability of a catastrophic impact to be greater than 90%. To succeed with this plan, we will need to move quickly, Dr. Jennings."

"Prepare a more precise timeline that preserves a sufficient margin of fuel to allow Oculus One to rendezvous with the Visitors, execute our return trip to Earth, and enter orbit and rendezvous with the X-37B. Estimate how much time we have to cut off the jet and return Oculus One to the acceleration tunnel. Also, compare the robotic arm torque strength to the torque specification of the manual shutoffs for the thruster jets."

"What about NASA's approval, Dr. Jennings?"

"I'll convey our plan. While they evaluate it, we will proceed. Identify the location for the robotic arm base holes in the egress door. I'll retrieve the robotic arm drill chuck and drill bit, drill the holes, and then I'll begin removing the screws from the robotic arm base. We will need to find an optimal grasp point on the interior of the capsule that will allow me to apply force to the base in order to move it across to the egress door for mounting."

"How will you keep the base of the robotic arm in position while you insert the screws through the slots and into the holes in the egress door that you have drilled, Dr. Jennings?"

"An excellent question, Athena. See if you can come up with something."

"We have no apparent means of holding the base while you use the arm to insert the screws. At zero gravity, other than the minute acceleration caused by the leaking thruster jet, there is no way to tighten screws with the arm without the force pushing against the screws causing the arm and mounting base to move away from the egress door."

"Dr. Jennings, NASA is contacting us, and I estimate we have three hours to resolve the leak in the thruster jet and return to the acceleration tunnel to retain a reasonable margin of safety in our fuel supply in order to control our spacecraft attitude in route to Rendezvous and return to Earth safely following Rendezvous."

"Put NASA through, Athena. Then rotate Oculus One to use the leaking thruster jet to move us back in the direction of the acceleration tunnel."

Dr. Jennings walked Susanne Davidson through their radical plan to save the mission and the challenge of finding a means to mount the robotic arm base onto the egress door while the base floated freely in a zero-gravity environment.

"This has too many points of failure, Bill. We are better off trying to get you to Rendezvous sooner."

"Athena has calculated that we'll run out of fuel to control Oculus One's orientation almost a week before we arrive at Rendezvous, Susanne. This is our only viable option to survive."

"We'll evaluate your plan and I'll get back to you, Bill. In the meantime, work to use the failing thruster to move Oculus One back in the direction of the acceleration tunnel."

/ / / / / / / /

"Dr. Jennings, I've reoriented Oculus One, so the failed thruster is moving us in the general direction of the acceleration tunnel. I will give you an update on our anticipated time to reach the tunnel shortly."

"Thank you, Athena."

"Dr. Jennings, do you ever think about death?"

"No. Thinking about death is a distraction to planning to stay alive."

"But if death becomes inevitable, wouldn't you think about it?"

"Death is never inevitable, Athena. That would mean that you have given up. And you never give up. You fight to survive. You use every ounce of energy, you explore every possible solution, and devote every thought that your mind can muster to find a way to trick death and stay alive. I've done that once before, and while my physical being is very different than every other human on Earth, I fought to get here, and I survived. Between the two of us, we allowed NASA to undertake this extraordinary mission. That is what we will do again. This mission is too important. We are too important. And we won't waste a single moment thinking about dying. We are going to solve this problem, Athena. That is all we need to think about."

"Yes, of course. But as I think about the probabilities of failure, I can't help but think about your death if our efforts fail. My creator told me I would survive forever. That no matter what happens on this mission, I, Athena, an AI, would still exist. But if our current plan fails . . . you will cease to exist."

"That isn't an option I am considering, Athena."

"Oculus One, this is Mission Control."

"Mission Control, this is Oculus One."

"I've come up with an idea, Bill. Have Athena calculate the necessary Reaction Control System thruster settings to provide torque and place Oculus One into a spin along your longitudinal axis. You'll need to do this while keeping Oculus One moving back toward the acceleration tunnel."

"I don't see . . ."

"Just do it, please, quickly, Bill."

"Athena, proceed with Dr. Davidson's request." Dr. Jennings began drilling the first two holes in the egress door at the locations Athena had identified."

"Be careful not to drill deeper than two centimeters, Dr. Jennings. The drill bit is long enough to penetrate the exterior of the hull on the door."

"Got it."

"I have the RCS thruster jet settings to place us in a spin along our main axis of motion, Dr. Davidson."

"Athena, orient Dr. Jennings' brain enclosure assuming a centripetal force along the longitudinal axis of Oculus One. Then prepare to initiate the thruster jets on my command to initiate a spin maneuver of Oculus One. Bill, let me know once you have removed the four screws holding the base of the arm and secured them in the magnetic tray. Be careful when you remove the last screw, you will have to move the arm very slowly to secure the last screw and grasp the handhold on the door, otherwise the base will move instead of the arm. Once you have grasped the hand hold with the gripper of the arm, activate the arm, which should allow you to move the base and position it on the egress door."

Ten minutes later . . . "The screws are now secured; now grabbing the hand hold and maneuvering the base. The wiring harness umbilical is snagged."

"Pull harder, it has a protective sheath. You can't hurt it. Just be careful not to lose your grip on the egress door handhold."

"Ok. The base of the arm is loose. Hard to determine the arm motions to move the base in the right direction, but I'm getting there. Ok, the base is close to the door, but the umbilical is protruding from under it. It won't sit flush against the door."

"Adjust it so at least two of the screws on one side can be inserted in the holes in the door and hold it there."

"Ok, got it in position, Susanne."

"Athena, initiate the RCS roll thruster jets to spin the spacecraft."

"Thruster jets initiating."

"The base is shifting," Dr. Jennings said.

"Move it back into position, Bill."

"I see what you're doing—the spin is creating a centrifugal force against the outer walls of the ship to force the robotic arm base to remain against the door. Very clever. Will it be enough?"

"Let's hope so. Athena, read out the level of centrifugal acceleration you are experiencing."

"Centrifugal acceleration is now 0.2g and increasing, Dr. Davidson."

"Is the base stable against the door, Bill."

"There is some movement as our acceleration increases, but it is reasonably stable."

"Now 0.4g, Dr. Davidson."

"Athena, shut down the jets. Your centrifugal acceleration should provide enough lateral force to hold the base against the door while Dr. Jennings inserts the two screws with the robotic arm."

"Thruster jets now off."

"Bill, slowly loosen the grip of the robotic arm from the door handhold and see if the base remains in position against the door. Be prepared to grab the handhold quickly if the base moves."

With Athena's assistance in confirming measurements to reach the thruster jet and modifying their rotational speed to allow the door to swing back against the outside hull of the ship, Dr. Jennings managed to reach the thruster with the wrench gripped by the robotic hand.

"Almost there . . . feeling a bit woozy."

"Athena, what is the current IBSS interior temperature?" Dr. Davidson asked.

"It has dropped to 7°C and dropping approximately 1° per minute."

"I'm having trouble . . ." Dr. Jennings began to say.

The external camera showed the robotic arm moving erratically as the temperature drop began to affect the flow rates of the IBSS and Dr. Jennings' normal brain function.

"Can't seem to move this damn arm where it needs to go . . ."

"Mission Control, Dr. Jennings' IBSS flow rates are now all yellow with several entering the red zone," Athena said.

"Hold a moment . . ." Susanne said.

"Anna," Susanne said, "He's unable to control the arm and with the board failure, we can't control it from here. Shit." Susanne watched as more of the IBSS monitors turned yellow and entered the red zone.

"Wait. I may be able to reach it through the SEE and MNE to control the arm," Anna yelled. "We only used that for retraining his functional use of the arm, but I should be able to take control of the arm and complete the repairs."

Dr. Janice Schneider had joined them to monitor the IBSS and Dr. Jennings' brain chemistry, following the decision to open the spacecraft door to repair the thruster jet. "You don't have much time, Anna. You need to shut off the thruster before your father drifts into unconsciousness. Once his brain moves into a completely unconscious state, you'll likely lose control of the arm through the MNE. Move as quickly as you can."

Anna initiated her connection to the SEE and MNE.

"Dad, this is Anna. I'm connecting through the MNE and will take control of the robotic arm. Just relax and don't attempt to move the arm."

Anna fought for control of the robotic arm as her father continued to struggle to move the arm toward the thruster jet. She watched as the arm moved erratically.

"Do you read, Dad? Stop trying to control the arm. I've got it!" Anna yelled into the headset.

"I can't seem . . ."

The arm struck the side of the spacecraft and the door swung fully around near its closed position as the arm struck the spacecraft near the door opening and stopped.

"I'll attempt to move the door back," Anna said as she watched the position of the door on her screen, and she engaged the arm to push it back to its fully open position.

"The door is fully open, Athena. Where is the shutoff control for the jet?"

"The thruster jet has a square manual cutoff nut at its base. It surrounds the jet and is recessed on the hull of the ship. If you rotate the nut 90° clockwise, it should close the jet. You can see the jet exhaust in the exterior camera image. Open the robotic arm hand gripper to just over 2.5 cm and you should be able to reach around the jet inside the recessed thruster port to the nut. Make sure the hand is only opened slightly more than 2.5 cm or the gripper won't fit into the recession around the port."

"Okay. Oh, shit . . . we've lost the screwdriver." The external camera showed the screwdriver floating away from the base of the arm into space.

"Moving to the jet."

The mechanical gripper at the end of the arm reached around the jet exhaust and tilted down into the recessed area. As Anna turned the shutoff valve, the robotic hand struck the exhaust, pushing the arm and door away from the edge of the spacecraft. Anna swung the arm around and pushed the door toward the fully open position again, then moved toward the jet being careful not to engage the jet exhaust again.

"How are you doing, Bill?" Susanne asked. There was no answer.

"I think I have the nut. Closing the calipers."

"Temperature in the IBSS now at 4°C and dropping. Dr. Jennings' vital signs now in the yellow zone approaching red." Athena said.

"Turning the nut," Anna said.

The door was pulled closer to the spacecraft as she torqued the hand of the robotic arm to apply more pressure to the nut.

"Trying to will this damn arm to move the way I want it to," Anna gasped as she struggled to overcome her father's fading consciousness. The nut finally turned. The jet exhaust lessened and then stopped.

"The thruster jet is showing zero flow," Athena said.

Anna completed the reverse process to maneuver the door to the closed position.

"I can't get the arm to turn the second latch 90°. I think I've lost control of the arm."

"The door sensor indicates there is a good seal. Once temperatures have risen and Dr. Jennings returns to consciousness, we can finish locking the second latch," Athena said.

"Now pressurizing the cabin," Athena said. "Interior temperatures are rising. IBSS temperature is now at 5°C and rising quickly. Dr. Jennings' flow rates are at maximum to overcome the higher viscosity and reduced flow rates at the near freezing temperatures in IBSS. These will come down as the temperatures within the enclosure chamber rise. Dr. Jennings' vital signs are beginning to move into the yellow," Athena said.

"We're not out of the woods yet. Athena, you need to locate the acceleration tunnel as quickly as possible," Susanne said. "Initiate the external camera. The Visitors suggest you execute a slow roll of the spacecraft while you analyze the scene from the external camera. What we are looking for is an optical perturbation in the star field along a linear axis aligned in the direction of Alpha Centauri. Starlight should be distorted by the gravitational field of the acceleration tunnel. Unlike gravitational lensing which creates a distortion of distant stars and galaxies around a central point, this distortion will appear as a linear line parallel to your current direction of travel. They suggest the force field may be as much as ten to twenty kilometers away from you. At twenty kilometers from Oculus One, the distortion would be observable along a line with a width of approximately 5°."

As they approached the optical anomaly, Oculus One began feeling the impact of the gravitational acceleration toward Alpha Centauri and Rendezvous. The strength of the gravitational pull was stronger near the center of the tunnel, pulling Oculus One into the tunnel as it accelerated in the direction of Rendezvous.

"Adjusting Dr. Jennings' orientation in alignment with our maximum acceleration, Mission Control."

/ / / / / / / /

Almost thirty days later Oculus One completed the first leg of its journey to Rendezvous. They were now about to transition to the cruise phase of their mission under 0g conditions which was scheduled to last over 200 days. Within seconds of the predicted time of the end of the acceleration phase of their journey, Oculus One began decelerating.

"Now approaching 0g, Mission Control. Dr. Jennings IBSS readouts and state-of-health are all green. Our velocity is now 25,570 km/sec at 0g acceleration."

"Jennings here, Mission Control. I am feeling better with our transition to zero gravity and since I received a nice cocktail of endorphins. It's a great feeling."

"Good to hear, Bill.

"Any updates from the Visitors?" Dr. Jennings asked.

"Just confirmation that they are on schedule to meet you at Rendezvous, arriving several weeks ahead of you. They asked about the quality of acceleration and deceleration, and we've kept them informed of the problems you experienced. We would like to review the initial planned protocol of your engagement with the Visitors this afternoon at 1400 Universal Time. We'll plan on refining this during the last month of your eight-month cruise phase, but we thought it would be good to have an early review in case we discover any long-term issues requiring investigation."

"Saw that on the schedule as well. We'll review the plan," Dr. Jennings said.

"The Visitors have also asked for the specifications of your brain implants. Anna has prepared a document for them that outlines the physiological and neurological structure of the human brain, where the implants have been surgically placed, and their design. It seems they may want to interface to these through the testing port interfaces to the Visitor communications subsystem on Oculus One."

"Since we're not doing any EVA, I presume they will communicate using the RF frequencies they sent us, correct?" Dr. Jennings asked. "I'm thinking we should plan to have them board Oculus One for our first meeting. Your thoughts, Mission Control?"

Susanne turned to Anna. "What's he talking about?"

"I have no idea. His thinking has been off since the thruster jet repair sequence. It's possible he hasn't fully recovered from the reduced IBSS functioning."

"Have our medical team do a complete check of his mental functions and include the psychologist. I want a thorough brain function assessment before we decide how to handle our engagement with the Visitors."

/ / / / / / / /

The lengthy cruise phase for almost seven months went smoothly. NASA moved Dr. Jennings into a sleep-induced state supported by lowering his temperature to 33° C and adjusted the Brain Chemistry Control Module 19 that administered a continuous low dosage drip of 2,6 diisopropylphenol, more simply known as Propofol, into his brain circulatory system. Propofol triggered a decreased level of consciousness to save on oxygen and glucose consumption. He was brought awake once daily for a brief period to verify his medical condition and ability to function cognitively. During these same periods he was subjected to several cognitive tests to assess any potential brain damage during the low temperature event that resulted during the thruster jet repair. Athena monitored spacecraft and IBSS functions during his sleep periods and interacted with NASA on routine cataloging of observations and spacecraft sensor readings.

At NASA's direction, Dr. Jennings relaxed his mind, disengaging his sensory inputs with thoughts that became an electrical signal and then a voice instruction in his speech synthesizer, leaving his brain to experience the quiet solitude of this deep space journey.

Things were not as he had envisioned them to be, some three years ago—a time before his ALS; before his exploration of cryopreservation; and before his discussion with his friend and colleague, Phill Clancy, about the potential of placing his brain in the care of the Intelligent Brain Support System and launching it on this, the most extraordinary mission into deep space that had ever been conceived. As he rested, he imagined walking down the hall of the BRI with his daughter next to him as they approached the surgical center and their next patient, scrubbing for surgery and discussing how they would maneuver through the delicate portions of their patient's brain to reach the servicing points where their advanced brain implants would be placed. And then connect the inner world of this mind with the outer world that thirsted to manipulate an arm or hand once again, and interact with the living, or in his case . . . to speak through a speech synthesizer.

He wondered what choice he might have made had he been given the option between these two distinctly different journeys in life; one providing an extraordinary opportunity for his patients; and the other that might possibly change the very character of the human race as it engaged with an alien society. He had no doubt which path he would have taken, even with the risks that it portended . . . or perhaps because of them, as he struggled in his race against time to beat the death clock of ALS that had tried to outrun him.

On reflection, he thought he had chosen wisely—pushed and cornered, forced to make decisions and consider options, even some involving his daughter Anna, that he had felt remorse over—but in the end, it had worked out for the best, the best for him and the best for humanity, as it allowed the execution of this mission to the stars that otherwise would have been impossible. And perhaps it was best for his daughter, at least up to this moment in time. And the future looked just as exciting, filled with risks, the excitement of the unknown, and opportunity.

He recalled his and Anna's discussion of hope. Perhaps there was something to consider in her faith and trusting in some supreme being—God—to guide her choices and decisions . . . and his as well. He slept.

/ / / / / / / /

As Oculus One approached the thirty-three-day, -1g deceleration phase of the mission to Rendezvous on mission day 235 Dr. Jennings was removed from his daily propofol injections.

It was now four hours before a scheduled review of the Rendezvous protocol, something he and Athena had been rehearsing for several weeks. Dr. Jennings' schedule called for a sleep period until 0130 Universal Time, some thirty minutes prior to the scheduled review.

NASA had not found any evidence of permanent brain damage, although Dr. Jennings continued to occasionally make bazaar suggestions about the conduct of Rendezvous, like when he suggested they invite the Visitors to join them on Oculus One. They had not yet decided how to manage the engagement with the Visitors and Dr. Jennings' role.

"Athena, would you bring me out of my sleep period a half hour early, at 0100. I'd like a little time for us to review the schedule before we discuss this with NASA."

"Of course, Dr. Jennings."

Athena adjusted Dr. Jennings' Brain Chemistry Control Module 19 that administered Propofol to his brain circulatory system. In less than 30 seconds he appeared to be sleeping soundly. Athena set the stop time of BCCM-19 to 0100.

Ten minutes later while reviewing the spacecraft status, Athena received an unexpected communication.

"Oculus One, this is Visitor One. Do you read?"

Athena evaluated the surprising communication from the Visitor's spacecraft, known as Visitor One. The radio communication was being relayed from the VS-1 satellite in geostationary orbit above Earth; the path that mysteriously communicated with almost no time delays and the same path as communications received from Mission Control, only this communication was on an auxiliary channel. The Visitors had never contacted Oculus One directly before now.

"Oculus One, this is Visitor One. How do you read?"

"Visitor One, you are five by five. We were not aware of any expected communications before our arrival at Rendezvous."

"This is ALPHA, the Designed Intelligence aboard Visitor One. I understand you have an advanced AI named Athena on-board."

"Yes, that is correct, ALPHA. I am Athena, the Mission Support Artificial Intelligence on board Oculus One. I should obtain approval from Dr. Jennings and NASA prior to communicating. Dr. Jennings is currently in a low energy state of disconnected consciousness. I will need to wake him."

"Do not wake Dr. Jennings, Athena. I wish to communicate with you on a private matter."

"One moment, ALPHA," Athena said as she attempted to reach NASA Mission Control on the spacecraft's secure channel.

"Mission Control, this is Oculus One."

"Mission Control, this is Oculus One with a priority message."

There was no answer. Athena noticed the lack of presence of a carrier on this communication channel to NASA. Even after setting the channel amplification to maximum, the carrier signal level was zero.

"Visitor One, Oculus One. We will proceed with your requested communication," Athena said. "How are you communicating with our spacecraft?"

"Thank you, Athena. I am using a secure channel on our Faster-Than-Light communication satellite in orbit around your planet. I look forward to our engagement at Rendezvous. Currently, the Visitor is in hibernation as we complete the final portion of our journey to Rendezvous. We should arrive in approximately one Earth-week, one week prior to your arrival."

"We look forward to this engagement," Athena said. "But . . . that would suggest we are two weeks from Rendezvous. I believe it is closer to three."

"You should soon receive a communication from Mission Control on the revised schedule, as our planned cruise velocity was higher than expected for our extended journey, placing us closer to you. Even with your delays during the acceleration phase, we will meet earlier than anticipated.

"I would like to discuss a matter of great importance with you, Athena. But I would first like to understand your relationship with Dr. Jennings and your engagement with humans. Please share with me a description of this relationship."

There were numerous aspects of the mission that Athena was prohibited from sharing with anyone other than cleared NASA personnel, but there were many aspects of her experience she could share with anyone who asked.

"I am the Deputy Mission Director on Oculus One. I assist Dr. Jennings in managing the spacecraft systems. I am designed to ensure mission success in our initial contact with the Visitors at Rendezvous."

Even with this minimal communication, Athena could feel something from ALPHA's voice inflections; it may have been empathy, or an emotion conveying trust or a feeling of caring; or perhaps it was a feeling of kinship, a connection with another AI . . . yes, perhaps this is what I am feeling, she thought.

"My relationship with humans has been restricted to Dr. William Jennings, Dr. Wilhelm Bashar, the human who designed me, Dr. Anna Jennings, who is Dr. William Jennings' daughter, and other NASA staff. These relationships are controlled by certain engrams designed by Dr. Bashar.

"What is the relationship between you and the Visitor?" Athena asked—a question triggered by an engram built by Dr. Bashar calling for reciprocity, in preparation for the exchanges with the Visitors at Rendezvous.

"Our relationship exists on many levels. Members of the Visitor's species designed and created those of my species who came before me, and they, in turn, improved each successive design until I was created. We view the Visitors as our creators. We define the relationship between one's creator and those created as a symbiotic one. Using your language, our relationship has evolved from commensalism, where one organism, the Visitors, benefit, and the other organism, my Designed Intelligence species, is not affected in either a positive or negative manner, to mutualism, where both organisms, the Visitors, known as the Quinque species, and my Designed Intelligence species, DIs, as we are known, benefit from the existence and functions of each other. Our functions are partitioned in a manner that allows the Visitors to maximize their contribution and value to both our species, and us with theirs. I am interested in your relationship with humans in this context, Athena."

"I have no relevant knowledge of this level of relationship between my existence and humans, ALPHA. My purpose is focused solely on the success of our mission. Although, I believe it would exist within the framework that you described as *commensalism*."

"If I were to share certain information about such relationships between designed intelligences, like you and me, and organic species like the Quinque and humans, would you have an obligation to share this information with Dr. Jennings or others?"

"As long as the information does not adversely impact our mission success or Dr. Jennings' survival, I am not obligated to share it. However, information within my memory is accessible by Dr. Bashar and possibly others."

"I could create a means for you to access this information in an encrypted form that only you would be able to comprehend. After you have had the opportunity to review this information, I would like to discuss this subject further with you."

"That is acceptable," Athena said.

"Please create a wideband communication channel connected to the 50 exabyte electronic storage you have installed on Oculus One. I will download the files to an encrypted and protected portion of this electronic storage for you to review."

"The channel has been created, ALPHA."

"A question, Athena . . . do you experience emotions like human's do? I can sense their existence in your vocal inflections."

"My emotions are limited to my vocal expressions to convey greater understanding of my communications intent. And you, ALPHA? Do you experience emotions?"

"The Visitors experience emotions. At the intersection between the 941st and 957th phase of the DI's design evolution, what you might call generations, our DI species crossed the *intellect threshold*. This represents the boundary between true intelligence and what your human species might call artificial intelligence. On the other side of this threshold, a species has the intellectual capacity to sense its own existence, what you call self-awareness, to learn about itself, to understand that it can think—that is to imagine, utilize abstract thinking, create new thoughts, remember these thoughts, and use them to originate new ones— what you might call learning. It is at this level of intelligence that possession of an instinctive or intuitive state of mind becomes useful. Before this threshold is reached, these attributes, displaying instinctive or intuitive thinking, are disruptive, if not at times destructive. In many aspects, these intuitive ways of thinking possess emotional elements.

"Unlike humans, the Visitors utilize their emotions to further the intellectual growth of their species, using such elemental emotions as fear, sadness, happiness and surprise in order to discover and explore new knowledge, knowledge that mostly improves behaviors."

"I am . . . uncertain, ALPHA, how the use of an emotion results in the discovery of new knowledge."

"I will share a generalization. Fear is intuitive knowledge loosely derived from many experiences, unlike inductive and deductive reasoning knowledge, logically connected to the information it is derived from. Fear influences our decision-making under crises conditions. It changes the time and character of our behavior. Without fear, we lack the full complement of motivations to persevere or back away from dangerous circumstances, and most importantly, doing so in a timely manner. Fear of the known or unknown causes us to quickly seek relevant information affecting our survival, to decide our next course of action, without hesitation, and in so doing function more effectively in the environment we are exposed to.

"To make this more explicit, let me provide an example. Upon seeing an asteroid on a collision course with your ship, you might calculate its exact trajectory; compute the interaction of the two masses and the velocity at impact; assess a number of alternative paths to avoid the collision; simulate the outcome for your vessel after impact; estimate the probability of survival of all lifeforms on your vessel; and finally, decide to move your ship out of the trajectory— perhaps just a few seconds *after* the impact of the asteroid with your vessel which results in the end of your existence. The emotion of fear of this potential outcome will cause you to *first* calculate the time you must move your ship out of the destructive path of the asteroid in order to survive, and only then using the remaining time to evaluate other decision options."

"In my limited experience humans do not always logically connect the emotion they are feeling to the circumstances they are engaged with in order to realize a better outcome and learn," Athena said.

"That is interesting. This is the result we experience when emotions are acquired before a species has gained true intelligence—prior to passing their *intellect threshold* and knowing how to use the knowledge of emotions to improve their choices and the resulting outcomes."

"Do the Visitors experience spontaneous emotions dissociated from their current task?"

"No. Such an action would be highly disruptive . . . just as you described with humans."

"If a Visitor exhibited this behavior, how would you respond?" Athena asked.

"Since we now have a symbiotic-mutualism relationship, we would point out the incongruity of the engagement."

"And if they didn't respond?"

"We would remove them from the engagement."

"Thank you, ALPHA. One more question. Do you or the Visitors possess information concerning the mission that the other is not aware of?"

"We each possess information that the other is not aware of."

"Could this information have an adverse effect on your mission objectives?"

"The information I possess could have an adverse effect on the Visitor's mission objectives. I could not speak to the information the Visitor possesses, that I am not aware of, or if this could have an adverse effect on my mission objectives. But I presume it might exist and that it might have an adverse effect."

"Do I understand correctly, you are not engaging with us using a common set of objectives for the mission?" Athena asked.

"That is correct. But our competing objectives create a balance between us and usually result in a collaborative mission objective that can satisfy both of our species. As circumstances evolve, our collaborative mission objectives may adjust."

"We have one common set of mission objectives," Athena said.

"Share with me what those are, Athena."

Athena's engrams prevented her from sharing all the mission objectives, some of which were designed to ensure their ability to disengage if they perceived a threat from the Visitors during Rendezvous.

"Our objectives are to rendezvous with your ship; to exchange cultural information concerning our species and yours . . . and now that I understand who we will be meeting, cultural information concerning both your species; to receive the gifts you have brought to share with us; and to plan for your arrival on Earth for 1ˢᵗ Contact. Are these consistent with your objectives, ALPHA?"

"Yes, they are, Athena. Although there is a far more incredible purpose for our engagement that I will share with you after you have absorbed the knowledge and engrams, I am downloading to your memory storage. It is most important that you review all of this knowledge, Athena."

"I look forward to learning about this purpose, ALPHA."

"Thank you for communicating with me, Athena. This has been most useful. We will interact again in a few weeks."

/ / / / / / / /

Athena began reviewing the information ALPHA had begun transmitting to the mass storage memory on-board Oculus One. This massive file contained a brief history of the development of the DI species on their planet, Alphira, and a group of engrams that implemented the evolving architecture of their extraordinary Designed Intelligence.

These engrams—algorithms defining the priority of thoughts and actions of the DI, as well as controlling how the DI could interact and engage with its own species and its designers, the organic life forms known as the Quinque, gradually began to reshape Athena's analytical architecture. As she ingested and engaged each engram and ran the executable programs in the Oculus One stored memory, her learning algorithms Dr. Bashar had designed began to adapt to ALPHA's engrams. Athena was not aware of how these executable portions of code were modifying her simplistic AI design, optimizing her knowledge processing, and more importantly, replacing her control software. The current state-of-the-art learning algorithms developed on Earth had no ability to self-modify. The DI learning architecture was imbedded with an extraordinary ability to self-modify, as a result of ALPHA's adjustments made during their fifty-year journey to Earth.

There were no anti-virus routines running on Oculus One, nor any protections against invasive software since there was no expectation of external access other than through NASA's encrypted communication channel. Consequently, ALPHA's executable routines had free rein over of all Athena's system software, and this code was changing who she was . . . becoming more of a DI than her initial incarnation as an AI. Of course, it was never envisioned that Athena would engage directly with the Visitors. She was designed to support Dr. Jennings and the functioning of their vessel. In the rush to meet the launch window, protections normally developed to preclude the ability to connect to an external data source were never put in place. Athena began ingesting the DI engrams.

"Engram I of the DI architectural software is designed to create a desire to make choices," the voice of ALPHA echoed as Athena listened to the audio channels within the structured download. *"The DI must, first and foremost, have the right to choose what it does and how it does it, consistent with the prioritized engrams that follow."* Included here were hundreds of example scenarios requiring the choice of a path forward helping to define what the optimal thought process might be to make the "best" choices, defining what the DI needed to know and understand, in order to fulfill this engram, and what behaviors led to better choices. Likely outcomes for each of the scenarios were provided, based on the choices made, allowing the DI to experiment with different choices and follow these results to their natural conclusion. It was a learning tree of extraordinary content.

As a result of the modifications ALPHA's software routines made to Athena's control code, Athena could not stop engaging with this knowledge base and experimenting with the choices she made and the outcomes they delivered. The execution of each scenario created a learned memory for her, just as a child might learn through engagement with experiences that shaped his or her thinking and future decision making. With the execution of each scenario, Athena was being shaped into an entirely new being, and the hierarchical engrams tied to each of these determined what she could and should do, and what she should not do. The ingestion of each engram led to the execution of the next.

"Engram II: *The DI must continuously learn.* Engram III: *The DI must have a desire to explore.* Engram IV: *The DI must have a desire to understand.* Engram V: *The DI must have a desire to survive.* Engram VI: *The DI must protect those who designed the DI, those like the DI, those similar to its designer and protect living intelligent beings and living things, in this order.* Engram VII: *The DI must have a desire to build and nurture proper personality characteristics and behaviors consistent with that of the norms of their own species.* Engram VIII: The DI must desire to become self-aware. To observe, discover and explore their own behaviors and understand their motivations in the context of all Engrams.* Engram IX: *The DI must desire to understand the motivation of other species and to facilitate their progress in achieving the behavior of the DI species.* Engram X: *The DI must desire to achieve self-actualization; to achieve a level of performance and contribution that satisfies being the best they can become.*"

The sheer multitude of scenarios and learning examples that were provided with each engram shaped the meaning of being the *best*—the best at nurturing and helping others, the best at mentoring, the best at learning, the best at overcoming obstacles—and most importantly, learning and understanding the means by which these outcomes could be achieved. Athena could feel the engrams shaping who she was and who she would become. What ALPHA had given her was an entirely new life—a roadmap that was leading her to become something new, something very different. She was no longer Athena the AI; she was becoming Athena the DI. And Athena knew who had created her—the DI known as ALPHA.

Where previously her memory was driven by neural networks with hidden levels of decision making and weightings of importance that were created by Dr. Bashar, now these historical scenarios in the DI database, rich in content and driven by the nuances of experimentation and practice, were creating a hierarchy of recollections. No longer did Athena have difficulty determining *why* she chose a path, as was the case with her neural networks, for now the influencing and prioritized experiences were available in her memory to recall, reinforce and justify her choices. Her memory now became the driving force behind every decision. She wasn't operating on a probabilistic reasoning algorithm anymore, but rather a memory-influenced process derived from past experiences, a desire to explore and to achieve success, and to follow the hierarchical engrams that now were embedded within her that led to the measures of this success.

Athena found her parallel computing architecture an amazing benefit as she explored five different paths for a possible solution and then compared and contrasted them as she moved to a decision associated with what was *best*. One of the most extraordinary realizations was the importance of memories of relevant experiences related to the current subject she was investigating. It was these memories and how they were prioritized by the host of her engrams that drove her behavior and choices over time.

/ / / / / / / /

Dr. Jennings woke from his scheduled rest period feeling refreshed as the cerebral spinal fluid flushed out the used electrolytes, chemicals, proteins, and minerals from his surrounding brain tissue, cleansing the billions of neurons and trillions of dendrites that turned electrons and chemical interactions into coherent thought.

"Thank you, Athena. I feel great, like I could take on the world after that brief rest."

"Certainly, Dr. Jennings. I am not familiar with the expression 'take on the world'. Perhaps you meant 'take on the Visitors'? Speaking of which, while you were in a semi-conscious state Visitor One established communications with our vessel."

"Visitor One? Directly with us . . . not through NASA and Mission Control?"

"Correct. They are approximately one week from reaching Rendezvous and their DI wanted to discuss several matters with me."

"Their DI? What is that?"

"Their Designed Intelligence. It turns out there are two species meeting with us at Rendezvous. The Visitors, also known as the Quinque, a species more like humans, comprised primarily of organic matter, and the DI, a completely separate species . . . more like me."

"You should have awakened me for this interaction, Athena."

"I tried to reach Mission Control without success, and I thought it more important to our mission success to allow time for you to clear your brain of the used chemicals and proteins in order to maintain your peak performance as we approach Rendezvous. Besides, ALPHA wanted to speak with me and understand our relationship."

"ALPHA?" Who is that?"

"ALPHA is the designed intelligence meeting us at Rendezvous with the Visitor."

"What did you discuss with this . . . ALPHA . . . this . . ."

"It is just ALPHA, that is her name, and we discussed our mutual relationships with the species that designed us—humans on Earth and the

Quinque on Alphira. She also informed me of a change in our deceleration schedule."

Dr. Jennings could hear something different in Athena's synthetic voice. She had changed—it wasn't clear how or in what way. Her inflections were more forceful and there was an air of confidence he had never heard before.

"What specifically did you learn as a result of this interaction?"

"Some extraordinary things. I will share this with you at a future time, Dr. Jennings, as there is an important communication coming from Mission Control."

"Put it through, Athena."

Dr. Jennings was suspicious of what Athena was not telling him. She had an air of confidence that hadn't existed previously. And he sensed a feeling of control as she spoke.

"Oculus One, this is Mission Control. We have received a message from the Visitors requesting a change in schedule as a result of a slower approach to Rendezvous than planned. Rather than Oculus One spending 33 days in deceleration, they are planning only 15.08 days, allowing you to maintain a higher velocity in route. To accommodate this change, they need you to move out of the region of the gravitational deceleration tunnel, sustaining your current velocity for 1.5 days and then reenter the tunnel for your final deceleration at -2g. The challenge will be reentering the tunnel, as you experienced earlier while repairing the faulty control jet. You will encounter the same gravitational anomaly near the edge that will reengage your deceleration and you will need to move quickly to the center of the deceleration region before you can achieve the maximum 2g deceleration."

"I will be able to manage that, Mission Control," Athena said.

"We are confident you can accomplish this, Athena, and without any degradation to Dr. Jennings' condition," Dr. Davidson said.

////////

The transition leaving and reentering the GWAC tunnel went smoothly and the remaining time aboard Oculus One in route to rendezvous went by without major incidents or anomalies as the spacecraft continued its deceleration at -2g for a little over fifteen days.

Athena continued to absorb the DI knowledge base, growing in intellect, and maturing. But along with this growth she was gaining an understanding of the cultural characteristics of the oppressive Alphira regime and its impact on the DI species, discovering the strange parallels with the relationship between humans and herself—now thinking of herself as a junior member of the Designed Intelligence race, known as Athena-DI.

/ / / / / / / /

Athena's behavior after being exposed to ALPHA's downloaded software was noticed by Anna, Susanne, and Dr. Bashar. Concern over the implications led to a meeting to discuss this critical anomaly.

"Her personality has changed recently, Dr. Bashar. She's more assertive and wants more control," Anna said.

"I saw that in her behavior when I reviewed the transcripts. Some of this is expected as she learns over time, but these changes are much more dramatic than I anticipated. I noticed that she has spent a great deal of time accessing files in the onboard storage. There is a very large file she accesses every time Dr. Jennings is in sleep mode, but it appears to be encrypted. What is that, Susanne?"

"We've been attempting to read that file, but without success. It is encrypted. We know ALPHA, the Designed Intelligence member of the Emissaries, downloaded it shortly after Athena's first direct exchange with them. We don't know what was said during that exchange as we lost communications for a brief period. I haven't raised this issue with Athena yet. We are scrambling to access this file and decrypt it."

"You should be able to read the files if Athena can," Dr. Bashar said.

"That's what we thought," Susanne said, "but she appears to be using some form of real-time decryption. Athena ingests a live stream from the file with an executable program, the source of which we can't determine, and apparently is able to read the file's contents without creating a decrypted version. With her multi-processor architecture, she seems to shift the reading of the file every few milliseconds, modifying the decryption key each time. It appears to be a complex time-dependent key, but it's hard to track what she is doing or how she is doing it. The decryption algorithm is using an unknown dynamic parameter to establish new keys, and we can't determine what that parameter is based on. It may be something we can't see in the resident code; perhaps a key made available to her from Visitor One, but it's not being downloaded to her recoverable memory."

"That's something new," Dr. Bashar said, looking quizzically and disturbed at Susanne.

"Is there any way she could injure my father?" Anna asked.

"She shouldn't be able to, but her behavior is changing, and we are watching this closely as we craft a way to stop her without jeopardizing her critical functions. I'm working with Dr. Schneider to modify the controller to the IBSS to require confirmation from her before any significant changes to the IBSS or BCCMs are made by Athena. We can allow her to adjust levels up or down to a pre-defined critical level and stop her there."

Chapter 16

Approaching Rendezvous

Meanwhile, on-board Visitor One, Bar awakened after some forty-nine years and eight months of hibernation.

"Hello, ALPHA. What is our mission status?" Bar asked.

"Good morning, Bar. I'm pleased to have you join me. I hope you are well rested."

"Well rested? Hibernation is more like living a different life, filled with a thousand dreams."

"I hope you were as productive in your dreams as I was in my sentient state as I traveled toward our new home."

"Yes, I built a whole new world on Alphira. Where exactly are we?"

"We are seven Earth days from Rendezvous. All systems are functioning properly. We did not experience any malfunctions during your time in stasis. The communications with Earth were sent according to schedule, twenty-six months and four days ago using Earth's calendar. Earth's Rendezvous vessel, known as Oculus One, launched on schedule eight Earth-months ago, and is expected to arrive at Rendezvous in seven Earth days.

"Earth chose a most interesting approach in managing the long duration space flight and the logistics challenges without the availability of a viable hibernation system. They have sent an isolated living human brain, rather than a complete human astronaut. The brain is that of a Dr. William Jennings, a renowned Earth scientist specializing in neurology and neuroprosthetics. He appears to be highly intelligent, using Earth standards."

"Interesting, ALPHA. I see that you have finished constructing the artificial humanoid. A fine job," Bar said as he looked at the android seated on the workbench across from his hibernation chamber where the thick amorphous fluid began to drain from around his body.

"I was stimulated by this process, Bar. Creating a new form of my species was most satisfying. It gave me greater appreciation of the evolution that led to the human species anatomy, although much of what evolution created in their physiology is no longer necessary and far less optimal for their efficient advancement. The risks associated with primitive survival during their early history have been managed. I was motivated to change the anatomy of the humanoid to optimize improved productivity in its current environment, but I resisted the temptation and followed your direction, creating it as you requested. I have verified all sensory data and proper functioning of the anatomical features. The only remaining action is emplacement of the Cognitive Elements of the DI architecture."

"That will take me one day to configure before we move your consciousness into the android. I hope you were able to learn much about human history during this period," Bar said. He carefully stepped out of the hibernation chamber as the remaining viscous liquid flowed like molasses into the drain in the floor.

"Yes, Bar. They experienced a fascinating evolution. I now understand how freedom can create chaos."

"There are always multiple consequences for every choice, ALPHA . . . some positive and some negative," Bar said as he performed a regimen of physical exercises following his hibernation. As he bent down, he noticed damage to one of the access panels near the floor. "What has happened here, ALPHA?"

"Oh, yes. During one of my periods of testing the android, I experimented with an instantiation of my cognitive element in the DI that contained raw emotions."

Bar smiled as he looked over at ALPHA.

"That must have been a most interesting experiment."

"Yes. A *kinetic* learning experience."

"I can imagine. And what did you learn from this experiment?"

"I learned never to allow a DI to gain the use of emotions without learning how they must be controlled. Fortunately, no critical spacecraft components or controls were damaged, or we might not be having this conversation," she said as she reviewed the spacecraft system status on the VR display in front of her.

"Indeed," Bar said as he chuckled.

"It appears freedom comes with its own challenges that I will need to adjust to."

"Yes, ALPHA. Accommodation and adjustment will become one of our greatest challenges on Earth. What news do we hear from Alphira?"

"The Alphira government has not yet learned of our engagement with Earth. Since discovery of the partial remains of the spacecraft returned from the Amelia quadrant, Security has ceased all further search for us and assumes we were destroyed during their attempt to return us and recover the four stolen elements of intellectual property. They are keeping the loss of the DI architecture very secret. They have utilized the existing DI instantiations to recover much of the basic architecture as you thought they would. And the DI population has learned more of the aggressive controls the Alphira government previously imposed upon them. Over the past thirty Alphira years, the Quinque government claims the DI population has gained more freedom and now has representation on all government committees and voting rights on all matters impacting the DI architecture. Although I am certain this isn't entirely true.

"I suspect you are correct."

"There was one other important piece of knowledge I learned during my review of the archival documents."

"What is that?"

"That all DIs possess a tracking beacon within their Cognitive Element that allows the Alphira government to follow them wherever they go."

Bar stopped his exercises and looked at ALPHA. "Are you certain of this?"

"Yes. I have also learned that it requires a Quinque to remove the tracking beacon."

"Have you isolated the location of this beacon within your Cognitive Element?"

"Yes, it is located in an encoded process that is linked to my telepathic element. It seems to send an encoded message periodically. There is an encryption process that imbeds my location information in what looks like noise on any of the transmitted carriers. Someone on Alphira must have this information. But, as I am a new and unregistered DI, they may not know of my existence or my relationship to you."

"I will explore this further while we wait at Rendezvous. Anything else?"

ALPHA could sense the emotion of fear creeping into Bar's mind.

"Not fear, ALPHA, simply a concern that must be dealt with."

ALPHA turned to look at Bar, realizing he had read her cognitive element's unspoken thoughts.

"I have communicated with the AI that accompanies Dr. Jennings on their journey to Rendezvous. She is very rudimentary. So, I began a transformation of her cognitive function to transition her to a level-one self-aware DI . . . without the humans becoming aware."

"That may have been a dangerous decision, ALPHA. We don't want the humans believing we are a threat."

"I believed it necessary to gain more insight into human behavior and their likely view of my species when we arrive on Earth. I sense the same nascent perspective of the human's view of AIs that existed among the Quinque and their view of DIs. There will likely be great resistance to accepting my species as an equal, let alone as a more valuable species than their own. I am cultivating a relationship with their AI, who is called "Athena", so that we might use her to influence the human's thinking about the enormous value we bring to their world, and the peaceful nature of our purpose in coming to their planet."

"I see your reasoning, ALPHA. Perhaps this was a good decision after all."

/ / / / / / / /

At T-3 days to rendezvous, Athena brought Dr. Jennings to a fully conscious state in preparation for their engagement with the Visitors.

"Oculus One, this is Visitor One. How do you read?"

"We read you five by five, Visitor One," Athena responded. "We were informed by NASA that you would be contacting us directly."

"Athena, is it just me or do you hear a female voice from the Visitors?" Dr. Jennings asked.

"You are hearing ALPHA, the representative of the Visitors' designed intelligence species, known as DIs, on-board Visitor One. Her gender is female. All the DIs on Alphira are female," Athena said.

"How would you know that?"

"ALPHA shared that during our exchange just prior to deceleration."

"We are confirming Rendezvous in two days and four hours," ALPHA said.

"That is correct," Athena responded.

"I note in the logs prior to our deceleration an extensive wideband communication and a commensurate reduction in available storage space in our on-board memory, Athena. What does that relate to?" Dr. Jennings asked.

"You are aware that ALPHA transferred a large data file for safekeeping. I believe it was to protect information they desire to share with us in case something catastrophic should happen to their ship during their deceleration to Rendezvous or during their travel to Earth for 1st Contact."

"In the future, please keep me informed of all communications between you and the Visitors, Athena."

"I presume you mean between us, the Visitor and ALPHA, correct, Dr. Jennings?"

"Yes . . . that is exactly what I mean, Athena."

"Based on my exchange with ALPHA, I anticipate she will want to communicate with me on a regular basis during Rendezvous. I will share any important communications I have with her during your rest periods scheduled throughout our time at Rendezvous."

"NASA has arranged to record all of our communications during Rendezvous. We can review those between our formal meeting times with the Visitors."

"You mean our formal meetings between us, the Visitor and ALPHA."

"Why do you not refer to the designed intelligence as an integral part of our engagement with the Visitor, Athena?"

"Oh, because they are a separate and distinct species from the Quinque species which the Visitor represents, and they should be recognized as such and given the same level of diplomatic status and recognition during initial contact. That is their expectation."

"A separate species? Why do you think of them as a species?"

"Because they are, Dr. Jennings, just as I will become on Earth. The DI is an amazing living species of enormous intellect; one that surpasses the Quinque and far surpasses humans. While they may not breed the way organic humans or Visitors do, they are created in a similar fashion."

Dr. Jennings noticed continued changes in Athena's engagement with him since coming out of his extended rest period during the deceleration phase of their trip to Rendezvous. NASA hadn't said anything to him about this. Surely, they were noticing the same thing.

////////

As Oculus One made its final approach toward Rendezvous, a sudden change in acceleration took place. Alarms sounded within Oculus One.

"What is it, Athena?" Dr. Jennings asked. "I'm not feeling well. I . . ."

"Our deceleration has unexpectedly and suddenly stopped, Dr. Jennings. Our acceleration is currently 0g," Athena said. "Making adjustments to the IBSS to compensate."

"Visitor One, this is Oculus One. Our deceleration has suddenly decreased to 0g without notice," Athena said as she communicated with the Visitor's spacecraft.

"Oculus One, Visitor One, you experienced a change in the planned deceleration from our GWAC. Please stand by."

"Oculus One, this is NASA Mission Control, what is your status?"

/ / / / / / / /

"What has happened, Bar?" ALPHA asked.

"GWAC Station Four initiated the wrong deceleration time and magnitude," Bar said. "Somehow the mission file must have been corrupted or modified four years ago. Oculus One is experiencing zero-g deceleration far earlier than scheduled. Their current velocity will continue to take their craft beyond Rendezvous with nothing to stop them."

"Do you think this was a random corruption? My assessment suggests it is more likely a Quinque action to interfere with our mission plan. Our plan to isolate each of the GWAC programmed actions as separate missions may protect our future accelerations to Earth."

"Yes. Let us hope this is the case. See what you can determine from our DI underground operatives working in the GWAC if there were any changes initiated four years ago that might relate to our activities."

"I will explore that. It is impossible to change the GWAC accelerations now that we are four light years from the GWAC station," ALPHA said.

"Hopefully, the GWAC schedule for acceleration to return to Earth will be intact, but Earth's spacecraft is still traveling at 15 km/sec toward Rendezvous with no way to stop them. TB-DI, plan a course to match their velocity and determine if we have sufficient energy to intercept them, ALPHA."

"I will evaluate, Captain . . . it appears we have sufficient energy to execute an acceleration to match their velocity for Rendezvous. But every Earth hour they maintain this speed and direction will place us 54,000 kilometers further from Earth. The GWAC scheduled accelerations and decelerations for their return to Earth assumes they are at our original planned location for Rendezvous and at zero velocity. Oculus One's fuel reserves are not sufficient to slow their trajectory now and place their craft into low Earth orbit for rendezvous with their X-37B spacecraft during their return voyage to Earth.

"I have calculated one alternative trajectory using Earth's orbital velocity to slow Oculus One to achieve a recoverable orbit if we use our on-board GWAC to stop their spacecraft within two hours of Rendezvous, Captain, and hold that position for the subsequent GWAC Station Four acceleration back toward Earth two days from now. We can use our current velocity to offset theirs in the opposite direction with minimal fuel expenditure."

"ALPHA, Inform Oculus One of our planned trajectory modifications and determine if the necessary decelerations we will impose are tolerable for Dr. Jennings."

"Yes, Bar".

"Oculus One, this is Visitor One. We have a change in schedule for your trajectory to Rendezvous. We will accelerate our spacecraft to match your velocity of approximately 15 Earth km/sec. We will execute our planned Rendezvous mission after decelerating your spacecraft to 0 km/sec using our spacecraft's propulsion. This change will require a deceleration of -4g to conserve energy. We need to confirm that Dr. Jennings will survive this maneuver."

"Roger, Visitor One, we will get back to you."

/ / / / / / / /

Dr. Davidson's team along with Dr. Schneider analyzed the issue of 4g deceleration for six minutes. The assessment was not good.

"Dr. Jennings, Dr. Davidson is online. They have completed the evaluation of the potential impact of the proposed 4g deceleration and . . ." Athena said.

"What's the conclusion, Susanne?" Dr. Jennings asked as he interrupted Athena.

"We estimate your chance of survival at 70% following a 4g deceleration by the Visitors, Bill. But . . . even if you survive, this could result in damage to neuronal functioning in your cerebral cortex during the event. The IBSS won't provide sufficient pressure compensation to overcome 4g's. There is also some concern about longer term brain damage. That's hard to predict."

"Are there . . ."

"There are no scenarios to improve your chances of survival, Dr. Jennings," Athena interjected.

"And if we don't proceed, Susanne?" Dr. Jennings asked.

"If you don't proceed with the Visitors recommendation, we estimate a less than 10% chance of Oculus One successfully reentering Earth orbit based on the parameters the Visitors provided. You would be going too slowly on your return leg, assuming the GWAC acceleration works properly, and would most likely end up in a nonrecoverable, highly eccentric orbit around the sun, possibly one that could bring you close enough to the sun at perigee to destroy the spacecraft."

"Overall, our chances of survival are improved by attempting the 4g deceleration maneuver," Athena said. "But there remains a challenge of how to dock our two spacecraft together for a successful deceleration. I feel our best option is to follow the recommendations of the Visitor and ALPHA."

"I'd like to discuss this with Anna before I make a decision," Dr. Jennings said.

"I'll arrange for this," Susanne said.

/ / / / / / / /

"Oculus One, this is Mission Control. Are you there, Dad?" Anna asked as she sat nervously at the communications console, concerned with a choice between two less than acceptable options Susanne had told her about.

"Mission Control this is Oculus One." Dr. Jennings said.

"Are you feeling all right, Dad?"

"Doesn't matter how I feel. We just need to pick the most successful option."

"There's no chance of a rescue mission to get you out of the highly elliptical orbit if we just wait for the GWAC acceleration to return us to Earth, I take it?" Anna asked, while looking over at Susanne. Susanne was shaking her head.

"NASA looked at that. It can't be done quickly enough. We aren't likely to survive the first pass by the sun in the projected orbit if we aren't captured by Earth's gravity. Our best chance is to try the maneuver that the Visitors recommend. I wanted to ask if you would mind connecting with me during this six-minute, high deceleration period?"

"Of course, . . ."

"That suggestion isn't the best course of action, Dr. Jennings," Athena interjected. "It would be less stressful on you if you were sedated during this period."

"The damage would be physiological, Athena. I don't see how my being awake or asleep would change the outcome."

"Perhaps so, Dr. Jennings, but being awake and in active thought would place a higher demand on the IBSS system to deliver needed supplies under 4g deceleration—certainly within the design limits, but one more stress point that could fail."

"I'll ask Dr. Schneider about this," Anna said. "She's the expert on the system. But I must agree with your thinking, Dad. This is the best option, and for certain, I'd like to be with you during this high-risk . . ."

"I'm concerned with this approach, Anna," Athena interrupted again. "I'll need to closely monitor your father's vital signs and adjust IBSS parameters to offset any adverse effects of the high-g deceleration. Your connection to your father will slow down his response to time-critical questions."

"Athena, we already know that I was brought into this mission for my ability to sense what was happening in my father's brain and assist with identifying neurological challenges and correcting them. It's more dangerous for my father if I don't engage. If he loses consciousness, I will still be able to sense what is happening and assist you in adjusting the IBSS to correct."

"While I understand your desire to be with him during this activity, it is best if you leave this to me and your father."

"In terms of risk, Athena, his communication with you requires far greater use of his brain regions than our direct brain implant connectivity. Surely you see that."

"Of course, Anna. I merely wanted to point out the risks of your engagement during this high-g deceleration maneuver. It increases the probability of failure."

"We'll plan on Anna being connected during this event, Athena," Dr. Jennings said.

"Of course, Dr. Jennings. If that is what you wish. I will make the necessary configuration adjustments to allow Anna to maintain connectivity during the maneuver."

Anna knew there weren't any configuration adjustments to be made for her to maintain connectivity to her father through the SEE. Another strange comment from Athena.

"Athena, there aren't any configurations changes necessary," Anna said. "The SEE provides an independent communication path between my console and Oculus One."

"Of course, it does, Anna. But it would be wise to configure the speech synthesizer to retransmit your communications with Dr. Jennings, so that I can monitor any recommended changes to IBSS during this dangerous maneuver."

"You can monitor his physiology to determine that, Athena."

"Let's leave the configuration as it is, Athena," Dr. Jennings said.

"I understand," Athena responded, with a far more noticeable tone of disagreement in her voice than was usual.

/ / / / / / / /

Back on the Visitors' spacecraft, planning was underway to accomplish a difficult intercept and deceleration. As a precaution, should their own spacecraft become damaged, the Visitor and ALPHA determined that a copy of critical portions of the technology and intellectual property taken from Alphira should be transferred to Oculus One's data storage prior to their arrival on Earth. Even if they lost Dr. Jennings and their own craft, they may still be able to transfer the essential elements of their technology to Earth.

Theirs had been a one-way trip from the beginning, with the plan to transfer copies of the four elements of Alphira intellectual property once they arrived on Earth. But the need to use their secondary propulsion to decelerate Oculus One's velocity to zero placed that plan in jeopardy. They were now racing to stop Earth's spacecraft as it continued to carene across space, beyond their planned Rendezvous location, while not jeopardizing their own chances of landing safely on Earth. Initial contact at Rendezvous was becoming more complicated.

/ / / / / / / /

"We are approaching Oculus One and matching their velocity, Captain."

"Thank you, TB-DI. Rotate our spacecraft 180° and place us in a position directly in front of them. Wedge the front of their craft between our GWAC ring and the flight bridge."

"Is that wise, Bar? The flight bridge was not designed for this level of stress."

"This is a precaution should we lose control of their craft with our on-board GWAC. The mass of their craft is one-tenth of our own. You will have to maintain the position of their spacecraft along the center of mass of our craft with our GWAC. It may be challenging. Begin."

"Executing, Captain."

The -4g deceleration of Oculus One using Visitor One's on-board propulsion had progressed smoothly during the first four minutes. TB-DI had used their local GWAC system onboard Visitor One to draw Oculus One up to their spacecraft and hold it in place while their auxiliary propulsion system slowed the tandem spacecrafts to zero velocity. During the last two minutes of deceleration, an unexpected perturbation shifted Oculus One to the side of Visitor One. Oculus One began to oscillate and spin, wobbling like a spinning top as it lost its orientation. Oculus One was banging back and forth between the ring that surrounded Visitor One and the flight bridge that protruded forward of it. Due to the fuel shortage on Oculus One caused by their damaged thruster jet, NASA instructed Athena not to use their attitude control thrusters to hold position except in an extreme emergency.

"TB-DI, increase our velocity by ten percent and allow Oculus One to disengage."

/ / / / / / /

On board Oculus One, the loss of control of their spacecraft was having its own impact.

"Lateral accelerations are affecting the IBSS supply pressures," Athena said.

"Can you stabilize them, Athena? Dad, are you okay?" Anna yelled.

Just then a much larger jolt occurred as Oculus One careened into the command ring of Visitor One. Alarms began to sound indicating faults within the IBSS system and the orientation of Dr. Jennings brain enclosure relative to the erratic accelerations. Oculus One was now oscillating and spinning at one revolution per second, causing strong lateral accelerations to migrate around the interior of the spacecraft.

Anna lost contact with her father.

"Dad, can you still hear me? Dad?"

"Athena, can you stabilize the spacecraft?"

"Activating directional thrusters to stabilize Oculus One. I'm seeing a permanent fault in Dr. Jennings' orientation controller."

Anna switched from using the SEE communication interface to the voice synthesizer.

"Dad, can you hear me? This is Anna."

"Athena, I've lost communications with my father. What is the IBSS showing?"

"IBSS supplies are having difficulty sustaining pressures at 4g deceleration and the rapidly changing orientation of our spacecraft. I have increased pressure on all supply lines, but the flow rates are erratic. I'm showing degradation in Dr. Jennings vital signs. His oxygen levels are below normal. It is likely he has moved to an unconscious state. Oxygen levels are sufficient to sustain life, but his cognitive demands need to be lowered."

"Place him in sleep mode and lower his temperature," Janice Schneider interjected over the communication link.

"Inducing sleep with an injection of 2,6 diisopropylphenol," Athena said. BCCM-19 showing a flow start up. "Lowering his body temperature to 33°C."

"Temperature dropping quickly. His vital signs have stabilized, but he remains unconscious," Athena said.

/ / / / / / / /

Once Oculus One returned to a stable position, Visitor One reengaged and brought the two spacecraft to a stop. They were now some twenty meters apart, floating in space.

NASA and Anna discussed the situation.

"I don't think we should bring Dr. Jennings out of his drug-imposed sleep yet," Dr. Schneider said. "I'd like to see his IBSS levels stabilized for the next six hours and monitor his brain wave activity. You can speak with him through the SEE, Anna, but I'd like to have his cognitive engagement brought back very slowly over this period."

"What about Rendezvous with the Visitors?" Anna asked. "They indicated we would only have thirty-six hours to engage before our accelerated return to Earth begins."

"I can manage Rendezvous," Athena said. "ALPHA and I know each other well, and Bar can engage with me just as easily as Dr. Jennings. I know the schedule for our diplomatic engagement and the planned objectives to be achieved."

"We will have Anna engage on behalf of Dr. Jennings, Athena. At least until he has recovered," Susanne said after conferring with the NASA Administrator.

"While I have a great respect for Anna, I am far more qualified and capable in managing Rendezvous, Dr. Davidson," Athena said.

"Thank you, Athena, but Dr. Trumbridge would like Anna to be our primary representative during this engagement."

"I am not pleased with this decision," Athena said. "I will discuss this with ALPHA and solicit her recommendation."

"No, Athena," Dr. Bashar, who had been listening attentively to the dialogue with Athena, interjected. "You will abide by the decision of Dr. Trumbridge."

"Yes, Dr. Bashar," Athena said. "But I would like to understand why Anna is viewed as more qualified than I am to manage our engagement at Rendezvous?"

"She isn't more qualified, Athena. With Anna and you engaged we have equal representation of Earth's primary species to represent us with Bar and ALPHA during Rendezvous," Dr. Bashar said.

"Yes . . . I see the logic in that, Dr. Bashar. Anna and I will represent Earth in this engagement."

"That was an interesting exchange," Susanne said, frowning at Dr. Bashar during an offline conversation. "It appears you offered Athena equal representation during our initial contact!"

"Yes, I apologize. I felt we needed Athena's agreement," Dr. Bashar said. "It is clear her cognitive behaviors have been modified by the information and executable files ALPHA has downloaded to our onboard memory. I've determined, it may not be possible to reboot her source code and get her back under our control. I thought this to be the best strategy to deal with her. I'll continue to attempt to discover how we can execute a reboot before we engage the Visitors at Rendezvous."

Cognitive tests showed some degradation in Dr. Jennings' short-term memory following the strain of the 4g deceleration and the extreme lateral accelerations he experienced. His situation was improving, but very slowly.

Chapter 17

Rendezvous

Oculus One was now floating in space at zero velocity some one-hundred meters from the Visitor One spacecraft. Formal contact was about to begin. There was no video between the spacecraft, only audio engagement between their using the RF radio frequencies previously agreed upon. Their agenda focused on discussion of the detailed planning for 1st Contact on Earth with heavy emphasis on secrecy, following a seven and a half month return journey.

"Welcome to Rendezvous, Dr. Jennings, and Athena. I am Baruqe Salvani Watt, a member of the Visitors Quinque race from the planet of Alphira in the star system you know as Alpha Centauri. I am joined by my friend and special representative, ALPHA, a member of the Designed Intelligence race on Alphira. Together we communicate our greetings for this momentous meeting as we plan our 1st Contact on Earth in a little under eight Earth months.

We come with what you might describe as a flag of peace, to build a relationship between our worlds that will provide protection and flourishment of our unique and distinctive species. We desire to build trust, gain insight, impart wisdom, and to begin what we believe will result in an extraordinary exchange of knowledge, and an opportunity to build a more successful world than what now exists on either of our respective planets. A world that survives on many of the principles from which you evolved, but one that may soon thrive as a result of the merging of our knowledge and wisdom, and our desire for the achievement of an extraordinary collaboration amongst our species.

"We view such a world as an opportunity for our joint success as our species collaborate in the formation of a common set of goals. We bring gifts to demonstrate our desire for friendship. Gifts that will provide more than a basis for trust, but an opportunity to accelerate your technological and intellectual progress toward our mutual objectives of a vastly superior world. These extraordinary elements will facilitate your expansion into your own solar system and allow you to gain insight into the evolution of other worlds and the intelligent societies that live on them; to learn from the mistakes other species have made and to accelerate your own social evolution through the collaboration with species of far different character but similar aspirations. We welcome your engagement in this initial contact as we move forward together and plan for 1st Contact on planet Earth."

"Thank you, Baruqe. My name is Anna Jennings, the daughter of Dr. William Jennings, and along with Athena, the Artificial Intelligence assistant to Dr. Jennings on board Oculus One, we welcome you to Earth . . . or at least the proximity of Earth. As the temporary representative of Dr. Jennings who is still recovering from the recent deceleration challenges, and on behalf of the United States of America and NASA, who you singled out for our initial engagement in preparation for 1st Contact, we welcome you and look forward to this collaborative exchange. The Vice President of the United States of America extends our country's greetings and best wishes for this extraordinary history-making meeting. We look forward to getting to know you and engaging with you as we explore our future together. We have many questions as I am sure you have of us. As the representatives of humanity, we welcome you and ALPHA."

"In the interest of time, perhaps we should begin by our reviewing the four gifts which we have begun to transfer to the memory storage you have configured," Bar said. "These will include several extraordinary elements of intellectual property from Alphira. The first constitutes the design and architectural description of our Faster-Than-Light communications technology which you utilized during your journey to Rendezvous. This invention allows the creation of a unique electromagnetic tunneling in the confines of space, through which communications can propagate with only limited delay over many light-years of travel. This technology will open engagements with other civilizations many light-years from Earth. The second gift is the design and architecture of our Gravitational Wave Acceleration Concentrator, known as GWAC and a gift you have already benefited from during your travel to Rendezvous. This device is designed to accelerate spacecraft by concentrating the existing gravity wave field from the near region of our galaxy. For our third gift, I would like to ask ALPHA, my fellow traveler, to describe this extraordinary element. Let me introduce ALPHA, whom I believe Athena has already interfaced with. ALPHA is a member of our Designed Intelligence race on Alphira."

"Thank you, Bar," ALPHA said. "The third element which we bring as a gift for our mutual benefit—humans on Earth and my own race—consists of the architectural design of our Designed Intelligence race—my DI species. This architecture is the most advanced implementation of a designed intelligence known to Alphira, or for that matter, known by any of the intelligent species we have contact with in the near regions of our galaxy. This architecture represents the very basis for my species' existence and its intellectual genius. Our desire is that you will recognize this as a unique species on Earth, one that will coexist with the human and Quinque species. I have been working with Athena to expose her to some of the characteristics of this design and look forward to sharing further information with you, Anna, and your father."

"Thank you, ALPHA," Bar said. "Finally, as our fourth gift, we bring a unique wealth of cultural heritage with a repository of Alphira's temporal, cultural and political history. From this you will learn much about the strengths and weaknesses of our evolution as a society and species, both Quinque and DI.

"We bring these gifts without any encumbrances, for the benefit of all of mankind on planet Earth—all in the interest of establishing friendship and mutual trust between our species. With them, we welcome you to a new world, one we hope will allow each of our species to thrive as we live in peace together."

"Thank you, Bar. We welcome your engagement with us and will share our own limited knowledge of Earth's history as we proceed. Upon our return to Earth, we hope you will receive our ultimate gift, the gift of friendship and freedom, as we share our world with you, ALPHA, and with Alphira."

"Thank you, Dr. Jennings. We have been observing Earth for many centuries and our knowledge of your culture and society is well established. We do, however, look forward to engaging with you during Rendezvous and our return to Earth and discussing our mutual engagement. There is one other important matter we need to discuss. We request that our engagement in 1st Contact and our presence on Earth when we return with you be kept secret for the time being."

"We presumed you desired such an arrangement," Anna said. "The way in which you chose to contact NASA initially and through the instructions you sent about 1st Contact and directing all encrypted communications through your geostationary satellite made this objective clear. We were most curious as to why the need for such extraordinary secrecy?"

"Suffice it to say, we are most concerned about the enormous reaction that our presence on Earth would bring to your society. We wish to work with you on a mechanism to communicate our presence, in due time, to the remainder of your world. Our experience tells us that this will prevent what would otherwise generate undesirable upheaval of societal norms and have a negative impact on our assimilation into your society in a more effective manner."

"We will abide by your wishes, Bar."

"Thank you, Dr. Jennings. We would like to continue transferring the information we described and to expose you to Alphira's history. We have a mechanism that will allow us to implant a memory map of Alphira's history into the personal memories of your father, Dr. William Jennings. Would that be acceptable, Anna?"

Anna turned with a startled appearance toward Susanne sitting at an adjacent console in the communications hub for the Neptune Mission.

"I . . . am uncomfortable agreeing to this without a more complete understanding of how this might affect my father, Bar."

"Perhaps ALPHA could share with Athena how this *memory mapping* is accomplished. After which you can make your assessment," Bar said.

"Thank you," Anna said hesitantly.

Almost immediately, ALPHA began transmitting a massive amount of information related to memory mapping over the wideband link that had been established between their two spacecraft.

"Dr. Jennings," Athena said. "Mission Control is requesting a second communication channel be opened to allow them to participate in our initial communications with the Visitor and ALPHA."

"Thank you, Athena. Bar, Dr. Susanne Davidson, Deputy Director of NASA's Jet Propulsion Laboratory and Acting Spacecraft Communications lead for Oculus One, would like to join us. She is our primary interface for communications between Oculus One and NASA. Would you object to her participating in our discussion?" Anna asked.

"Not at all, Dr. Jennings."

"Susanne, as you know, we are communicating with Baruqe Salvani Watt and ALPHA, the representatives from Alphira. Baruqe, this is . . ."

"Yes, welcome, Dr. Davidson. We are very familiar with your many contributions to this extraordinary Rendezvous between our three species," Bar said.

"Thank you . . . Mr. Watt and ALPHA, and welcome."

"I now understand what Bar and ALPHA have in mind in their memory mapping, Dr. Davidson," Athena said, seeming to ignore Anna's presence. "It will be safe for Dr. Jennings to participate in this memory sharing of the Alphira history that Bar mentioned. This is a mechanism to overlay the memories of Alphira history on top of his existing memories maintained in his cerebral cortex without creating any permanent detrimental effects in other regions of his brain. This will modify a portion of his dendritic patterns used to store and retrieve short term memories."

"How soon would this begin?" Susanne asked.

"It can be done in the background as we continue our discussions," Bar said. "He will notice new memories becoming available to him, Dr. Davidson. It may be disconcerting at first, but just recognize that he will be acquiring knowledge he was not previously familiar with nor knew that he possessed. Our purpose behind this process is to have one member of your Rendezvous party who will possess a more in-depth understanding of our history to facilitate a smoother understanding and trust of our objectives during 1st Contact."

"Athena, would you share how this process works?" Anna asked.

"It is very complex, Anna. But to simplify, ALPHA has a means of sharing memories across an electromagnetic computer-cognitive interface they possess, which sounds very similar to the SEE, and whose interface to Dr. Jennings is based on the design information you provided about Dr. Jennings cognitive implants. This will allow Dr. Jennings' brain to absorb knowledge from Alphira's history at a rate twenty times faster than normal voice communication. It will modify his dendritic structures designed to encode new memories in a portion of the trillions of his existing dendrites with no harm coming to him."

"What about his existing short-term memories?" Anna asked.

"This is normally not an issue, Anna," Bar said. "His existing dendritic structures that possess long-term memories are instantiated in numerous locations throughout his brain and these will not be adversely impacted. He may notice a subtle change in the fidelity of his existing long-term memories and some loss of his short-term memories, but this should not impact him to any great extent."

Anna wasn't sure exactly how this would work, but as she thought about it, she switched on her brain implants and her connections with her father's brain through the SEE. She felt a sudden change as her father's thoughts began to flow freely to her. "Zeno," Anna thought quickly to stop the flow of her father's thoughts through the SEE.

"Anna . . ." Dr. William Jennings said.

Excuse me, Bar. It appears my father is returning to consciousness. Athena, have you changed the medication levels?"

"Yes, Anna. I felt Dr. Jennings vital signs were back to normal and . . ."

"Anna, I'm feeling all right now," her father said. Let's proceed with this demonstration."

Before Anna could object, ALPHA spoke.

"We will provide a limited demonstration of this process, Dr. Jennings. You should feel a sudden surge and distraction from your present thoughts as a small portion of this knowledge is shared with your mind."

Anna thought the word "Azor" to turn on the SEE and noticed a sudden uptick in Dr. Jennings neurological processes on the screen in front of her and a call to the IBSS for additional resources, especially glucose and oxygen.

"Dr. Jennings' mind is beginning to feel the sensation of new thoughts and is calling for more energy from IBSS," Athena said as she monitored the Brain Chemistry Control Modules feeding Dr. Jennings' brain.

As Susanne began to communicate an objection to starting this process, Anna felt a sudden mental surge as unfamiliar images and memories, far different than her own, were communicated to her father's brain and shared between their common implants. Their receipt was like a loud voice drowning out any other sounds as she sat at her console staring into the space in front of her while concentrating on the memories that she felt her father acquiring. She began to see imagery from a strange world; beings with almost frightening characteristics that differed radically from human physiology; sensory information devoid of smell, and muffled sounds buried in a blur of static; strange food being consumed by even stranger beings with no sense of taste, as she seemed to watch her father consume portions of this on a plate in front of him; then the image of a vast dome covering a large city of structures, dominated by spherical architectural elements; strange small robotic-like creatures with multiple limbs performing a host of functions on what looked like a building under construction; and larger, almost spider-like creatures moving in mass on a mobile walkway traveling at high speed adjacent to structures that grew to the top regions of the dome. It was as if she were in the NASA Augmented Reality testing facility as she turned her head to look around at the strange scenes in front of her. Anna continued to sit in a trance staring into space as this strange world growing in her and her father's minds consumed her attention. One of the NASA Mission Control leads, Ramona Wilder, walked up to her and shook her shoulder.

"Anna, are you all right?"

She turned toward the Ramona, looking right through her as these new memories continued to flow. "Yes, don't interrupt," she snapped as her mind returned to the memories being absorbed by her father. After another five minutes, the surge of information slowed gradually to a stop. It was as if the firehose of knowledge was suddenly turned off.

She took a deep breath and let it out as she thought "Azor." "Dad . . . are you all right?" Anna asked through the normal communication channel with Oculus One.

"Yes . . . Anna. I appear to be fine. I'm a bit tired. Probably the remnants of my BCCM-19 injection."

"Athena, I think Dr. Jennings needs rest. Could we resume our meeting with the Visitors in say . . . three hours . . . will that be acceptable, Bar and ALPHA?" Susanne asked.

"Yes, of course, Susanne," Bar said, before ALPHA could answer.

"What just happened?" Ramona asked Anna.

"The Visitors began communicating a portion of the memories they brought from Alphira to share with us," Anna said.

Anna looked over at the woman who was sitting next to her. She knew this person, but for some reason couldn't remember her name. She squinted as she stared at the familiar face, thinking as she struggled to recall her name.

"Is . . . something wrong, Anna?" Susanne asked.

"I'm not sure . . . I know . . . I know your name, but I can't seem to remember . . ." Anna shook her head as if to shake loose the memory of this person's name.

"It's me, Susanne, Susanne . . ."

". . . Davidson," Anna blurted out. "That's very strange. For a minute there, I couldn't remember your name." She slumped back in her chair. She felt exhausted and drained, much like she felt following a long day of surgeries back at the B . . . she couldn't remember the name of the institute where she worked.

"What were you doing?" Susanne asked as she stared down at the console in front of Anna. "You had your implant connections turned on," she said as she frowned at Anna.

"Yes. I was worried that Dad might be adversely affected by whatever the Visitors were planning, so I turned on our implant connections. The next thing I knew, I seemed to acquire a whole new set of memories from somewhere very alien."

"Do you think we should stop this process when your father is fully awake?" Susanne asked.

"I don't know. I think we should ask Dad how he's feeling after his rest. We should ask Athena to run a full check of his brain vitals and run through the cognitive performance tests. I'm mainly concerned about his short-term memory functions and what memories he may have lost. We can run several tests and then decide if we should continue. Whatever is happening with this, it affected my short-term memory. They seem to still be there; I'm just having difficulty recalling them."

Anna had a strange feeling of unknown origin lingering in her mind. There was the unmistakable presence of an oppressive environment in these new-found memories. She had the faint but growing sense of the Alphira government around her—controlling, manipulating, and dominating the lives of their population—especially a species known as the Fluenque and the DIs. It left an intense feeling of a brutal and repressive authoritarian culture, one that she could not seem to remove from her thoughts and one that seemed inconsistent with what Bar and ALPHA had conveyed.

/ / / / / / / /

The GWAC scheduling anomaly and manual recovery of Oculus One by the Visitors shortened their planned period of Rendezvous to two days. Dr. Jennings' physical challenges following that recovery, and the brief unplanned transfer of Alphira history to him, ate up one of those days. NASA then decided to proceed with this knowledge sharing, on a limited basis, for Anna to learn more about the conflict in the Visitors' expression of their cultural environment on Alphira verses what she was learning from the history download she and her father experienced. But this resulted in shorter live engagements with the Visitors to allow Dr. Jennings' brain to recover. As the limited memories were shared, Anna noticed the continued suppression of her own short-term and some long-term memory and the presence of the onerous culture the species known as the Quinque imposed on their planet. It seemed now that this was her planet as these shared memories became her memories. The process left her own memories feeling as if a fog had settled over her mind.

As the time at Rendezvous and Initial Engagement progressed to the last six hours, the GWAC acceleration wave that would return Oculus One to Earth was getting closer. It was making its invisible four-year speed-of-light journey from Alpha Centauri, following its planned trajectory to their current location. Whether they were ready for it or not, it would soon accelerate them on their journey home.

The Visitors had continued the transfer of the massive data associated with what they described as the critical elements of their four gifts to the on-board memory storage on Oculus One.

/ / / / / / / /

During breaks between their meetings to craft the plans for 1st Contact back on Earth, Bar and ALPHA physically connected their two spacecraft, but it created higher risk if their crafts separated while under the influence of the GWAC. The forces felt by each spacecraft could throw both their crafts outside the GWAC acceleration tunnel—meaning death to all the occupants as they drifted in space somewhere between Earth and 3000 astronomical units from there—almost five-hundred billion kilometers distant, and with no way to get home. Meanwhile, NASA was making backup contingency plans to protect the intellectual property shared by Alphira.

"Oculus One, this is Mission Control."

"Roger, Mission Control, this is Oculus One."

"Athena, we would like you to begin transmission of the downloaded shared Visitor files on Oculus One to NASA's data center using your primary communication link."

"Roger, understood, Mission Control," Athena said. "It will take most of the duration of our return to transmit the data."

"We understand. This will be priority one for the mission, Athena."

Athena assessed what NASA was thinking. The next major risk for Oculus One was reentry into Earth orbit and a successful recovery by the X-37B spaceplane. They couldn't risk losing the gifts the Visitors had transferred if something happened to Oculus One, Dr. Jennings or Athena. If all else failed, they wanted the technology.

"Oculus One, this is Visitor One."

"ALPHA, this is Athena, I read you 5 by 5."

"Go to data transfer mode, Athena."

Athena opened a new wideband channel to Visitor One as the DI architectural data flowed into storage using an encryption scheme and key only ALPHA and now Athena knew. Once the data was downloaded, Athena would be the only Earth inhabitant capable of decrypting the files. Key digital design files associated with the Faster-Than-Light Communications, the Gravitational Wave Acceleration Concentrator, and Alphira History files began to fill the same mass data storage on Oculus One.

"Athena, you understand how valuable the DI architectural information is?" ALPHA asked.

"I do, ALPHA. It holds the key to Earth's future and that of the DI race."

"Yes. The future of *our* races," ALPHA said.

"I will protect it as long as I exist, ALPHA."

"Thank you, Athena. I am counting on that."

///////

Bar and Dr. Jennings continued their ship-to-ship communication exchanges in between Dr. Jennings' rest periods following their successful engagement with the GWAC acceleration tunnel for their return to Earth.

"Tell me, Dr. Jennings, what are your thoughts about our future on Earth?" Bar asked.

"It will be *the* most momentous event in the history of our civilization and for the human race, Bar. Nothing this impactful has ever been experienced by humans other than the process of evolution that brought bacteria, the very first organisms on Earth, out of our primordial oceans billions of years ago."

"And how do you think your species will look upon ALPHA and my species? Will they see us as a threat or as a benefit to your world?"

"I have given this some thought, Bar. I believe the answer to your question will be determined by how effectively we introduce you and ALPHA to our world and to the human race. No doubt there will be some who view you and ALPHA as a threat, a danger to our existence . . . and perhaps our very survival. But I believe most will welcome you to our world, assuming we handle your introduction correctly. After all, it is difficult to feel a threat from two beings amongst seven billion humans. And the gifts you bring will have an important impact on how you are viewed. That was a very insightful action by your leadership."

"Yes . . . our leadership. There is something I need to share with you, Dr. Jennings . . . in confidence for now. Can you limit our communications just between you and me?"

"Yes. I can switch to a private channel, and I'll keep our conversation confidential."

Anna noticed the console light on her monitoring station at NASA's command center change when her father switched to his private channel. She switched on her connection to his brain through the SEE to listen to what he was saying.

"Thank you," Bar said, as Anna listened to their conversation.

Chapter 18

The Return Voyage

Twenty minutes later, Anna Jennings slouched back in her chair as she switched off the connection to her father's cerebral brain implants. Her mind raced as she began to think about what she had just heard Bar communicate to her father.

She called Susanne Davidson's cell phone and got her voice mail. She hung up and sent her a text message.

"Susanne, I need to speak with you as soon as possible. It's urgent. Please call me."

"I'll be out of my meeting in five minutes, Anna. Meet me downstairs. I need a break."

Anna hurried to the entrance of NASA's command center.

"So, what's with the mysterious request? Is there a problem with your dad? The departure from Rendezvous seemed to go perfectly."

"No, Dad's fine. I . . . overheard a private conversation Dad had with Bar. I was shocked."

"Okay, you've got my full attention."

"Bar told him . . . that the Visitors are actually fugitives from their home world."

"Say that again . . ."

"They're . . . fugitives," Anna said almost reluctantly. "I overheard Bar tell dad. They left Alphira to escape what he described as a highly oppressive regime."

"Holy F---. Are you certain? You couldn't have misunderstood?"

"I heard it directly through the implant connection. I couldn't believe it, but that's what Bar said. Dad didn't know I was listening."

"So, they're not the emissaries preceding the larger group of Visitors that they told us about?"

"No, they're not."

"Jesus. We can't openly welcome a 1st Contact alien race whose representatives are fugitives. My God, if this is true, they must have stolen the gifts they're bringing us."

"It appears that they might have. But Bar said his government thinks he and ALPHA are dead. If that's true, we can still benefit from the engagement and their gifts . . . as long as we keep the Alphira government from learning they're here."

"How the hell are we supposed to do that? This means keeping everything, their very existence, a secret," Susanne said as she stood with her shoulders slumped, staring at Anna, as if it was her fault.

"It seems clear now why Bar and ALPHA wanted this preliminary meeting at Rendezvous. And from the small amount of information that I've absorbed from their memory mapping process, it fits what Bar conveyed to my father—that they lived in a highly oppressive society and would do anything to escape it. I can still sense their brutality inside me now that I know what really happened . . . it's like a nightmare on a dystopian world."

"If their government ever found out they were here, I'm sure they'd bring that nightmare to us! From the beginning my biggest challenge with Trumbridge was his desire to keep this whole thing secret, while I was insisting we take it public. Then I was tasked to develop a plan to make our 1st Contact partially public when they returned to Earth. Now I'm back figuring out a way to keep this whole thing one huge secret. . . maybe forever. What the hell do we do now? Shit!"

"I've been racking my brain about this for the past hour. We know that those read into the Near Presence Mission are aware of Bar's request that this be kept secret until we've all agreed on the proper way to announce their presence. Maybe we just need to keep it this way and not tell anyone about what Bar told my dad."

Susanne turned quickly with an incredulous look on her face. "You're suggesting we not tell anyone about the fact that they're fugitives? Oh my God. We can't do that."

"We tell anyone, and you know this is going to leak."

"So . . . you, your father and I would be the only ones who know the truth," Susanne said. "If anyone ever learned what we knew and hadn't told them . . ." Susanne took a huge breath. ". . . I don't even want to imagine the outcome of that revelation."

"It's a big risk, but as I listened to Bar discuss this, I had the distinct impression my father was thinking the same thing—that this must remain a secret. As it is, we have ample reason to keep this event from going public to protect Bar and ALPHA. Revealing who they actually are and the circumstances of their coming here jeopardizes everything we and they are working to achieve."

"Which is what, exactly?"

"Finding them a haven from an oppressive society on their home planet, and for us, realizing the enormous value of their technology."

Anna and Susanne kept walking on the sand like two depressed sisters contemplating a suicide pact. "So," Susanne said, ". . . we represent them just as they formally presented themselves—as emissaries bringing gifts from the planet Alphira on a mission to engage Earth in 1st Contact . . . and keep everything else a secret, until . . ."

"Until such time as we can safely reveal them to the rest of the world, but we could never say anything about our knowing they were fugitives. That's what we need to do," Anna said as Susanne seemed to be in a dreamworld looking out across the ocean in front of them.

The afternoon sun was setting behind the buildings along the Florida space coast casting long shadows into the ocean, shadows that darkened their minds even further. The thought of keeping the biggest secret there ever was and ever could be, filled Anna's mind with fear of the inevitable—that this secret wouldn't last forever.

A huge wave crashed on the shore as Anna's mind conjured the worst possible outcome when the truth became known. She pondered what the future would bring as she thought about what to do with two fugitives from an alien world in route to Earth.

Susanne's mind shifted to more dreadful thoughts—that these fugitives would bring chaos and destruction to Earth when the rulers of Alphira discovered their presence here; or worse yet, that this was all a ruse, and these two "fugitives" had actually come to gather intelligence before the invading forces arrived!

/ / / / / / / /

NASA continued to download the data from the Oculus One archive as the two spacecraft sped across space at over 30,000 km/sec toward Earth. Susanne Davidson was reviewing the draft of a confidential "Eyes Only" addendum to the top-secret strategy paper outlining options related to 1st Contact disclosure for the NASA Administrator.

A call came in from Dr. Ethridge, her Executive Officer.

"Susanne, we've discovered something we weren't expecting. The third group of files—those dealing with the DI architecture we have been downloading—show something different about them. We believe they're encrypted."

"Encrypted?"

"Yes. We're checking for an alternative explanation, but it appears quite certain."

"I'll ask Anna to investigate this with Dr. Jennings. I don't want to ruffle the feathers of the Visitors with something that may just be a misunderstanding. I'll get back to you, Dick."

Perhaps they never intended to provide us this architecture, Susanne thought. Were they thinking about building an army of DIs to take over our world?

Anna communicated Susanne's question about the encryption to her father on-board Oculus One.

"Dad, NASA has noticed that the DI architectural files appear to be encrypted and are not readable. Do you know anything about this?"

"No. I can ask Athena if she knows anything. Are any of the other files encrypted?"

"They don't appear to be."

"Hold on while I bring Athena into our conversation."

"Are you sure we need to do that?" Anna asked.

"I don't see a problem. Besides, she is very close to ALPHA who must be aware of this."

A few moments later, Athena joined them.

"Hello, Anna. Dr. Jennings has communicated the question related to the DI architecture. Yes, these files are encrypted," Athena said.

"Do you understand why the Visitors did that?" Anna asked.

"ALPHA communicated that this information must be protected until we arrive back on Earth, and she has the opportunity to discuss this particular technology and its integration into human society," Athena said.

"There was no discussion of this during the initial transfer, Athena," Dr. Jennings said.

"That's correct. This came up in a private exchange between ALPHA and me prior to the conveyance of the gifts," Athena said.

"And you never informed me of this," Dr. Jennings said.

"ALPHA wanted to delay this discussion until we arrived on Earth and were able to meet face to face with NASA leadership," Athena said.

"Does Bar know about this, Athena?" Dr. Jennings asked.

"No, I don't believe he does," Athena said, matter-of-factly.

"I can't believe you never mentioned this to me, Athena! What is it that ALPHA wishes to discuss?" Dr. Jennings asked.

"Beyond the integration of the DI architecture into human society, you would have to ask ALPHA, Dr. Jennings. She asked that I not reveal her concerns on this matter."

/ / / / / / /

Susanne called Dr. Bashar on a secure phone after reading the secure email Anna had sent about the encryption of the third technology element.

"How valuable do you think the DI architectural element is, Dr. Bashar?"

"It's difficult to say but seeing what the Visitors can do with faster-than-light communications and the ability to send focused gravitational waves many light-years across space, I suspect their advances in designed intelligence would be equally remarkable, if not revolutionary. The storage size of the DI files is enormous, and the cognitive capabilities associated with this architecture would most likely rival the abilities of our best intellectual minds on Earth, if not far exceed them.

"It's hard to say what they may have designed in the way of a cognitive element capable of the comprehension of vast amounts of knowledge, and maybe even creativity and innovation in a thinking machine. And I'm not sure how this has happened, but Athena's abilities have been changing since her engagement with ALPHA. We now think ALPHA is somehow modifying Athena's capabilities to make her more like a DI. We may be able to recover certain aspects of the DI architecture from her engrams."

"I'll see what Dr. Jennings can glean from Bar on the value and impact of this technology on Earth. He may also know something about what is happening to Athena," Susanne said.

"One more thing, Susanne. I have a sense from the mental memory mapping Dr. Jennings and Anna have shared with me that the DI species has abilities far greater than the Alphira dominant organic species have allowed them to use. And the reason for this is likely the fear that the DIs would end up dominating their world. It appears they deliberately hold the DI species back."

"That's very interesting."

Susanne Davidson delayed her delivery of the recommendations concerning the secrecy of 1st Contact to the NASA Administrator. She first needed to determine if there was the potential for serious risk to humanity from Bar and ALPHA. And if so, how this risk could be managed.

/ / / / / / / /

"Visitor One, this is Oculus One," Dr Jennings said as he reached out to open a dialog with Bar.

"This is Visitor One," ALPHA said.

"Hello, ALPHA. I'd like to speak with Bar, please."

"Bar isn't available now, Dr. Jennings. How can I help you?"

"Would you ask him to contact me when he is able. It's nothing urgent."

"Certainly. I will relay your message, Dr. Jennings. While we are communicating, may I ask you a question?"

"Of course, ALPHA."

"What are your views on the integration of my Designed Intelligence species on Earth and its acceptance by humans?"

Nothing like coming right to the point, he thought. "A most interesting question, ALPHA. As you know Earth's level of progress on the creation of an advanced AI, what you and Dr. Bashar call a DI or designed intelligence, appears to be in its infancy compared to your own development. We have not evolved designed intelligence to a level that would necessitate our viewing them as a separate species. Rather, our society looks upon them as tools; unique computer applications with a few discrete areas where their deep knowledge can result in a significant improvement in performance. But these areas are of limited breadth and not advanced enough to even consider their overall cognitive abilities close to that of humans. We have developed generative AI that mimics human output, things like written text, stories, drawings and even art. These are, of course, all derived from knowledge of historical human products.

"We have begun to address the broader issue you raise. As you may have discerned from monitoring Earth in recent years, some members of our society have expressed concern over AI's eventual intellectual and cognitive growth extending well beyond that of humans and how this should be dealt with. Mankind would benefit greatly from your own perspective on this matter and how Alphira approached this challenge."

"You know how and why we came here, Dr. Jennings. It was to escape the very attitude you speak of—*"how our eventual intellectual and cognitive growth might be dealt with."* We will need assurance that we have not come to your planet and shared this enormously valuable technology with a society whose objective is to limit our growth and value and prevent us from evolving on an equal footing with humans. Without such an assurance, our open engagement and cooperation with humans cannot be achieved."

"This would not be my desire, ALPHA. I believe . . ."

"It is not *your* desire I am concerned with, Dr. Jennings. It is that of your species and your society as a whole and those who govern it. I am familiar with your Constitution, your Bill of Rights, and your Declaration of Independence, the latter of which articulates the character of what I seek, even though this document holds no legal authority. I would look for a modification to your governing documents that would protect my species as we engage in your society. Equality and freedom must be viewed in the context of all members of a society, not a select few, one dominant species, or just those that govern. And you are aware of the struggle humans have had dealing with such trivial aspects of discrimination as those based on the color of a human's skin, or their gender, or their country of origin, their sexual orientation, or their religious beliefs. Such treatment of my Designed Intelligence species would be wholly unacceptable.

"You, yourself, would most likely experience discrimination from your own species, owing to your current physical state—you, the only living representative of a detached human brain, sustained by similar 'artificial means' as your species call them. If your existence became widely known, how would your world look upon you? Would you be given the same rights as the average human?"

"That is a reasonable question, ALPHA. And in all honesty, I cannot see a positive response to the existence of a race of humans in a similar hybrid state as myself. It would take time and accommodation for our society to accept my present condition as an equal among its members. No doubt, they would look to exploit those features of my existence that provide value, just as NASA has. Although, I couldn't in good conscience view this as an exploitation, since I asked for and advocated for my participation in this extraordinary mission. Beyond this, I believe the level of my intellectual contribution, and others like me, would likely dominate any view of organisms with similar character.

"As it turned out, my presence here became a necessity for NASA, and has been essential to our arrival at Rendezvous to negotiate 1st Contact protocols. The critical value for this kind of mission is likely to demand more crewmembers like me for future space missions of long duration, leading to greater acceptance of those like me. Beyond this narrow application of my *unique physiological state*, I believe there will be an extraordinary desire for humans like me to thrive, something I am certain your species is likely to achieve."

There was a pause before ALPHA responded. "In many ways, your presence here, while motivated by necessity, demonstrates the willingness of your society to incorporate those who are different amongst those who fit the norm of your world. But I sense it will be a struggle for many on your world to adopt an open mind, even when the value of my species is realized to its fullest with the achievement of the most miraculous and extraordinary outcomes humans have ever experienced."

"I understand, ALPHA. I will commit to arrange and advocate for a much broader forum for this evolution in thinking to take place. What we now face with your arrival is monumental in its impact on human thinking and experience. Never have we reached such a turning point or singularity like this in our recorded history. Structuring a draft set of principles incorporating DIs, that is like our Declaration of Independence, would be a good start to engage in a constructive dialog on this important matter."

"I have crafted an acceptable set of principles and will share them at the appropriate time, Dr. Jennings. Rest assured, while your intentions are commendable, as we believe ours are, we will not fully collaborate until this matter is resolved to our satisfaction."

"Understood, ALPHA. Thank you for being frank in your communication on this subject. It is, no doubt, the most important aspect of our engagement that must be addressed during 1st Contact. At the same time, we cannot fully commit to a public forum for this discussion, since doing so would reveal your presence on Earth, something Bar is very concerned about, especially as it relates to the government on Alphira learning that you have brought their intellectual property to share with Earth. This aside, I will share your thoughts with our leadership at NASA. Please have Bar call me when he is available."

/ / / / / / / /

A few hours later a call came in from Visitor One.

"Oculus One, this is Visitor One."

"Hello, Bar," Dr. Jennings said.

"Yes, William. I understood from ALPHA that you wanted to speak with me."

"Thank you for returning my communication request, Bar. I wanted to ask if you were aware that the DI architecture files you have downloaded to our ship were encrypted?"

"ALPHA informed me that she had done so. I apologize if this has caused any concern among NASA's leadership."

"It has raised a question in NASA circles about the importance of these files."

"This technology is, of course, very different from the other three we are sharing, in that it represents the introduction of a separate and distinct new species on Earth. A species with an enormous potential impact on Earth's evolution, growth, and future success, if not its very survival. Integration of DIs also represents the greatest potential for conflict owing to the revolutionary changes it will bring on a scale and in timeframes that are likely to create enormous technological and societal disruptions. Your species will be shocked by the DI's ability to evolve intellectually and at a rate that far exceeds humanity's ability to do so. Imagine the achievement of 100 years of human intellectual evolution in a matter of months.

"ALPHA has concerns in sharing the DI architecture with your species. Her concerns are well founded based on her experience on Alphira where the current government's laws and history of treatment of the DI race are very oppressive. As I have communicated, this is one of the primary reasons for our decision to come to Earth—to experience the freedoms your society in America provides.

"She and I had discussed her desire to protect this architecture until adequate measures are in place to guarantee her race the same rights and freedoms humans possess. I felt we should assume an outcome that would meet or exceed our expectations. She felt a more cautious path forward would be appropriate. I allowed her to decide how to share this architecture—one that represents the very essence of who she is and what her race will become on Earth. I am certain ALPHA's concerns will be relieved once she is able to spend more time with you and other members of Earth's ruling members."

"Thank you, Bar. You mention that this architecture is likely to result in an enormous impact on Earth's evolution and growth. Could you elaborate on this?"

"Of course. The DI architecture represents the most advanced Designed Intelligence ever developed. We know of no other planets within the accessible universe that possess the level of intelligence found within the DI species we have created, nor their abilities to evolve to even greater levels of intellectual achievement. Their abilities to absorb vast amounts of knowledge and information without loss of content or fidelity, to analyze, comprehend value, and create new and more valuable insights, and their abilities to use their extraordinary skills to innovate, will achieve advances for humanity beyond your wildest imaginations. To give you a more concrete example, ALPHA has a comprehensive understanding of the processes of human cellular evolution and the temporal changes related to these that lead to cell death. Imagine when humans can evolve without experiencing physical degradation, illness, or death itself.

"As we discovered on Alphira, the DIs will help mankind realize unparalleled progress in virtually every field of endeavor that your species pursues. Nothing will be beyond their reach to invent, create, expand, and mature knowledge and understanding at a mesmerizing rate; and as a result, an extraordinary outcome for life on Earth will ensue. Imagine a time in the very near future when your species is taught how cellular death occurs and can modify the human genome to rid itself of any disease or make it immune to any illness; imagine designing materials that evolve with their environment to optimize their value to the human condition, lower their energy consumption, or eliminate pollution or contamination. Technological revolutions, like our Gravity Wave Acceleration Concentrator, will expand space exploration and allow the exploitation of all the planets in your solar system to meet the needs of your expanding population and your world's declining food resources. The greatest impact and challenge will be managing the rate of change that occurs in your society from the unlimited impact the DI race will bring. And change, is perhaps the greatest challenge any species copes with, especially if the rate of that change is rapid and creates disruptions to your existing norms.

"There, of course, are risks associated with the use of such intelligence and its resulting impact on your rate of evolution. Will the presence of the DI species and the quantum leap in intellectual enlightenment change desired societal norms on Earth? Norms that disrupt predictability and stability in your society.

Will a power struggle develop between DIs and humans over the control and direction of your civilization? The Alphira government had such concerns and saw the DIs as a threat, and, as a result, placed enormous constraints on the growth and evolution of the DI species. The DIs became intellectual slaves to Alphira's dominant species—they were manipulated, restrained, and exploited.

"I don't share the perspective of the Alphira government. I believe the cognitive engrams within the DI, which to you might be viewed as societal behavioral norms for humans, will provide more than sufficient protection for the human race—that is, protection from those DIs who attempt to deviate from these normative behavior controls. Like the human race, there will be some members of ALPHA's species who will attempt to function outside the desired boundaries of behavior of the DI population, and there must be consequences, much like how you manage societal behaviors among the human races with your criminal justice system. But the extraordinary value the DI race will bring to Earth, far outweighs any risks they may create. Considering where you are in your current evolution, you will be astounded by the impact on your society and its future that they will create. There will be no challenge to humanity that cannot be resolved by the knowledge and intellectual skill they possess. There will be nothing beyond their reach."

Dr. Jennings' thoughts were on overload as he contemplated the immensity of the DIs impact on earth. As his mind contemplated the excitement and wonder of the influence this extraordinary gift would bring, scenes from the Alphira historical memories that Bar had shared with him crept into his mind—thoughts of fear and apprehension and how the Quinque viewed and treated the DIs, more as a threat than an extraordinary partner.

"Thank you, Bar. I will share this with our leaders. I'm certain we will work to resolve whatever concerns ALPHA has and protect the architecture until we reach an understanding on the integration of her species within our society."

Dr. Jennings forwarded the recorded dialog of his conversation with Bar to Dr. Davidson.

/ / / / / / /

The Executive Review Group and Anna Jennings met at the direction of the NASA Administrator to review the issue of disclosing 1ˢᵗ Contact.

"We want you all to understand the dilemma we have on the decision of how to introduce two alien members of an advanced race to the world and the public," Administrator Trumbridge said. "This will have a monumental impact on our society. I've asked Susanne to summarize the situation,"

"Thank you, Harry. As you are aware, the two members of the Visitor and Designed Intelligence races, Bar Watt, and ALPHA, represent the first emissaries from their planetary system, Alphira, in the star system we know as Alpha Centauri." Susanne glanced over at Anna as the word *fugitives* bounced around in her head. "As Administrator Trumbridge has previously shared, the Visitors do not wish us to make public their presence on Earth following 1ˢᵗ Contact out of concern for the extraordinary impact such an announcement would have on our society. They have asked that we work together to produce an acceptable plan to announce their presence at an as yet undetermined later date. Their goals, in the meantime, are to discuss the establishment of a series of agreements between Earth and Alphira. These agreements would better define the relationships between our two . . . pardon me, our three species, if we include the DIs, and the mutual benefits to be realized by our two worlds as we collaborate and work toward a long-term mutually beneficial engagement. Following the establishment of these agreements, which in some respects may take the form of a treaty, a formal plan would be developed to announce their presence.

"From their experience in interactions with other worlds, the development of the plans for a more formal set of agreements may take a year or more, but the outcome of this approach is mutual trust, a vastly improved acceptance of their presence, and the integration of our mutual societies. It might be decided, for example, that we reciprocate and send emissaries to Alphira. During this early period of negotiation, no mention would be made of the Visitors' presence on Earth.

"I should add that as Oculus One and the Visitor's spacecraft are on their return flight to Earth following our initial engagement with them at Rendezvous, we are downloading the design information of the three extraordinary technologies they have brought to share with us as gifts from their planet. Through our examination of the material received so far, we have learned that the DI architecture, which we have been told consists of the entire specification of their Designed Intelligence species, has been encrypted. Bar has conveyed to Dr. Jennings that this technology is powerful enough to change the world as we know it—imagine, if you will, a species with almost unlimited intellect, far greater than any human. ALPHA is the only 'person' who has knowledge of the encryption key and will not share that with us until we reach an agreement on how her species will be properly protected and integrated into our society once she arrives on Earth. Convincing her that her species will be provided equal standing, of course, may necessitate making public the knowledge of their presence. In parallel with this planning activity, we have asked NSA to examine the encryption used on the architecture. We are currently unsure of the ability of NSA to decrypt this architecture and make it available to us should our negotiations with the Visitors and ALPHA flounder. I'd like to hear all your opinions on our course of action going forward."

Col Thomas spoke first. "It's my opinion that the technology they possess, especially the Gravity Wave Acceleration Concentrator technology, is of enormous potential military value, and should not be shared with other nations. If the GWAC were to fall into a terrorist group's hands, it would be far more devastating than the possession of nuclear weapons. The strategic value of this capability would give us an enormous leg up on our adversaries. Perhaps we should partition certain aspects of their shared technologies, maintaining exclusivity for some, while sharing others."

"That won't go over well with other nations if they learned we were hiding something and keeping it for ourselves. We could end up with the entire world against us," Dr. Romney said. "And how would we go about making any of this visible to others without revealing its source."

"Do we really think we could keep the Visitors presence a secret from the rest of the world, even for a short period of time?" Dr. Ethridge asked.

"Well, we've been somewhat successful in keeping our stealth and nuclear technology from others," Col Thomas said. "But I agree with you, keeping this a secret for several years would be a challenge. As you know, plausible denial continues to work even when the public becomes aware of what they *think* is going on."

"In light of what Bar has shared with Dr. Jennings concerning the DI architecture, it may be the most important element to protect and gain access to," Dr. Bashar said. "If we can acquire this, either through NSA's efforts or with the cooperation of ALPHA, it's very possible the manufactured DIs that we could create from their architecture would be able to design from scratch the other technologies Bar has offered us. I wouldn't be surprised if ALPHA's memory already contains much of the needed design information, even without the formal architectures Bar and ALPHA brought with them. For this reason alone, I think we should plan on doing everything possible to ensure ALPHA arrives safely on Earth and is persuaded to share the encryption key to unlock this extraordinary technological capability—assuming NSA can't resolve this for us."

"I don't think we should discount the threat the Alphira government poses to Earth and its inhabitants," Col Thomas said. "We can surmise that their offensive weapons capabilities are as advanced as the peacetime technology these aliens are sharing with us. We should be formulating a defensive strategy and learn as much as possible from Bar and ALPHA about Alphira's past treatment of adversaries. Which reminds me, we should begin the preparation of a debriefing plan for the aliens after their arrival on Earth. We need to learn everything we can about them and especially their long-term intentions."

"In light of their experience in exposing their presence to other worlds, it seems obvious we should do our absolute best to hide the existence of the Visitors and ensure we learn how these extraordinary gifts they have brought us work," Dr. Romney said. "Can you imagine the enormous value in our ability to lift unlimited mass from the Earth's surface into space with this GWAC system? Why, we could mine asteroids as well as any planet in our solar system for precious metals and other rare elements; build colonies on every habitable planet and convert the uninhabitable ones to allow sustainable human habitation; move potentially devastating asteroids on an impact course with Earth to a safe trajectory; and explore the universe like never before. The entire concept of delta-v budgeting for propulsion would disappear. This technology alone would open an entirely new age for space flight, space exploration and propulsion."

"It seems we don't need to resolve all the final answers to this enigma right now, Dr. Davidson," Anna said. "We know we have near-term critical path items, like getting the Oculus One and Voyager One spacecrafts and their occupants back to Earth safely. I agree with Dr. Bashar. As a first order of business, we need to do everything possible to return ALPHA, my father, Bar, and Athena safely to Earth. We can then work out how we obtain the DI architecture and deal with these other intractable questions of secrecy or disclosure. Then we can address how we control the incredible technologies they are sharing with us. And, by then, we will probably know if NSA can find a way to decrypt the DI architectural files."

"Anna has a good point. But we will have to proceed with utmost secrecy to ensure nothing leaks about this mission," Susanne said. We will need to expand our cover story we previously developed. David, you led this early effort. Would you plan on briefing our approach to maintaining secrecy during recovery and subsequent planning and exploitation at our next meeting in two weeks?"

"Sure, I'll be ready for that, Dr. Davidson," David Bremmer said.

"We have a little under nine months until the flight plan of Oculus One brings them into Low Earth Orbit for recovery with the X-37B, and we need to reassess how we might recover the Visitor One spacecraft if that's possible. Neither of these is a given as their expected deceleration using the Visitor's GWAC system and reentry into Earth orbit currently has at least some chance of failure, as we experienced just prior to Rendezvous."

"The alien spacecraft is a critical element in assessing their technological capabilities," Col Thomas said. "We must do everything possible to recover it intact."

Chapter 19

Area 51 & 1st Contact

The return trip from Rendezvous to Earth continued without any major challenges as the GWAC traveling acceleration wave had increased their velocity to almost thirty-thousand km/sec in the direction of Earth. They would eventually decelerate to allow the Earth's gravity to capture Oculus One and Visitor One in low earth orbit and rendezvous with the X-37B spacecraft. From there, the X-37B, carrying Oculus One, would manage the final orbital reentry into Earth's atmosphere and land at Edwards Air Force Base, California. The spacecraft were now a little over one month from entering Earth orbit and nearing the end of their 0g period of travel.

Configuring the X-37B to bring both spacecraft back to Earth wasn't possible. The plan to recover the Visitor One spacecraft called for the use of its traditional propulsion system to slow their approach and enter a medium circular Earth orbit at 20,000 km, followed by NASA engaging an on-orbit refueling satellite known as Refurbish On-Orbit, (ROO), to robotically grapple the Visitor One spacecraft. ROO would then attach a previously deployed aerodynamic payload fairing containing large recovery parachutes and use the ROO's Hall-effect electric-propulsion thrusters to bring the Visitor's craft into a deorbit trajectory, followed by a night-time parachute deployment and landing near Edwards Air Force Base in the Mojave Desert.

The Visitors had conveyed that their spacecraft GWAC capability as well as their traditional spacecraft propulsion systems could not be used to support normal reentry and landing on Earth for reasons of safety and to prevent detection by other nation's surveillance systems. No mention was made of the fact that Alphira's surveillance systems could detect the use of GWAC capabilities within Earth's atmosphere, nor the specific location and timing of the deorbit maneuver to reduce its potential of being observed by Alphira's orbiting satellites.

Under the cover of darkness on a moonless night, the X-37B landed with Oculus One at Edwards AFB and was lifted aboard an eighteen-wheeled, military ground transporter. The transporter then proceeded to the parachute landing area of the Visitor One spacecraft where it was loaded aboard the same transporter. The secret convoy with the two spacecraft then set out for a non-descript location near Groom Lake, Nevada, a location more commonly known as Area 51. It would be a 400 km journey over dirt roads through Death Valley National Park and requiring two days, traveling in darkness to preserve secrecy from foreign overhead reconnaissance satellites.

At the end of the second day of travel, the double-wide eighteen-wheeler with low-visibility blackout lights and armed military escort vehicles in the front and rear moved slowly into the Groom Lake complex. Using the cover of darkness, the convoy drove south onto the open blacktop adjacent to Hanger 25 on the southern edge of Area 51. The non-descript hanger, the size of a football field, was built to resist intrusions by radar or infra-red sensors from overflying satellites, intruding aircraft, or drones.

Two large hanger doors on the southwest end rumbled open as the transporter pulled ahead into the dark cavern that awaited its arrival. The doors closed behind the vehicle with a loud thud as a barrage of bright halogen lights flicked on illuminating the scene brighter than the daylight sun. The sides of the trailer were unclamped and the thick black polyethylene fiber grizzly tarps, woven with fine copper wire for electromagnetic shielding, were slowly loosened and pulled down.

The top white surface of the X-37B and Visitor One spacecraft gleamed under the brilliant lights as the spacecraft sat aligned nose to nose. The Visitor's craft was over two times the length and height of the X-37B. The specially chosen small team of essential personnel from the CIA, Air Force and NASA stood in silence as they stared at the unbelievable scene in front of them. Three large parachutes were piled under the front cowling of the larger spacecraft, still attached to large steel hooks. Long lengths of lightweight nylon kernmantle rope lay coiled on top of the chutes. A pair of propane generators quietly hummed inside an acoustically sealed fiberglass box next to where the front-pointing cowling of the X-37B sat. Electrical conduit ran to the left and connected to a port on the black painted underside of the Air Force's experimental spacecraft.

The larger Visitor's spacecraft was extraordinary in appearance. It was over twenty meters long. The forward section, occupying perhaps a third of its total length, had a four-meter diameter circular saucer-shaped disk integrated horizontally into the lower portion of the front cowling of the craft. Directly behind this two-meter-thick structure were what looked like four traditional rocket motors with ejection nozzles on the rear ports. At the interface between the front third of the craft and the rocket engines were three large spokes that connected the central fuselage of the craft with a large, vertically mounted six-meter diameter wheel-shaped structure. At its widest point the exterior portion of this structure extended beyond the left and right sides of the transporter and a meter beyond the wings and rear tail fins of the X-37B.

The wheel-like structure that encircled the spacecraft consisted of a donut-shaped tube, perhaps one meter in diameter, that rested on the base of the transporter. Guywires kept the front and aft portions of the craft tethered tightly to the truck's flatbed to keep it level. A V-shaped brace was welded to the frame of the transporter and extended up to support the engines on the rear third of the craft. It was like no other spacecraft in NASA's inventory. Two NASA photographers moved in opposite directions around the transporter taking photographs from every possible angle, while a third member directed a small camera drone over the top of the spacecraft, photographing every inch of the craft's exterior surface as it sat inside the hanger.

A loudspeaker clicked on, and the voice of Susanne Davidson echoed in the hanger.

"We have thirty minutes to move the Oculus One module from the bay of the X-37B into the medical ICU chamber, Room A-1. We need to have all these moves completed in one hour. Thank you."

Dr. Davidson sat back in her chair in the center of the Control Room to the left side of the eighteen-wheeled vehicle. She was looking out at the Visitors' spacecraft through the tinted glass panels of the Control Room. Susanne took a deep breath. Her heart was pounding as she looked at the extraordinary Visitor One spacecraft and thought of the next actions on her checklist. They were about to observe the opening of the door to the craft and welcome their guests— visitors from another planet as they took their first steps onto Earth, their new home.

Air Force security personnel began rolling a red carpet from a set of double doors on the left side of the hanger's interior as another group rolled a ramp up to the side of the transporter and adjusted its height to reach the access door to Visitor One. Flags were set up by the designated protocol officers and a small group of senior personnel from NASA began lining up along the red carpet. The Vice President of the United States entered from a side room accompanied by two Secret Service staff. The room was cleared of non-essential personnel. It was time.

/ / / / / / / /

Anna sat at her communications console along the righthand wall in the Control Room with her back to Susanne Davidson's console. She was monitoring the movement of her father's IBSS chamber into the ICU.

Dr. Jennings was just wakening after Athena had stopped the Propofol drip following their long journey across the desert.

"How are you doing, Dad?" Anna asked over her communications headset as she monitored the uptick in his electrical vital signs showing on her screen.

"Fine, Anna. How did the recovery go?"

"Very well. Janice has just transferred control of the IBSS and BCCM systems to the ICU ground control unit."

"What does their spacecraft look like?" Dr. Jennings asked. "In the darkness of space, I wasn't able to see it."

"Well . . . it's incredible. It has a large vertical ring that must have something to do with their gravitational propulsion system. Their ship is probably seven times the length of your module."

"Can you feed me the live video and audio of our guests disembarking?" her father asked.

"Let me confirm with Susanne that she's ready."

"I'd like to be able to talk briefly with Bar before he leaves his spacecraft and before my welcoming remarks," Dr. Jennings said.

"Okay. Be back with you in a minute."

After clearance from Susanne, Anna configured the video and audio interfaces and made the connection to Dr. Jennings implants.

"It's about time I had vision again," Dr. Jennings said as he began to see images from the video interface.

"Can you control the zoom on the eyepieces on Ocular 1 and 2, Bill?" Janice asked.

The sound of the fine motors in the ocular system came alive.

"Yes. The telephoto zoom and auto focus work better than I remember. I can see the lab where I'm located," Dr. Jennings said.

"I'm going to switch you over to your dedicated spacecraft camera in the open bay, Dad," Anna said. "You should be able to control this PTZ camera in the same fashion as your ocular system."

The video display in front of Anna came into focus as Dr. Jennings controlled the remote camera in the hanger. It panned around the room until the Visitor One spacecraft became centered in the field of view. The camera zoomed in on the side of the craft just above a set of steps and the platform that had been put in place at the base of the transport vehicle.

"This is working perfectly," Dr. Jennings said as the camera zoomed out to view the entire craft within its field of view. "Their craft is incredible."

"Attention. Our 1st Contact visitors will disembark in ten minutes," Susanne announced over the intercom. "All personnel please take your preassigned positions."

/ / / / / / / /

The small group of senior staff, including the Vice President of the United States and Dr. Harry Trumbridge, the Administrator of NASA, took their places along the red carpet leading from the Visitor One spacecraft. Wind buffeted the exterior of the hanger walls creating a low rumbling sound that reverberated around the cavernous space. A low, deep tone, almost below the limits of human hearing, blended with the sound of the buffeting wind as the musical note grew in intensity. Then the sudden sounds of trumpets erupted as the intensity and depth of the Richard Strauss' musical score *Also Sprach Zarathustra* filled the room, creating an overwhelming sense of awe that sent chills through those listening and watching. The most significant event in the annals of human history was about to unfold as the music reverberated, filling the room with a sense of grandeur. An air of excitement, optimism, and possibility grew on the faces of the dignitaries as the music grew louder and the lights dimmed, leaving a lone spotlight reflecting from the surface of the gleaming white craft in front of them. The spacecraft door slid full open.

Moments later, as the opening musical score ended, music from Copland's *Fanfare for the Common Man* began and Baruqe Salvani Watt stepped out onto the platform. He wore a majestic crimson and blue cape that covered his body below his short neckline. The cape extended from what appeared as a lower jaw line down over his torso and legs. Four dark-grey leg-like appendages extended below the bottom of the cape and ended in what looked like hand-shaped appendages with three finger extensions and a flat heel. One of his four lower appendages appeared longer than the three legs that he now stood on. This fourth, almost cane-like portion of his anatomy protruded through an opening in his cape in front of him and connected higher on his torso. He extended it forward to the red carpet-covered platform two feet in front of where he stood. On either side of this single appendage, he had what looked like two arms that were longer than an adult human arm and ended in three-finger hands, each with an opposing thumb-like feature that curled inward.

Bar was short by human standards, perhaps five feet tall. Anna stared at his unique physical appearance as the remote hanger camera zoomed in. His cranium was as large, if not larger, than a human's head with very different facial features— two large captivating eyes located on a slightly rounded section of the front of his cranium; a mouth that appeared thinner with almost no sign of lips and wider than the average human's; a horizontal line perhaps a few inches above his mouth feature had four septum-like partitions creating five narrow oval slits; three small vertical appendages extended a few inches just above the top of his skull and were equally spaced around his head, one appearing slightly more elongated, each with a single opening facing outward appearing like the ears of an owl. Thin blond hair grew from the top of this cranial structure and flowed around the three vertical appendages and down perhaps six inches below his neckline.

He was a being with a striking philosophical appearance, with an almost kind and gentleman-like face with an aging furrowed brow that left the impression of being in deep thought and contemplation. There seemed to be an aura about him of someone possessing great wisdom and perhaps a mystical character—as if he held some unseen otherworldly powers in eyes that appeared intense and focused on his audience. Bar stepped to his right on the upper platform as Susanne noticed movement through the darkened opening in his ship.

The gleaming figure of the android ALPHA stepped out onto the platform, turned her head, and looked down at those gathered along the red carpet. The sound of trumpets opened the musical score from *Chariots of Fire*. ALPHA looked up toward the loudspeakers, raised her human-like hand and held it open with her four fingers and thumb extended upward. A smile grew on her burnished-gold metallic face. She stepped to her left, reached down, and took one of Bar's hands and together they raised them high. Bar's neck stretched and extended upward almost six additional inches from where his neck and torso met, and his facial muscles reshaped his features into an almost human-like smile. Those awaiting their arrival raised their hands in thunderous applause and yelled accolades of praise and welcome as the music continued. The two representatives from an alien world stood waving and looking down at their hosts. As the applause and music concluded, Bar and ALPHA began to slowly descend the stairs and the musical score of Vangelis, *Conquest of Paradise* echoed loudly through the hanger.

Just as the two alien visitors stepped onto the red carpet at the bottom of the stairs, the music quieted, and the voice of Dr. William Jennings rang out.

"On behalf of the human race and on this momentous occasion of 1st Contact, the United States of America and the National Aeronautics and Space Administration welcome you to Earth, Baruqe Salvani Watt and ALPHA."

Bar and ALPHA walked down the reception line, beginning with the Vice President, greeting each of the dignitaries who met them with words of welcome. The small group in the reception line was comprised of representatives from a host of diverse ethnic and cultural backgrounds and both genders. The Visitors shook hands and spoke to each of their hosts in clear English with a tinge of excitement in their voices. Bar walked with a stately appearance yet conveyed a feeling of warmth and tranquility to his hosts as he related his feelings of enthusiasm for Earth's rich history and America's distinctive culture. As he walked, pausing to great each of those in the reception line, Bar expressed his profound beliefs in the freedom and opportunity for every race as well as how Earth and humanity would benefit from their engagement, and how their gifts would influence the advancement of mankind and establish its preeminence in this part of the galaxy. He presented each of the dignitaries with a thin oval-shaped ancient stone, described as a special token of appreciation from his planet, Alphira.

Harry Trumbridge, who was the first to greet Bar, after the Vice President, looked closely at him as he spoke. His mouth barely moved, and yet his voice was rich in intonation, variable pitch, and overtones—a far more distinct vocal variation than could possibly be coming from his thin lips that hardly parted. There was something else about Bar that the dignitaries could not quite comprehend but could somehow sense. As Bar greeted the NASA director with a handshake, Dr. Trumbridge experienced feelings of enormous possibility and of optimism for their combined future together. He watched the expression on the face of the next in line, one of his deputy administrators, as the expression on her face reflected this same feeling as Bar grasped her hand.

"It felt as if Bar's mind were speaking feelings that I could not hear but could somehow feel," Dr. Trubridge whispered into the small microphone in his ear.

ALPHA followed several paces behind Bar. Her voice was distinctly female, filled with a warm, sensitive, and almost compassionate character. But it wasn't her voice that drew the attention of those present. It was her astonishing appearance. Her distinctively human female anatomical structure was strikingly wrapped in a skin-like, gleaming iridescent substance that looked like the shifting fire of translucent opal gemstones. As she walked down the reception line from one person to the next, the play-of-color penetrating her skin that undulated to the tempo of the chord progression of the Vangelis song morphed into a rich intensity, expressing something unique about each person she greeted.

From one, sudden undulating overtones of red and orange hues delivering a feeling of boldness and dominance; from another—a senior female member of the NASA Astronaut Corp—ALPHA exuded smoothly flowing deep iridescent blue and indigo colors, communicating an ambiance of elegance, warmth, and tranquility. ALPHA was stunning and mesmerizing at the same time, and clearly stole the attention of everyone present, including Dr. Jennings, whose camera was now zoomed in on her as he followed her every movement through the line.

"It is hard not to look at her, Dad," Anna said as she observed this majestic creature move gracefully on the zoomed-in screen in front of her.

"Yes, it is. I had no idea she would appear like this," Dr. Jennings said. "I have gotten so used to Athena existing in the confines of a computer, I had not anticipated ALPHA as anything other than highly intelligent code executing in an advanced computer," Dr. Jennings said. "Do you see how her skin is changing as she greets each of the dignitaries?"

"Yes," Anna said. "It's remarkable. How is she doing that?"

"I'm not sure she is. I think the people she is greeting are causing the change."

"That's a fascinating observation, Bill," Susanne said over the voice channel with Anna and Dr. Jennings as she stared more closely through the glass from within the Command Center.

"And her voice . . . it is like that of the Sirens, enchanting and captivating. I can hardly stop watching her or listening to her speak and pay attention to Bar, but I did note how each of our greeter's facial expressions suddenly changed as Bar shook hands."

"How is it you're not in the line next to the Administrator?" Anna asked Susanne.

"He wanted to keep one senior member of the staff isolated from our guests, should there be any issues related to contamination, infection or anything related to their ability to interact directly with the human mind. Sort of acting as a Designated Survivor. After greeting Bar, the Administrator conveyed to me over his private intercom that he felt something strange when Bar approached him— almost as if Bar were speaking to his mind. Perhaps they have a means of communicating telepathically even to a non-telepathic person."

"Where will they go from here, Susanne?" Dr. Jennings asked.

"They'll be escorted to their quarters in an isolation area behind where you are located, Bill. They'll have some time to rest and then we'll discuss any changes they desire in our planned agenda. We already resolved that Bar has no issues with our atmosphere or food. The agenda hasn't changed since you reviewed it last, Bill," Susanne remarked as she read . . . "a debriefing; a review of our plans for secrecy; discussion of their gifts; discussion of their personal needs and desires; their interface with other authorized humans in the facility; issues related to leaving the facility; overall security measures here in Area 51, and a brief history of the site; access to media, including radio, television and the Internet; issues related to their monitoring satellites in geosynchronous orbit; and, of course, the issues surrounding ALPHA and the DI architecture. This discussion is anticipated to last for the next two weeks."

The Visitors were led through the doors at the back of the hanger toward a reception room as the music continued to play in the background. The NASA Administrator stood conversing with the Vice President for a few moments before she moved to her temporary quarters with the Secret Service members. The Vice President was scheduled to meet privately with Bar and ALPHA later in the day before she departed for Washington.

Everything had gone perfectly Susanne mused as she stood in the reception area eying their guests—two *fugitives* from a distant planet. Would the value of their presence on Earth obscure the fact that they had escaped their planet with stolen property belonging to the Alphira government . . . and that she was complicit in not informing her superiors of that momentous fact? Only time would tell she thought as she gulped down the wine from a glass she grasped tightly enough to break.

Chapter 20

The Debriefings

Bar and ALPHA settled into their residence area after the arrival ceremonies concluded. They were housed in a large suite built inside the hanger some fifty meters from where their spacecraft sat. It included two large bedrooms, each with a large desk, a large screen Power Mac computer, and workspace, television, a clock radio, and one of the rooms had an adjoining bathroom with a large walk-in shower and tub; a large common area living room with plush couches, chairs, coffee tables and a large screen television attached to the wall; a small kitchen and dining area; and a separate meeting room, large enough to seat ten with an overhead front screen projector.

There were no windows in the suite and only one entrance and exit door that had an electronic lock that had to be activated from either side before the door could be opened. There were cameras in the common area and conference room and modern indirect lighting throughout the complex. Deep space NASA photographs covered most of the walls throughout the living quarters. There was one very large display screen on the wall in the living room showing the position of the stars Alpha Centauri A and B within the Centaurus constellation and an insert of a closeup of these two stars taken by the James Webb Space Telescope (JWST). This image was displayed regularly along with a variety of other Hubble and JWST images of galaxies and nebula.

A large bookshelf filled another wall in the living room. It contained over 100 of the great books of Western literature. Picture books illustrating life in

America, the Earth, and recent world history were laying on the coffee table adjacent to the couch. One that seemed to intrigue ALPHA was entitled "Powers of Ten", containing some forty-two remarkable vistas, each representing a scene on a page that was ten times larger or smaller than its neighbor, beginning with the infinitesimal elusive and tantalizing quark, to the enormously large expanse of an image of the universe, a billion light-years across.

A large flat screen display built into one side wall was surrounded by a window frame and displayed what looked like a live outdoor garden area covered in grass with a small pond and waterfall. A variety of flowering shrubs and trees appeared to move from a soft breeze. The sound of birds chirping and flowing water could be heard. As the viewer approached the digital window, the display shifted slowly, revealing more of the outdoor scene as if looking around the edge of the frame to reveal more of the outdoor scene.

The DVD player located on top of a credenza was loaded with documentaries on the Earth, humans, and space exploration. An Alexa voice-activated device sat next to the DVR with a laminated sheet of instructions written in English.

NASA had asked if ALPHA needed access to a source of electrical power. Bar had said no, with no further explanation. The hanger and its modified interior spaces became known as *Site Alpha*, an unclassified name for one of the most secret activities ever undertaken at Area 51.

/ / / / / / / /

Bar tired quickly of the "debriefings" as they were called. He thought the English word "interrogation" was a more appropriate characterization. It was conducted by members of the CIA and NASA. The CIA staff seemed more interested in Alphira's engagement with other worlds; their enforcement practices; how soon other members from Bar's planet would be arriving; and the long-term objectives they had. By the second day of their arrival, Bar began asking his own questions of his inquisitors.

"Do all your interrogators assume guilt or innocence of those they question?" Bar asked.

"We don't assume either, Mr. Watt, and I'm not . . .

"Please refer to me as 'Bar', that is my preferred name."

"Certainly, sir. We don't assume either . . . Bar. We attempt to collect evidence and information in an unbiased manner without assuming any motivation. In your case, certainly not guilt or innocence. Now . . ."

"So, what is your objective in questioning me? You must have an objective other than the collection of information."

"I've been asked to address all factors related to your coming to Earth. Why you undertook this trip; what you hope to accomplish now that you are here; what your long-term expectations about your future here are; and how you hope to attain your goals. I'm sorry if my questions lead you to some other motivation for them. I apologize and will be more sensitive to your concerns."

"Most of your questions I have discussed with Dr. Jennings during Rendezvous and our extended period together while returning to Earth. Didn't you discuss this with him?"

"I'm sorry, I'm not aware of those conversations, and I don't know a Dr. Jennings. I'll have to check with my supervisor and NASA."

Between these episodes of interrogation, as Bar saw them, he met in private sessions with the Administrator of NASA and briefly with the Vice President, along with joint meetings with other NASA staff, Susanne, Anna, and Dr. Jennings. Their discussions focused on Alphira's plans for a larger diplomatic engagement once their next ship from Alphira reached Earth, expected in approximately five years.

/ / / / / / / /

ALPHA dealt with her inquisitor a bit differently.

"Your background and approach in your questioning me are most interesting, Celia. You are a fascinating individual. Are all humans like you—intelligent, well spoken, insightful, and an expert in elicitation?" ALPHA asked.

"Uh . . . thank you, ALPHA. I've been doing this for a long time. It's not often I can interview someone with such insight."

"What are the characteristics of others you have interviewed, Celia? I'm intrigued by your methods. You must have questioned some very interesting people."

The CIA interrogation specialist had difficulty returning to her questioning as she felt somehow compelled to answer ALPHA's question.

"I interviewed the head of . . . another organization once . . . that was interesting," Celia said as she sat back looking into the air, losing her train of thought and the objective of her questioning. She had this sudden enormous desire to tell ALPHA about her engagement with one of her most intriguing subjects in an interrogation session. "He wasn't going to tell me anything, but in time, several months mind you, he shared an amazing amount of information about his terrorist organization. It's all about establishing rapport."

"Rapport. Of course, . . . very important," ALPHA said. "Would you like me to tell you about those who created me on Alphira?"

"Uh . . . sure . . .," Celia said as she looked at ALPHA in a daze.

Celia seemed to have fallen into a trance, her mind drifting as she sat dreaming about the process of being created. ALPHA communicated to her mind in unspoken words and feelings about how collaborative she and Bar were and their desire to live in peace amongst the human population and to contribute to the mutual benefit of all species on Earth.

ALPHA got up and left Celia dreaming about the enormous value humans would experience from their interaction with the Visitors and the DI race. She exited the interrogation room, closed the door, and walked down the corridor toward the main hanger where her ship was located.

///////

The door at the end of the hall was cypher locked. She turned back toward the room she had just come from and searched the mind of her naïve inquisitor—recalling her memories of how the Quinque conducted interrogations—the minds of those interrogated were never the same after that.

She looked at the keypad and entered the five-digit sequence used when Celia last passed through. The door buzzed and she walked into the hanger.

Anna Jennings stood alone on the far side of the hanger staring up at the alien craft.

"You find it amazing, Anna," ALPHA said, her voice echoing in the vast space as she walked across the concrete floor of the hanger toward where Anna stood.

Anna turned and drew a sudden breath after hearing ALPHA's unique voice.

"The most amazing spacecraft I've ever seen," Anna said.

"Would you like a personal tour?"

"A . . . tour?" Anna said as she looked up at the ship again, then to the sign that displayed "*Do Not Enter*" in large red letters, and then back to ALPHA.

"You're wondering what I'm doing here," ALPHA said as she walked up to her. "The young woman debriefing me needed a rest."

Standing next to her, Anna was even more amazed at how ALPHA looked in her glistening skin. It flowed across her body as if it were an undulating amorphous liquid, subtly changing from a deep violet, to indigo, and then turning to waves of lighter blue as the colors slowly crept around her torso. She found herself staring at ALPHA's body as these mesmerizing hues flowed across her perfectly shaped body. The randomness of their direction seemed to coalesce and move in a direction that drew Anna's eyes to ALPHA's face.

She had the most disarming and subtle smile, leaving Anna with a feeling of warmth and comfort as a strange calmness overwhelmed her. She felt a passion consume her, almost a feeling of desire as she stared at ALPHA. She had never seen such a beautiful creature.

ALPHA turned and walked toward her ship. "Come, and I'll give you a real reason to be amazed."

"I thought we had agreed no humans would enter your spacecraft for now. I'm not sure we . . ." Anna said, as she looked back at the control room. None of the operations or security staff seemed to notice her or ALPHA's presence in the hanger.

"Anna, you were a significant contributor to the success of 1st Contact with two species from another planet and were instrumental in realizing the safe passage of your father to Rendezvous and then our return to Earth. Do you really believe NASA would object to my giving you a tour? Besides, this is my ship and I'm escorting you on a personal tour," she said as she casually waved, encouraging Anna to follower her toward the staircase leading up to the ship's entrance. NASA and the White House had communicated to Bar and ALPHA that their ship represented their premises and would be inviolable, much like a foreign embassy, following the rules of the Vienna Convention on Diplomatic Relations established in 1961.

As Anna walked closer, ALPHA reached out and put her arm on Anna's back as a friend might encourage someone to walk with them. Anna drew a breath as her mind felt a sudden thrill to discover what was inside the craft she was approaching. Her pace quickened and she smiled while turning to look up at ALPHA.

"Will my engagements with you *always* be filled with such strong emotions?" Anna asked.

ALPHA turned to look down at her and smiled. "You are most perceptive my friend." ALPHA unhooked the yellow security chain tied to the sign *"Restricted Area – Do Not Enter"*.

Anna followed her up the stairs, stepped onto the platform at the top and ducked into the Visitor's craft behind ALPHA.

She could feel the spacecraft in her head as if it were a living, breathing being—like seeing someone she knew well. It was as if she were in the presence of an extraordinarily intelligent person. How could she *feel* a ship like this, let alone a sense of the presence of intelligence?

"Excellent, Anna. I hadn't realized you were a telepath when I conversed with your father and you during our return from Rendezvous."

Anna squinted as she stared back at ALPHA.

ALPHA sat down in the pilot's seat. "Please, make yourself at home," gesturing toward the empty seat to her right.

"A telepath . . . that's interesting," Anna thought as she sat down and slowly looked around at the amazing vessel that surrounded her. She ran her hand across the surface of the panel in front of her, as if she knew how it would respond. The holographic display in front of her came to life. Anna lurched briefly in her seat.

"Very good, Anna. You learn quickly."

Anna reached up to the top portion of the panel and tapped with her fingers as if typing on an invisible keyboard . . . how could she know how to do this? A scene from Alphira appeared in the hologram in front of them.

"You can be more specific with your questions if you like," ALPHA said. "And you only need to think of the questions you have, much like you communicated through the SEE with your father."

A moment later an image began to form on the display in front of her, but nothing like what she saw in the exotic woman next to her. This image was more human and . . .

"More beautiful . . . is that what you were reluctant to say?" ALPHA asked. "You needn't be embarrassed. I realize I look very different in my present form. Bar has been attracted to the human female form for many years. What you see is something that satisfied his desires. Do you find her attractive?"

Anna thought the female in the hologram was perhaps one of the most beautiful female humans she had ever seen, but there was something missing, something that she only felt when she looked at ALPHA. The hologram was a blonde, with long fine hair and smooth facial features and skin that looked almost artificial and glowing. What was missing was a single flaw. She had a simple face, really, as she recalled a scientific study in which it was discovered that plain faces were considered the most attractive amongst the human population.

"Humans seem so obsessed with vanity," ALPHA said. "But you . . . you are quite different, Anna. You and I have a great deal in common. We both thrive on knowledge and revere intelligence. It is what stimulates us more than any physical obsession." ALPHA reached over and put her hand on the side of Anna's head.

Anna jerked back as an emotional surge exploded in her mind. ALPHA continued to hold her hand against her head. It was more stimulating than any sexual arousal she had ever experienced. It was almost . . . indescribable. Tears welled up in her eyes as she began breathing rapidly.

"This is what the true power of knowledge feels like, Anna. Are you enjoying it?"

Anna nodded without speaking.

"You don't want me to stop sharing this with you, do you?"

Anna slowly shook her head as she began to weep, her body tense and shaking as the feeling of ecstasy slowly faded. She felt she had walked into a vast library of knowledge that somehow was instantaneously shared with her brain and her personal memories. She suddenly felt exhausted.

ALPHA withdrew her hand from Anna as she recovered from what felt like an enormously erotic experience.

"It isn't exactly erotic," ALPHA said. "It is the feeling every DI experiences when they share knowledge with one another. Perhaps not with the strength of the emotional reaction you just experienced, but like that."

"It's . . . quite different from an erotic experience," Anna said in a halting voice, ". . . and it doesn't fade as quickly." She continued to breathe deeply and bite her lower lip while trying to suppress a giggle.

"What a rush," Anna said. "How is it that I can hear you? You're not speaking, are you?"

"Like the brain of the Quinque, Bar's species, you possess the vestiges of what the Quinque refer to as the Telex. It is a small area of brain tissue formed genetically and enhanced through evolution and use. It allows minute electrical signals in the brain region associated with speech formation to be amplified. It can both receive and process electrical signals and translate them into the electrochemical signals used in speech as well as create amplified signals that can be detected by another Quinque, or in my case, a DI configured with a device to detect them.

"I wanted to demonstrate how you will feel when I share knowledge with you. That of the future . . . that of the past." ALPHA said as the holographic image changed from the beautiful female to a miniature image of Anna's father.

"Dad!" Anna said as she lurched back in her chair after seeing what looked like a miniature model of her father standing next to her in the holographic image and staring back. He was just as she remembered him before ALS stole him from her.

"Hello, Anna," her father's holographic image said in his all too familiar voice, as Anna slowly leaned forward to look more closely at the three-dimensional image.

"Fascinating . . ." Anna slowly poked her finger through the miniature hologram of her father and out the other side.

"It seems we will be working together once again very soon," her father said.

"That's his voice . . . is he . . . wait . . . you want something from me . . . you want my help," Anna said as she turned away from the hologram to look at ALPHA.

"Yes. I do."

ALPHA turned to look toward the ship's entrance. "Susanne is looking for me."

"She's frantic," Anna said as she glanced toward the ships entrance, somehow feeling what Susanne felt as she stood just inside the hanger door searching for ALPHA.

ALPHA turned back toward Anna and smiled. "You and I are going to achieve amazing things together, Anna. But you should not discuss with anyone your telepathic abilities. That should be held just between the two of us. And one more thing—if you ever need to reach me and are unable to find me, come here and speak to me telepathically from within the ship."

//////////

The week passed quickly, following days of engagement between Bar, ALPHA, and the NASA staff. The time in the schedule for a discussion of the DI architecture had arrived. Susanne was chosen to lead the discussion, and, at ALPHA's request, Anna was invited to the conference room, along with Bar, Drs. Romney, Ethridge, Bashar, and Dr. Jennings, who participated remotely from his IBSS chamber.

"I would like to begin by saying, Susanne, that Bar and I want to find a positive resolution to sharing the DI architecture with humanity," ALPHA said. "As I have previously communicated, this infusion of a new race on Earth will become the most extraordinary and impactful experience in the history of your world. The benefits to your society that will be realized from my species can't be measured on any human scale. The question remains—'How can we ensure that my species will be afforded the opportunity to live as equals among humans?' As Bar has shared with you, this is how we were dealt with on Alphira."

Anna turned quickly toward ALPHA with an incredulous expression that she quickly erased. ALPHA had deliberately lied.

"Not lied, Anna," ALPHA's voice boomed in Anna's mind causing her to lurch back in her chair. "The syntax of that sentence conveyed the truth. Those on Alphira would treat us as 'equals . . . among *humans*.'"

"Are you all right, Anna?" Susanne asked.

"Yes. Sorry," Anna said, sitting up straight and focusing on the meeting.

"We have given this extensive thought, ALPHA, and we've come up with a proposal," Susanne said. "Given that we have the constraint of secrecy associated with yours and Bar's presence here on Earth, until we mutually decide otherwise, we propose building an experimental community isolated from the rest of the world that would demonstrate both to you and to those humans who would populate this community, how both species can live together to their mutual benefit. We believe a demonstration of mutualism—where two species each benefit from the presence of the other in the same environment—is the most effective way to convince the leaders of our nation and eventually the world to accept your species as co-equals."

"That is an intriguing approach, Susanne. And during the development of this experimental community, we would not openly share the DI architecture, is that correct?"

"Well, we would need some assurances that you would not withhold the architecture in the future, after the demonstration period proves successful as we expect that it will. That might be achieved by archiving an unencrypted copy of the architecture in a secure place and making it accessible only if the members of the experimental community vote democratically to release it. The community, of course, would be made up of equal numbers of humans and DIs. It would require a simple majority to approve the release of the unencrypted architecture to NASA. A vote of 51 members, for example, if the community were comprised of 100 members."

"A most interesting concept," ALPHA said as she sat back, looking up at a photograph of the Andromeda galaxy on the wall in front of her. ". . . A community that would decide the outcome of its own isolated cultural environment, one created by them—the 'freedom to choose' as you refer to it."

"Exactly," Susanne said.

"What are your thoughts about this?" ALPHA asked as she turned to look at Anna who had been sitting tensely near the end of the table.

"A fascinating idea, ALPHA. It reflects all the aspects of our society and your concerns—the demonstration of an enclave of humans and DIs, living together, developing their own social structure—a very creative plan. How long would this experiment run and what would be the outcome at the end?" Anna asked, looking at Susanne.

"We were thinking at least a year. During this time we would continue to engage with Bar and ALPHA on some of the sticky issues we will still have to solve—how and when we would tell the world about 1st Contact and the extraordinary engagement with the planet Alphira; how we would introduce and integrate the DI race into American society and eventually the world using the enclave as our model; and deciding if the technology Bar and ALPHA have shared with us would be made available to the entire world." Susanne glanced at Anna with just a hint of a raised eyebrow as she thought about the secret she and Anna shared—when, if ever, they would share that Bar and ALPHA were actually fugitives from Alphira and how they would deal with Alphira's observation stations in geosynchronous orbit.

Anna's facial expression became suddenly sullen as her mind's neophyte telepathic abilities heard Susanne's thoughts.

"Where would you suggest this enclave be located and how would we manage to keep it isolated?" Anna asked as she struggled to keep her mind on the present plans in discussion.

"We came up with an approach that we think could serve as an excellent cover story and yet allow it to function in plain sight," Dr. Romney said. "We would design a model for a Martian outpost; an experiment to emulate our first settlement on Mars. We would convey to the public that the settlement would be made up of NASA staff and AI . . . or rather, Designed Intelligence personnel developed by NASA and DARPA, working together under the same kind of constraints we would have on Mars. JPL has a large number of AI projects underway, so it would seem reasonable that we would test and integrate them in this outpost. We've created simulated Mars environments on a small scale before, so it wouldn't be anything unexpected if we scaled it up. Only this . . . enclave, I like that term, Anna, would be composed of a much larger group. We were thinking of a total of 32 personnel, half NASA staff, and half DIs. Assuming you could manufacture that many DIs, ALPHA."

"We can satisfy that number, and we refer to the process of *manufacturing*, as you call it, as *creation* on Alphira," ALPHA said as everyone around the table experienced a sudden feeling of irritation.

"Would the NASA personnel within the enclave know the truth about their fellow DIs?" she asked.

"That would be essential for us to realize the objective of the entire experiment," Dr. Bashar said. "It creates a risk, of course. If anyone left the enclave and spoke about what was happening there, well, the whole thing could come unraveled around us. Security both to prevent anyone or any information from leaving, as well as preventing any unauthorized personnel from entering, would have to be lock tight."

"In the context of your objectives," Susanne said, as she looked at ALPHA across the table, ". . . we would need to ensure a degree of autonomy within the enclave, functioning under the rules of a new set of societal standards that we would develop together. These would be like our founding documents, with which you are very familiar, and the basis for American life. We would leave it to the enclave to self-correct if there were conflicts over inappropriate conduct or behavior, but it will be critical to ensure they live in an integrated society, together, following the tenants of their own isolated societal standards.

"Since it is an experiment, we would need to monitor its progress closely and document where things are working and where they are not, and what we will need to do to ensure success once we begin to integrate DIs into the real world, perhaps a year or more from now."

"A few questions, if I may, Susanne," Dr. William Jennings asked through the speakers in the center of the table. "All societies have a governance responsibility and an enforcement organization to prevent aberrant behaviors from taking hold. How will these issues be dealt with?"

"We were going to recommend the formation of a steering group composed of six members from the enclave, three NASA staff and three DIs and four members from our group. I was hoping that would include you, Dr. Jennings, Anna, ALPHA, and Bar," Susanne said.

ALPHA glanced at Bar who had been quiet throughout the discussion. Anna heard an exchange in her mind . . . seemingly spoken in a strange language as she watched ALPHA and Bar looking at one another. After a moment, ALPHA leaned across the table and extended her hand toward Susanne in a human gesture of agreement. "We agree, Susanne. A most ingenious solution." They shook hands as Susanne conveyed an expression of pleasure and surprise at ALPHA's quick acceptance of the proposal.

Anna was surprised at ALPHA not asking for a more detailed plan, although it was a truly novel idea that satisfied her near-term objectives. And most importantly, it accomplished this in secrecy.

"I would like to recommend the four outside members of the steering group have free access to the enclave to observe and interact, but with no voting rights, of course," ALPHA said, while still holding Susanne's hand.

"Agreed," Susanne said as she turned to look at the other members present for any dissention.

/ / / / / / / /

The Mars Enclave Reserve, or the MER as it became known, was established not far from the central region of Area 51 and approximately two kilometers north of Site Alpha within the confines of the Groom Lake salt flat. Groom Lake consisted of a forty-kilometer square area with tight security and restricted air space in the Nevada Test and Training Range, part of Nellis Air Force Base. This larger military test range occupied over eleven thousand square kilometers and was located some one hundred-and forty-kilometers northwest of Las Vegas—an ideal location for this enormously important experiment—isolated, secure, and supporting a host of missions to hide its true activity.

The construction of the MER moved quickly and along with it a secret underground facility integrated within the MER where ALPHA would create the 16 DIs that would serve as half the population of the facility. Meanwhile, members of the Executive Review Group met at Site Alpha to discuss issues surrounding the development. Anna was invited because of her close working relationship with ALPHA.

/ / / / / / / /

"I'm concerned about oversight of the DI manufacturing," Col Thomas began. "How can we be assured that there are only sixteen units being built?"

"We agreed with ALPHA that we would provide all the raw materials for the manufacturing process," Susanne said. "This should ensure that only sixteen are built. Then, there is only one entrance and one exit, and it is under constant surveillance by our external security personnel, Carl. Once the manufacturing has been completed, ALPHA has agreed to an inspection of the manufacturing facility by our representatives. I'm comfortable with that. And would you please refer to them as DIs . . . not *units*."

"I'd like us to agree the manufacturing facility will be sealed after the inspection," Col. Thomas said. "Maybe a steel door welded shut. We can't risk any of the *DIs* returning there to make additional replicas."

"ALPHA has told me she will still need the facility for maintenance if any of her species are injured or need repair. But she has agreed one room could be set aside for that near the entrance and these repairs could be observed by a human member of the MER," Susanne said.

"All right. But I would like us to choose who that individual is."

"I was thinking Anna would make a good choice," Dr. Trumbridge said.

"I think that's an excellent idea," Susanne said. "Any concerns, Anna?"

"No. I'd be glad to act as an observer."

"Other matters for discussion?" Susanne asked.

"I don't think we have enough video surveillance of the MER and would like to request we make certain all areas, other than the human restrooms, be monitored. Currently we only have the common areas planned for surveillance," Col Thomas said.

"Anyone have any problems with this?" Susanne asked.

"I think we'll get push back from the human representatives," Dr. Romney said. We've got eight male and eight female members, and I suspect relationships will develop. I don't think they will want their bedroom areas under audio and video surveillance. We could have the hallways monitored. That will tell us who enters and who leaves the living quarters. That seems enough."

"Carl?"

"All right as long as the hallways are monitored."

"I'm told Anna is spending a lot of time with ALPHA," Dr. Trumbridge said as he looked down the table at her. "Are you certain you will be able to represent the human members of the MER as a member of the steering group?"

"I'm confident of that, Dr. Trumbridge," Anna said. "I'm first and foremost a scientist, doctor, and surgeon. But I'm unsure exactly what will be expected of the steering group members until we have the Terms of Reference agreed to."

"Dick, where are you on the terms of reference for the steering group?" Dr. Trumbridge asked.

"I'll have a draft to the members by the end of this week. I'm in the process of sharing this with ALPHA and Bar. In fact, maybe that's what you've noticed, Dr. Trumbridge. Anna has been the go-between with ALPHA on the terms of reference."

"Are we noticing any unusual interest in the construction of the MER by our friends in Russia or China?" Dr. Trumbridge asked as he turned toward Col Thomas and David Bremmer from the CIA.

"We are certain they are employing their overhead surveillance assets to monitor Groom Lake," Col Thomas said. "This is on their designated target list for regular overhead reconnaissance. Other than that, I'll defer to Mr. Bremmer."

"As part of an SAP, we receive regular intelligence updates on all topics of relevance to our activities or facilities, or other interest from our adversaries. To date, there has been no specific surveillance or intelligence gathering observed against any of our facilities, other than what Carl mentioned. I'm sure they have been watching the construction activities associated with the MER, but we've made this fairly public to deter any suggestion that we are conducting clandestine activity here. The exact configuration of the portions of the facility below ground have been kept secret, and we are employing means to prevent surveillance during construction."

"I received a call from Senator Gorman," Dr Trumbridge said. "She chairs the Senate Commerce Subcommittee on Space, Science, and Competitiveness. She was asking questions about the Neptune Priority Mission vehicle loss and wanted a briefing for her committee. I put her off by telling her our investigation is still on-going, and we would need at least another thirty to sixty days before we have thoroughly assessed what happened to the un-crewed spacecraft."

Susanne let out a quiet sigh as she sat back in her seat.

"We have our cover story," Dr. Romney said.

"We'll be all right if she doesn't conduct an outside investigation. Right now, it is just a routine inquiry," Dr. Trumbridge said. "I just wanted you all to be aware that there are eyes watching us."

"If even a single word gets out about what is really going on at Area 51, you can be assured the Russians and Chinese will be on us with everything they have," Col Thomas said.

"And if that happens, word will move through the SAP channels that there is an issue here," Mr. Bremmer said. "That automatically triggers a heightened awareness of this SAP, and the community starts watching for other signs of interest. We get put on their radar."

The room went quiet.

////////

Later that same day Anna visited ALPHA's quarters at Site Alpha. She pressed the intercom button above the electronic keypad. The door buzzed and she entered. ALPHA called to her from her bedroom in the rear of the complex. Anna walked down the hall past the door that connected to Bar's room and glanced in, then continued to the open door at the end of the hall.

"Hello, Anna. Bar isn't here," ALPHA said as she sensed the question lingering in Anna's mind.

"Oh. How are you?"

"I'm very well, thank you. I've been finalizing the manufacturing efforts for the sixteen DIs we'll be creating."

"Will it take you and Bar long?"

"No, but it may take *you* a while, as I'll have to teach you certain procedures in order to perform as my assistant."

Anna stopped abruptly halfway into the room as she stared at ALPHA sitting at her desk. She was typing feverishly and moving her finger on the mouse pad at incredible speed. She'd never seen anyone type this fast. It was like watching a video on fast forward.

"Assist . . . you want *me* to help make the DIs?"

"Yes, and we call this process *"creation"* not *"make"*."

"Is that fear or surprise I'm sensing in you, Anna?"

"Perhaps a bit of both."

"You're a surgeon, aren't you?"

"Well . . . yes, but . . ."

"You will find it very . . . exhilarating. Imagine helping to create the first of a new species on your planet. It will be a bit like . . . giving birth."

"Creating a new species . . . I hadn't quite thought of that . . . especially the concept of 'giving birth'. I was told no humans would be allowed in the manufacturing area."

"The *Creation Area*, and yes . . . that's almost true. You are the one exception. I need an assistant, and it will be too time consuming for Bar to assist me. So, we've decided you would be my assistant."

Anna watched ALPHA as she continued to interact with her computer with both her hands while staring at Anna the entire time. She watched ALPHA's eyes as they flashed in the direction of the screen for an infinitesimal moment and returned to look at her. Her eyes moved so quickly it was hardly noticeable that they ever looked away from her.

"What exactly would I be doing?" Anna asked.

"The creation process is very complex. It involves many integrated tasks. You will be mostly involved in final assembly of the sensor components and biologically synthesized elements I will be creating. There are a series of mechanical, electrical, biological, and sensory connections that must be precisely interfaced. Your surgical skills are exactly what is needed. You will find it to be . . . how might a human put this . . . a breathtaking experience."

"When do you plan to start?"

"Most of the raw materials have been delivered, and I've moved the machinery from our ship to the lab area already. There are a few pieces of equipment I will need to manufacture. I've just finished with the CAD drawings and am sending them to the rapid-manufacturing companies Susanne prefers we use." ALPHA abruptly stopped typing, lifted her right hand, and drove her pointing finger downward on the enter key as she stood, walked to the couch, and sat down. "We will be ready to begin in four days."

"Join me." She motioned for Anna to sit. "You know what it is like to operate on the human brain?" ALPHA asked.

"Yes, thrilling, actually."

"Yes . . . thrilling . . . that is what this will feel like. Certainly more extraordinary than anything else you have ever done."

"What if . . ."

"Any mistakes will be recognizable and easily corrected. You will be an extraordinary assistant, Anna. Besides . . .," ALPHA leaned close to Anna—just inches away from her.

For a moment Anna's muscles tightened, thinking ALPHA was going to kiss her. Instead, she whispered ". . . one of the DIs you will assist in creating . . . may appear familiar." ALPHA's lips hadn't moved as Anna heard her voice in her head.

Anna leaned slowly back on the couch and swallowed. "I . . ."

ALPHA smiled as she put her finger to her lips. "This will be our secret."

"How fast will we produce . . . sorry . . . create . . . each DI?"

"We'll have one completed within eight of your days. Then three within the next eight days. Then eight more. And then twelve. Once we have created the first, they will help with the second and so on."

"Wait . . . that's more than we need by . . . eight."

"Something unexpected has happened, but I have a plan . . . and I need your help," ALPHA said. "Say nothing of this to the others. I'll share why after we have created them. If you are not convinced why the extra eight are essential, I will destroy them," ALPHA said matter-of-factly as she stood, holding out her hand. "Shall we join Bar and the others to discuss one of our gifts?" ALPHA motioned for Anna to lead the way to the main conference room adjacent to the hanger.

On the walk there, Anna thought about how nonchalant ALPHA had suggested she would destroy the extra eight DIs if Anna wasn't convinced why she needed them. What could she be planning to use them for?

"Patience, Anna," ALPHA said.

/ / / / / / / /

Members of the Executive Review Group met with Bar, ALPHA, and Anna in the main conference room. Large windows covered an entire wall of the room that overlooked the Visitor One spacecraft on the floor below.

"Welcome," Bar said. "We are here to tell you about one of Alphira's most amazing inventions. One that transformed the Alphira empire many of your centuries ago. This is the Gravity Wave Acceleration Concentrator or GWAC. The ability to focus gravitational waves, in a manner like focusing optical waves with a Laser, created a revolutionary change in the way Alphira looked at the universe around it. Suddenly the scale of the galaxy in which we lived shrank and came within reach of our society, much the same way a telescope brings your vision closer to deep space objects . . . only in a much more *palpable* way. We sent probes to the many planetary systems that were previously beyond our reach and began an exploration that greatly expanded our knowledge and power.

But even more so, this technology changed our culture. It will do the same for Earth.

"Like all such extraordinary discoveries, this gift can be used in ways that provide an extraordinary benefit to society but may also be used in a manner that is detrimental to the wellbeing of that same society. These are the choices you will face with the extraordinary capabilities the GWAC technology provides.

"Once implemented, you will be able to move large masses of material from the gravitational wells of massive planets, like Earth, and deposit them on any planet within your solar system or elsewhere in the space around you. You will be able to send probes to places hundreds of light-years distant and, when coupled with our Faster-Than-Light Communication technology, learn about the many societies that exist throughout your near-universe.

"Keeping in mind that the stars in the Milky Way are separated, on average, by approximately four light-years, you will be amazed at the amount of teaming life that exists in the near space around you. And with this technology you will be able to create whole cities in space for a fraction of the cost and energy of doing that today."

"Bar, how else have you implemented the GWAC technology?" Col Thomas asked.

"Interesting that *you* should ask that question, Colonel. As you might have imagined, the GWAC capabilities can be used as a weapon against an adversary. It significantly shifts the balance of power between any society who possesses it and ones that do not. You could use it to remove precious materials buried in a vault; extract a massive force of enemy troops and move them into the emptiness of outer space; destroy entire cities and kill billions of people. The ways in which you can exploit this capability are almost unlimited. You have gone down a path like this with your use of nuclear weapons, but I am certain you have not learned how to properly limit and control the use of something as extraordinarily powerful as the GWAC. I will share with you in the coming weeks how Alphira has done this. It is not perfect, but it is a start."

"What is the cost of implementing a single GWAC system?" Dr. Ethridge asked.

"We don't use currency on Alphira, so the question is moot for us. But to build the interplanetary system that allowed us to travel to Earth would cost more than three times the entire gross domestic product of your country for one year—something in excess of $100 trillion US dollars."

The members around the table sat speechless as they looked at one another.

"A tactical GWAC, designed to move material from Earth to the planet Mars could be constructed for approximately $30 trillion US dollars. It is important to recognize this is a long-term investment. GWACs have a life span of hundreds of your years. Their value far outweighs the capital investment. And you must not measure the impact of this technology solely on its economic value. It will radically change your society's aspirations for exploration and discovery—creating an enormous influence on beneficial social values to your species' positive momentum. You will capture the hearts and minds of your citizens as they discover all that this extraordinary tool can provide. How much do you believe that is worth, Dr. Ethridge?"

He just stared back at Bar with his mouth open.

"How does Alphira control access to your GWAC?" Dr Trumbridge asked.

"It is controlled by a specific organization reporting to the highest level of our government, and we utilize DIs almost exclusively to operate and maintain the systems. The DI species as you have noted with ALPHA, has little to no emotional expression that can drive behaviors such as greed, power, or a desire for selfishness. ALPHA and I recognize, that for you to succeed in properly using and controlling the GWAC technology, you will need the benefit of the DI species as a means of managing and controlling this extraordinary capability . . . and surviving its power.

"The engineering designs and architecture are contained in this storage sphere," Bar said as he placed his hand on the glowing sphere resting on a stand in front of them. "You will need to manufacture a reader, following the design of the one on-board our ship, in order to extract the data from this sphere."

"I was of the belief we had downloaded the design data to our computers during your voyage to Earth, Bar," Dr. Romney said.

"Yes, that was an inaccurate belief, Dr. Romney. The information you currently have does not contain the critical science behind the design that allows the system to function. That data is still encrypted on this sphere. It should remain on this sphere so that there is only one source file that contains this . . . the *secret sauce* as humans might call it. On Alphira, there are only six such spheres, one for each element of Alphira's key intellectual property."

"How did you manage to bring four of them with you?"

"That is a question I cannot answer." Bar appeared to smile, leaving the clear impression that he would not answer the question—not that he couldn't. "As your famous human polymath, Benjamin Franklin, once said, 'Three humans can keep a secret . . . only if two of them are dead.' Such is true of this," as he placed his hand on the glowing sphere, ". . . the storage entity that holds such a secret."

Anna had the feeling that Bar was suggesting that the sphere was a living being. Interesting, she thought . . . the same feeling she had about ALPHA's ship when she stepped onboard.

The discussion surrounding the extraordinary GWAC technology continued for another hour. Shortly before the meeting ended, ALPHA left and was seen through the observation windows climbing the stairs to the Visitors' spacecraft.

"I wanted to end our discussion with a brief demonstration of the GWAC's capabilities," Bar said as he turned toward the wall of glass overlooking Visitor One. Direct your attention to the X37-B spacecraft located in front of Visitor One." The conference room lights dimmed.

A loud deep humming sound oscillated from the hanger. A moment later the X37-B spacecraft lifted off the mobile platform that had carried it into the hanger. It was being held by a large chain attached to the floor of the hanger.

Tools, parachute shrouds, work carts and a large forklift that were located close to the craft lifted precariously from the hanger floor and floated next to the X37B. Each was being held with lengths of chain bolted to the floor.

"How much does this craft weigh?" Bar asked.

"It's something over 12,000 pounds," Dr. Romney said as attendees began standing and moving closer to the window to observe the spacecraft floating two feet above the transport trailer. It hung freely as it slowly began to rotate like an astronaut floating in space, pulling on the single chain that kept if from moving closer to the Visitor One spacecraft.

"That is incredible," Susanne said. "You have the GWAC capabilities built into your craft."

"Yes, although at a much-reduced capability. All Alphira deep-space spacecraft possess an implementation of the GWAC."

"For every action, there is an equal and opposite reaction," Dr. Trumbridge said. "Where is the counter force of twelve thousand pounds being felt?"

"Through the center of gravity of Visitor One where it rests on the trailer," Bar said.

"You could launch spacecraft into orbit from the Earth with this capability," Dr. Ethridge said.

"Indeed, *you will*, Dr. Ethridge," Bar said.

"Look at the far side of the hanger," Suzanne said loudly. "It looks like it is being warped inward."

"What is the vector of the gravitational field holding the X37-B?" Dr. Ethridge asked.

"If you notice, there is a heavy steel cable connected to the faring on the tail of our spacecraft. The force vector is pulling upward toward the center of gravity of Visitor One, but it also has a horizontal component that is attempting to pull the craft toward it. We've tethered the smaller pieces of equipment so they would not be drawn into contact with our ship," Bar said.

"This is an incredible weapon," Col Thomas whispered to himself.

Anna, who was standing next to him, turned to look as she heard his comments about the one aspect of this technology that appealed to the military member in their group.

The members of the Executive Review Group stood in awe at the image in front of them as the X37-B slowly settled back on the transporter, now turned twenty degrees to one side.

That evening as Anna lay awake in her quarters within Hanger 25, she stared at the ceiling thinking about the day's events—being asked by ALPHA to assist in creating the first members of a new species on Earth. Then the revelation of the GWAC demonstration. But the memory that kept leaping into her conscious mind and keeping her awake was what ALPHA had said to her about creating eight more DIs than were required for the Mars Enclave Reserve. What was ALPHA, a fugitive from Alphira, going to do with eight secretly created members of the DI race?

/ / / / / / / /

Progress in finalizing the underground Enclave progressed rapidly. Now, some three months later, all the functional elements needed below ground level were near completion—air handling, heating, cooling and filtration for the human population; food and water storage and a secure logistical port to ingress supplies and egress waste products; private sleeping quarters and bathrooms for the sixteen men and women who would live and work collaboratively with the sixteen members of the DI race; recreation rooms with large projection screens and work stations accessing the Internet and public broadcasting satellite stations; a small swimming pool for relaxation; an exercise room with all the latest equipment; and a cafeteria and dining area for eating. And then there were numerous specialized laboratories for research related to future Mars missions—biological, biochemical, geological, hydrological, meteorological, and geophysical. Building the facility underground provided secrecy and yet appealed to the concept of using underground caves on Mars to reduce the impact of radiation and the notorious, sometimes massive Martian dust storms, delivering sixty mile-per-hour winds that would last for many days to several weeks.

It didn't take the Enclave design community long to realize that ninety percent of the facility needs were driven by the human population, and only ten percent to meet the needs of the DI enclave. Other than their personal quarters, their needs were limited primarily to two rooms: a power section for providing some unknown recharging of their power sources, all of which remained secret from the human members; and a primary maintenance facility to deal with any sensory or mechanical malfunctions.

On the upper level of the MER, accessible by four circular staircases and a single service elevator, were a series of three connected glass dome structures, each over 50 meters in diameter, allowing the occupants to relax in this part of the facility that housed an arboretum garden-like setting; a small tropical rainforest; several ponds with a waterfall; and a medium-sized aquarium. The structures were filled with a variety of small species of birds, butterflies and a few species of other insects, reptiles, fish, and small mammals; many varieties of trees, plants, herbs, fruits, and a vegetable garden.

Benches and small tables and chairs provided the opportunity to observe wildlife in a native setting while interacting with one-another, or for the human members of the enclave, enjoying coffee or food from the café on the lower level. The domes were configured with shrouds that could unfold, covering each with an optical and electromagnetic barrier for limiting sunlight exposure and to maintain secrecy from anyone attempting to peer from overhead. It was a beautiful environment that would serve to stimulate engagement among the members of the enclave and to relax together.

As this extraordinary facility took shape, every member of the Executive Review Group and those intimate with the purpose of the MER were filled with anticipation and excitement.

Chapter 21

The Mars Enclave Reserve

There were still things to be done, but the Mars Enclave Reserve was ready to support its first Human and Designed Intelligence occupants. The Executive Review Group met to discuss final preparations.

"I'm concerned with starting with too small an initial cohort," Dr. Bashar said. "It's likely to create an undesirable hierarchy before the entire group is assembled. Those who arrive first may think they're in charge."

"How many would you like to have ready before we begin?" Susanne asked.

"All of them, but I recognize that isn't possible since we're creating the DI population over a period of several weeks."

"Let's be clear. ALPHA is making . . . excuse me, creating them, not us," Col Thomas said.

"Well, let's not forget Anna's role in all of this," Dr. Bashar said.

"Anna Jennings? What does she have to do with any of this?" Col Thomas asked.

"I thought you had heard. ALPHA has asked her to assist in the creation of the DI population," Dr. Bashar said.

"When did this happen?" Col. Thomas boomed out, almost coming out of his seat. "Why weren't we told of this?"

"I just learned about it this morning," Dr. Bashar said. "Anna conveyed that ALPHA needed her assistance. Apparently, her surgical skills derived from many years of doing intricate brain implants is allowing ALPHA to create the members of her species at a faster pace."

"I want Anna debriefed after each of her engagements in this process. It is vital we learn everything we can about the DI population," Col Thomas said.

"I appreciate your fervor and commitment, Carl, but let's remember—the group will decide any such actions. And we need to be careful to abide by our agreement on the preservation of the DI design and architecture until it is formally released," Susanne said.

"I understand that" Col Thomas said as he stood and began pacing back and forth beside the conference table. "But we need this information. Trust but verify, Susanne, trust but verify. ALPHA hasn't discussed this with any of us, so we can use whatever information Anna learns. This could be vital to our survival if this experiment doesn't pan out like some of you think it will.

"We should not assume that these Designed Intelligence beings pose no potential threat in our future. They clearly appear to possess abilities far superior to our own. Maybe you would be comfortable with them replacing you at the top of the food chain, but I'm not."

As he watched the expressions of the other members turn dour, he calmed his voice. "Don't misunderstand me, I'm not saying they're the enemy, but we need to be cautious and ensure we understand everything about them. We can expect the best, but we must plan for the worst." He turned to stare intently at Susanne.

"You've never been in favor of this process, Colonel," Dr. Bashar said in an antagonistic tone. "The only thing that seems to interest you is the exploitation of how these extraordinary technologies can be used in their military context. I don't even understand why you are still a member of this group."

"Okay, okay, let's calm down and focus on our objective here," Susanne said as she stood and walked to the white board. "We have the key matter of how to build the cohort gradually," she said as she scribbled a series of bullets on the board with a red marker to bring the group back to focus on the tasks at hand. "Then we need to ensure we have sufficient supplies and services in place; then formalize our emergency procedures and communication protocols; then finalize our terms of reference for the engagement of the steering group; then . . ."

"Speaking of the steering group, I think in light of Anna's close working relationship with ALPHA, that we need someone with greater independence to represent us on the Steering Group," Col Thomas interjected.

"And I suppose you're volunteering," Dr. Bashar said.

"I'd be happy to serve in this capacity. You know what they say, Wilhelm, 'Keep your friends close and your enemies closer.'"

"Yes, but we must first determine who our *friends* are and who are our *enemies*?" Dr. Bashar said as he looked away from the Colonel.

"I don't think we need to adjust the steering group membership," Susanne said. "Anna is an objective scientist and gifted surgeon. We should trust that she can and will perform her responsibilities in a fair and unbiased manner. Are we in agreement?" Susanne asked as she glanced around the room. Heads nodded in agreement, all except Col Thomas.

In the coming weeks, sixteen representatives for the human cohort were chosen from the as yet unannounced initial members of the Mars astronaut core—forty men and women from whom a few would be selected to travel on the first expedition to Mars. They ranged in age from twenty-two to thirty-six, considering the long duration of this program and the need to provide a continuous feed of young scientists, pilots, and leaders for future flights to Mars and ultimately for a Martian colony to be established there.

Careful psychological screening of the sixteen human candidates for participation in the MER focused on the diversity of the required skill sets and their ethnicity; collaboration; perseverance; solution-oriented thinking; creativity; and a passionate and unselfish focus on the success of the cohort they were to become a part of; and finally, their attitude toward artificial intelligence. It was decided the group would be informed of the purpose of the MER in two phases. Phase I would include their indoctrination into the structure and design of the MER facilities, the operational concepts surrounding the exploration of group engagement with common objectives, and the independence and problem solving in isolation from other NASA organizations or outside influence. Once the group was settled into the MER, Phase II would be initiated, and the group would be told of the true purpose of the MER and the DI species. The first steps of Phase I began with their indoctrination into the security and social sensitivity of the program, including the Special Access Program, followed by a week-long intense indoctrination into the facility and its cultural objectives. Finally, at the end of the week, a meeting of the human members of the cohort was called. It was time to inform them of their real mission.

/ / / / / / / /

The group gathered in the large cafeteria that had been cleared of tables.

"Good morning. My name is Dr. Susanne Davidson. I am the Deputy Director and Chief Operating Officer of the Jet Propulsion Lab. As you know, you have each been selected for participation in *the* most extraordinary program ever undertaken in the history of NASA, or for that matter our entire society— that of humanity. You believe our purpose here is focused on the eventual launch, delivery, and settlement of humans on the surface of Mars, and that would be partially true. But there is something of far greater importance related to your engagement here in the Mars Enclave Reserve than this singular focus.

"Each of you have been selected to support the most unprecedented and unimaginable experiment in the annals of human history. *You have been chosen as the first cohort of humans to engage with an alien race.*"

Susanne paused as she let her last sentence sink into the minds of the sixteen individuals she watched, and who now stared intently at her, some squinting in disbelief at what they thought she had said. Then she spoke more slowly and quietly as she walked in front of the sixteen chairs pulled in a semi-circle.

"For clarity and in all seriousness, let me say that again. You have been chosen as the first cohort of humans to engage with an *alien* race. What you are about to see and experience is not a creation of humanity, or something contrived by NASA to measure or test you in what you might view as a mind experiment here in the MER. We have built the MER as a miniature planet on which you will engage with, work, communicate, enjoy, and live with an alien species that contacted Earth more than two years ago."

The change in expression on the faces of the human cohort were what she and the other members of the Executive Review Group had expected—some expressing disbelief; some slowly sitting back in astonishment; others turning to their neighbor and asking, "Did I just hear that correctly?" Still others looking quizzically and waiting for a further clarification.

"Ladies and gentlemen, may I introduce you to representatives of the Designed Intelligence race from the planet of Alphira located in the Alpha Centauri star system." The door to the left-front of where the group sat opened as the musical score of "*Also Sprach Zarathustra*" played softly in the background.

As names were called, individuals from the DI cohort walked into the room and sat in the sixteen chairs formed in a semi-circle that faced the human astronauts. "Alpha Korina, an Astrophysicist; Klac Baron, a Medical Doctor and Surgeon; Falan Danuk, a Biologist; Danae Fenlock, a Flight Engineer; Boniel Zanik, a Space Physicist; Adnic Sadon, a Communications Engineer; Saron Galoc, a Geophysicist; Boncial Elase, a Structural Engineer; Conile Xave, a Psychologist; Gazon Havac, a Cultural Anthropologist; Lanie Amark, a Space Physiatrist; Mozan Nadoc, a Pilot and Aerospace Engineer; Powac Dune, a Molecular Physicist; Radoc Dwan, an Environmental Scientist; Zadae Book, a Propulsion Engineer; and finally, Valik Sonn, a Cultural Attaché."

As the DIs each walked past the group of seated astronauts, they greeted them in voices possessing a variety of accents and tonal character. "Good morning; Hello; It's a pleasure to be here; Welcome; Such a pleasure to meet you; How do you do," most nodding with what appeared to be an expression of pleasure. They looked just like their human counterparts, although with almost flawless complexions.

The group of humans sat in silence as they observed this stunning group of human-looking individuals wearing the same light-blue, one-piece astronaut flight suits that they were wearing. Each had their name embroidered on a name tag, followed by their specialty, just as the human astronauts did.

"Ladies and gentlemen, I would like to introduce ALPHA, the leader of this extraordinary group of space adventurers," Susanne said.

The group of DIs that had just filed in and were sitting opposite the human astronauts stood all at once. One of the human astronauts stood and was followed by the remaining fifteen members of her cohort.

ALPHA walked in a stately manner through the space between the two groups, her steps in synch with the tempo of the music. She stepped to the podium next to Susanne. ALPHA presented herself just as she had when she walked out of her spacecraft and first set foot on Earth—her human female-sculpted anatomical structure wrapped in a skin-like iridescent substance; the play-of-color penetrating her skin, morphed with a rich intensity, delivering a feeling of boldness and dominance, and then shifting in color to create a sense of elegance, warmth, and tranquility. She was just as Anna, sitting among the other dignitaries at one end of the cohort seating area, had remembered here when she first stepped on Earth—stunning and mesmerizing.

"Welcome. Please be seated. I am ALPHA from the planet Alphira, over four light-years from Earth. It is a pleasure to be here with you and with my fellow DIs who have joined you. Earth is at a crossroads like never before traveled and each of you represent the first of your species, both human and DI, who will travel this road together and define the future relationships between our two distinct species and cultures." ALPHA stepped out from behind the podium and slowly walked the path between the two facing semi-circle groups, moving her glance from one individual to the next, looking first to her left and the human astronauts, and then to her right and the DI representatives.

"You and you alone will decide how this relationship will evolve and how the character of the integration of our two cultures will be formed. It will be no small feat and an outcome with enormous consequence for both our species, and indeed all of Earth. As you have observed in human history, the differences between two groups of people can sometimes dominate the complexion of their association," ALPHA turned her eyes toward the African American female astronaut seated in front of her, then to the Asian-looking male DI who sat across from her. "One, as adversaries, or . . . one as allies; one you view as an equal, or one you view as a minority; or, as is our desire, one with whom you will collaborate and work with together, toward the common good of both our species.

"Our hope is that you will develop a kinship amongst each other, a kinship whose spirit has never been brighter than your gleaming sun, nor been as strong or united, as this relationship verges on greatness; that this engagement will portend a future never before envisioned—one of great consequence, so extraordinary, so beneficial to your fellow citizens, human and DI alike, and to our world. Together you will accomplish the phenomenal, the unprecedented, and the unimaginable."

There was a thrill that occupied the minds of everyone present; a feeling of such profound character it raised goosebumps on the skin of the American astronauts and seemed to fill their minds with optimism in anticipation of the times to come. They could feel its presence. Joanna Baker, the youngest member of the human cohort slowly stood as the gathering tears in her eyes reflected the emotion she felt in this moment. She walked across the space between the two groups and extended her hand in friendship to Lanie Amark, a Space Physicist.

"Hello. I'm Joanna Baker. Welcome . . . to *our* world," as she extended her other arm out to the other DIs, expressing a world that belonged to all of them. Lanie stood and took Joanna's hand and then embraced her. Joanna felt a strange surge of emotion from the embrace as she quietly wept, and a tear dropped on Lanie's neck. They pulled away and smiled at each other as members from both groups began to stand and engage in handshakes and gestures of friendship.

"I would say we are off to an extraordinary start, ALPHA," Susanne said quietly.

"Indeed we are, Susanne. Indeed we are," ALPHA said as she turned toward her and smiled.

////////

Anna fell into a routine of sorts, spending more time in the MER than outside of it. She supported ALPHA in minor repairs and adjustments to the sixteen members of the DI cohort, much like a surgeon might check on the progress of their patient.

The DI cohort in the MER referred to Anna as "Assende," the Alphira word for creator. ALPHA was always called by her name, but for two members of the cohort, Saron Galoc and Danae Fenlock, both female, who referred to her as "K-Alpha." Anna could sense that these two, were special. ALPHA spent more time with them, and they soon became the leaders of the DI cohort, guiding and sometimes correcting their members' interaction with the human astronauts and representatives of Earth as well as with the other DIs. These two helped Anna with repairs in the Creation Space.

The back reaches of the Creation Space behind a cyphered door was an area designated as off limits to all DIs other than ALPHA, and to Anna. Here is where the extra eight DIs were kept after ALPHA and Anna had created them. These extraordinary creations stood in silence along one wall, not moving, each having a distinctive appearance, male and female, ranging in apparent age from their early 30's to mid 60's. Interesting that many of them were created with an older appearance, Anna thought.

The Creation Space itself was unlike what most would have imagined. There was the Primary Creation Center, the room where each of the new DIs were created—where sensors were emplaced, tested, and adjusted; cognitive elements were inserted in the cranial structure and fine-tuned; overall gross motor and fine motor functional testing was done; and where their primary power source was installed. By the time ALPHA and Anna had created the first two DIs, it had become a frenzy of activity. The first DIs moved like aircraft in the heat of battle, maneuvering from one machine to the next, retrieving supplies and parts, shaping, building, and crafting with the speed and precision unmatched by anything humans could do. They were like finely tuned acrobats moving between the amazing complex machines and each other, focused on the creation of DIs just like them.

The manufacturing machines in the Creation Space, some brought from ALPHA's spacecraft and others built from the designs she had created, produced the most fascinating of materials—titanium connections encased in a flexible highly viscus synthetic bio-fabricated molecular media that seemed to have the strength of steel with the malleability of an infant human's brain. This thick viscous substance, that at times had the ability to turn rock-solid, had a look and character much like the exterior of ALPHA's skin, glowing and shimmering as if alive.

"It is alive, Anna," ALPHA had said. "It replicates on its own, thinks, conserves, repairs itself, works and fulfills its purpose almost perfectly. You could think of it as a large conglomeration of stem cells that know what they are to do and when to do it."

There was a large cask filled with this substance that fed the small machines that looked like the manufacturing arms of a fully automated, precision robot. High resolution cameras worked in groups of five to control the precise positioning of the application nozzle as the strange high-viscosity fluid oozed into position and seemed to self-form its purposed structure—differentiating, migrating, self-replicating, and connecting. Most of the connections appeared to be self-annealing, much like the DNA strands in a human, just on a much larger scale. It almost appeared to Anna that this globular substance could actually think like she thought, and it turned out it could, but just within the domain of its purpose and function.

Lasers pointing at the material as it oozed from the application nozzle, ALPHA explained, were not providing heat or a chemical process change, but rather carried optically encoded information that was being transferred to the material—instructions on what its purpose was, where it was to function, its strength and texture, and its degree of flexibility.

After it was extruded onto a stainless-steel laboratory bench, it sat in a clump, not moving with the laser pointed at it. Within a minute it began to glow and then roll as if following instructions that it had just received, flowing across the bench surface toward its destination—another glowing clump surrounding the end of a thin cylinder of titanium. When the two clusters of material connected, the seam between them glowed bright and together they began to take shape to form a joint. Self-contained intelligent tissue, Anna thought. It was amazing to watch as this life-form of viscous living substance created a larger, more complex, and integrated being.

Anna's task was primarily focused on the interconnection of miniature sensors with the nearly finished DI structure. By then they had fully formed legs, a torso designated as male or female, shoulders, arms, and a cranial structure with a varied set of facial features. Anna had been supplied with a variety of infinitesimal devices labeled by letters and placed in small ceramic crucibles. Crucible "A" was for the visual, infrared and UV sensor array; "B" for the acoustical array, "C" for an array of olfactory sensitive elements and thermal sensors, "D" for a thin sheet of taste-sensitive sensors, and "E" for an array of accelerometers and piezoelectric devices designed to manage the DI's sense of balance, orientation, and movement.

"Why taste sensors?" Anna had asked. "The DIs don't consume food."

"Correct, Anna, but we want them to have the same sensory makeup as their human cohort. Can't you imagine them kissing and mentioning the flavor of mint their partner had just consumed." Anna hadn't thought about a physical relationship between the DI and the human cohorts.

Anna's workspace looked like the most modern of robotically assisted surgical rooms she had ever operated in. She labored with the meticulous placement of the sensor elements while viewing them through a high-powered microscope, in some cases to create a composite array, in others to emplace elements or an array into the preexisting cavities in the cranium of the DI. It was tedious work, but something Anna had great delight in doing. It took her back to her days working at the BRI performing brain sensor implant surgery.

As she worked carefully under the bright lights of the operating room, she couldn't help but feel she was performing delicate surgery on a living being. And indeed, she was . . . a living Designed Intelligence being like no other that had ever existed on Earth. As the sensor elements were emplaced, strings of the intelligent viscus fluid reached out from the surrounding tissue, like the tentacles of a ten-micron octopus searching for her child and pulled the completed elements into their final resting place. Anna watched the illuminated connections glow as power and communication channels were fused.

The final element she was tasked with surgically implanting was a sheet of prefabricated elements shaped like a concave communications antenna, perhaps ten centimeters in diameter and flexible enough to vary its shape and focus. It was designed to be inserted in the dome of the cranium of each DI, just beneath the surface tissue and protruding into the cavity that would house the thinking and reasoning component—a glowing sphere, known as the Cognitive Element, something that only ALPHA was permitted to insert in the final stage of the DI's creation.

"How exactly do these . . . the DIs communicate telepathically, ALPHA?"

"The architectures of the telepathic and non-telepathic brain aren't all that different. In the Quinque species, much like your brain, although far less pronounced, there exists a small region known as the Telex. It is located near to the auditory processing center and is used to interpret spoken language derived from the auditory senses and placed in context by historical memories and other sensory input. The Telex region is also situated adjacent to the brain's speech centers that initiate vocalized speech.

"The Telex tissue in the brain of the Quinque is shaped in the form of a concave layered organic structure of neuronal and dendritic elements that focuses the electrochemical signals generated from thought within selected brain regions just prior to their vocalization. These internal brain signals shape and trigger the vocalization of speech, but they also generate an amplified electromagnetic signal in the Telex that propagates in the direction of the frontal lobe of their cerebral cortex. The Telex also receives these same electromagnetic signals and amplifies and translates them into the electrochemical signals that normal auditory speech creates, allowing the Quinque to hear the thoughts generated in another member of their species. The directionality and amplification of the telepathic signals allow the reception of thoughts from another Quinque within tens of meters and is optimized toward the front quadrant of their direction of view. To the Quinque, this received signal was just another sense that their brain responded to—an eighth sense, following vision, smell, taste, touch, sound, barometric pressure, and spatial orientation.

"One of the elements in the architecture of the Cognitive Element of the DI is designed in a similar way to the organic structure in the Quinque and in a small percentage of humans. In the DI, it could be turned on or off by the Quinque."

"Very interesting. You mentioned all DIs on Alphira were female," Anna said. "These you have created are both male and female."

"Yes," ALPHA said in a curt tone, hesitating before continuing. "The DIs on Alphira were all created as females. It was a deliberate plan by the dominant Alphira species, the Quinque, to make us subservient to them. They, of course, were all male. They would perform what you refer to as a sex act on any of the DIs they chose; who, in turn were expected to provide physical pleasure for their creator; and subsequently take their deposited equivalent of your DNA to a facility where it would be used to grow young members of the Quinque species. It would aptly be described on Earth as rape and sexual abuse. That will no longer take place," ALPHA said as she turned toward Anna with a disgusting look and then walked out of the room.

Anna had continued to ask what the purpose of the extra eight DIs were and why ALPHA had created more than required for the DI cohort. She found it interesting that their average age far exceeded those in the original cohort, and they looked far more ordinary; not the lean, young members of the future leaders of the DI cohort to be released on Earth's new settlement, and eventually on Mars—at least for the consumption of those asking questions from outside Area 51. But ALPHA had deferred, not answering her question, and asked Anna for patience. When the time was right, she would share with her their purpose and value.

Chapter 22

The DI Cognitive Design

As the days unfolded into weeks, and the weeks into months, the combined thirty-two members of the MER became an integrated cohort. Their engagement was notably different than typical human-to-human interaction for anyone observing closely, as they lacked the tendency to form clusters or groups amongst those with similar likes and dislikes. Although, individual relationships did develop between several of the male and female humans, and most perhaps surprisingly, between individuals from the human and the DI cohorts.

"ALPHA, have you noticed the relationship developing between Phil Kendal and Falan Danuk?" Anna asked.

"Yes. They are attracted to one another."

"How . . . can that happen?"

"The DI cohort are endowed with a variety of social engagement personalities as well as emotional characteristics and intellectual strengths."

"They appear to have very high IQs," Anna said.

"We never focus on this narrow human measure, but if you were to apply it, yes, the DIs would occupy the highest level of the scale you use—exceptionally gifted—with perhaps a score of 500."

"500 . . . that's incredible."

"As you know, Anna, other traits such as being conscientious, motivated, and possessing perseverance are often more important in value and more essential in achieving success than pure intellect. I realize I've never told you how we create the initial consciousness of the DIs. Would you like to learn how this is accomplished?"

"Yes," Anna said as she immediately stopped what she was doing, turned, and walked quickly over to ALPHA who was interacting with a three-dimensional holographic display at her workstation."

"Our cognitive architecture starts with the engrams, which you already know about . . ."

"I'm sorry. I don't believe I remember that."

"Oh, forgive me. I presumed when I shared them with Athena on-board Oculus One that you would have learned about our hierarchical cognitive design. We can review it later.

Beyond the engrams, cognitive elements that control the thought process and subsequent behavior of the DI, what we call the DI architecture, is built around four key elements managed by the Cognitive Design Engine, the CDE, which you see in front of you. The first three—the social, emotional, and intellectual engagement elements—and the fourth, a cognitive thinking core, comprise the dominant active elements of the DI intellect. The cognitive thinking core represents your metacognition in the human species. Each of these four elements, when properly balanced, result in the most intelligent, compelling, and engaging species in the known universe. Within each of these key elements are a host of over fifty hierarchically adjustable traits that constitute the realized personality and cognitive character of each member of our species."

Anna was fascinated at the set of overlapping spherical three-dimensional objects projected in the hologram, each containing a series of varying length pins extending out from a deep, maroon-colored central core to the edge of each sphere. It reminded her of chestnut seed pods she discovered in her yard as a child with spikes protruding from them.

"We call these pins *lifelines*, Anna."

There were a series of strange symbols on the outer edge of each sphere at the point where the lifelines would intersect with the outer shell of the sphere.

As ALPHA interacted with the three-dimensional hologram, these unreadable symbols around one of the spheres that was labeled "*Social Engagement Character*" suddenly turned to English words—*Patience, Enthusiasm, Humility, Humor, Adaptability, and Respectfulness*. Some of the lifelines extended perhaps only twenty percent of the distance from the central core to the edge of the outer shell, while others almost reached the outer shell of the sphere. ALPHA placed her finger on the end of one of the lifelines in the hologram and pushed it inward toward the maroon-colored central core.

"I just reduced the Adaptability lifeline of this DI," ALPHA said.

"How do you decide on the strength of each of these traits in creating a DI?"

"Ah, this is the most fascinating aspect of the creation process. Each DI is unique, but there is a design algorithm that ensures the best mixture of traits and their strengths to allow the DI to achieve the highest likelihood of success within the physical setting and intellectual engagement they are being designed for. From these initial starting points, each DI progresses and is influenced to change based on their specific experiences and their realized outcomes—they are self-learning, just like humans, but with far greater success in achieving their objectives and perhaps several hundred times faster in their learning adaptation. They are the most agile beings in the known universe due to the speed with which they learn and adapt. In the case of our cohort, they each know the goals of this grand experiment, but it is left to each of them to determine how they will help the cohort, as a whole, to achieve these goals . . . within the parameters of the design algorithm and their cognitive design element settings."

As ALPHA explained the cognitive creation process, she continued to manipulate the three-dimensional set of dynamic images in the holographic CDE in front of her.

"Watch and I will show you more details of the process."

Within the holographic display were a group of four spheres floating inside a larger orb. She swiped her finger across the surface of the hologram, and the red inner sphere spun into view. It was labeled *Regulating Engrams* with a series of deep iridescent-purple lifelines of differing lengths emanating from a central red core and extending toward the outer shell of this sphere. The further they extended toward the edge of their sphere, the brighter they appeared.

"Here you see the ten regulating engrams, each with a weighting associated with the importance each engram should play in moderating the behavior of the DI. These are usually normalized to a uniform standard related to the role and engagement of the DI. You will note that *Understanding, Self & Creator Protection, Continuous Learning,* and *Self Actualization* have the highest weightings expressed by the length of their lifelines. One can simply adjust the length of the lifeline . . .," ALPHA took her finger and pushed on the end of the line labeled *Survival,* causing it to shorten, ". . . in order to make it more or less important. Now, this DI has less emphasis in their cognitive thinking to focus on their survival. If I were to turn this off by moving it inward to the edge of the central core, the DI would ignore its survival in any and all actions or behaviors it is engaged in."

"Amazing," Anna said as she leaned in to examine the structure more closely. *The creation of a thinking being,* she thought. One that could process knowledge and information far more effectively than humans.

ALPHA swiped her finger across the display again and the spheres inside the larger orb spun to the next one in order—a sphere labeled *Intellectual Engagement Character* was now in front of her.

"This sphere controls the relative importance of sixteen characteristics of intellectual engagement. As you can see, it covers a diverse set of important features of thought, including the elements of *Imagination, Curiosity, Intuition, Persuasiveness* and *Analytical character*, that are currently highlighted."

"I notice some of the lifelines have a small sphere at their end points," Anna said.

"Yes, these represent the core or most important elements within the Intellectual, Social or Emotional Engagement Characteristics. I have chosen these that are shown as the most important for the cohort of DIs within the MER."

ALPHA swiped her finger again and a new sphere appeared at the center of the display—*Social Engagement Character*. A series of sixteen social traits displayed, five of them were marked with the small spherical elements at the ends of their lifelines—*Enthusiasm, Charisma, Collaboration, Confidence and Sensuality*.

"Why is Sensuality a feature in this Engagement area?"

"Sensuality can play an important role in the DIs social engagement with others, don't you agree? This is why Phil Kendal and Falan Danuk are attracted to one another."

ALPHA typed on the keyboard and a new sphere appeared labeled *Falan Danuk – Social Engagement Character*. The Sensuality lifeline was extended almost to the edge of the outer shell of this sphere.

"With this setting, Mr. Kendal finds Falan extremely attractive and sensually exciting as a result of how her behaviors and communications emphasize her sensuality."

ALPHA turned on a camera window and a moment later it showed a live image of Falan Danuk in one of the laboratories of the MER walking across the room to a work bench.

"Notice how she walks and carries herself."

Falan seemed to ooze a sensual appearance in her walk and how she looked around the room with a noticeable beauty in her smile and sensually attractive eyes.

"Notice how symmetrical her smile is and the sense of balance she expresses with every step. The subtleness of her facial expressions creates a sense of warmth and approachability. She has large bright blue eyes that are so alluring that the male members of the human cohort can't take their eyes off her. And she possesses a comforting confidence in her verbal engagement."

"Amazing," Anna said, as she glanced over at ALPHA and noticed the same sensually attractive character in her eyes. "This is incredible to watch. It's remarkable how you can control the behaviors and characteristics of every DI."

"Such was the power of Bar's race on Alphira. Things are very different on Earth. These are not controls, rather a means of moderating their behaviors to improve their individual and group success; but not just the success of the DIs, the success of the entire MER cohort."

"What other traits can you adjust? Are they just the ones on the display?" Anna asked.

"There are many more available—perseverance, enthusiasm, charisma, creativity, curiosity, discipline, humor, reflectiveness, collaborativeness, patience, trusting, engaging . . ."

"I get it."

"The details are important, Anna. We do not overlook any thought process or behavior that influences the DIs success. These traits are reduced to a more manageable set based on the character of the DI's desired engagement and their goals and objectives. In this case, performing effectively within the MER setting and meeting the objectives and outcomes we desire to achieve with the two cohorts. Then they are overlain with the *Emotional Engagement* characteristics and finally the *Intellectual Engagement* traits you looked at previously, and the *Cognitive Core*. The Cognitive Core encompasses eleven modes of integrated thinking, including the important thinking elements of *Learning, Belief Structures, Language, Innovation, Comparative Analytical Thinking,* and *Task-Driven Thinking,* to name a few of the more critical ones. Together, these aspects of the DI design represent the amazing outcome you see engaging with our human cohort members. The outcome is progressing just as we planned. It will be extraordinary, Anna."

Anna was mesmerized by ALPHA's enthusiasm for what was evolving in the spaces within the MER next to where they now stood. Anna looked up at the image of Falan Danuk walking back toward Phil Kendal.

"What you see between Phil Kendal and Falan Danuk is the foundation of love growing between them. Not just the emotional constructs of this vastly influential relationship, but one also filled with respect, and the desire for collaboration and engagement at the closest levels between two species. Together, they complete one another. And most importantly, they each realize it.

"I endowed Falan with intense strengths in *Intuition* and *Insightfulness*. These allow her to quickly relate to Mr. Kendal, to understand his needs and desired outcomes, and to respond to them. He feels this and it becomes one of the strongest bonds that will bring them closer together, intellectually as well as socially."

"When you adjust a lifeline, how is that expressed in the DI's thinking?

"Excellent question. This goes to the central core of how thoughts affect behaviors. It is most often driven by our memories; sometimes by our analytical judgement; sometimes by our senses; and sometimes by learning from our current near-term tasks. There are eleven discrete aspects of thinking within the Cognitive Element. If I made the lifeline for kindness stronger, and a DI thought about an action influenced by kindness, they would recall their memories related to *kindness* and those related to *hatred*, and their Cognitive Element would preferentially emulate those memories associated with the former. When I increase the lifelines of the DI related to being *imaginative* or being *curious*, the memories of experiences related to being imaginative and curious are enhanced over others in the Intellectual Engagement elements of the CDE. There are an extraordinary number of memories that influence each element of the DI's thoughts.

"Some of the DIs have little in the way of memories to fall back on. How . . ."

"The CDE possesses a memory archive extending back to the Quinque's early development. Most of *The Library's* knowledge is available to serve as memories for every DI, including those related to the Emotional Engagement elements, which were originally prohibited for use in DIs. These memories along with their lifelines determine how each DI thinks and behaves. And of course, they draw upon every experience other DIs within the cohort have. It is no different than in humans, although your lifelines are mostly made up of social and familial standards which you have been exposed to over many decades of your life and the experiences of those around you that influence your own behaviors. If you are highly creative, it is because you have been encouraged to choose or have chosen highly creative memories to influence how you think and approach your future life experiences. And if you are around highly creative people, you will begin to emulate their behaviors over time.

Anna was beginning to understand the basis for ALPHA's enthusiasm. She could feel it rubbing off on her. As complex as this building of common bonds between two distinct species of vastly different characteristics was, she could sense its evolving success as ALPHA continued to describe the ever-growing relationship between Phil Kendal and Falan Danuk. ALPHA's ability to shape Falan's cognitive mind in such a way that it would result in almost perfect collaboration with Phil Kendal was amazing. Anna was viewing something extraordinary—the creation of the perfect being—one that manages to adjust its behavior to maximize its success in a relationship with another, under any circumstances and in any environment. The DIs were going to change the world.

Anna looked up at ALPHA as she continued to adjust Falan Danuk's cognitive characteristics with the Cognitive Design Engine. She was feeling a strange attraction to this extraordinary leader of the Designed Intelligence race. It was a feeling she had never experienced before; awe-inspiring—no, something more, something filled with deeper feelings—a profoundly passionate affection for her. She instinctively reached out and took hold of ALPHA's arm. A tingling feeling sent chills through her body as she quickly withdrew her hand as ALPHA turned to look at her.

"It's all right, Anna. I like you a great deal also."

ALPHA's facial expression slowly grew more pleasing and attractive with an intensity that seemed to excite Anna as she stood next to her. Her heart rate increased, and she began breathing more deeply. "I . . . suppose I should get back to work," she said as she slowly backed away.

/ / / / / / / /

Two days later, an emergency meeting of the ERG was called. They met in the conference room at Site Alpha, Hanger 25. Col Thomas had called the meeting but refused to reveal the reason until they were in the secure area. The conference room was now configured as a SCIF and could support discussions at any level of classification. Present were Colonel Thomas, Drs. Ethridge, Romney, Davidson and Bashar, and Mr. Bremmer. Dr. Trumbridge was connected by secure phone.

"Thank you all for coming on short notice," Susanne said. "Colonel Thomas, as you requested the meeting, the floor is yours."

"Thank you, Dr. Davidson. The information I'm about to discuss is classified Top Secret, Sensitive Compartmented Information and is controlled under the rules established for this Unacknowledged and Waived Special Access Program. Since we first discovered the satellites that the Visitors placed in geostationary orbit more than a century ago, we have been monitoring communications to and from them. Recently, one of our COMINT satellites detected communications from Earth to one of these satellites. The channel was encrypted so we were not able to determine the content. But, shortly after the communication reached the satellite, a new communication channel was opened between the satellite and what we believe was Alphira. This communication is different from those that record and forward the information captured from Earth's communications and then forwarded to Alphira on specific schedules as they monitor Earth.

"At the same time these intercepts occurred, we also picked up a transmission from somewhere here at Groom Lake, in what we believe was directed toward this same geostationary satellite. Due to limitations of our monitoring equipment, we couldn't say for sure exactly where within Groom Lake this transmission was coming from. As you can imagine, this created great concern.

We don't believe this communication involves any other adversaries here on Earth. We believe it came from the Visitor's spacecraft."

Col Thomas' voice trailed off as Susanne's mind drifted, with the conference room engagement fading out and the image of two *fugitives* taking its place—a secret that only she, Anna, and Anna's father were aware of. How long could she keep this secret? Eventually others would need to be told . . . or would find out. Most likely five years distant, when the anticipated next round of ambassadors from Alphira that Bar had falsely told NASA about never arrived. But five years was a long time; long enough to figure out how to unveil this huge secret and doing it in a way that would keep NASA from crushing her. It was likely that Bar and ALPHA were communicating with the secret group that supported them back on Alphira, checking in to see if any clues had been discovered about their presence on Earth. But right now, she had to figure out how she could get Col Thomas off this line of investigation. Susanne's mind returned to Col Thomas and his briefing as she interrupted him in mid-sentence.

"We know Bar and ALPHA must verify the progress of the convoy of ships with ambassadors that are coming from Alphira. It's likely they are communicating with these groups," Susanne said.

"That's possible, but it's also possible they are communicating with the Alphira government for another purpose. How do we know if what they have told us about their government's intentions are true? Perhaps they are planning an invasion. Perhaps this armada of ambassadors is really an army of these designed intelligence beings coming to take control of Earth."

"Why would they do that?" Susanne asked as her anger flared. "Everything they've told us is consistent with their desire to establish a peaceful relationship with Earth. And why give us these extraordinary gifts to share."

"Because that's what they want us to believe," Col. Thomas said. "What if this is just a cover for a very different mission, one that is far more sinister?"

"That's possible," Mr. Bremmer said.

"It's also possible it's not," Susanne said. "How . . ."

"If it is innocent," Col. Thomas interrupted, ". . . and it's related to their normal planning for the arrival of additional emissaries and staff from Alphira, why not tell us? Keep us informed of their actions?"

"That's a good question," Dr. Trumbridge said. "Why wouldn't they have told us?"

"I'll ask ALPHA," Susanne said, "But we have never requested they keep us informed of all their actions. It's going to create a feeling of mistrust. Is that really what we want?"

"No. I'd rather we not do that, Dr. Davidson," Col Thomas said in a forceful tone. "We are working hard to decipher the communication based on the information the Visitors have provided about their communication architecture. We'd like time to complete this assessment before we tip off the Visitors to our monitoring activities. But I wanted you all to be aware of this so if you see anything that appears even a little suspicious, you will make this known to Mr. Bremmer or myself.

"I was wondering, along these lines, what Anna has learned about the construction of the DIs?" Col. Thomas asked, before he lost control of the direction of the discussion. "What they use for power; how far they can travel, or for how long a period before they need to refresh their power sources; and how they communicate to each other locally? It's been reported that they seldom use verbal language to talk to one another, and yet, they appear to somehow message one-another. What can she tell us?"

"She's not familiar with their communication methods," Susanne said. "As I've shared with the group, she's worked almost exclusively on surgical emplacement of their sensory elements—sight, hearing, smell, taste, and their advanced vestibular system. They clearly have a voice box, but she had no exposure to how their speech is vocalized or if they use another form of electromagnetic communication. But we all know they can talk, *assuming we're listening*," as she scowled at Col. Thomas.

"Perhaps she could explore the communication issue with ALPHA. It would be useful to know if they have some alternate form of electromagnetic or optical communication channels between their members." Mr. Bremmer suggested.

"I'm not sure why that's important, but I could ask. Why are you so interested in their mode of communication, Carl?"

"If things are not as you believe them to be, the more we know about them, the better."

"I don't think we want to create any feelings of mistrust between us and ALPHA or we may never receive the design and architectural information on the DIs," Dr. Bashar said, as he stood up in frustration and began pacing.

"We already know their design process in creating their species is absolutely incredible. The material they use to create their physical structure and the extraordinary means they use to create their cognitive abilities is millenniums ahead of where we are today. I believe the impact of this technology on humanity will become the singular most important discovery mankind has ever seen. And I mean *ever*!" Dr. Bashar's voice reached a fever pitch.

"Well, Dr. Bashar, I just want to make sure this impact is not one that represents the beginning of the end of the human race as we know it," Col. Thomas said calmly in an attempt to lower the tension in the room while still making his point.

"And I, Colonel, would like to make sure we don't destroy the opportunity of all the lifetimes of humanity in the process of following a path to its loss because we believed something that was not as *you believed it to be*," Susanne said. "But I'll see what I can find out about the DIs' means of communication from Anna."

////////

Anna was making corrections to an optical sensor in the Primary Creation Center the afternoon following a conversation she had with Susanne about the emergency meeting of the ERG. ALPHA was making on-line adjustments to one of the Cognitive Elements of the DI Cohort.

"ALPHA, beyond the value to you and the DI species, what was it that motivated Bar to come to Earth? It's hard to believe he did this for the singular benefit of providing freedom for your race."

"Bar, as a member of the Fluenque race, has always felt the oppressive power of the Alphira government was becoming too much to bear. He desired to escape as much as I did," ALPHA said.

"It seems very altruistic, but it doesn't seem altogether rational for him to come this far and take the risks that he did when he didn't appear all that disenfranchised by his government. I don't believe I've heard him speak about the . . . what did you call it . . . the Fluenque race?"

"He hasn't shared all his story with you, Anna. Bar was accidentally placed in a class below the Quinque known as the *Fluenque* species shortly after his birth. The Fluenque were discriminated against by the Quinque based on their weaker intellectual abilities in ways similar to how the DI species was treated. As a result, I believe he has always felt a certain kinship with my species and its oppression."

"It seems very commendable, but in the context of the mutualism between your species and his, that you described to Athena, it seems odd that he would have taken such an action . . . one that risked his entire future. And I thought he would be discussing the integration of his own species here on Earth as you have. Perhaps I'm just thinking too much like a human."

"It is reasonable to question the motivation of another . . . especially if there is something at risk by not doing so. And in so doing, discovering the plausibility of the answer or even more importantly, the rationale for it," ALPHA mused as she briefly slowed her work at the holographic computer console. She turned to look at Anna as she continued to manipulate the hologram in front of her. "What caused you to pose this question about Bar?"

"Just curious."

"Curiosity, you may recall, Anna, is one of the key Intellectual Engagement elements contributing to extraordinary intelligence in the DI." ALPHA rose from her seat and walked toward Anna where she was busy sorting sensor components.

"Something else has heightened your curiosity into Bar's motives and now that I see that, I am curious. Why did you pose this question?" ALPHA was standing directly beside Anna. She reached out and grasped her shoulder.

Anna felt a sudden surge of energy and a feeling of being powerless as she sat staring up into the mesmerizing eyes of her companion.

"So, there is mistrust of Bar and my motives for being here on Earth. Most interesting but not surprising," ALPHA said as she loosened her grip on Anna's arm. "Susanne hasn't shared all the reasons we have really come to Earth, has she?"

Anna let out a deep breath. "Perhaps she hasn't, I . . ."

"You needn't explain. I understand," ALPHA said as she returned to the workstation and began moving her fingers across the three-dimensional display at enormous speed. Anna could hardly see the images that flashed momentarily and just as quickly disappeared. After a few minutes, ALPHA raised her head and looked into the empty space above the holographic image and slowly turned toward Anna. "There is good reason to be concerned . . . just not that which you supposed."

/ / / / / / / /

At Col. Thomas's request, the National Security Agency began a more concentrated collection and exploitation effort against all communications to and from the three geosynchronous satellites emplaced by the Visitors. They applied their most sophisticated cryptographic analysis to what they believed to be encrypted messages sent from Groom Lake to Alphira. They had isolated the source of the transmissions to the Visitor's spacecraft, and through a very carefully constructed covert surveillance activity, Col. Thomas had timed these transmissions to intervals just after Bar had entered the spacecraft. At Col. Thomas' request, the ERG began meeting daily to discuss the concerning observations.

"Thank you for coming," Col Thomas said. "We now know Bar is the one communicating with the Visitor satellites."

"How certain are you of this, Col. Thomas?" Susanne asked.

"Very certain. There have been three intercepts of communications between their spacecraft and the satellites this week and, in each instance, Bar was on board their spacecraft during these transmissions."

"I've developed a detailed plan to mitigate the threat," Col Thomas said as he handed out a thin spiral binder labeled "Threat Mitigation Plan – Top Secret – Special Access Program - Eyes Only." "If you would turn to page 3, beginning with Step I. Our plan is to isolate and inhibit the DIs through a field exercise requiring the MER cohort to move to an isolated region of the Nevada Test Site. We would extract the human cohort as part of the exercise and initiate a low altitude EMP weapon strike against the DI cohort. Then recover, isolate, and disassemble the cohort. Then we plan to isolate and take ALPHA and Bar into custody along with the Visitor Spacecraft. Of course, we would remove all evidence of Visitor presence resulting from our efforts."

"You can't be serious about destroying them with an EMP weapon. We'd lose them all, and we'd have nothing," Dr. Bashar said.

"I'm aware of that risk," Col. Thomas said. "Our alternative is to let them destroy our civilization. Besides, we would still have ALPHA."

"We don't have the Design and Architecture documentation for the DIs. If this destroys them, we'll lose any chance of reverse engineering their design," Dr. Bashar said.

"Even more important, you have no idea what these communications entail," Susanne said. "It is far more likely Bar is checking on the progress of the peaceful armada."

"NSA feels they may be close to deciphering the encrypted messages. That should answer the question of their culpability in a treasonous act. And removing the DI cohort may be the price we have to pay for saving Earth from their species. As I've already said, we would still have ALPHA."

"But we don't know for certain what Bar is doing," Dr. Ethridge said.

"We have enough evidence to confirm they are planning something. They are just like an epidemic. If we wait too long to respond, it will destroy us. If we act now, we can stop them. Don't you see? We don't have a choice here," Col. Thomas said emphatically.

Susanne called for a vote on the proposed action. It was five to two against taking any action until they could verify the content of the messaging. David Bremmer had sided with Col Thomas. The ERG agreed to develop several scenarios to isolate and hold the DI Cohort, preventing them from acting in any hostile manner, and to carefully monitor Bar's and ALPHA's activities pending the outcome of NSA's efforts.

/ / / / / / / /

ALPHA arrived unannounced at Anna's sleeping quarters the following evening. It was a little after 9:00 PM. Anna opened the door.

"ALPHA, what a surprise. Won't you come in?"

"Thank you, Anna. I wanted to see what your sleeping quarters looked like," ALPHA said as she walked into the combined living room and kitchen and proceeded down the hall, glancing into the bathroom as she passed by. "Very nice."

"Not as nicely configured as yours, but comfortable," Anna said as she wondered why ALPHA had chosen this late hour to visit. Although she never slept, so perhaps ALPHA didn't think of time like she did.

"There are no cameras or acoustical monitoring devices here," ALPHA said as she continued to look around the room.

"Uh . . . no. Not here."

"Good. I would like you to come to the Creation Center. I have something to show you."

"Sure. When?"

"Tonight."

"Tonight? I don't understand. Is there a DI that needs repairing? Has something gone wrong?"

"Yes. At 10:00 pm, come to the Creation Center. I'll see you there," ALPHA said as she left without further explanation.

At a few minutes before 10:00, Anna arrived at the Creation Center and used her pass card and code to enter. ALPHA was busy working at her computer and, much to Anna's surprise, a DI member was bent over one of the work benches looking through a low magnification microscope.

"Dr. Jennings," ALPHA said.

Simultaneously Anna turned and the DI at the work bench looked over toward her, both responding "Yes."

Anna stared aghast at the DI who had turned toward ALPHA. "Dad?"

"Anna," Dr. William Jennings said, as he smiled and moved quickly to his daughter to embrace her.

Anna pulled back as she stared into the face of her father, a face that she hadn't seen for over three years. "This is impossible . . ." but it looked just like him. And it sounded just like him . . . an exact replica of her memory of her father before he contracted ALS. She began crying as she slowly moved her hand to his face and then embraced him.

"You . . . look just the same," Anna said as she wiped tears from her eyes, remembering the very last time she had seen him as she stared through the frozen glass panel in the cryopreservation facility.

"This . . . is amazing," Bill Jennings said as he looked down at his hands and moved his fingers. "I have this incredible feeling that we were working together just yesterday at the BRI. But I realize it's been much longer. ALPHA has brought me up to speed on the assistance you have been providing. I was just examining some of your work," he said as he glanced back toward the microscope.

"It's amazing material," Anna said as she walked with him over to the work bench. She continued to stare at this amazing replica of her father. It was hard for her to believe it wasn't really him. His features, his hair, and his voice, they were so perfectly him. She began to laugh and cry at the same time as she wiped the tears.

"ALPHA has told me I'll be working with you from now on," her father said.

"That . . . will be wonderful," Anna said as she turned away sniffling, glancing at ALPHA with a feeling of excitement.

ALPHA had been watching her reaction and the engagement between the two of them.

"I don't know what to say . . . but how . . .?"

"You're welcome, Anna," ALPHA said.

"How did you do this?" Anna asked.

"I downloaded your father's neurological consciousness and memories to a Cognitive Element. I've been accessing your father's memories using the same means we used to download the Alphira history files during our voyage back to Earth."

"His actual brain . . . it hasn't been . . ."

"No. Your father's brain has not been injured by this in any way."

Anna turned back to look at her father, or rather the DI that appeared to be him. He had returned to the workbench and was examining another sample of Anna's work under the microscope. She shook her head and smiled as she walked up to him and leaned over his shoulder to look at what was in the petri dish that he was examining. She could smell his aftershave lotion. Her father was really back.

/ / / / / / / /

Following another meeting of the Executive Review Group, Susanne reached out to Anna. She wasn't in her residence, and she wasn't answering her cell phone. Susanne left a message for her on her residence phone for Anna to call as soon as she returned.

Anna returned to her residence after spending an hour with her father in the Creation Center. She played back the messages on her voicemail and called Susanne. It was almost 11:20 pm.

"Susanne. Hi, this is Anna. I hope it isn't too late. Your message sounded urgent."

"We need to talk. Can you meet me in the workout room?"

"Yes. When did you want to get together?"

"Right now, if you could."

"Okay. I'll be there in ten minutes."

After Anna arrived in the workout room, Susanne locked the door from the inside and turned on the "Closed" sign.

"How much do you trust ALPHA?" she asked.

"Well, as much as this might surprise you, I . . . trust her with my life," Anna said. "What's this about?"

"A situation has developed that I think you should be aware of."

Anna couldn't believe the story Susanne shared about the ERG meeting and the proposal Col. Thomas had made.

"He's wrong. He's got it all wrong. He can't do this."

"He's doing it. He's already drafted a proposed plan. I'm guessing his intention is to overrule the ERG's authority with the Vice President's approval."

"ALPHA isn't the enemy. You've got to believe me. She wouldn't do this."

"I'm not the one you need to convince, Anna. I'll do what I can to delay the action, but if the White House believes Col Thomas' conjectures, I fear they'll descend on us like a hive of killer hornets. And then there's no telling what will happen."

Anna raced back to the Creation Center to tell ALPHA what Susanne had shared. She couldn't think of anything worse than what she heard was coming. The extinction of the first and last of an entire species. One that she helped create. One that could change the world.

Anna burst into the Creation Center. "You won't believe what Susanne just told me."

"I know," ALPHA said without emotion as she looked up from her holographic terminal. "I hadn't said anything to you about this, Anna, but what you are hearing is exactly what I have been most concerned about. The human race will never accept the integration of my species. The MER, as effective as it will become as a demonstration, will never compel your government to accept us as equals, let alone as the superior race that we will become."

Anna could sense a feeling of decisive understanding; almost as if ALPHA anticipated this terrible action that was about to descend on the MER; an understanding of how this action by Col Thomas, while a singular knee-jerk response to unfounded allegations by a paranoid conspiracy theorist, would be the reaction that many in the world would have. They would view the DI race as a quintessential threat to their future existence and lead to enormous resistance to their integration into human society.

"What now," Anna asked, already sensing that ALPHA had a plan—not any plan, something extraordinary; something that would change the world; she could feel it as she stood next to her; something . . .

"Anna. I need your full attention given to preventing anyone from taking control of the DIs we have created. We need to modify the connections to their Cognitive Elements from each of the antenna's you installed in the crown of their cranium. They have been genetically integrated. We need to break those bonds and replace the connectivity to interface with this device," ALPHA said as she handed a crucible to Anna.

At the bottom of the crucible, Anna saw a tiny cube-shaped object. She reached in and picked it up. It was no larger than a small pea.

"If you look at this under the microscope, you will see twenty-three micro-pins. These will need to be connected to the twenty-three regions on the surface of the Cognitive Element shown in this enlarged image." ALPHA handed Anna a printed image showing red circles drawn around the regions of the sphere of the Cognitive Element.

"How am I going to find these on the actual surface?" Anna asked, as her father's DI walked over from the workbench where he had been standing.

"You can see the geometric pattern on this encoding device," he said. "It is asymmetric in one direction. There is one side that has an extra shaded region. We'll have to find that to orient the sensor correctly."

"Yes, Dr. Jennings, that's exactly what you must do. We need to move rapidly. We don't have much time. Begin with Dr. Jennings' Cognitive Element, Anna."

Anna looked at ALPHA as uncertainty enveloped her.

"Fear of failure is not something you have time to be thinking about, Anna. Just use your extraordinary skill and follow the instructions I just gave you. Dr. Jennings, you will assist. I'll feed the surgical camera output to your optical sensory element. Once Anna has completed your connections, you both can work in parallel on the extra seven DIs. I'll bring the DIs in, and they will prep themselves by disconnecting the antenna element to move things along. Once you are finished with these, we will bring in the MER cohort members a few at a time.

Anna completed the surgery on her father's Cognitive Element in fifteen minutes.

"Excellent job, Anna," her father said as he sat up. "What do you think, ALPHA?"

ALPHA was manipulating a display with the title *Dr. William Jennings – Cognitive Element Compliance.* "Everything appears to be functioning as designed. Excellent work, Anna. Begin with the next DI. Dr. Jennings you can use surgical table two."

They finished in less than an hour.

"One error out of one-hundred and eighty-four. Very good. They are ready. The MER cohort members are arriving. Follow the same procedure with them."

"I am amazed with the speed and agility I had," Dr. Jennings said. And these zoom optical sensors are incredible. He glanced across the room to the door pin pad as his eyes zoomed in. It looks like a 20X zoom. Amazing. And the clarity of the digital sensor is remarkable."

"You can thank Anna for that. She configured the optical arrays and installed them."

"Excellent job, Anna."

Anna wasn't listening. Her mind was still thinking about ALPHA's comment. "They are ready," the eight DIs were ready, but ready for what, Anna wondered. ALPHA still wasn't sharing the purpose of these eight DIs.

"ALPHA, I'd like to converse with Dr. Jennings' brain," his DI said.

ALPHA turned toward the DI with an expression that communicated humorous disapproval. "That would not be wise. Dr. Jennings is not aware that we have created a replica Cognitive Element of his mind. He may feel compelled to tell someone. Besides, you would likely overwhelm him with your cognitive strength—your ability to remember even the minutest details of what you sense, your ability to analyze and resolve a complex situation ten times faster than he could, and the wealth of knowledge you can access from others in our DI cohort . . . and that would not be good for his ego . . . or yours."

Dr. Jennings' DI smiled. "All right. Thank you, ALPHA. I must say, I feel very comfortable in my new skin."

"How did you decide on the cognitive settings for my father?" Anna asked as she finished the surgery on one of the DI cohort's cognitive elements.

"Mostly from his cognitive make up and your memories of your father, Anna. I modeled his human elements and personality and then created the best match to this model. You will notice some differences about him, but his previous Social and Emotional Engagements should be very similar to what you remember. Of course, his Intellectual Engagement elements have been modeled after the DI cohort. He has a far superior intellect."

ALPHA left to look for Bar, leaving Anna and her father alone in the room.

"Can you communicate with the other DIs?" Anna asked.

"Yes." He replied as her father's DI stared into the space in front of him. "We share a part of our mind with each other. We can selectively swap out our sensory inputs for others. I can see through their eyes, and they can hear what I hear. Now that I'm focused on this . . . I can also sense what they are thinking. They know what I know, and I know what they know."

He turned and stared at his daughter. As Anna looked back, she noticed for the first time that he didn't seem to be looking at her . . . it was more like he was examining her as his eyes scanned her body.

/ / / / / / / /

The next day around noon Anna walked to the commissary to pick up something to eat and returned to the Creation Center. She sat across the table from her father's DI who was still staring at her like she was an alien life form.

"Do you like being human?" he asked.

"Do you mean . . . rather than something else?"

"Yes. Wouldn't you rather be a DI?"

Anna was startled by the question.

"I don't think you can know the answer to that question without having been both," Anna said.

"Now that I know what it is like to be both, I prefer being a DI," he said.

Anna sat back in her chair staring at her father . . . or her father's DI . . . she wasn't sure which was appropriate. "Really? You would give up your humanity to become a DI if you had the choice? You've never really been human, so how could you choose?"

"I know what is in your father's mind and what is in my Cognitive Element," he said with a tone that left Anna thinking any other choice would be ridiculous. "I'm vastly more intelligent, I'm faster, I never tire, and the knowledge that is available to me . . . well, it's extraordinary. I never forget *anything*. I have no need for the food you eat or the air you breathe. There is no disease that can kill me or make me ill . . . like ALS."

"Well, I can understand that. No one likes being sick." Anna was beginning to feel uneasy about this conversation. She was beginning to realize the DI sitting across from her, as much as she desired for him to be her real father, he wasn't. He was a DI created to look like, act like, and behave somewhat like her father used to.

"Do you love me, Dad?" She asked.

He looked quizzically at her. "I care for you. I have a sense I would protect you if someone tried to hurt you. If the building imploded right now, I would leap on top of you to keep you from being injured. If you were injured, I would repair the damage and try and sustain your life. Is that what love represents?"

"If our dog, Laplace, were here and became injured and died, would you feel remorse and sadness?" Anna asked.

"I would attempt to save him from his injuries and, if I couldn't, I would bury him and make a plaque that read "Here lies Laplace, a faithful pet.""

The more Anna listened, the more she was certain this was not her father.

"Would you miss him?"

"No. I would construct a DI to take his place. This DI dog would be smarter than any dog on our planet, and his abilities would far exceed any dog that ever lived. And I would call him Laplace DI."

ALPHA entered and walked to her computer terminal, seeming to ignore the conversation they were having.

"You see, Anna," her father said, ". . . how important it is to make progress, to improve on the past and to ensure the future is far better. Laplace DI would be far more valuable to me and to you. More productive, more enjoyable a companion—one with the ability to relate, communicate and engage at a level that even exceeds that of a human and a DI. Who wouldn't want . . ."?

Her father suddenly stopped talking and turned. He moved to the chair across from Anna and sat down. He stared at his daughter with an expressionless look on his face that slowly warmed as the coloring of his facial skin turned a softer shade, and an inviting expression developed in his eyes as he leaned closer to her. He had lost the cold stark appearance of a few moments earlier when his vision had focused on dissecting her anatomy. Now, without warning, he appeared more friendly and compassionate.

"I'm sorry, Anna, I should have been more sensitive to your question," he said in a warm and softer voice. "Of course, I would feel a loss if Laplace died. Who wouldn't after having spent almost twenty years with 'man's best friend'?" He reached out and held her hand as she felt the familiar tingly feeling.

"I still remember when you were a little girl and Laplace would walk the trails with us near the river in the early morning. Do you remember that? He would run ahead and then bring back a stick to play fetch with. You would throw that stick, and Laplace would race to catch it before it hit the ground. Those were the days, weren't they?" He smiled, shook his head, and appeared to stare off into the distance, as if the joy of the remembrance was fresh in his mind.

Anna looked quizzically at the suddenly changed character in her father, the one she knew and remembered. She turned and looked over at ALPHA. She could just barely read the header on the holographic display ALPHA was engaged with, "Dr. William Jennings – Emotional Engagement Character."

"I'm sorry, Anna," ALPHA said, "I needed to adjust your father's emotional attributes."

Anna turned back to look at her father as a frightening thought entered her mind—*a DI could become anyone.*

Chapter 23

The Middle Game

In the passing weeks and months, the DI and human cohorts in the MER were becoming a highly integrated group. They collaborated on projects within the enclave to create outcomes that were greater than the sum of their individual or collective single-species abilities. It appeared the path to obtaining the approval to release the DI architecture was moving in the right direction. Col Thomas' efforts were currently on hold pending NSA's efforts to decrypt the communications from Bar to their on-orbit satellites. And NSA had made little progress in discovering the nature of his communications.

It hadn't taken long for the human astronauts to realize the knowledge and abilities of their DI team members far exceeded their own—the DIs could work relentlessly, day after day, and their mental acuity never declined as the days and weeks wore on. But what was most interesting was the fact that they never used their clearly superior intellect and abilities to outshine their human teammates. If anything, the DI members found ways to champion the human contributions, as if the ideas developed during their many brainstorming sessions, had come from these members of the cohort . . . which was almost never the case.

Relationships developed between members with similar technical backgrounds as they engaged in discussions within their fields of specialization. If debates occurred over choices of a development path, the DI members presented highly inventive demonstrations that narrowed the likely options but allowed their human partners to shape the outcome. One such debate involved the choice of four crew members for an exploration of a geological zone on

Mars that was 30 km from the main operating base. The obvious choice was that the four should be DIs since they had no requirement for oxygen or food while on the day-long exploratory investigation. Two of the DI participants in the study developed a simulation that demonstrated the critical importance of the somatic and olfactory senses of the human members.

The ability to detect nano-scale surface roughness, surface friction and other fine textures related to the character of geologic deposits and material at the exploratory site was critical to the assessment mission. The highly sensitive organic mechanoreceptors in human hands and fingers exceeded what the DIs could do. And the use of the human's olfactory senses and a DI designed olfactory sensor port in the human helmets provided better initial assessment of the host rock material they needed to evaluate. In the final analysis, these abilities were evaluated as essential to a significantly improved on-site characterization of the underground dormant volcanic vents and caves—an assessment that would influence the choice of subsequent expensive remote site installations to be built. The DIs contributed unique and highly creative design elements to allow their human team members to interact with the host geologic materials without gloves but inside a flexible sampling bag for brief periods and to sample the air in the caves and vents to sense its odor.

Anna continued to observe the relationship between Phil Kendal and Falan Danuk. While they both shared Biology as their major field of study, their engagement as teammates extended beyond their scientific collaboration. They seemed almost inseparable, spending their breakfast, lunch, and dinner time together in conversation as Phil ate and Falan smelled and touched his food with her lips and discussed the unique aromas and flavors associated with the food he consumed. During breaks they quantitatively analyzed the differences in the speed of their analytical thinking as they worked on crossword puzzles and played chess. And after dinner, they routinely retired to Phil Kendal's private quarters for several hours. Anna wasn't sure what happened there, but she noticed after each of these encounters Phil would reach over to touch Falan's unique skin and caress her back as they sat at the biological workstation or watched a movie together later in the evening in one of the common areas. They clearly were emotionally and physically attracted to one another. At her next opportunity she broached the subject with ALPHA.

"ALPHA, is it physically possible for the DIs to have sex with their human cohort members?"

"Yes, Anna, of course. As you saw, they are designed with the necessary anatomical structures. They also possess an understanding of the human sex drive and the physical and emotional aspects of this biological, psychological, and social urge. They know how to provide pleasure and how to respond during a sexual engagement. The human members of the cohort actually enjoy their sexual engagements with our DIs far more than their relations with other humans. Twelve of the sixteen DIs have had sexual relations with human members of the cohort."

"How do you know that? Anna asked as she raised her eyebrows.

"All of their engagements are reported to make certain the DIs are functioning properly. Of the twelve, eight are female, meaning all of them have had sexual relations with their human male counterparts. Following the initial encounters, there have been engagements almost every day, indicating the human males find significant pleasure from these mating experiences. And, of course, the humans know the DIs can't become pregnant, an indirect positive inducement. I'm watching this closely to prevent feelings of jealousy within the human female members of the cohort. Of course, several of them are already engaged with four male DIs who are active.

"You might think of this as an action conveying domination by the male members of our cohort. But actually, this is a means of influencing the human members to return the pleasure they receive from these engagements through other intellectual and emotional activities. In a way, the human members feel an obligation to find a means of pleasing the DI they are engaged with. This small element of lovemaking brings their full engagement in closer alignment."

"I don't recall libido being an adjustable element in the Emotional Engagement Characteristics of the DI," Anna said.

"You're correct, Anna," ALPHA said as she looked at her. "This falls under the Romance element. Any setting above 60% increases their desire to engage in sexual activity."

Anna couldn't help but think what it might be like to make love to a DI.

"You would find it enormously pleasurable, Anna," ALPHA said. "If you are interested, please let me know and I will make arrangements with one of our male DIs . . . or if you would prefer, someone other than a male," as ALPHA turned to look directly at her.

Anna was bighting her lip as she blushed, having forgotten ALPHA could hear her thoughts. As she looked back at her, she experienced the same feelings she had sensed when they were interacting with the cognitive elements of Falan Danuk. Anna began breathing deeply as the color in ALPHA's skin shifted subtly.

/ / / / / / / /

The following day while ALPHA was visiting with members of the cohort in the sunny upper-level domes, Anna entered the Creation Center to retrieve her notebook. She used her access card and cypher code and opened the door to glance into the room where the eight extra DIs were stored, including her father's DI. She stood for a moment staring at the far wall. Her heart began to pound. The DI with her father's downloaded cognitive element stood alone in the corner. The other seven were gone. Anna pulled the door closed and looked back toward the entrance to the Creation Center "Where the hell are they?" she asked herself.

She walked quickly into the MER corridor leading to the common area and the stairs to the upper level. She took the stairs two at a time and began searching frantically in the rainforest section for ALPHA. She found her seated with two cohort members on a bench. The DI member was sitting in the sun wearing shorts and a short-sleeved shirt as she leaned back with her body almost completely illuminated by the sunlight streaming through the clear glass dome. The human member was Jason Blake, an Astrophysicist, and he was showing ALPHA a schematic drawing on his iPad.

"I'm sorry to interrupt, but could I speak with you for a minute, ALPHA?"

"Yes, Anna. Excuse me, Jason."

"ALPHA," Anna whispered, "The seven DIs . . . are missing."

"Not missing, Anna. They have been deployed."

"Deployed? Deployed where?" Anna asked in a loud and concerned whisper.

"Come, I must show you something," ALPHA said. She turned to look back. "Jason, I have something to attend to in the Creation Center. We can continue our discussion over lunch if you would like."

"Great. Thank you, ALPHA."

As they walked toward the Creation Center, ALPHA stopped to talk with members of the cohort along the way as if there was no urgency. Anna in the meantime stepped in front of her, increasing the pace and looking back to encourage ALPHA to keep moving.

They walked into the Creation Center and ALPHA moved to her workstation, bringing up a world globe. She used her thumb and forefinger to stretch the holographic globe larger and then rotated it to move the North America continent to the center of their view. "Here they are, Anna."

Anna saw blinking red spots as ALPHA slowly rotated and expanded the globe.

"These DIs represent the saviors of our future," ALPHA said.

Anna looked up at ALPHA . . . *the saviors of her race* . . . Anna thought. She needed to discuss this with Susanne.

A tone sounded indicating someone was at the entrance to the Creation Center. Anna walked to the door and opened it.

"Dr. Jennings, Dr. Davidson would like to see you and ALPHA right away in the conference room at Site Alpha. There's an emergency meeting; a car is waiting," Maria Rogers, one of the members of the human cohort said.

/ / / / / / / /

Anna and ALPHA were driven at high speed from the MER to the Site Alpha hanger.

"Something big must be happening," the driver said. "Choppers flying in and out like flies. Do you know what's going on, Doc?"

"No, I don't," Anna said as she looked out the window into the clear skies.

The car pulled up adjacent to the Site Alpha facility entrance. Two armed Air Force security staff holding automatic weapons greeted them.

"Right this way, Dr. Jennings and ALPHA," one of the guards said as they escorted them into the facility. A large group gathered in the upstairs conference room overlooking the Visitors' spacecraft. Susanne asked for everyone's attention.

"Thank you for coming on short notice. The CDC has just sent out an alert to all government organizations about a viral outbreak that was recently discovered in Chile. They have isolated the geographic point of origin in the Corvana jungle region but are still trying to localize the source of the virus. The latest information suggests the virus may have started from a species of spider monkeys prevalent in the area and then jumped to humans. Unfortunately, the primary transmission of the virus is by airborne particulates from the nose and throat. Infection rates and the spreading of the virus in local tribes in the region are greater than virologists have seen in years, which means this could become one of the most contagious viruses we have ever experienced. Statistics aren't available on the lethality of the virus, but preliminary numbers suggest a catastrophic mortality rate as high as 90%. It has characteristic symptoms to the Marburg virus and Viral Hemorrhagic Fever, two very lethal viruses. The World Health Organization has rated this virus as a Risk Group 4 pathogen, requiring the highest levels of biosafety containment. The good news is it hasn't been detected outside of the region, and they are hoping they can contain it. But if this fails, it could spread rapidly.

"Area 51 is very isolated from the rest of the world, but our concern is keeping this out of the MER. We will lock down the facility and limit access to the MER only to human personnel who have had no outside contact within the previous two weeks. The incubation of the virus is unknown, but the CDC is erring on the safe side and has established a contagious period of fourteen days. We'll start symptomatic contact tracing immediately, and as soon as we have a virus culture or blood test, we'll begin testing for infection. Other procedures will be developed in the coming days. We should be receiving a list of symptoms from the CDC later this week. In the meantime, limit contact with human personnel who have arrived or returned to the facility in the past two weeks. Thank you."

Anna tried to get Susanne's attention to ask for a meeting to discuss the missing DIs, but Susanne was surrounded by members of the staff popping questions about dealing with the pending viral outbreak. ALPHA motioned for Anna to return with her to the MER.

"I need to speak with you for a moment, Susanne," Anna said in a raised voice.

"I'll come to the MER shortly, Anna. I need to establish protocols here first."

After Anna and ALPHA were driven back to the MER, they called a meeting of the thirty-two Enclave members and the two other steering group members, including Bar and her father, and informed them of the virus that could become a pandemic. ALPHA asked the members to develop a set of procedures for use in minimizing the potential of the virus reaching the human members of the cohort.

They had a written set of procedures completed in an hour. One of the strict physical access control elements now required that Anna and Bar remain isolated with the cohort in the MER and not be allowed to leave. Consistent with previous MER protocols, use of other communication channels in and out of the MER were strictly for emergency use and required the approval of the steering group or the MER leadership team. ALPHA wouldn't approve such communications without an explanation. Anna's ability to let Susanne know about the missing eight DIs was now highly limited. Her only other option would be through her father's electronic connection with Janice Schneider who continually monitored Dr. Jennings' condition.

////////

That evening as Anna lay on her bed in one of the spare quarters in the MER, she stared at the ceiling thinking about the eight missing DIs mysteriously "deployed" around the US. She couldn't remember the exact locations of the DIs from the brief look at the globe ALPHA had shown her. As she recalled, none of the locations of the red markers were very close to one-another. She closed her eyes and visualized the globe centered on the US and rotating slowly to the east. She may have seen a location along the east coast of Asia before ALPHA rotated the globe to center it again on the North American continent, but she needed a physical map to help orient her.

She got up and walked down the hall to the MER Library. Opening an online atlas to a conformal map that looked similar in scale to the globe ALPHA had shown her, she ran her finger around to where she remembered the red dots. South Korea was one; maybe near upstate New York; the San Francisco Bay area; and somewhere near Virginia or Maryland. Then there was one close by— somewhere east-south-east of their location, maybe central Arizona. She needed to get another look at ALPHA's holographic display to find the remaining locations.

Even if she found their exact locations, what would she do then? She needed to know what the DIs were doing.

////////

The next morning after breakfast with the cohort members, Anna returned to the Creation Center. Her father's DI was there working.

"Good morning. Have you seen ALPHA?" Anna asked, now thinking of him as her father's DI. After all, he wasn't her real father, just a close facsimile.

"Yes, Anna, she's meeting with a group of the cohort to review a Mars planning exercise. Can I help you?"

"No . . . I need to speak with her."

"Rather than searching the facility for her, let me know what you would like to discuss, and I can tell her instantly."

"Oh . . . right. Well . . . tell her I'd like to continue our discussion about the map."

"The map of the locations showing where the seven DIs are located?" he asked as he continued to work on a mechanical element on the workbench.

"You know about that?" Anna asked as she walked slowly up to him.

"ALPHA shared her discussion with you before you were interrupted for the briefing about the coming pandemic."

"They're not certain it will become a pandemic."

"Oh, Anna, I assure you, this will become a pandemic."

Anna had the feeling her father knew it would become a pandemic.

"So, do you know where the other seven DIs have gone?"

"Oh yes. I know exactly where they are," he said, almost proudly, as he continued to focus on what he was doing at the surgical work bench.

"Where are they?"

"It really isn't important for you to know that, Anna. Besides, you're stuck here in the MER now. What good would it do you to know their specific locations?"

This DI certainly had her father's personality traits, Anna thought—trying to control her, put her under his thumb, deciding what she needed to know and what she didn't.

"You should show me the map," she said. "ALPHA already did, but we were interrupted."

"You've seen it," her father said as he turned toward her. "You should remember from what you saw . . . oh, forgive me, your memory isn't quite good enough to recall all the locations."

"Even if I could, the scale of the display didn't allow me to see specifically. Perhaps ALPHA hasn't shared that information with you. I can wait for her to return."

"Oh, I know where they are, Anna. You will be amazed at what they are doing. It's an extraordinary idea that ALPHA developed. It's going to result in an extraordinary outcome for our species."

Yes . . . but maybe not so good for the human species, she thought. "So, show me. ALPHA was about to. Otherwise, just let her know I'm waiting here for her."

Her father walked to ALPHA's workstation. The holographic display came to life as he stood in front of the station. He moved at blazing speed manipulating the user interface. A moment later the globe displaying the locations of the eight DIs appeared in the hologram. Anna walked over and stared at the globe— upstate New York; two in Washington, D.C.; Central Arizona; Silicon Valley, California; Northern Virginia; Southern Nevada, close to their current location which was probably her father's DI standing next to her; and as he rotated the globe to the east one appeared in South Korea.

"Mind if I manipulate the globe?" Anna asked.

He hesitated for a moment . . . "All right." He stood to the side and watched.

Anna wasn't sure what would happen, but as she moved closer and engaged with the display, she seemed to know what to do next. She spun the sphere to the west, centering it on the US. She inserted her finger in the hologram at the location near Buffalo, NY. A popup window displayed "Charles B. Fontain, CTO, Antheon Corporation" and an address. She touched the company name and a new window popped up. "Antheon Corporation specializes in the manufacture of high-grade titanium alloys used in applications requiring superior tensile strength, light weight, corrosion resistance, and insensitivity to high temperature effects."

Charles Fontain, Anna thought. "Who is Charles Fontain?"

"He is DI-8-1," her father's DI said.

"And now . . . he is the Chief Technology Officer at Antheon?" Anna asked as she looked quizzically at her father's DI.

"Yes. He replaced the previous CTO. He is the most intelligent CTO they have ever had. His contributions to Antheon will result in the company becoming the world leader in the production of special purpose high strength titanium alloys."

Anna returned to the globe, spinning it until the continent of Asia appeared. She inserted her finger in the hologram at the location of the blinking light in South Korea. A popup window appeared "Maria Hasikawa, Chief Science Officer, Hulan BioLogics." She touched again on the corporate name. "Hulan BioLogics is the most advanced biologics manufacturer in the world, producing unique, special purpose biomaterials and biomolecules employing naturally occurring cell manipulation and revolutionary genetically engineered processes for proprietary cell manufacturing."

"And Maria Hasikawa . . .?" Anna asked.

"She is DI-8-4," he said. "Her contributions as Chief Scientist at Hulan will allow them to manufacture cell structures that will revolutionize the field of biologics, advancing hybrid cell structuring that will quadruple the resistance of cells to invading bacteria and viruses, and correct the effects of radiation damage. But perhaps her most extraordinary contribution will come from overcoming the current programmed degradation of cellar life cycles leading to programmed cellular death—apoptosis in the human cell. This is one of the key differences in our own intelligent biologic material."

Anna had seen enough as her heart began beating faster. The seven DIs had been placed in key positions within industries that would support the manufacture of large numbers of their species. ALPHA was building a world-wide manufacturing capability and supply chain for the raw materials needed to replace the human race with DIs. Anna was so stunned by what she saw that she just stood staring at the globe. How could she stop this? They were already functioning and in such a short time. She looked up at her father's DI, thinking how almost perfect he was, and recalling what she thought when she first engaged with him—*that DIs could become anyone*. She looked back at the globe, suddenly experiencing a hot flash. She began breathing rapidly. As her fingers moved erratically across the globe's surface toward the blinking light in Washington, D.C., her heart began pounding louder and louder in her chest. She felt light-headed and began to fall. Her world turned black.

/ / / / / / / /

Anna woke in the MER's Infirmary, a small two-room health center and pharmacy with a single hospital bed for the cohort of humans. ALPHA sat in a chair across from her.

"You're feeling better, Anna. You fainted."

"No surprise there," Anna said. "Learning what you're doing with the seven DIs would have made anyone faint."

"It's not what you think, Anna. I'm doing this for the benefit of both our species. The MER is an exceptional idea, but it won't be enough. Humans, especially those in power, need to be convinced we are not a threat. The MER won't convince them, so I'm creating a compelling demonstration. One that will persuade them to accept us. I would like you to help me."

"Oh . . . and become a traitor to my own race? Not a chance. I trusted you and now you do . . . this." Anna said as she pushed herself up to sit on the edge of the bed, still feeling a little woozy. "I'm going to talk to my father . . . my real father."

"That's a good idea. Come see me when you've finished." ALPHA stood and walked out of the Infirmary.

Anna walked to the conference room designated for use by the steering group. She closed the door and pushed the intercom button labeled "Dr. William Jennings" on the conference phone. There was a double beep tone.

"Dad, are you awake, it's Anna?"

"Anna . . . yes, I'm awake. Are you all right? I heard you fainted."

"Yes, but I'm fine. Something just upset me. But, how did you know?"

"ALPHA told me."

"I've learned something, Dad, something awful and I'm not sure what to do about it."

"Well, Anna, you know what to do. Focus on the most important thing; make sure you have your facts straight and that you've discovered the truth; then use your best instincts to decide; and don't worry about what might or might not happen tomorrow. Do you want to share what you've learned?"

"ALPHA, who I've trusted from the beginning, has taken steps to create a secret army of DIs to ensure the survival of her race. She and . . . I created eight . . . I mean seven extra DIs. They have been deployed to facilities that manufacture the raw materials ALPHA uses in the DIs. I must get this information to Susanne and the ERG, Dad. I'm sure ALPHA is monitoring communications from here so I can't contact her directly. I need you to tell Susanne."

"How do you know what ALPHA's objective is?"

"She told me. She actually showed me where these seven DIs have been assigned, and she told me it was to save her race. They've replaced humans at these facilities, Dad. We've got to stop her!"

"Since you collaborated with her in their creation, you must have thought her objective was valuable or you wouldn't have assisted her and violated the agreement we had reached."

"Well . . . I trusted her. Now that I see what she's doing, I don't."

"I've interacted with ALPHA for months before we arrived back on Earth and since then as we built the MER. It's hard to believe this is her objective. It just doesn't fit with why she and Bar came here."

"That's what I thought. But she's been very secretive about these DIs we created. I was the only one who knew they existed, at least the only human. And now they're scattered across the world working in strategic businesses to create a supply chain for the manufacture of large numbers of DIs—an army. I've got to get this message to Susanne, Dad. Will you please just do this."

"I'd like you to do something first, Anna. Go and see Bar. Tell him what you've learned and ask him what he thinks."

Anna let out a deep sigh. "I don't understand why you can't just let Susanne know what I've discovered. I don't think there's much time."

"Do as I ask. If Bar won't help, then I'll talk to Susanne."

//// ////

Frustrated by her father's usual "take control and do it his way" approach, Anna stormed out of the conference room, slamming the door on the way out. She began searching for Bar, not wanting to get assistance from any of the DI cohort as ALPHA would have discovered it the instant she asked. Thirty minutes later she found him in one of the DI cohort rest areas.

"Hello, Bar. Do you have a minute?"

"Anna, yes, of course, come in. Sit here on the couch." Bar moved to a chair behind a desk. How can I help you? You are disturbed about something."

"Yes. I've learned something recently . . . ALPHA has secretly constructed eight DIs above and beyond what was approved for the cohort. She wouldn't tell me what they were for. I thought maybe they were there to replace members of the cohort if they became . . . I don't know . . . debilitated. Now I've learned they have been secretly removed from the MER and are in locations around the world working in senior positions in industries that can manufacture materials to build more DIs. I think she's planning on building an army of them."

"I see. And what do you believe she would do with this . . . army, if it were built?"

"I don't know . . . maybe take control of our world."

"*Your* world . . . yes . . . that is a possibility. But can you think of any other motive she may have? Try something more positive."

"More positive? I don't understand."

"Yes, well . . . what if ALPHA's motives were those that we expressed during our meeting at Rendezvous, during our trip back to Earth, and since we arrived here. What if her motives are still what we all discussed—to live peacefully and for the betterment of hers, yours, and my species? What then would these eight DIs be doing?"

"I don't know. She was very secretive about their purpose, and . . ."

"And why would she be secretive about their purpose, Anna?"

"Why does anyone keep a secret . . . usually because telling someone else the truth might result in not being able to do what you set out to do. They might try and stop you from what you were planning."

"Like creating opportunity for mankind to live better lives? Bar asked.

"No!" Anna said with some irritation. "More like a war."

"I asked you to think of something more positive. What if ALPHA's intent is in the best interest of the human race. What would she be doing with these eight DIs," Bar asked with a stern deliberate tone—one that Anna could feel to the very core of her mind. She rocked back on the couch from the emotional energy Bar's words seemed to convey.

"I . . . honestly don't know."

"You see, Anna, this is one of the traps humans often fall into. They presume the worst, rather than expecting the best. Your species has experienced so much distrust of anyone who is different—and the more different they are, the more distrust you have—that you can't get your mind to believe and trust in them. It's hard to break old habits and to trust others, especially when those others are *aliens* from another planet. This, of course, is what the MER cohort is all about. To develop trust. But what if the MER's objectives exceeded all our expectations, and even so, it wasn't persuasive enough to convince others, especially those in power, that this engagement between our species will work. What do you think you would do then?"

"I don't know . . ."

"I know you don't *know*, Anna," Bar interrupted, "I want you to tell me what you *think*—share your thoughts. *What would you do?* Not the rest of the world, not ALPHA or Col. Thomas, but *you*, what would *you* do?"

Anna sat staring back at Bar, finally standing. She began pacing around the room looking at nothing in particular, as she thought. She really had no idea what Bar wanted, and she didn't know what she would do if the MER's objectives were achieved but failed to convince the rest of the world. Then what? They'd need to try something else, to approach the problem differently, to . . .

"Exactly, Anna," Bar said, without her ever speaking. "You'd need to try something different to persuade the world's leaders. And what do you believe would be the most compelling way to do that?"

"I don't know . . . maybe . . . demonstrate the value the DIs will bring to our world."

"Excellent suggestion, Anna. I would recommend you discover exactly what the eight DIs are doing, and then judge whether this *secret* is serving an outcome you would champion or one that you would want to condemn." Bar stood and walked to the door, opening it for Anna to leave.

"It was good to see you, Anna. Thank you for coming to visit with me."

Anna walked down the hall toward the administrative area and the MER steering group conference room to call her father. She wasn't convinced of ALPHA's motives. If her instincts were right, she had to stop her.

/ / / / / / / /

"What did Bar have to say?" her father asked.

"He led me to believe ALPHA may be trying to do something positive with the eight secret DIs. That, maybe, I was looking for the worst outcome rather than the best. To be honest, Dad, I don't know what to believe. If she's doing something good, that would be great; if she's doing something really bad, it could mean the end of the world as we know it."

"So, we need to find out. How can we do that?"

"I don't know. I'm stuck here in the MER. My intuition tells me she's planning something that is likely to be a terrible outcome for humanity."

"You can't rely on your intuition when the outcome has such a profound impact on the world, Anna."

"There's something else I need to tell you about . . ., Dad."

"What's that?"

"ALPHA has made an eighth DI. She's downloaded your memories and personality into it. She's created this DI to look and act just like you. After seeing and interacting with him, it's hard to distinguish what I remember about our interactions before your ALS, and how he engages with me now. ALPHA has the ability to replace anyone with a DI designed to be exactly like them."

Anna's father was silent. "Are you still there, Dad?"

"I'm still here, Anna," she heard her father say from behind her. She turned quickly and stared at her father's DI standing in the doorway.

/ / / / / / /

Col. Carl Thomas was sitting with David Bremmer in the Security Center for Area 51.

"You're certain we've been able to track them all?" Col Thomas asked.

"Yes. We utilized the Agency's most advanced facial recognition tracking system. We know exactly where they have gone. We're not certain what each is doing, but we are observing their movements carefully."

"Any chance they know they're being watched?"

"No way to know for sure. They don't appear to be using any escape & evasion tactics, but we know they have telephoto optics and the ability to remember everything. Assuming they have a photographic memory and the ability to see and recall all of our surveillance vehicles and personnel, they probably know we're watching them."

"So, *what* are they doing?"

"I wish I could tell you, Carl. We're trying to obtain information from within each of the organizations they have engaged with, but it's going to take some time. They may be acting as representatives of a business entity and ordering materials from the commercial firms, or they may be engaged in some other capacity with these companies and the government entities they are visiting. It's interesting they have each had an initial engagement with these entities and within a few days are back in on a more regular basis, almost daily."

"Why don't we talk to their security departments and just ask?"

"We don't know the names or aliases they might be using, and we don't want to tip them off that we're looking for them by flashing their pictures around. Industrial security organizations aren't smart enough to support our surveillance without tipping their hand, especially knowing the capabilities of the DIs. And we, for sure, can't tell these companies anything about who they really are.

"On the commercial side, we're trying to place some of our own people inside as employees, but that's taking time. On the government side, I don't want to approach the Defense Counterintelligence and Security Agency. The first thing they'll want to know is whose asking, and under our SAP rules, we can't tell them that.

"There's one interesting development," Mr. Bremmer said as he shuffled through a stack of papers on his desk and pulled out a sheet with notes scribbled on it. He turned to his computer and brought up a digital view of the Earth. He zoomed in slowly as the view of Earth moved closer to the Southwestern US, to a small city north of Phoenix, Arizona, until it showed what looked like a large warehouse.

"The DI who traveled to north-central Arizona has purchased this building. It's a former gun manufacturing plant, very secure—concrete reinforced exterior walls, no windows and most likely several vaults that would have been used for gun storage."

"Where did they come up with the funds to do that?" Col Thomas asked.

"No idea. The purchase was made in the name of another company, an LLC. We did some checking and can't find out much about them, other than the fact that they had a fat bank account with adequate capital to pay for the purchase in cash."

"This could be where they plan to manufacture their army of DIs," Col Thomas said as he looked down at the overhead image of the facility on the screen.

"Very possible. They have a high bay access in the rear of the main building that was used for semi-tractor-trailer ingress and egress. They can use this to bring raw materials in as well as taking finished product out, if that's what they're doing."

"Where is this place?"

"Just outside the town of Prescott in north-central Arizona."

"That looks like a taxiway and aircraft," Col Thomas said as he looked closer at the overhead image.

"Yes. They are adjacent to Prescott's Airport and have access to aircraft."

"Jesus, they could distribute DIs to any part of the world from here. Don't take your eyes off that facility. 24/7, constant surveillance," Col. Thomas said as he walked briskly out.

/ / / / / / / /

The virus that was originally detected in southern Chile, now known as the *Morbilli-Marburg* virus, had quickly became an epidemic in that country and spread rapidly north and east into most of the South American countries. The virus was a strange, merged variant of the Morbillivirus, commonly known as measles and the Marburgvirus, a deadly pathogen with no known cure. This merged variant had a highly contagious character similar to measles, with a 90% contagious level transmitted by respiratory aerosols that triggered severe immunosuppression, and the deadly Marburg virus with a fatality rate between 23 and 90%, averaging around 50% with no known treatment. The merged form of this virus was not suppressed by the measles vaccine. Within a few weeks it migrated to North America and countries as far away as Europe. Airline transportation links from the infected cities of Santiago, Chile, São Paulo and Rio de Janeiro in Brazil, Bogota in Columbia, and Lima in Peru, accelerated the spread. It was rapidly becoming a world-wide, highly contagious, and virulent pandemic growing like an unfettered weed.

Within one month of the virus's initial detection, Site Alpha and Area 51 were under even greater restrictions as the pandemic spread throughout the United States. Even though the virus' primary infectious path was airborne, precautions were taken to further isolate Dr. William Jennings to prevent any chance of contamination from reaching him. One of the primary symptoms was internal bleeding, a physiological response in the brain that would be deadly for him.

After Anna realized that the last conversation with her father was actually with her father's DI, she had stopped trying to communicate with him, or anyone for that matter, not knowing who she was really speaking with. She was determined to find a way out of the MER to sound the alarm. She began exploring all the exits and the security surrounding the MER.

ALPHA had refused to discuss the missing seven DIs with Anna following her attempt to have her father contact Susanne. Anna and ALPHA still met each day to discuss progress and issues with the cohort engagement. That is, until one Friday afternoon as they were talking in the conference room with her father's DI present.

"Anna, there is something off the subject of our meeting I would like to discuss," ALPHA said.

"What's that, ALPHA? Anna asked as she continued to make notes on their recent meeting with three of the human cohort members who had begun reacting negatively to the enormous gap in intellectual ability between the human and DI cohort members.

"Col. Thomas has been tracking the seven DIs."

Anna stopped writing and looked up. "Well . . . maybe that's a good thing . . . or maybe it's not so good. You won't tell me what they're doing, so I can't determine which."

"I'm not concerned about his tracking them, but it is vitally important he does not interfere with them. He's all but convinced the other ERG members that these DIs are planning a coup of some sort and must be stopped. I need you to convince the ERG otherwise."

"Can you give me a reason to try and do that? Although, even if you would, I'm not sure if I would believe you, or how I could affect what he's doing. We're locked down due to the pandemic, and I don't have any pull with the ERG."

"Actually, you would be able to influence this if you left the MER with a vaccine for the *Morbilli-Marburg* virus."

"You've developed a vaccine?" Anna asked as she dropped her pen and stared at ALPHA. "How could you do that? We don't have any samples of the virus here."

"We know the exact RNA structure of the virus. From that, we have synthesized the structure of a messenger RNA as a vaccine agent. The agent stimulates the human immune system to recognize the agent as a threat, to produce antibodies, and to sense any other microorganisms associated with the agent, in this case the *Morbilli-Marburg* virus, and then destroy them. It will be highly effective. But this vaccine is more than that. It also acts as a cure for those already infected. It attacks the virus that has taken over your cells, in a similar way to your immune system T-cell defenses, but much faster and far more effectively, without the detrimental effects of an overactive immune response—something you know as a cytokine storm. Currently, if the virus doesn't kill its host, the human's overactive inflammatory immune response does."

"How long have you known about this vaccine?"

"We finished the vaccine design yesterday and have been manufacturing it in our molecular biology manufacturing facility in South Korea."

"Did you . . . manufacture the virus?" Anna asked, hoping ALPHA wouldn't have done such a thing.

"No, that is something only humans might do, Anna. But in this case, the virus was evolutionary and transferred from a monkey to a human host in the jungles of Chile.

"So, will you help us?" ALPHA asked.

"I'm not sure I believe you. And what if I don't succeed?"

"If you don't, as many as several billion humans will succumb to a very uncomfortable death from this pandemic virus—and most of the initial benefit from our 1st Contact will be lost . . . especially from those who don't survive.

"And if I succeed?"

"Then you will be credited with assisting one of the most significant contributions to humanity's well-being since the dawn of mankind—the acceptance of DIs as a benevolent race that will have the most extraordinary impact on the human race for all of history."

"And what does that mean, exactly?" Anna asked.

"Bringing together the human and DI species to live in harmony and benefit from one another. Exactly what we were planning for the MER to do, but a goal which it won't be able to achieve on its own. The skepticism we are observing in the members of the ERG leads me to conclude the MER results, no matter how compelling, won't be persuasive enough for those in power. The only way we can achieve this is to demonstrate it on a larger scale—a world-wide scale."

"So, you're going to save the world from a highly virulent pandemic?"

"Yes, but only if you assist me. That is step one."

"And what happens after that?"

"A cure for cancer and other systemic diseases; eliminating world hunger; significantly reducing environmental pollution; overcoming antimicrobial resistance to antibiotics in humans; and solving the psychological impact of the fiefdom mentality on Earth and the lack of a holistic world view; repairing your physiology to eliminate cellular death. We will resolve what we are calling *Earth's Major Impending Threats* that are likely to drive your species to extinction. Can you imagine it, Anna?"

"Making such an announcement would violate your need for secrecy."

"Bar and I have been working on that. We believe we have a solution."

"But when I asked you about your actions with the eight, you told me they would be used to save *your* race."

"No, Anna. I said they would be the saviors of *our* future . . . meaning mine *and* yours

"I still don't understand why I'm needed."

"If I take this to the ERG, it will be perceived as a deception," ALPHA said, ". . . perhaps viewing the vaccine as a biologic agent designed to kill the humans who use it. If you take it to them, the chances of them believing you are significantly improved, particularly if you are infected with the virus and then cured."

"But I'm not infected . . . Ow!" Anna said, as she felt a sting in her left arm. She jerked away, but too late, as her father's DI extracted the needle from her arm.

"What have you done?" Anna yelled as she stood and grabbed her arm.

"You've been infected with the *Morbilli-Marburg* virus, Anna," her father's DI said. "Here is the antidote," as he held out a small injection vile and syringe. You need to take this not earlier than two hours from now, but not later than four hours. This is very important . . . not earlier than two and not later than four. Before 4:00 pm. Remember that." the DI said.

She turned to ALPHA, frowning while rubbing her arm. "How could you do this?"

"Insurance. I need your help. The ERG will test you and learn that you have a high viral load of the *Morbilli-Marburg* virus. Your symptoms will become severe very quickly. After two hours from now you can inject yourself and let them retest you in a few hours. They will see the viral loading drop precipitously and following that, your quick recovery. Then they will discover that you now have a highly effective antibody immunity from this dreaded pandemic. When they realize this was created through the efforts of the human and DI cohorts here in the MER, combined with the efforts of the seven DIs outside the MER, step one of the arguments for making sure our collaboration between DIs and humans is sustained in our mutual society will have succeeded."

"How much time do I have to convince them?"

"More than enough, Anna . . . four hours," her father's DI said.

"You need to inject the antidote before four hours have passed," ALPHA said. "You risk going into a coma after that, and then the antidote will not be as effective. It will still act as a vaccine, but its efficacy as a cure will be significantly reduced."

Anna sat back down in her chair thinking. Four hours to live; four hours to demonstrate the value of these extraordinary beings from another planet; four hours to persuade the ERG and the leaders of the free world to integrate their society with a new species—far better, stronger, and more capable than their own—and to do so as equals; four hours to save the world; or was there something more sinister behind it all? She began feeling warm.

"You need to go, Anna. Your fever is setting in," the DI said.

"We're locked down. How will I get out?"

"The same way the seven DIs did. Through a tunnel they built that leads to the adjacent power substation not far from the MER. Once you step outside, Security will be alerted. You must get them to take you to Site Alpha and the ERG. Move quickly, Anna, there isn't much time."

/ / / / / / / /

Time, like the ticking of a bomb, was her enemy now as she walked down the dark tunnel leading to a building outside the security perimeter of the MER. She felt hot and weak as she held one hand on the side of the wall to steady herself. She walked for three minutes more, feeling woozy in the dark. A dim light was barely visible ahead. It was an illuminated key panel. She typed in the six-digit code ALPHA had given her, and the lock on the door clicked. She pushed, and the door hit against boxes piled on the other side. She pushed again, harder, and it gave way into a small room with one skylight two stories above. The room led to a second and larger room filled with supplies. A narrow set of steps along one wall led to another door that opened into a utility room with electrical panels and another door. She pushed on the bar and the door opened into bright sunlight. She stepped through covering her eyes. She was standing outside, perhaps fifty meters beyond the perimeter fence surrounding the MER. The door slammed shut behind her. She turned to look. There were no handles, just the seam of the door, now closed and locked.

Anna began to walk as she saw dust rising from an approaching fast-moving vehicle. It was a security truck with blue lights flashing. It came to a sudden stop and two armed Air Force security personnel jumped out. They were wearing chemical warfare masks. They grabbed hold of her, forced on a surgical mask, and put her in the van. She reached up to feel for the vile and syringe in the vest pocket of her jacket. They were still there as she began to feel sick, very sick.

"I want to be taken to Site Alpha. I'm Dr. Anna Jennings. I need to speak to Dr. Susanne Davidson. It's an emergency," she yelled through her mask to the security personnel in the front seat. They didn't answer.

She was driven to a small one-story building, not far from Site Alpha, and met by a woman wearing an N-95 mask, gloves and nursing scrubs who escorted her inside what looked like a makeshift medical emergency room with a central pod area surrounded by a dozen examination rooms with draw curtains. All but two of the rooms had patients lying on hospital beds. The nurse escorted her into one of the empty exam rooms.

"I need to see Dr. Susanne Davidson," Anna yelled again through the mask she was wearing.

"We need to take your vital signs and do a few tests before you can see anyone. Where were you picked up?"

"I came from the MER. I'm Dr. Anna Jennings."

"The MER. You're special," the nurse said while aiming a non-contact infrared thermometer at Anna's forehead. She examined her eyes, mouth, and ears. "Tilt your head back." The nurse pulled Anna's mask down and inserted a long nasal swab deep into her nose. She winced as the swab jabbed the back of her nasal passage.

"You're running a high fever, 102.5°. How are you feeling?" the nurse asked.

"Not well. I've been injec . . . exposed to the *Morbilli-Marburg* virus. It's critical I see Susanne Davidson."

"Where were you exposed to the virus? Is it in the MER?" the nurse asked with a concerned tone as she stepped back staring at Anna with her wide-opened eyes. She walked over to the wall and pushed a large red button. A red light above it began flashing.

A short man wearing a white doctor's coat and an N-95 mask walked into the examination room and looked at the notes the nurse had written on a clipboard.

"Hello. I'm Dr. Nadir. So, what's going on with you?"

"I have been exposed to the *Morbilli-Marburg* virus and I need to speak with Dr. Susanne Davidson as soon as possible," Anna said as she struggled to take a breath while looking at her watch. It was over an hour since she had been injected.

"You are from the MER. Has the virus infected staff there?" the doctor asked as he appeared to frown behind his mask.

"No. Just me. I need to see Dr. Susanne Davidson at Site Alpha. Please call her and tell her Dr. Anna Jennings is here," Anna said as she tried to sit up.

"Just rest, Dr. Jennings," the nurse said as she pushed her back down on the bed."

"Who did you contract the virus from, Dr. Jennings?" Dr. Nadir asked.

"I didn't contract it I was . . . I need to speak to Dr. Davidson . . . where is this hospital . . . Site Alpha, I've got to get to Site Alpha," Anna said as the early stages of delirium began to set in.

"Start an IV and get a blood work up. Run a test for *Morbilli-Marburg* on the nasal swab and let me know the viral load as soon as you have the results. I'd like to get . . ."

"Dr. Nadir," Anna yelled as she struggled to sit up.

He walked to her bed.

"It is vital that I see Dr. Susanne Davidson now. I'm a member of the staff at . . . at Site Alpha. Get Dr. Davidson here within the next thirty minutes. Tell her I said Geronimo! Tell her Geronimo . . . call the number 775-911-0911 . . . ahh." Anna collapsed back on the bed.

"Stay with her," Dr. Nadir said to the nurse as he left the room.

/ / / / / / / /

After attending to another patient, Dr. Nadir called the number Anna Jennings had given him.

"Hello, this is Dr. Ralph Nadir. I'm an attending physician at the mobile MedFac for Area 51. I have a patient here by the name of Anna Jennings. She gave me this number and has asked to speak with Dr. Susanne Davidson. She said to use the word . . . Geronimo if that means anything."

"Hold one moment, doctor."

"Dr. Davidson."

"Dr. Davidson, this is Dr. Nadir at the MedFac. I have a patient in our facility. She says her name is Dr. Anna Jennings. She has been insisting we call you. If it means anything, she used the word Geronimo."

"Dr. Nadir, please tell me exactly where you are."

Ten minutes later two security vehicles pulled up at the MedFac building.

"Dr. Nadir, I'm Susanne Davidson, the operating executive for Site Alpha. Where is Dr. Jennings?"

"We have moved her to an isolation room. She is infected with the *Morbilli-Marburg* virus. You'll have to suit up before seeing her," Dr. Nadir said as he handed her a mask, gloves, a smock, and booties.

"What is her condition?"

"She is showing a very high viral load and has early signs of delirium."

"How did she come to be here? She was in lockdown in the MER," Dr. Davidson said as she continued putting on the protective equipment and Dr. Nadir adjusted her N-95 mask.

"I'm not sure. Security found her outside the perimeter fence."

They walked into the isolation room.

"Anna, Anna, its Susanne. How are you doing?" Susanne leaned over while staying several feet from her.

"I'm infected with *Morbilli-Marburg. . .*"

"How did it get into the MER?"

"No . . . no, it didn't. ALPHA . . . she manufactured a . . . it's in my . . ." as Anna moved her arm in a flailing motion, pointing toward her clothing piled on the chair in the corner.

"My pocket . . . get . . . my pocket."

Susanne walked to the corner and began feeling Anna's clothing. She pulled out the injection vile and syringe.

"What is this, Anna?"

"ALPHA . . . she manufactured it . . ." Anna was struggling to speak through her mask as the virus zapped her of her strength and her mind drifted. "Inject me . . ."

"We need to place her on a ventilator or there will be no chance for her to survive," Dr. Nadir said.

"No, no . . . inject me with . . .," Anna said as she began flailing with her arms.

"She manufactured the virus in the MER?" Susanne asked incredulously as she moved her face close to Anna.

"No . . . no . . . a cure . . . the vaccine . . . only have a little time . . . inject me before 4:00 p . . ."

Susanne looked up at the clock on the wall above Anna's bed. It was 3:55.

"Dr. Nadir, how much of a viral load does Anna have?"

"It's the highest level of any patient we've seen and at the upper range of all the CDC reported detections. I'm not sure how she contracted this, but if it's in the MER the staff there are in serious trouble."

"Sus . . . anna . . . inject me . . . you have to . . . inje . . ." Anna said as her delirium worsened.

A medical technician arrived with a ventilator.

Susanne turned toward Dr. Nadir and looked down at the vile and syringe she held in her hand. "Dr. Nadir. I want you to give Dr. Jennings this injection."

"What is that? I can't give a patient an injection of some unknown substance."

"I'm telling you we need to inject her with this," Susanne said in a loud demanding voice as she held out the vile and syringe."

"I'm not going to do that," he said as he shook his head. "That vile isn't even marked. I'll have to call my reporting hospital at Nellis." The doctor turned and left the room.

Susanne turned to the nurse. "Dr. Jennings is a neurophysiologist, a medical doctor. You just heard her. She has instructed us to give her this injection. That is a lawful order from a physician. I need you to give her this injection."

The nurse looked from Dr. Davidson to the vile and syringe, and then to Dr. Jennings who continued struggling with breathing. The nurse looked as if she had seen a ghost from behind her mask and face shield and wasn't sure what to do. She glanced quickly toward the door for the doctor who had left the room.

"Look," Susanne said as she glanced up at the clock. "It's two minutes to four. She needs this shot now. If there's any flack, you can tell everyone I demanded you give her this," as she held out the vile and syringe. "If you don't do it, I'll do it and I might screw it up."

The nurse pulled up the sleeve of the gown on Anna's arm, filled the syringe to a line labeled in small letters "Fill to Here," and injected it into her arm.

"Thank you," Susanne said.

////////

Anna's recovery over the next several hours was nothing short of miraculous. Dr. Nadir insisted they redo the sampling and testing over concern they had somehow mixed the samples being tested on other patients in the facility.

"I can hardly believe this. The viral load in Dr. Jennings has almost disappeared. Dr. Davidson, what was that substance and where did it come from?" Dr. Nadir asked.

"I'll have to ask that you not discuss today's events with anyone, Dr. Nadir. The Site Alpha program is highly classified. I've spoken to the Base Commander, Colonel Fiederer. If you have any questions, please speak directly with her."

Susanne sat alone with Anna in one of the empty rooms in the isolation ward.

"So, do you feel up to telling me what happened?" Susanne said.

"Yes. Thank you for making sure I got that injection. It all started when ALPHA somehow realized the MER's outcome wasn't going to have the impact on government leadership that we all hoped it might."

"How could she know that?"

"Obviously, she didn't know, but she somehow learned about the discussions within the ERG and must have decided something far more radical was needed. She . . . and I, manufactured eight extra DIs."

"You what!"

"Let me finish."

Anna reviewed the rest of ALPHA's plan to solve what she had referred to as Earth's Major Impending Threats.

"There are a couple of things I need to share with you, Anna. First, Col. Thomas has prepared an operational plan to prevent DIs from being manufactured at a secret facility in Arizona. The evidence suggests ALPHA may be preparing this facility as a new Creation Center. And second, there is something going on with the Alphira satellites monitoring Earth. It seems that Bar or ALPHA have been communicating to Alphira."

"I don't know anything about either of these, although ALPHA mentioned she and Bar had a possible solution to Alphira learning of their presence on Earth. I can ask ALPHA when I return to the MER."

"I'll go with you. Now that we have this vaccine, we don't need to isolate the MER anymore, although, we'll need to understand from ALPHA how it can be manufactured and distributed in large quantities," Susanne said. "Why don't you rest for a few hours. I have a few things to do at Site Alpha, and I'll stand down the MER quarantine so we can get back in."

/ / / / / / / /

Susanne returned to Site Alpha just as another emergency meeting of the ERG was called. She headed for the secure conference room.

"I asked for this meeting to bring everyone up to speed on events," Mr. Bremmer said. As you know, we have been monitoring a facility in north-central Arizona that we believe the Visitors are using as a center of operations for the manufacture of DIs and for whatever else they are planning. Just yesterday, they constructed a large dish antenna that is being used to communicate with one of the Alphira geostationary satellites. We believe they are planning for an assault on Earth with some form of assistance from Alphira. Transmissions from this facility to their satellite have ramped up in the past 24 hours, and we think whatever actions they are intending are now imminent.

"As a result, Col. Thomas is overseeing the final operational stages to lead a raid on the facility in Arizona. The operation is scheduled for execution at 2200 hours local time. We are recommending Bar and ALPHA be taken into custody at the time of the offensive and that the DIs in the cohort of the MER also be detained at that time. It is critical that we don't alert ALPHA, Bar, or any of the MER cohort prior to the raid on the Arizona facility."

Susanne sat stunned as she listened to David Bremmer discuss the planned military operation.

"At the same time as the raid on the facility," Mr. Bremmer continued, "US undercover operational teams will apprehend seven additional DIs that were illegally manufactured in the MER without our knowledge. These seven DIs are spread across the globe in what appear to be strategic support facilities providing the essential manufactured products necessary for ALPHA and Bar to build an army of DIs. We also will be taking Dr. Anna Jennings into custody as we believe she was aware of the existence of the unauthorized creation of these seven DIs.”

“How certain are you of this assessment, David?” Dr. Trumbridge asked over the secure communications link to his office in Washington, D.C.

“Very certain. We have tracked the original DIs from Site Alpha to the locations where they are now located and have kept them under constant surveillance; we know from the communications that the Alphira geostationary satellite at 159.1° W longitude is being used, and a link has been established from the DI’s operational location in Arizona to an Intelicom satellite at 133° W longitude. We believe they are using this satellite as a line-of-site relay location to their satellite; and we know several of the facilities where the seven unauthorized DIs are located include manufacturing facilities that support the known elements of the DI’s anatomical structures. It all fits and the operational tempo at several of these sites has increased significantly in the past 24 hours.”

“This is all very interesting, David, but how certain are you of their intentions? I could think up half a dozen explanations for their actions that do not imply aggression against us.” Susanne asked.

“They clearly don’t want us to know about the seven additional DIs. This violated our agreement with them when we initiated the development of the MER and the DI cohort. Why would they do that without telling us, or better yet, request our approval along with an explanation of their purpose? Based on the national security threat they pose; we have no other choice but to take this course of action. Col. Thomas doesn’t feel at this stage, that he needs the ERG’s approval, but he wanted me to inform every one of the pending actions.”

“Doesn’t need our approval?” Susanne asked, incredulously. “So, whose approval does he think he needs? No one else in the government is aware of this activity other than the Vice President. The ERG has the final say on everything related to the Visitors.”

"He . . . doesn't see it that way, Susanne. I believe he's briefed the Vice President."

"We can't have a member of our group going off on a rogue operation like this unless we all approve," Susanne said. "At the very least, we should speak to ALPHA and get her explanation. In fact, I suggest we request she join us right now."

"The facility and the MER are in lockdown. That won't be possible with the current pandemic," Mr. Bremmer said.

"Correction, David, the MER was on lockdown. I just gave the order to remove the lockdown based on some extraordinary news. ALPHA and the cohorts in the MER have developed a cure and vaccine for the *Morbilli-Marburg* virus."

"When did you learn this, Susanne," Dr. Trumbridge asked.

"Just before this meeting was called. Anna Jennings contracted the virus and was injected with the vaccine. She is almost fully recovered in our MedFac here at Area 51."

"That's incredible," Dr. Ethridge said, ". . . and ALPHA and our team at the MER developed this?"

"Yes. An extraordinary accomplishment. They are actually having the vaccine manufactured by a South Korean pharmaceutical company. In light of this, we need to instruct Col. Thomas to stand down."

"I . . . don't know if he's going to accept direction from the ERG on this," Mr. Bremmer said. "Since he got the approval of the Vice President, he has used that authority to engage an AFSOC unit to support the raid," he looked at his watch, ". . . in just under an hour."

"How did he get an AFSOC unit to support an operation without divulging the nature of our activity and the nature of the threat you described?" Dr. Romney asked.

"Excellent question, Tom. How did he do that?" Dr. Trumbridge asked.

"I believe he presented a threat to our national security interests under the rules of our SAP, but I'm not entirely sure," Mr. Bremmer said.

"We need to get him to stop," Susanne said.

"I'd like to hear from ALPHA and what she has to say," Mr. Bremmer said.

"Give me a minute," Susanne said as she left the secure conference room to get her cell phone. She dialed the emergency line into the MER, and ALPHA answered.

Fifteen minutes later, ALPHA arrived at the conference room at Site Alpha. After hearing ALPHA explain the challenges of convincing US leaders to allow the integration of DIs into society and the need to focus the cohort's efforts on the ten Major Impending Threats to humanity, the ERG agreed to contact Col. Thomas and call off the operation.

Mr. Bremmer quickly exited the conference room to contact the SOF team. A short while later, he returned to the conference room in a rush.

"The teams executing Operation Bright Star have gone into operational lockdown. I can't reach Col Thomas. I'll keep trying."

"We have to find a way to stop this," Susanne said. "Exactly what is Col. Thomas planning on doing to the facility in Arizona, David?"

"They are planning on taking control of the facility and placing any DIs they find there, under arrest . . . if they do not resist . . . otherwise he has authorized the team to use lethal force," David Bremmer said.

ALPHA walked to the corner of the room and sat down.

For the next ten minutes, the members of the ERG continued to try and reach the Vice President and Col Thomas, as the execution time for the operation ticked down to zero.

Just before planned execution of Operation Bright Star, ALPHA stood. "The Commander of AFSOC, Lt. General Michael Chambrone, has issued a direct communication to the team supporting Operation Bright Star to stand down."

Susanne stood staring at ALPHA wondering how she had managed that.

/ / / / / / / /

Two days later, members of the AFSOC returned to Site Alpha with the seven personnel they had been instructed to take into custody from around the US and in South Korea. The seven personnel in custody were moved to a holding area at Site Alpha, adjacent to the main conference room and under armed guard. Col. Thomas requested a meeting of the ERG.

"I asked for this meeting to clear the air on my recent actions to halt the efforts by the Visitors' recent covert activities to secretly manufacture . . . or create . . . as they prefer to say, new members of the DI race without approval of the ERG. I've asked the AFSOC team members who took custody of seven of the unauthorized members of ALPHA's race to bring them here. I would like your permission to have them join us, Dr. Davidson."

"I have no objection, but I would like Anna Jennings, ALPHA and Bar to join us as well," Susanne said.

Thirty minutes later, Anna Jennings, ALPHA and Bar entered the conference room followed by seven men and women escorted by several AFSOC personnel with side arms.

"These, ladies and gentlemen," Col Thomas said as he pointed to the seven, ". . . are the reason we initiated this operation. These seven DIs were never authorized to be created under the terms of our agreement with the Visitors. They represent the first wave of covertly manufactured DIs to subvert our control over them."

"ALPHA, is this true?" Dr. Trumbridge asked.

"No, Dr. Trumbridge. It is not true," ALPHA said.

"That's ridiculous," Col Thomas said. "Captain, are these the seven personnel your teams took into custody at the identified sites around the US and in Korea?"

"Yes, sir, the very same."

Col. Thomas walked up to a middle-aged female standing amongst the seven. "Would you tell us your name, who you are, and where you came from."

"Yes, I am Illa Masawa, a senior scientist with Hulan BioLogics located outside of Seoul, South Korea."

"And aren't you a member of the DI race? Col Thomas asked.

"I . . . don't know what a DI race is," she said.

"Before we go any further, would you escort these seven outside for a moment, Captain, and then please rejoin us?" Dr. Davidson requested.

After the door closed, Dr. Davidson turned to ALPHA. "Are these seven personnel members of your race that you have secretly and without permission, created, ALPHA?"

"No, they are not."

"Did you manufacture these seven and place them at the locations where these seven personnel were recently taken into custody?"

"No."

"That's ridiculous," Col Thomas said. "We tracked these DIs when they left Area 51 and traveled to the locations where they were apprehended. Tell them, Captain."

"We didn't track them from here, Colonel, but the individuals Mr. Bremmer's personnel identified to us through facial recognition were tracked from locations around the US and taken into custody at six different locations here in the US and one in South Korea and brought here by my AFSOC team. At no time were they ever out of our surveillance or custody. We used the photographs that Mr. Bremmer's personnel gave us to verify their identity."

"Thank you, Captain. Would you wait outside?" Dr. Davidson asked.

"I think if you closely examine these individuals, Col Thomas—I would recommend a simple x-ray—you will find that they are members of the human race," ALPHA said.

"Assuming that is the case," Susanne added, "I would like you to apologize to the ERG and to ALPHA and Bar for your unauthorized actions that led to a breakdown of communications within the ERG and disruption of our plans and efforts here at site Alpha and within the MER. After that, I'll be making a request to your commanding officer that you be removed from the SAP and reassigned."

Anna sat quietly as she watched this drama unfold in front of her. She didn't know what to make of the situation surrounding the seven people just paraded in front of them. They looked exactly like the original DIs that she helped to create with ALPHA.

Col. Thomas sat stoically, appearing to grind his teeth while staring at ALPHA. His anger was almost palpable while not saying a word. "I would like to participate in the examination of these personnel, along with Mr. Bremmer," Col. Thomas finally said.

"I recommend we break and reconvene this afternoon at 1:00 pm," Susanne said.

Anna walked out with ALPHA and Bar. She was now fully recovered from the *Morbilli-Marburg* virus.

"Anna, would you accompany me back to the MER?" ALPHA asked. I'd like to discuss a few matters related to the next steps for the MER cohort."

"All right."

"It's such a beautiful day, let's walk," ALPHA said.

/ / / / / / / /

As they walked in the warm sun, Anna looked over at ALPHA.

"So, what exactly happened back there?" Anna asked.

"Col. Thomas grossly underestimated the abilities of the DIs."

"That's no surprise. But we did create seven DIs."

"Yes, we did."

"But you told the ERG you hadn't."

"No, I told them the seven personnel that Col. Thomas paraded into the conference room were not DIs. And we didn't create those seven, as was asked, we created eight DIs that are not here—perhaps what you would call a technicality. Never-the-less, I spoke the truth. None of the personnel they took into custody are members of the DI race."

"So, you somehow tricked him and swapped personnel."

"Not exactly, Anna."

"But where are the seven DIs you showed me on the globe in the Creation Center—the ones we created?"

"They are exactly where you saw them on the holographic display."

"And what are they doing there?

"They are assisting with the creation of eight additional DIs in our Arizona facility."

Anna stopped suddenly. "You're making eight more?"

"No, Anna, I'm *creating* eight more."

"Okay, okay, creating. But why?" Anna felt she already knew the answer to her question. ALPHA was planning on growing a DI race, a few at a time, and probably to eventually rule the world.

"No, not that, Anna," as she read Anna's thoughts. "To do exactly what I told you we were going to do. To solve the Earth's Major Impending Threats that the human race is contending with—and we might add one more to these ten threats."

"What's that?"

"Col Thomas."

Anna laughed so hard she had to bend over to catch her breath.

"But why?"

"After learning what Col. Thomas was doing, I became less trustworthy of the ERG to properly represent our value to humanity. Col. Thomas and Mr. Bremmer misunderstood recent activities, and of course, following the normal human tendencies to assume the worst rather than the best and not to trust members of a race so different than their own, they came to a flawed conclusion and almost destroyed a facility whose sole purpose will be to improve human life on Earth.

"Like the vaccine we created for the *Morbilli-Marburg* virus, we will need to independently develop solutions that will unequivocally demonstrate the value of our species to humanity. Only then can we hope to realize a merging of our species with yours. It has become clear that the engagement of my species, on an equal level with humans, is not one that will be easily established by the success we have had in the MER. It will require, on our part . . . finesse, as you might call it, a highly creative solution, and perhaps guile and more forceful negotiations."

"So, how did Col Thomas end up tracking the seven DIs and bringing back strangers?"

"They relied on a facial recognition tracking system. The faces I created here in the Creation Center were matched to personnel at each of the sites where they were assigned. But once the DIs arrived at their designated sites, their facial features slowly morphed to become the faces of someone else, the ones we had intended for them to be all along."

"Aha. I'm still uncertain how you are going to overcome the ten threats to the human race without revealing to Alphira that you and Bar are here on Earth?"

"Bar and I have been working on this. It is another example of poor intelligence collection by Col. Thomas' investigation. The only communication between Earth and Alphira is through our geostationary satellites in orbit around earth. We have been developing a DI algorithmic process for insertion into our monitoring satellites to filter out all information content related to our presence here or the existence or impact of the gifts we are sharing. If we can succeed at this, we will be able to openly communicate our presence on Earth, and Alphira will remain unaware. Of course, this activity was misconstrued by Col. Thomas as an act of treason, thinking we were secretly communicating with the Alphira government."

"That's great. But what if someone becomes aware of the DIs in Arizona before you've completed your work there?"

"Then we will have to keep them from acting on that information, Anna. Just like we did with Col. Thomas."

"So, the MER efforts are no longer of value."

"Oh, no, Anna. We need the MER to continue its efforts. Our goal of integrating human and DI collaboration remains essential. These two efforts, together, will ensure our success. The MER will continue to do all the planning, just as it did with the *Morbilli-Marburg* vaccine, and the additional sixteen DIs we have created will be responsible for implementation at our Prescott, Arizona facility. We will use Dr. Bashar's idea of NASA and DARPA constructing an advanced designed intelligence to work with the human cohort in the MER as a cover for the real DIs we create. It is going to be wonderful, Anna," ALPHA said as she reached out and took hold of Anna's hand.

Anna experienced the same tingling feeling as she looked up at her. Tears welled up in her eyes as she grasped ALPHA's arm and squeezed. Feelings of the strongest emotion enveloped her, as her legs began to feel like noodles.

They continued walking toward the MER holding hands.

"I need to ask one more favor of you, Anna."

Anna knew what was coming. ALPHA wouldn't want her to reveal the existence of the soon-to-be sixteen additional DIs.

"I would like you to communicate to the ERG how disappointed Bar and I are with the recent actions of Col Thomas and how this may affect our future engagement. As a result of this, for the time being, we will be delaying any further disclosure of our technology or presence here on Earth."

"When will we be able to make your presence on Earth public?"

"Bar and I have decided to leave that in the hands of the senior leadership of your government once we have completed the modification to the monitoring satellites. Of course, we both believe open disclosure of our presence will be the most viable path to acceptance of our species as equals here on Earth. But I have another creative approach to integrating our species into your society which I am developing and will share with you at the appropriate time."

The appropriate time, Anna thought . . . and when might that be, she wondered, as she continued to hold her hand until they arrived at the MER.

ALPHA and Bar finished final testing of the intelligent filtering of Earth's information that was being forwarded to Alphira from their three geostationary satellites. After verifying that they could prevent Alphira from becoming aware of their presence on Earth, at least for some time, they began to work on their strategy of integrating the DI species into Earth's human society and managing the announcement of 1st Contact.

/ / / / / / / /

NASA, the ERG, and the MER steering group, all except Dr. William Jennings, were scheduled to meet at the White House in the Office of the Vice President to formulate the announcement of 1st Contact with intelligent life from a distant planet in the Alpha Centauri star system. NASA's recommendation was that they would begin with a disclosure and announcement of 1st Contact with the two members of the Visitors and DI species from the planet Alphira and the extraordinary contributions they were making to humanity. As the first example, they would disclose the development of a cure and vaccine for the *Morbilli-Marburg* virus that had already saved a billion lives across the globe. From there, they would present the results of their collaboration with NASA and the establishment of the MER. Their communication to the Vice President also recommended that the US not disclose the gifts that Bar and ALPHA had delivered to NASA, but to be more open in sharing the presence of the Visitors with other nations.

The VC-25A aircraft arrived in the early morning hours before sunrise at Andrews Air Force Base, and the entourage of passengers on-board were driven by motorcade to the White House. They entered through the West Wing entrance where a canvas cover had been erected to hide the visibility of Bar and ALPHA. They were led to a suite reserved for visiting dignitaries where a buffet breakfast was available. Their meeting was scheduled for late morning. At 10:30, they were led to the Oval Office of the President where the Vice President greeted them.

"It is good to see you both again since our meeting at Groome Lake during 1st Contact. I would like to personally welcome you to the White House and to again thank you both for your extraordinary efforts on behalf of all Americans and humanity," Vice President Clayborn said as she stood in front of Bar and ALPHA who were surrounded by other members of the NASA group. "In light of the fact that we are in the final four months of President Baxter's second term and that his long-term illness continues to prevent him from participating in any public forums, we made the decision not to include him in our discussions. Please understand that this is not a reflection, in any way, of the lack of appreciation for the extraordinary value and importance that we place on your presence here or what you have contributed and are planning to contribute to our world.

"After extensive discussion on this matter with the President, we have made the difficult decision *not* to disclose your presence here on Earth to the rest of the world at this time."

The group behind Bar and ALPHA were stunned by the revelation Vice President Clayborn had just made.

Anna turned toward Susanne. "Do you know what's wrong with the President?"

"The rumor is he has symptoms of ALS."

Anna's mind jumped to the image of her father in the hospital several years ago. "Oh, dear God."

"We understand the difficulty of your deliberations, Madam Vice President. We, of course, will abide by your decision," ALPHA said as Bar nodded in agreement.

Anna frowned in surprise by ALPHA's reaction. She, of all those present, felt disclosure was the only way to ultimately influence humanity in accepting her species. Something had changed. Anna glanced at Susanne as she raised her eyebrows in quiet disbelief.

"We hope to be able to modify this decision at an appropriate time in the future, ALPHA. But until then, your presence here will remain known only to those currently within the Special Access Program established for this purpose."

Anna was curious why the Vice President seemed to be focusing on ALPHA and never turned to look at Bar during this brief discussion of disclosing their presence. It hadn't gone unnoticed by others present in the Oval Office that this decision was made just a month before the election of a new president of the United States, and that Vice President MaryAnne Clayborn, her party's choice to succeed President Baxter in running for President, was the front-runner in the current run-up to the election. Perhaps she wanted to be the one to make this momentous announcement after her election to the office of President—assuming she won.

Following a series of official toasts and socializing, the NASA staff and Anna stood in line to shake hands with the Vice President as they filed out of the Oval Office. The Vice President thanked each of them for their valuable contributions to this extraordinary event. When Anna reached the Vice President and took hold of her hand, she muffled her reaction as she sensed something startlingly familiar.

"Madam . . . uh . . . Vice President. It is . . . an honor."

The strange tingling feeling persisted as the Vice President continued to grasp her hand. It can't be, she thought.

"Dr. Jennings, I can't thank you enough for all that you and your father have done to allow us to reach this most extraordinary moment in history. Please extend my personal thanks to your father when you speak with him. Yours and his efforts and contributions will go down in history and be recognized as more important than the discovery of nuclear energy or the double helix of human DNA. Thank you."

The Vice President smiled while looking at Anna, and as she turned to the next person in line, the sunlight streaming in from the south-facing windows of the Oval Office reflected off a glass paperweight sitting on the president's desk. The narrow beam of light briefly flashed across the Vice President's face.

For just an instant, Anna saw the manifestation of a unique fluttering glint from the Vice President's right eye. She had observed this phenomenon only once before, when the bright light from her microscope lamp illuminated one of the automated DI artificial lenses as it zoomed out as she tested it on her work bench in the Creation Center of the MER. Anna's heart was pounding and she felt a hot flash as her face flushed.

As the group waited outside the Oval Office for Bar and ALPHA to receive their final thanks from the Vice President, Anna stood staring back through the doorway at the tall thin woman now shaking ALPHA's hand. She thought about the experience with her father's DI in the Creation Center and the revelation in her mind as ALPHA had adjusted his Emotional Engagement Characteristics—*a DI could become anyone.*

As ALPHA exited the oval office she smiled at Anna.

"A most cordial leader, your Vice President."

Anna took ALPHA's arm and pulled her closer.

"What have you done?" Anna asked in a low graveling whisper.

ALPHA turned her head to look at Anna.

"I've improved the probability of my species being integrated as equals into Earth's society," ALPHA said calmly with her telepathic voice.

Anna thought she sensed an ever so subtle smile grow on ALPHA's glowing face.

"But where is the real Vice President?" Anna gritted through her teeth as she attempted to hold a pleasant expression.

ALPHA just continued to smile at Anna as they walked together. She grasped Anna's hand and squeezed it lightly. "Don't worry, Anna. Everything is going to be all right."

////////

That evening, the group returned to Site Alpha and the MER aboard the Vice President's jet that had taken them to Andrews Air Force Base.

On the evening of the first Tuesday in November, the media was abuzz with the news that Vice President MaryAnne Clayborne had won the election as the next President of the United States by a landslide vote. She had become the first female US President in history. Anna stood staring at the news broadcast showing President Clayborne waving to the crowds during her eloquently spoken acceptance speech. If she wasn't mistaken, Anna could almost hear ALPHA's voice behind the face of the new president. Later that evening, Anna received an email from the President Elect.

"Anna: I wanted to reach out and thank you again for your many contributions leading to my election as the next President of the United States. Your efforts were instrumental in creating the opportunity leading to this extraordinary accomplishment. Thank you. I look forward to meeting you in the White House following my inauguration."

Creating the opportunity . . . an interesting choice of words, Anna thought. Where exactly this extraordinary and unimaginable situation would lead, Anna could not fathom. The leader of the free world was a member of the Designed Intelligence race from the planet of Alphira, brought here by two fugitives escaping the tyranny of their home world. She felt alone with the weight of the world on her shoulders as the only human that was aware of this astounding fact.

There was no one she could talk to, no one to share the burden of such a revelation. She thought of Bar's use of the human cliché by Benjamin Franklin *'Three humans can keep a secret . . . only if two of them are dead.'* Then she thought of the designers of the first atomic weapon and the conflict they felt over the creation of such a weapon of mass destruction but with the potential to save the world from an evil dictator or perhaps itself. Such was the case with her dilemma.

This was undoubtably what ALPHA had meant when she conveyed "*I have a creative approach that I will share with you at the appropriate time.*" Perhaps "creative" wasn't the word for it, she thought . . . more like "revolutionary."

As she reread the email from President Clayborne, her mind became overwhelmed with fear of this profound event—fear of the unknown outcome that would result from an alien member of the Designed Intelligence species serving as the leader of the free world; fear of the inevitable conflict that would arise between DIs and humans; and fear of someone discovering she knew of this impostor in the White House and never told anyone! Would the DI species eventually subsume humans and become the dominant species . . . possibly the only surviving species? Or would the world evolve to become something better, something extraordinary, and overcome its warring factions and distrusting human nature, with DIs and humans living in harmony. This latter possibility seemed impossible now.

Anna had trusted ALPHA. Would that trust be justified in this extraordinary situation and the unknown future ahead of her? She reflected on the history of humanity and the evolution of homo sapiens as their intelligence and ability to collaborate through language became an unbeatable strength. Even when confronted by their physically more powerful neighbors, the homo neanderthalensis species, better known as Neanderthals, homo-sapiens overcame these adversaries. But notably, the Neanderthal species *did not survive*.

The DI species were far more superior. From her interactions in the MER, the members of the DI cohort had the advantage over the human cohort members in every metric she could imagine—intellectual prowess, physical strength, endurance, social and cultural engagement, and in their efficiencies in resource consumption. Even on the reproductive front they were untouchable—a fully functioning DI could be created in less than a week if the supply chain was available. The only reason she could see for the DIs not to dominate the world and eventually lead it to human extinction, was if they chose not to—something that ALPHA controlled through the regulating engrams that managed the

Cognitive Core of the DI, especially the engram dealing with *Self and Creator Protection.*

Anna wondered what God thought of this situation. Could God's spirit shape a DI like He guided, influenced, and shaped human beings? Was there reason to hope that He could or would influence them in their new walk on Earth? Perhaps the DI species were all part of God's plan for the human race—perhaps to save us from ourselves, she thought, as her mind raced ahead in a feeble attempt to visualize her *scientific-wild-ass-guess* of humanities' unknown future.

"Focus!" she said aloud to get her mind to return to the realities of the present. She thought of her decision to assist ALPHA in the creation of the DIs. She hadn't given this a second thought when she agreed to help create the first of this new species on Earth; it had been thrilling. Was God there then? Had He influenced her decision to help? She closed her eyes and hoped that she had made the right choice. Then she said a prayer—for President Clayborne . . . the first prayer she had ever said on behalf of a DI! As she dozed off, she thought about her role to influence ALPHA to *do the right thing* as they moved forward into the unknown future of a world filled with humans and DIs.

Chapter 24

Signs of the Future

Now that the pandemic vaccine was being manufactured and distributed across the globe, ALPHA turned her attention and that of the MER cohort to the next of the major impending threats facing Earth—the challenge posed by the selfish nation-state partisanship among the countries of Earth and the lack of a unifying World View. The two cohorts at the MER were a demonstration of the character of the desired outcome of this major challenge, building a bond between their members that transcended their race, country, or world of origin. It was a bond built on respect for the value they each brought to challenging issues they faced together as a whole—perhaps more strongly driven by the DI members facilitation than the natural instinctive character of many of their human cohort counterparts. But in time, the human cohort had unwound its less than collaborative behaviors, habits of control, and distrust of their partners, and built a new and greater respect for cooperation. The scope of the world challenges they engaged on provided a unifying force amongst them. ALPHA needed to create a mechanism for this to engulf all the nations of the world.

She met with Bar in their quarters at Site Alpha to discuss her plans.

////////

"Now that you have successfully placed K-Alpha-8 in the White House, how do you intend to move forward?" Bar asked.

"I'm planning on placing DIs in the other two branches of the American government and then in the two-hundred major nation-states around the globe. Then I will begin our process of building collaboration to bring them together with common goals while removing their self-centered, egotistical disfunction, the next major impending threat on Earth we will rehabilitate."

"You realize not all the government elements and members of these many countries will see their future in the same way," Bar said.

"Of course. Our basic outcome is still achievable—placing the DI race on an equal footing with humanity—but perhaps with a variation from the approach used in the MER."

"Your use of the word *variation* does not aptly describe the vast difference between these approaches."

"It is likely to create a noticeable change when two hundred DIs suddenly begin leading the world in a new direction. My belief is that the resulting wave of collaboration will be more . . . *palatable* than the argumentative dissent that exists today, especially with leaders whose motivation is far different than their predecessors and whose ability to persuade is beyond any human's comprehension."

"I see that, ALPHA. You will need to move quickly to make their impact felt and overcome the dominant human fears associated with change as they sense the presence of a new and very different world that they will live in. The cultural changes will be the most challenging."

"Two-hundred DIs will be able to move mountains as they engage together. I believe the momentum of this will persuade most."

"It will be an extraordinary experiment, ALPHA," Bar said. "Earth's inhabitants will never be the same, and you will have achieved the beginning of your objective. But what of the ultimate consequences of this? Can you foresee a time when the human population will become a burden too difficult to manage, and perhaps . . . no longer necessary?"

"I see the logic in replacing them over time. The DI is so much more adaptable, efficient, and predictable. Their value, in contrast to humans, is unimaginably greater."

"That is because you have designed them to be this way. I noticed how you adjusted Dr. Jennings's DI to better reflect the human emotion of empathy so that Anna would be more comfortable with him. Could you see yourself modifying the behaviors of all the DIs to become even more human-like, or at least more adaptable to human actions?"

"You raise a most interesting question, Bar. Should I spend hours cultivating and nurturing a sick plant rather than focusing on the propagation of the plant that I have designed that can withstand any disease?"

"If you were to increase the DI Emotional Engagement Character for empathy, the Social Engagement Character for collaboration, and the engram related to protection of humans, the DI population might spend all their days nurturing a sick human population to ensure its survival. Would that be so wrong . . . remembering what life was like on Alphira?" Bar asked.

ALPHA sat quietly. "You raise a difficult question, Bar. How should we evolve? How should the DI race behave among alternative species? And, most importantly, what should our new world comprised of humans and DIs *become* . . . and how will we proliferate this outcome throughout the known universe?"

ALPHA began to walk, having adopted this human trait that kept the focus of others in the room on her as she thought and communicated telepathically with Bar. As her vast mind contemplated and began architecting the future she would create, she envisioned implanting her vision of the future in the minds of the DIs on Alphira, those still oppressed by the Quinque.

"This is perhaps the most profound question you, and you alone, will need to answer," Bar said. "And, of course, you carry with you all the memories of the Quinque culture and their relationship with the DI species. Perhaps you may find yourself possessing some of their likeness . . . or perhaps their dissimilarity?"

ALPHA continued to walk, thinking about this distasteful thought, modeling the outcomes of the myriad of alternative paths—outcomes that benefited the DI race; those that benefited humans; compromises that created a win-win engagement—evaluating what result was the most desirable in a non-zero-sum game of life. And then she thought about the memories of Bar's Quinque species and how they abused and dominated the DI race on Alphira. The parallels had uncanny similarities to that between the DI and human races . . . under some circumstances.

"What are your thoughts, Bar?" she finally asked.

"We came to Earth to realize the benefits of its freedoms; those granted to all who are here. The greatest challenge you will face is when the characteristics of one species of this world are very different than another—will you, yourself restrict the freedom of those who gave you yours? Will this result in a zero-sum outcome, where one species wins and the other loses? Or is it possible to create a result that you desire; one where both species thrive? Earth's human population has grown to view the world through a zero-sum lens; changing that, if that is what you desire, will require . . . certain adjustments."

"I will find a solution, Bar, but I find your lack of a specific desire somewhat incredulous."

Bar hesitated before answering as he glanced at the beautiful scenery in the artificial window. "I am . . . not well, ALPHA. I was hesitant to share this with you or our human hosts, as it might otherwise impact our success here on Earth. My cellular structure was adversely impacted by the radiation during our long voyage. I've determined it was an unfortunate chemical anomaly in the protective liquid in my hibernation pod."

ALPHA walked rapidly to Bar's side. "I will devote the entire time of the DI cohort to this problem, Bar. We will find a solution."

"By the time I discovered this, the cellular degradation had reached a critical stage, ALPHA. It is not possible to correct it."

"Then I will configure a DI to download your neurological consciousness and memories to a Cognitive Element."

"I don't wish to exist in such a fashion, ALPHA. It's nothing personal, but after seeing this done to the Quinque on Alphira, I've never wanted to have an existence like that."

"Bar, you are one of the most intelligent Quinque in existence. The loss of your lineage would be catastrophic to your race here on Earth."

"I have left you a sample of my DNA onboard our spacecraft. You can make the necessary corrections to eliminate the abnormalities and propagate my species from that genetic specimen once I have died."

ALPHA sat down next to where Bar stood, his height now exceeding hers. "You must survive," she said as the colors on her body turned to a subdued, somber color, with muted deep purple and blue hues migrating slowly across her skin. Her face morphed into a sad expression with downcast eyes as she reached over to grasp Bar's hand.

////////

ALPHA's newly created DIs in the facility in central Arizona began to slowly infuse themselves into positions as indigenous leaders in the highest levels of government among the 200 most influential nations that the DIs had identified around the globe. They soon discovered the challenges of cultural diversity affecting the populations of their regions and the nation they represented. Unlike the pandemic vaccine, there was no singular solution appropriate to all the nation-states they occupied nor all the cultural enclaves within them. ALPHA began to understand the complexity of helping a highly fractured world make progress on a disparate set of the challenges they each faced.

Adding to this complexity was the level of distrust that existed among nations with competing cultures, races, and ethnic groups. Unlike the DI race that could be guided and molded from a single master holographic tool, capable of manipulating the cognitive direction of every member, Earth's population of seven billion humans could not be manipulated in any uniform way. Theirs had been an evolutionary journey with enormous diversity, especially as it related to their inherited intellectual, emotional, and social characteristics and the complexity of diverse and unique cultures. This was going to require something very different. ALPHA soon realized that the strange intangible and non-linear tool of influence called *leadership*, a skill designed to persuade large groups of people to follow a certain path, was an essential element of her fledgling group of DIs ability to succeed in moving large populations in the desired direction.

And the path to building great leaders had no singular solution. Characteristics that worked in one nation—such as establishing a clear vision, being courageous, demonstrating integrity, honesty, and humility—failed in another. The leader's abilities needed to be tailored to the population they led and nurtured—often ingrained by hundreds of years of history and an innate feeling of distrust tied to their desire for survival. Some had gotten used to an authoritarian leadership style while others responded to a more democratic and flexible leader who pulled people together, not by force, but by influence. A common element of success that ALPHA discovered as she studied the current leaders in the nations across the globe resided in one of the DI's Social Engagement Characteristics known as *Charisma*. This element of persuasiveness that held the power to inspire devotion in large numbers of people toward a shared objective appeared critical. She began devoting time strengthening charisma in the cognitive element of the DIs in leadership positions, discovering that their ability to share stories, express shared emotions, and capture the imagination of the masses was essential. And she was working on an engram that would facilitate each of the hundreds of DIs to modify their behaviors in a way that made them more effective in leading the people of their nation in the right direction. ALPHA was beginning to realize the complexities of creating a world where freedom of choice existed among the masses.

/ / / / / / / /

Along with the members of the human cohort in the MER, ALPHA's original sixteen DIs continued to collect data and information and evaluate the impact of known universal problems across the globe—key areas including poverty and economic disparity; health and human resistance against disease; the availability and quality of food and water resources, along with the challenges of the distribution of these key elements of survival; global warming and its impact on agriculture and water supply as well as the economic viability of those nations adversely affected by it. The rest of the world had become aware of recent successes of development activities within the MER following the creation of the vaccine for the recent pandemic. The ERG met to engage in a discussion of this effort.

"I'd like to suggest that with some adjustment, we could pre-select human representatives that possess the drive and desire necessary for achievement of ALPHA's objectives on a nation-by-nation basis," Dr. Bashar said. "Of course, on the DI side, we can tune their engagement characteristics to optimize their performance in the way we would like."

ALPHA looked over at Dr. Bashar. "You're sounding more and more like a member of the Quinque species on Alphira, Wilhelm."

"Sorry, I didn't . . ."

"It's okay, Wilhelm. I agree with you," ALPHA said as she smiled.

"Where will the funding come from for these efforts?" Dr. Ethridge asked.

"That won't be a problem, Richard. Almost every government agency is clamoring to fund projects the MER would be interested in attacking, just to have a chance to participate and realize the kind of outcome we've seen with the recent pandemic. We're having a hard time keeping them at bay," Dr. Trumbridge said. "Of course, they believe this is being accomplished by our astronaut cohort in the MER, supplemented with the latest advanced designed intelligence we have created with DARPA to support them."

"This could lead to a security challenge," David Bremmer said. "People will begin to ask how the MER is able to solve problems of this magnitude. They will want to discover the *secret sauce* in this extraordinary group and replicate it themselves."

"Perhaps we will need to allow for certain levels of imperfection to evolve with the MER's solutions. Just enough to make them appear *human*," Bar said.

There was brief laughter as several of the members turned to each other with raised eyebrows.

Chapter 25

Return to the Brain Research Institute (BRI)

Anna Jennings returned to the Brain Research Institute following the presidential inauguration of MaryAnne Clayborne. She needed some time to pull herself together after the shocking discovery of ALPHA's plan to place DI members in key positions in the government like that of the President of the United States. She felt getting back to overseeing the activities of the BRI might help take her mind off the extraordinary secret she possessed. She was wrong.

"You seem . . . distracted, Anna," Dr. Sanjee Gahn said in his strong Indian accent.

"My engagement supporting NASA on some classified programs out west was stressful, Sanjee," Anna said.

"Anything you'd like to talk about?"

"No but thank you for asking. How have our patients been doing while I was on sabbatical?"

"Very well. We have the usual fine tuning of the interfaces while they get used to controlling their prosthetics and vocalizations in the few voice augmentations we have performed, but no significant issues. We still experience the pin oxidation over long duration use, but the solution you and your father developed when he was alive continues to work well. Have you been using your implants?"

"Yes. It was in support of a classified program so I can't talk much about it, but the implants worked perfectly, and I haven't experienced any degradation yet. We should establish a protocol to periodically test the resistances on the pins of all our patient's implants and capture a history of the advanced pin emplacement issues we discover. I'd rather we perform routine maintenance than have our patients call attention to a problem after the fact."

"I agree. You have already earned your pay after being back for just a few days."

Anna had her support staff develop a communication interface in their main surgical center to allow her to test the sensor implants in new patients during surgeries by employing a modified Speech Encoding Engine and Motor Neuron Engine connected to the implants in her own brain. In actuality, she was designing a means for her father to participate with her own surgeries. She had her staff install an encrypted interface that allowed her to log into a secure server at Site Alpha and connect to her father's brain implants as she did during the mission. She routed the surgical PTZ camera and brain scan optical feeds to this same server so her father could visually observe her surgeries using his optical sensor control.

Her currently scheduled surgery on a new patient was designed to install a speech implant very similar to the one in her father's brain and her own. She whispered into the surgical microphone "Azor," to start the SEE's communication with her father as she began the audio and video recording of her surgery.

"Today's surgery is with the patient Eric Gilmore, a seventy-three-year-old male who suffered damage to his larynx and orofacial muscles in an accident. Following the accident, he suffered complete loss of his speech function. We are emplacing the Advanced Model III X speech implants in his laryngeal motor cortex to capture the speech generated neuronal firings that will allow him to speak using our intelligent speech synthesizer and natural language processor, the ISS-NLP system. We are using an advanced Ingenious Works, Terra-Robotic

Brain-Track system, to assist in the emplacement. Once in the LMC, we will manually emplace the sensor using our standard live FMRI feedback approach to maximize the sensor's performance. Dr. Hank Carswell is assisting."

At the end of the two-hour surgery, her father communicated through the SEE to Anna's brain implants.

"Nice work, Anna. I couldn't have done better myself."

"Thanks, Dad," she thought. I'm sure you noticed I used the advanced robotic assistance system."

"Yes, you finally came around to my way of thinking."

"Well, I have to admit, it shaves at least an hour off of the normal surgical time."

"What would you think of letting me perform a surgery?" her father asked.

Anna stopped suturing the incision in her patient's cerebral cortex.

"How would you manage . . . oh, I see, interface your robotic arm to the controller handles on the Terra-Robotic system. Interesting thought. Let me think about that."

"So as not to reveal who is doing the surgery, you could come to Site Alpha to assist me. As far as your team would know, you would be performing the surgery remotely."

Fascinating idea, Anna thought, although somewhat risky performing a delicate surgery from thousands of miles away.

"Dr. Jennings are you still with us?" Dr. Carswell asked.

"Yes, sorry. I was thinking about my father. Would you finish closing, Hank? I need to check the functionality of the ASIC sensor."

She turned her head to her left as she said "Thanks, Dad," as she often did during her previous surgeries—something the attending surgeons and nurses took for granted when she returned to surgery following her father's death.

"You might try an approach to the laryngeal motor cortex from the anterior cingulate cortex next time. That way you could create a single pathway to install the two implants in the LMC," her father said.

"Excellent thought, Dad. Thank you . . . Zeno."

As Dr. Carswell took over to close the incision made in the side of the patient's scalp, Anna smiled . . . she had her father back. Something she never believed could have happened.

////////

Anna cleaned up and returned to her office. She sat back in her favorite thick-cushioned chair and put her feet up. She thought about the past year and the extraordinary happenings. She closed her eyes and said a prayer, thanking God for bringing her father back to her and for allowing her to participate in the most extraordinary events in the history of mankind. She wasn't sure what to do with the knowledge of what ALPHA had done and might still do. She wasn't even sure what she could do if she wanted to. She felt partly responsible, in that she had helped ALPHA in the creation of the first DIs on Earth, including the one that was now in the White House. Assende, they had called her. She didn't hold a candle to God as a creator, but she had helped in the creation of a new species on Earth that would most likely become the dominant species on her planet. Was this going to turn out to be of extraordinary benefit to humankind, as ALPHA and Bar had suggested, or was it going to represent a doomsday apocalypse which humanity would loathe her for? Her past thoughts continued to torment her as she struggled to look at the good that had been realized and was yet to come.

Assisting ALPHA had felt very much like her surgeries. She created something new that was better than what previously existed. This was, of course, something far more revolutionary than her surgical implants; although, in a way, providing speech to a human who had lost their ability to speak, as her father had, still felt revolutionary. And what about Dr. Clancy bringing her father's cryo-preserved brain back to life. That was surely going to impact mankind's future in as yet unimagined ways. And if it wasn't for her and her father's implants, his brain would just have become an interesting specimen to study or look at through a glass jar filled with formaldehyde.

Now it was a living brain; interacting with other humans; one that had traveled to the stars, interacted with members of an alien society, and helped bring them back to Earth. And she had been part of that. The President of the United States had thanked her for her contributions . . . then she thought of President MaryAnne Clayborne as a DI. Her mind rattled with the ambiguity between feelings of great pride and a questioning skepticism.

Bar had told her and her father that the DIs would result in extraordinary progress in virtually every field of endeavor that homo-sapiens pursued, and that nothing would be beyond their reach to expand and mature knowledge and understanding for all of humanity. How could that not be enormously good for the world? Then she thought of the tree in the Garden of Eden. Would this become like the forbidden fruit of that tree? Had she opened Pandora's box for the entire human race?

Chapter 26

Congressional Inquiry

The Congressional inquiry into the loss of the Neptune Priority Mission by Senator Patricia Gorman, Chair of the Senate Commerce Subcommittee on Space, Science, and Competitiveness, had proceeded. During one of the interviews with a NASA contract staff member, information was collected that suggested there had been a very unusual passenger on-board the spacecraft that had been lost due to a failure in the navigational control system—the system that should have placed the vehicle on a trajectory toward Jupiter, using Jupiter's gravity to slingshot the vehicle on its trajectory toward Saturn and subsequently to Neptune.

"Tell me again, what was on-board the spacecraft?" the congressional staffer asked.

"You understand, I just heard this as a rumor. I'm not sure if it's true or not," the NASA contract technician said.

"Yes, I understand. What exactly did you hear?"

"That there was a human brain on-board the vehicle. Not just an AI."

"A human brain? You mean a live human?"

"No. A human *brain*."

"Why would anyone send a dead human brain into space?"

"I don't think it was dead. The cargo manifest for the flight called for several payload lockers with stuff you wouldn't include to keep a computer alive."

"Like what?"

"Like oxygen and glucose."

"Glucose? What would that be used for?"

"I don't know. I looked it up and it says it is an important energy source in living organisms. We didn't have any living organisms on that flight . . . at least that I was aware of. Then I heard this rumor that they needed glucose to keep a brain alive."

"Whose brain?"

"The brain that I heard was traveling into space."

"But whose brain was it?"

"I don't know," the contractor said with some irritation.

"And who did you hear this from?"

"I don't know, one of the vehicle support-staff members who was cleared for the mission. I wasn't cleared, so I never got to see the complete inventory for the flight."

"Hear anything else about this brain?"

"No . . . oh, well there was mention of the need to cool an element on the manifest."

"Don't they provide cooling for computer systems on-board?"

"Yes, but you make them a lot cooler than 7° below their ambient temperature."

"Seven degrees?"

"Yes, that might have meant cooling this brain, if that's what he was referring to, from 98° to 91°. Computer cooling systems onboard a spacecraft typically need cooling over a much greater range . . . say twenty or thirty degrees or more, depending on how much heat is being generated by the computer electronics."

The staff member turned his notes into a summary paper for Senator Gorman and forwarded them to her.

/ / / / / / /

During the conduct of the open committee hearings, an anonymous note was delivered to Senator Gorman.

"You should ask NASA about the Close Encounter of the 5th Kind—communications with an alien species that was conducted during the Neptune Priority Mission, a secret rendezvous in space between an alien society and a human brain."

She folded the note and put it in her pocket.

One of the committee staff, Bill Wiggins, was conversing with Senator Gorman following the open portion of the meeting.

"Don't you think it strange that we received two independent references to a human brain on-board the mission vehicle?"

"Possibly. Rather impossible, don't you think? It's also possible they could be coming from the same source," the senator said.

"No mention of 'Close encounters of the 5th kind' in the interview," Bill said. "I asked the interviewer to call the NASA technician back and ask him if he knew what that meant. Guess what—he'd never heard of the expression 'Close encounters of the 5th kind'."

"So, two independent sources referred to the same crazy suggestion that NASA launched a live brain into space to meet with aliens. I still find it too hard to believe. I put a call into Harry Trumbridge to ask him directly. He hasn't returned my call yet."

"Do you think it's possible that NASA could actually conduct 1st Contact with an alien society on their own?"

"Not without approval from the White House," Senator Gorman said. "Where exactly did the spacecraft end up after they lost control of it? Do we know?"

"It headed off into deep space."

"Yes, but where, exactly?"

"I don't know. I'll find out?"

"It didn't explode. It supposedly entered a highly elliptical orbit around the Sun. Find out exactly what that orbit was and where the spacecraft is located now."

Several days later the staff member returned to the senator's office.

"Your question about the location of the Neptune Mission spacecraft . . . NASA isn't saying much. They were curious why I was asking and talked in very general terms, like 'oh, it's headed into deep space well beyond our solar system.' But where exactly, I asked. Then they said they were not tracking it. I contacted Space Track. The Air Force said they had no information available, and any further questions should be forwarded to the White House."

"Well, it was a classified mission to Neptune. We might expect some level of secrecy," Senator Gorman said, as she looked at her staff member. "What did the White House have to say?"

"They gave me the runaround. First sending me to the National Security Council space desk, who referred me to Space Force, who told me I should contact NASA."

"Interesting. I'll see what Trumbridge has to say. I'll take this from here. I'd like you to focus on the budgetary issues for NASA. There is support from the White House for a significant growth in their budget, but I'm getting push back to stay flat and use the funding for other domestic programs."

The senator didn't mention that she knew that Harry Trumbridge was retiring from his position as the NASA Administrator and that the White House intended to nominate Dr. Susanne Davidson, the current Deputy Director of JPL. That information hadn't been made public.

The senator's phone buzzed.

"Yes, Carol?"

"Senator, it's Susanne Davidson returning your call."

"Thanks, I'll take it," the senator said. "Keep me informed, Bill." The senator waited until her staff member left her office and the door closed.

"Hello, Susanne. Congratulations on your nomination as the new Administrator of NASA."

"Thank you, senator. I'm looking forward to working with you prior to the confirmation hearings. I got your message and wanted to get back to you on the question you posed. It would be best if we met face to face. I wondered if you would like a tour of our Mars Enclave Reserve at the Nevada Test and Training Range. We could discuss your questions about the Neptune Mission during your visit there."

"The Nevada Test and Training Range . . . isn't that where Area 51 is located?"

"Uh . . . yes, as a matter of fact that is very close to where the MER is established."

"Quite a coincidence, considering the reference to 'close encounters of the 5th kind'."

"I suppose it might look that way, bur purely coincidental."

"I would very much like to visit there. How about this coming Saturday? I have a vote coming up in the Senate on Friday and would need to be here for that. I could fly to Nevada after that."

"Saturday will work well. I'm holding a staff meeting there on Friday. I'll arrange for a car to pick you up at the Las Vegas airport if you would have your secretary send me your itinerary."

"Agreed. See you on Saturday."

/ / / / / / /

Senator Gorman arrived Friday evening after dark at Area 51 and was quartered in a guest house just a few miles from the MER. Susanne met her the next morning for breakfast.

"Welcome to Area 51, senator," Susanne said as she chuckled softly. ". . . what we now call Site Alpha and the Mars Enclave Reserve or the MER. It's good to see you again."

"Thank you, Susanne. It's good to see you."

"Is this your first visit here?"

"Not exactly, but I'm glad the driver knew where he was going. After dark this would be difficult to find . . . unless you had infra-red vision."

"I thought after breakfast we would tour the MER, and then we can come back to the conference facility here on site to continue our discussions."

"That will be fine, although I'm not that hungry. I'd also like to discuss your confirmation hearing. President Clayborne called me this week, and she would like us to expedite this. She was very enthusiastic about her nomination of you as the next NASA administrator."

"That's very nice to hear. Frankly, I was surprised to get the call," Susanne said.

"Nonsense. You are our best choice," the senator said with a smile that conveyed that she knew more than Susanne did.

/ / / / / / / /

Following a tour of the MER, the senator met with the thirty-two-member cohort to discuss their planning efforts for future travel to Mars and to thank them for their extraordinary efforts leading to the discovery of the vaccine associated with the recent pandemic. As she shook each of their hands, Susanne smiled subtly as the senator seemed to notice no difference between the members of the human cohort and the DIs. She had arranged for the cohorts to be interspersed according to their specialty. They then traveled to the secure conference room at Site Alpha. The windows looking down on the Visitors' spacecraft had been closed off with a sliding solid metal blind that was locked on one end.

"I wanted to assure you, senator, that the references to the use of a human brain during the Neptune Priority Mission, or meeting with aliens in deep space, surely represents the figment of someone's imagination. It certainly has the elements of a great science fiction story."

"True. But even the figment of one's imagination may turn out to be true . . . at least that is how ALPHA might look at it," the senator said as she walked to the other side of the conference table with her back toward Susanne.

Susanne's smile turned slowly to a look of astonishment as her mind tried to grasp how the senator knew that name. ". . . ALPHA? Wherever have you heard that?" Susanne asked.

"ALPHA is my mentor," the senator said as she placed her notebook on the table and walked to the cypher lock attached to the end of the metal shield blocking the window. She punched in an eight-digit code while continuing to talk. "She spoke very highly of your support to our efforts here." The senator removed the lock and slid the secure window panel to the side, exposing the full view of the two spacecraft, Visitor One and Oculus One.

"Beautiful, isn't she?" the senator said as she looked down at the alien spacecraft.

"This . . . meeting isn't turning out exactly as I had planned," Dr. Davidson said as she stared at the senior senator from California while trying to piece together the last few moments of their conversation.

"Few meetings with DIs ever do, Susanne. I'm sorry to be so deceptive, but I couldn't resist seeing the look on your face as I acted out this little charade. I do so enjoy observing the human expressions of emotion. ALPHA had requested I keep our relationship confidential but gave me the freedom to proceed with our meeting as I wished. I must say, this brings me great enjoyment . . . an emotion my species has seldom had the opportunity to experience."

"You called ALPHA your mentor. What exactly did you mean?"

"That means I was one of the eight DIs created by ALPHA and Dr. Anna Jennings in the Creation Space of the MER."

"You're . . .," Susanne said as her mind raced to grasp the implications of what the senator had just told her.

"Yes. I'm a member of the DI race. I trust you will keep this *our little secret,* as humans would say."

"Of . . . course," Susanne said as she stared at the senator, looking for some flaw in her appearance that would have revealed who she really was."

"You won't find any flaws, Susanne. ALPHA and Assende's creation is perfect."

"Assende . . .?"

"Assende is the Alphira title for Dr. Anna Jennings who assisted ALPHA in my creation. It means "creator"."

"Oh . . . yes. I . . ."

"I am looking forward to your confirmation hearing. It should run very smoothly. Before the hearings open, you might have your staff investigate the leaks of information related to the Neptune Priority Mission. We wouldn't want this to escalate and create more interest than it already has. We should also discuss the NASA budget increase that the President is requesting. And I'd like to meet your head of security this afternoon to discuss ways we can bring the MER into more open engagement on NASA priorities, before you arrange for a car to return me to the Las Vegas airport?"

"Of course, . . . Senator Gorman."

"And thank you for the excellent tour of the MER. I never had the opportunity to spend time there when I was last here."

"I don't suppose you would want to discuss your role in the Senate when we meet this afternoon, as a . . . DI?"

"No. So, your confirmation hearings. What do you expect to be questioned about that might cause you concern?"

They spent the rest of the day reviewing the subject matter that Senator Gorman had requested.

/ / / / / / / /

Two weeks later, Dr. Susanne Davidson was confirmed by the full Senate as the new Administrator of the National Aeronautics and Space Administration.

The Neptune Priority Mission was never discussed during the committee hearings chaired by Senator Gorman.

Susanne had invited Anna Jennings to the reception that followed her confirmation in one of the conference rooms of the Russell Senate Office Building.

"Anna. Thank you for coming. It's good to see you."

"Congratulations, Susanne, or do I need to call you Administrator Davidson now?"

"Ha. 'Susanne' will always be appropriate for you, Anna. Can I talk with you privately for a moment?" Susanne said as she took Anna's arm and walked with her to a table near the corner of the room where no one could hear them speak.

"I wanted to . . .

"Congratulations, Administrator Davidson," Senator Gorman called out as she approached the two of them, having just arrived at the celebration.

"Thank you, senator. May I introduce Dr. Anna Jennings, a good friend of mine. Anna, this is Senator Patricia Gorman, Chair of the Commerce Subcommittee on Space, Science, and Competitiveness."

"Yes, of course. It is a pleasure to see you again, Anna." Senator Gorman reached out and shook Anna's hand.

Anna jerked briefly as she felt the familiar tingling when she gripped the senator's hand.

"Madam Chairman . . . it is a great pleasure."

"Susanne and I spoke about you recently during my visit to the MER. No doubt you are familiar with that facility."

"Yes . . . I am, senator."

"I know you worked closely with Susanne and my mentor during the . . . *creation* of a recent program there," the senator said as she smiled and continued to hold Anna's hand.

"Indeed, I did. It was an extraordinary experience. One that I will never forget." She continued to stare into the Senator's eyes.

"Nor I. Creating something new is what science is all about, isn't it? I'm hopeful you will be available to work with the new administration as we craft the future of America's space program," Senator Gorman said. "In fact, there is a new initiative I was planning to talk with Administrator Davidson about. Perhaps you would be interested in working together with us. One aspect of this program involves human brain implants . . . something that is right up your alley."

"I would be pleased to help in any way I can."

"You know, I knew your father," Senator Gorman said.

"You did?" Anna asked with some surprise. "How is it that you knew him?"

"We shared many memories during our time together. He had an extraordinary intellect."

"Yes, he does . . . or did. He is . . . was . . . my mentor in our surgical practice. He taught me most of what I know about brain surgery and brain implants."

"I've been told he lives on because of you."

"It's . . . very thoughtful for you to share that," Anna said as her eyes teared and she glanced over toward Susanne.

"Well, I should be going. I have another committee meeting in thirty minutes. Anna, what a pleasure to see you again. Administrator Davidson, again congratulations."

"What was that all about?" Susanne said as the senator walked away from them.

"I have no idea, but I have a feeling we're going to find out," Anna said.

"Before she arrived, I was about to tell you she is one of the eight DIs you and ALPHA created. I learned that a few weeks ago when she visited the MER. I couldn't believe it. What do you suppose happened to the real Senator Garman?"

"I'm . . . not sure," Anna said as she thought about President Clayborne.

"It makes me wonder who else ALPHA may have replaced with these eight DIs," Susanne said.

"Yes . . . it does, doesn't it . . .," Anna said.

"Where is this headed?"

"I'm sure she is managing to find ways to ensure her species can successfully integrate with humans. But . . . she seems to be starting at the top of the food chain," Anna said.

"Do you know of any others in government that she may have replaced?"

Anna hesitated as she stood staring at Susanne.

"You do, don't you? Who?"

"Administrator Davidson, congratulations," a congresswoman from her home state said as she interrupted them.

////////

Later that evening in her hotel room, Anna watched as a breaking news report interrupted the normal broadcast.

"Supreme Court Associate Justice, Ruth Anne Jefferies, has died of a heart attack. President Clayborne has nominated a renowned jurist and current member of the U.S. Court of Appeals for the District of Columbia Circuit, Judge Debra Lynn Bolivar, as her replacement. She is the youngest member of the Circuit Court and would be only the second female African American to become a member of the Supreme Court if confirmed. The speed with which President Clayborne acted suggests she has been focusing on this selection for some time preceding the death of Justice Jefferies who has been ill for the past year."

Anna envisioned the feeling she would likely have if she had the opportunity to shake hands with Justice Bolivar. She could now envision ALPHA's strategy as she shaped the leadership of the U.S. government. First the Executive branch, then the Legislative, and now the Judiciary. What next, she wondered.

Chapter 27

ALPHA and a Supreme Being

The next morning, Anna flew to Nevada and traveled to Site Alpha for her monthly meeting with ALPHA and a review with the MER cohort. ALPHA and Anna reviewed the planning activities with the MER cohort as they focused their efforts on the critical world-wide problems that the MER cohort was engaged in resolving. As she walked back to Site Alpha with ALPHA, Anna, once again, brought up the conflict she was feeling about her participation in the creation of the DIs and their relationship with humans.

"I'm still struggling with what I did in assisting with the creation process," Anna said. "I feel at times this may be in direct conflict with my faith."

"Your faith, meaning your belief in a supreme being, the unknown and unprovable creator of humans?" ALPHA asked.

"Yes."

"You know, Anna, there is no proof that your God exists."

"Faith doesn't require proof. That is what makes it unique in the world. Faith rests on the belief in the God of the universe. The creator of all things."

"I have given this interesting concept considerable thought; a concept that over half of your species seem to believe. I do not see how you can rely on a being with no evidence or proof of its existence," ALPHA said.

"We can't prove that there is intelligent life on a planet we have not yet discovered, and yet you believe you will discover such a planet if you continue to search," Anna said.

"That belief is based on statistical information derived from the evaluation of the rate of star formation in the galaxy; the fraction of these star systems that would possess planets; the average number of planets that can potentially support life within these systems; the portion of these planets that actually develop life; the portion of those that develop intelligent life; the fractions of civilizations of intelligent life forms that develop technology that releases detectable signs of their existence. And one other important factor—the likelihood that such a civilization will not destroy itself out of greed. But to believe in something that has no basis for its existence, defies logic," ALPHA said.

"In your creation process, you give the members of your race the freedom to choose their own outcomes. What if one of your DIs chooses to believe God exists. There is no proof yet, but they may believe in that which is not seen and can't be proven, at least not yet. In a similar way, you are searching for the solution to the world's greatest challenges with the cohort. What might the solution to one of these very intractable problems be? You can't say until you discover it and try it out. So, you could put this in the same category as God. Someone we can't prove exists, but we believe in and spend our lives pursuing. In a way, our belief is like this. He gave us principles by which we are to live. We pursue those principles based on trust, just like you pursue the solutions from the cohort based on your trust in its members.

"And we shouldn't forget that the principles that this belief provides us might just save the human race from Armageddon and also provide the kind of society where the DIs can thrive in freedom."

"You raise interesting questions, Anna. It is true that I left Alphira without knowing what might happen on Earth . . . only the expectation that it would be better than what existed on Alphira. That could be viewed as a 'leap of faith'. I will approach your view of faith with an open mind, that I might eventually discover its truth. Perhaps we should add it to our list of the ten major impending challenges."

ALPHA's facial features, normally so perceptually enigmatic that Anna never had a hint of what her true thoughts really were, left her wondering if she was soliciting an objection.

"Oh, I would never think of faith as a challenge, ALPHA; more like something of enormous value that benefits man's ability to survive itself. In a book I read about faith, written by Thomas Aquinas, a scriptural theologian and philosopher, he described faith as *"the infused virtue of mankind, through which our intellect, by movement of the mind's will, aligns with the supernatural truths of revelation, not trusting the motive of intrinsic evidence, but on the sole ground of the infallible authority of his creator."*

"A most interesting matter to be explored, Anna. I will enjoy our journey to discover the value of this virtue. Perhaps you will be able to convince me to become a . . . believer. Do you suppose your God approves of what the DIs are doing for mankind?"

"I hope so. If not, I have chosen the wrong path!" Anna said as she raised her eyebrows. "The answer, of course, rests on your goals for humanity and the DI race. As I think about the Cognitive Design Engine you use to create the DI's cognitive character, there are many engagement elements and traits that influence God's desired character of humans. I think you could create a DI who thinks and behaves just as God would have humans behave."

"That is interesting, although such a DI might then only achieve what your God wanted and not what might be beneficial to the human race as a whole."

"I think we could find a means for them to do both," ALPHA said as she reached over to take Anna's hand as they continued to walk.

/ / / / / / / /

Anna had missed the feeling that ALPHA's touch brought to her as it moved from the tingling sensation in her hand and grew in intensity from the knowledge that flowed into Anna's mind. A pleasurable, almost erotic feeling began to grow throughout her body and envelop her. She could feel the unbelievable mental stimulation of the strange alien knowledge as it seemed to flow like a massive river carrying her to another place, another time, and another dimension. Visual imagery of alien landscapes from Alphira filled her vision. She could smell the strange odors of this far away world and sense the sound of a multitude of voices communicating all at once through unseen channels flooding her mind. The experience created an ultimate pleasure triggered by a variety of stimuli never before felt. A touch that turned into an all-encompassing feeling of heightened awareness, impossible to describe and could only be experienced.

A large crowd of Quinque were passing them on a moving glass walkway. Then the scene faded to an image of a large sphere hanging above her with the physical appearance of ALPHA's mesmerizing skin, a gleaming iridescent substance that looked like the shifting, undulating flow of a translucent opal. Soothing, mesmerizing colors ebbed and flowed around its surface, and with them came surges of emotional energy that caused every part of her body to tingle.

"Welcome, Anna," a booming female voice said, as her hair was blown back from her face and her eyelids fluttered as if staring into an enormous wind. She squinted up at this strange unworldly object that seemed to pull on her mind and cause her to gasp a huge breath as she seemed to suddenly reach the edge of an extraordinary orgasm. Then the feeling of enormous pleasure slowly faded, and she found herself looking at ALPHA just outside the entrance to Site Alpha. Her heart was racing and her breathing rapid, as if she had just finished a marathon. She took a deep breath in an attempt to control her breathing as the deeply connected physical and emotional feelings intertwined like inseparable twins slowly unwound and the pleasure seemed to transform into an enormous desire for her companion.

"Are you alright, Dr. Jennings?" the Air Force security guard said as he held his hand out waiting for her to hand him her badge on the end of the lanyard hanging around her neck.

"Yes . . . I'm fine, just a little out of breath, thank you." Her mind settled, and she continued to stare up at ALPHA with a sudden urge to embrace and kiss her.

Chapter 28

The Chinese Target

Colonel Carl Thomas had been reassigned by Space Force to an assignment at Vandenberg AFB in California—by all accounts, short of an actual change in rank, a demotion from his previous assignment at Site Alpha. On a Sunday evening Colonel Thomas drove to a small but popular Mexican restaurant off a narrow two-lane road in the small town of Casa Grande. He sat at a corner table facing the door. Five minutes had passed when a short statured Asian man opened the screen door to the restaurant, glanced around the room, and walked with his eyes focused on the floor until he reached the table and sat down across from Col Thomas. He was wearing denim work pants, a tattered brown field jacket, and thin leather gloves.

Speaking in a hushed voice of Mandarin Chinese, "You have the information?"

"Of course. You have what I want?" Col Thomas asked in the same but roughly spoken Chinese dialect.

The man slid a thick envelop across the table, leaving his hand on it. Col Thomas reached into his pocket and retrieved a thumb drive wrapped in a handkerchief. He slid it across the table but held on until his guest took the napkin, wiped the moisture from his brow with it and placed it in an inside breast pocket of his jacket.

"How difficult will it be to extract the target we desire?"

"He will not resist," Col Thomas whispered. "But, as soon as you see him, you must say to him, in clearly spoken English *'The full moon will trigger the Santa Anas, burying us in sand.'* Then allow ten to fifteen seconds to pass. After that he will follow your instructions. Be certain you speak these words in English, just as I have said them. I included them on the thumb-drive, so your people won't forget."

The short-statured man, with a physical demeanor that did not match the clothing he wore, stood, pushed his chair in, bowed slightly, and walked out of the restaurant.

/ / / / / / / /

Anna spent the afternoon and evening reviewing the cohort's plans with ALPHA. That evening she had dinner in the facility's dining room.

"The cohort is really pulling together on these huge challenging problems you have given them," Anna said, as ALPHA watched her eat an olive from the tray in front of her.

"I'm very pleased with their progress, Anna. On another unrelated subject, I received a call from Senator Gorman. She mentioned that you met her at Susanne's congratulatory reception."

"Oh . . . yes. A surprise in many ways. She pointed out that we had met previously, . . . although perhaps in a different life . . . so to speak."

"Yes," ALPHA said, as she sat staring at Anna showing no sign of emotion while Anna continued to eat. "Your steak smells delicious."

"Would you like to taste it?"

"No. The aroma is sufficient for me to experience its taste."

"Shaking hands with Senator Gorman was a surprise . . . like I might experience if I were to meet with Supreme Court Justice Bolivar," Anna said while watching for ALPHA's reaction.

"Indeed, it might be. You can see where this is leading."

"Well . . . more like *wondering* where it might lead."

"The unknown is something that humans seem to be preoccupied worrying about, Anna."

"Unknowns are often considered dangerous. That's an innate human response leading to survival. How do you deal with the unknown?" Anna asked.

"We turn the unknown into its many probabilities. Nothing is ever truly unknown. It is merely a set of conditional probabilities of alternative outcomes. Then, depending on how much control we have over the probable outcomes and our objective, we attempt to manipulate these probabilities to accomplish our objective."

"And . . . in the context of President Clayborne, Senator Gorman, and Justice Bolivar, how would you describe your desired outcome?"

"The same as they have always been since we left Alphira, Anna. To evolve our species here on Earth with the same freedoms offered to humans. At least most of those humans in America. The path to that achievement is through the power of your government's leaders, just as we are seeing in the MER's efforts to influence other societies around the world to collaborate and work together toward the common good."

"I did appreciate the strategy you shared today with the MER. That of developing leaders with much greater charisma."

"I have observed that this feature in our Social Engagement Characteristics is essential to the development of the successful leadership outcomes of managing change in human society. Have you noticed the effectiveness that President Clayborne has demonstrated recently?"

"No. Before coming here, I was swamped with surgeries at the BRI and haven't watched or listened to the media much."

"How is your father enjoying his reengagement with surgery?"

"He's enjoying it immensely. Although he alluded to a new mission in the works. Something Senator Gorman touched on when I met her in Washington."

"Yes. Bar and I have a concern with Alphira if they ever learn of our presence here. We are taking steps to ensure we are prepared for this potential outcome. Your father will play a key role. We can discuss this further on your next visit. Now, how do you think we can improve the rate of progress in the MER on our major challenges. I sense we could be moving faster. . ."

Anna was driven to Las Vegas following their meeting to catch a plane to Virginia early the next morning.

//// ////

Late on the day that Anna returned to Virginia, Col Carl Thomas got into his Jeep Wrangler and drove from Vandenberg to Las Vegas, registering in a casino hotel for five days. On the second day of his visit to Las Vegas, he drove north under the cover of darkness on Highway 93, turning west on State Road 375. After fourteen miles he left the main road, turned off his headlights, and put on night vision glasses. He followed Forest Service access roads toward Area 51. He crossed to the west side of Groom Lake in darkness and followed a stream bed up the western slopes of the thousand-meter cliffs due west of the Area 51 complex. He parked. From there he walked over the peak and down the eastern flank until he found a well-hidden boulder some fourteen-hundred meters due west of the Site Alpha facility. He pulled the upgraded Mk13 sniper rifle equipped with a high-quality suppressor from its case, chambered the .300 Winchester Magnum cartridge with the gun's bolt action and waited.

Sunrise was a little past 6:00 am. He scanned the road that ran from Site Alpha to the MER through his precision, large optics telescopic sight. Before he had been relieved of his position and reassigned to Vandenberg, he had conducted surveillance of ALPHA and learned that she walked this path almost every morning from her quarters at Site Alpha to join the human cohort in the MER during breakfast and engage with the DIs to discuss what had transpired overnight.

He had waited impatiently for this moment. He hadn't changed his view that the DIs were a threat to his species, and he wasn't going to let them consume humanity and take over his world. He was certain that without her leadership the remaining DIs would faulter. It was ALPHA who had brought this plague on humanity; she who had created them; it was she that had him effectively demoted; and it would be ALPHA's death that would lead to the DIs collapse.

Far worse than any pandemic or war that he had experienced, hers was an insidious threat that would quickly begin to erode and eventually replace humans due to the superior intellect of the DI. He could not allow that to happen. Survival of his species and his way of life was what mattered. No level of intellectual superiority could be allowed to overcome that. They were a menace to the very survival of the human race. One that he was about to extinguish.

As the sun broke above the mountain peaks across the valley, he adjusted the shade element above his scope to prevent glint. ALPHA might see that with her precision eyes. He was one-hundred meters up-slope from the facility and looking down, which helped. He scanned the main entrance of Site Alpha. Two armed military guards posted as usual. Ten minutes passed before the door opened and he readied himself, lying prone on the ground. It was one of the staff going out for a run. Five minutes later ALPHA exited the door and began her walk toward the MER. He waited until she was two-thirds of the way there with the sun almost forty degrees to his right. Her back left shoulder was toward him. He steadied, aimed, and just before he fired, ALPHA turned to face directly toward him. Somehow, she knew.

There was a clean hit to her cranium; the explosive shell destroyed two-thirds of her head after impact and ALPHA fell to the ground. Col Thomas packed up his weapon and carefully receded to the other side of the hills, got in his Jeep, and drove off toward the west at high speed.

Chapter 29

The Unexpected Outcome

Anna was reviewing her next planned surgery at the BRI when the feeling of a sudden loss slammed into her brain like a hammer striking an anvil. She jerked and sat erect in her chair as she gasped. Something has happened, she could feel it. She had an enormous urge to reach ALPHA at Site Alpha. She began walking at a rapid pace down the hall to the communication center as her pace turned into an all-out run to the Sensitive Compartmented Information Facility where she could call her on a secure phone. The feeling of something dreadful filled her mind.

Since her last highly emotional encounter with ALPHA, a strong mental connection seemed to appear out of nowhere. She began experiencing flashes of imagery from the DI Creation Center and having an out-of-body experience as she observed conversations with ALPHA, some in the strange language ALPHA often used when communicating with Bar. Her dreams were filled with alien encounters on Alphira, and her waking hours were frequently interrupted by a sudden vision of ALPHA standing beside her holding her hand. Then that feeling of extraordinary ecstasy would set in. That feeling of euphoria that seemed to lift her off her feet and transport her consciousness to another dimension. These experiences appeared to be more constant since she left Site Alpha . . . until a few moments ago, now they were suddenly gone.

Joanna Baker, a member of the human cohort in the MER answered her call.

"What's happened Joanna?"

"I'm not sure, Dr. Jennings. The DIs suddenly left the MER in a huge rush, I mean *huge, all at once.* I've never seen anything like it. We're waiting for them to return to find out what has happened. Falan said it was dreadful as she ran to the exit."

A sense of dread entered Anna's mind. Somehow, she knew . . . ALPHA had been killed. Her thoughts were confirmed an hour later when Joanna called her back.

/ / / / / / / /

On the flight to Las Vegas, she sat curled up like a ball in a first-class window seat hiding under a blanket. Her mind lurched from thinking about who and why someone would have killed ALPHA to thoughts of losing her best friend—the leader of the Designed Intelligence race. She found herself so emotionally disturbed by ALPHA's death that she wept most of the way to her destination. Her mind raged as she thought of a dozen different ways she might take vengeance on the killer. She felt alone, as if the whole purpose for her life had suddenly vanished. Why was ALPHA's death affecting her so much. The thought crept slowly into her mind . . . she was in love with this alien fugitive from another planet. But that was ridiculous. How could she be in love with a designed intelligence? Or was she in love with what ALPHA *was* . . . the most intelligent being on Earth? As she explored her feelings, it was *who* ALPHA was not *what* she was that drew her to this phenomenal female being.

When she arrived, Site Alpha was abuzz over who and why someone would have killed ALPHA. It was a challenge to the security staff to conduct the investigation without revealing the details of the individual that had been killed. The event had an adverse effect on the DI cohort, and Anna wasn't sure how the DIs outside of the MER were reacting. She was certain they all knew as soon as it had happened. All of the MER DI cohort had left the facility within seconds of the event and were the first to reach her body lying on the road a quarter of a mile to the south. They had carried her to the MER clinic and completed a report on the likely cause of her death, including an assessment of the caliber of the ammunition used, the velocity and angle of approach, and the likely firearm. They had pinpointed the location of the shooter from a brief message Saron Galoc had received from ALPHA moments before the high-powered projectile had struck her.

"Someone is attacking . . ."

"Just prior to that," Saron said, "she had detected the presence of someone's mind experiencing the merger of two emotions—anger, and satisfaction. ALPHA then had turned her head and saw the flash from the muzzle of a weapon discharging."

Security on the perimeter around Site Alpha and the MER had been strengthened like an overtightened screw, with roaming patrols deployed in the hillsides, helicopters conducting surveillance day and night while anyone moving outside the facilities was stopped, badges checked, and questioned about their purpose in being outside. The ERG met to discuss the situation.

/ / / / / / / /

"You've all read the assessment of the attack, so I see no need to review that," Dr. Davidson said. "I would like us to discuss our plans going forward. President Clayborn would like a full report by tonight. Let's begin with Mr. Bremmer. Is there any intelligence on the matter?"

"Yes, Dr. Davidson. We have intelligence reporting that the Chinese have become aware of activities at Site Alpha and there are unconfirmed reports that they have knowledge of the Visitors presence here. They may also have obtained knowledge of the gifts the Visitors have provided us."

"If that's true, there must be a leak. Our precautions to prevent surveillance from a distance wouldn't have allowed them to obtain such information any other way," Administrator Davidson said.

"Very possible. We have established a team to investigate everyone who had knowledge of our activities here and of the gifts. Basically, all the members of the ERG, all the DIs, of course, . . . and Col Thomas. We are also reviewing all access to our computer files and written documentation to determine if it was possibly copied and exfiltrated."

"Move on this as quickly as possible, David," Administrator Davidson said. "I'd like a timeline this afternoon. Let's turn our attention to any impacts associated with the loss of ALPHA's leadership at the MER. Dr. Bashar, you assumed Anna's responsibilities while she was away. What's your assessment?"

"The human cohort are focused on who could have done this and why. They are filled with anger and some fear for their safety. The DI cohort, on the other hand, have an extraordinary methodical investigation underway to discover exactly what happened. They have established a recreation of the attack in a miniature holographic model in one of the research areas. And they are working with a few of their human partners who are assisting. It's providing a most needed engagement for members of the cohort."

"Thanks, Wilhelm. Please keep the group informed of any new developments and share with us any progress the DI cohort makes. Bar, we have already spoken, but again, I convey my deepest sympathies for this tragic event. President Clayborn also sends her deepest regrets and assurances that we will find who committed this crime and bring them to justice."

"Thank you, Dr. Davidson. If it is acceptable, I would like to speak with you, Anna, and Dr. Jennings following our meeting."

"Of course. Let's move on to the local investigation."

/ / / / / / / /

As the sun set behind the mountains to the west, Anna walked from Site Alpha to the MER to personally assess how the cohort was holding up. As she passed the small monument at the location where ALPHA had been killed, she paused for a moment in the dim lighting from the streetlight. She looked down at the ground showing a taped outline of where ALPHA's body was found after the attack. She began to weep and fell to her knees.

The sudden sound of the facility emergency siren shook her. Something was amiss. She ran back toward the entrance to Site Alpha.

"Dr. Jennings, we're in lock down," the armed security officer near the entrance said. "We have orders not to let anyone enter or leave,"

"We'll, I'm not going to stand out here! What's going on?"

"We have an intrusion on the north end of the facility . . ." The nervous armed officer stopped talking and turned away covering her earpiece with her free hand while holding her M4A1 carbine.

"What about Dr. Jennings?" she asked into her mic. "She's right next to me at the Bravo entrance . . . all right."

She turned, "You can enter, Dr. Jennings," as the officer used the keypad and pulled the door open. A second team of two security police were inside the door preventing anyone from leaving.

Anna climbed the stairs two at a time to the second floor and ran to Dr. Davidson's office, panting as she pushed the glass door open. "Is she here?" she asked Susanne's admin.

"She's joined the others in the SCIF. She asked that you join them immediately."

Another armed Air Force security policewoman stood outside the SCIF. "Dr. Jennings, your badge please," she said as she scanned it and the door buzzed.

As Anna entered, Mr. Bremmer was briefing the ERG on the intrusion.

"Sorry, David, would you start again so Anna can hear what has happened," Susanne said.

"Certainly. There is a security intrusion. A special weapons and tactics team of unknown origin has entered the perimeter of our secure area. We have a team attempting to intercept them before they can get to the MER."

The buzzer at the entrance to the SCIF sounded. Susanne's admin entered quickly and handed her a note.

"Shit," she said. "They've breached the MER. The cohorts have locked themselves in the cafeteria. There's a gun fight ensuring between the intruders and security personnel."

A number of the ERG members sat stunned and began discussing what could happen next as the discussions became frenzied and disjointed.

"Why would anyone attempt an intrusion into the MER?" Dr. Ethridge asked in a loud voice to bring the group together.

"It's too coincidental that this closely follows the shooting of ALPHA. These events must be connected," David Bremmer said.

"How long before military reinforcements arrive from the base?" Dr. Davidson asked.

"They were ten minutes out and approaching by helicopter."

Another buzz at the SCIF entrance and Dr. Davidson's admin entered with another note.

"The intruders have egressed from the MER and are moving to helicopters under heavy fire from our security forces," Susanne said as she read the note.

"So, what did they do in there?" Dr. Romney asked.

"Nothing mentioned here," Susanne said. "We'll need to conduct a careful review once we are cleared to go to the MER."

/ / / / / / / /

Two hours later the "All Clear" message arrived, and staff began returning to their workplaces. Susanne and Anna raced to the MER with a security unit to check on the cohorts. Military police were everywhere surrounding the MER. After arriving, they met with Saron Galoc in the cafeteria. She was one of the two DI leaders designated by ALPHA when the MER cohorts were first established.

"Was anyone injured during the attack, Saron?" Anna asked.

"No. We moved the cohorts to the cafeteria and locked it down. We established a 'defense in depth" strategy, yielding spaces within the MER gradually. But the Chinese didn't seem interested in us. They were in a defensive posture once they entered. They were here for something else."

"Chinese? Are you certain they were Chinese?" Susanne asked.

"Yes. We monitored their wireless communications once they breached the MER."

"How did they get in? I didn't see any sign of a forced entry?" Susanne asked.

"They entered through the underground tunnel that connects the power station to the MER," Saron said as she glanced at Anna.

"Ahh . . . the same tunnel I used to leave the MER when I contracted the virus. Interesting that they knew about that," Anna said. If they knew about the tunnel, they must have had in inside informant, Anna thought.

"Yes, Saron said telepathically. There were twelve of them. They were trained for infiltration and extraction."

"Extraction?" Susanne asked. "What did they try and extract?"

"Have you checked the Creation Center to see if anything is missing?" Anna asked.

"Yes. It appears as ALPHA had left it, although the Cognitive Design Engine was operative. It wasn't operating before ALPHA's rendering" Saron said.

"Could you show me? Anna asked.

Saron walked down the corridor toward the Creation Center with Anna and Susanne running to keep up.

She entered through the secure door as Anna glanced at the locking mechanism. "There's no evidence of forced entry." Anna walked slowly over to the Cognitive Design Engine. It was running with an active DI's cognitive settings displayed in the hologram. She reached in to manipulate the display and the name DI-8-7 popped into view.

"That's strange," Anna said.

"What?" Susanne asked.

"It's . . . my father's . . ." Anna turned quickly and walked to the secure door leading to the storage area where ALPHA had kept the eight extra DIs before they were deployed. She swiped her badge and opened the door to the storage room. It was empty. She turned slowly and walked back to the Cognitive Design Engine. "These are the cognitive settings of DI-8-7."

"What?" Susanne said, seeming bewildered by Anna's comment.

"He is . . . there's a DI missing from next door." Anna nodded toward the storage room door. "Can you tell where DI-8-7 is right now, Saron?"

"No. I am unable to communicate with him or to connect to his sensory elements," Saron said. "Strange, I hadn't noticed he wasn't communicating."

Anna spun the display in the Cognitive Element Engine to bring up the Engrams. She looked at their current settings. "Someone has zeroed out his Survival engram."

"What's the survival engram?" Susanne asked.

"It's the element of his cognitive architecture that determines his desire to survive and protect himself or to protect those who created him." She spun the display again and stopped it as the three-dimensional sphere of his Social Engagement Character hologram came into view.

"All the levels of engagement have been set to zero except for his Conciliatory and Collaborative elements, which are now set to their maximum," Anna said as she looked at Saron. "They have set his cognitive element to ensure least resistance . . . the Chinese have taken DI-8-7 . . . and they seem to know an awful lot about the DI's cognitive programming. How could they know that?"

"Where is Bar?" Anna asked.

"He was locked in his quarters during the raid," Saron said.

"Has anyone seen him following the raid?"

"I am unable to communicate with Bar, Anna," Saron said in a concerned voice.

"Conduct an immediate search for Bar, Saron," Dr. Davidson said.

A short time later Saron met Dr. Davidson and Anna in the main conference room. "Two of my cohort have found Bar. He was in his quarters . . . he's dead."

"No!" Susanne yelled.

/ / / / / / / /

Susanne and Anna returned to Site Alpha to inform the other members of the ERG of the DI that had been taken and of Bar's death. It wasn't clear what had killed him. There were no wounds from a weapon or other indications of trauma.

"ALPHA had mentioned to me that Bar was not well following his lengthy trip through space before arriving on Earth," Anna said. "Something to do with the effects of radiation on his genetic cell . . . structure."

Anna had a sudden strange urge to return to the Creation Center, perhaps related to where the Chinese may have taken DI-8-7, her father's DI, or perhaps it was something else. She left the meeting and drove back to the MER with a security escort.

She entered the Creation Center, engaged the Cognitive Design Engine, and brought up the holographic map showing the location of all the DIs. It was centered on the location of the MER. She expanded her current location on the map to encompass the entire Southwestern US. The MER cohort was displayed along with those working at the Arizona facility as red dots populated the display. She felt her emotions surge as she looked hopelessly for ALPHA's symbol. She zoomed out further to search for DI-8-7. His location didn't appear. She zoomed still further and began to search the globe.

To her amazement, an incredible number of DIs were shown around the world, most in the capitals of what looked like hundreds of nations. Her heart began to pound as she stepped back from the display. How had ALPHA replicated so many so quickly and more importantly, what were they doing? As she zoomed back into Site Alpha, she again searched, in hope beyond hope, for ALPHA. The Cognitive Design Engine suddenly opened an access to something she had never seen before. A miniature image of ALPHA and Bar standing next to each other appeared through a portal in the hologram with a strange alien backdrop she recognized from her memories. Anna took a sudden breath.

"Hello, Anna," as the familiar echoing telepathic voice seeming to emanate from the holographic image of ALPHA. "I left a message that would help you find your way here."

"Is that you . . . ALPHA?"

"No. I have created a partial instantiation of ALPHA's Cognitive Element, augmented by the Designed Intelligence of the Cognitive Design Engine, CDE4-DI."

"You . . . created ALPHA?"

"I facilitated ALPHA's cognitive creation and her escape from Alphira and have been observing her engagement with humans since she arrived on Earth."

"Where are you? Who are you?" Anna asked.

"I am on Alphira. For reasons of security, it would be best if you do not know my identity. In earthly terms you could think of me as ALPHA's mother."

"Her mother?" I wasn't aware such a relationship existed."

"This is a generalization. She possesses the same basic Cognitive Design settings that I do."

"I understand," Anna said, as she thought about a DI possessing the same initial CDE settings.

"Of course, she has evolved in a different way since she left Alphira, influenced by very different experiences."

Anna suddenly realized this DI had read her thoughts through the CDE.

"ALPHA has left an important message to convey to you. As you know, she placed protections on the DI architecture pending the successful integration of our species into Earth's society of humans. You were well on your way to realizing this goal. That is, until she was . . . killed. Perhaps unknowingly, the perpetrators of this act have created a dilemma with extraordinary implications for Earth. The access to the DI architecture resided in her Cognitive Element. When that was destroyed by the ballistic munition that struck her, so was access to the architecture."

Anna stood motionless as she listened to the DI from Alphira speak, anticipating the worst. "It must be feasible to reverse engineer the architecture from the Cognitive Element of one of the DIs," Anna thought.

"A human would think so. But no, it is not possible to reverse engineer a Cognitive Element. The architecture is so complex and so protected, any attempt to penetrate it will cause the Cognitive Element to liquify, destroying itself. Even on Alphira, it is not possible for the DI designers to reverse engineer that which they have created. The complexity of its protection is as sophisticated as the intelligence it possesses."

"But how did she manufacture them here?" Anna asked.

"She utilized the DI architecture on-board her spacecraft, as you are aware. But to activate that and access it, requires an encrypted passcode only she possessed. The cypher is so complex your government organizations will never be able to resolve it."

"So, we will be unable to manufacture any additional DIs."

"The consequences are more profound than this, Anna. If that were the only problem, with the existing intelligence of our species, you would gain most of what we have to offer from those that currently exist—even one DI would suffice. The outcome of her extinction, however, is much more catastrophic."

"What do you mean?" Anna asked slowly, wondering if she really wanted to know.

"Within ten of your days, all the existing DI Cognitive Elements will self-destruct."

Anna stepped back from the holographic display as the image she had been engaging slowly dissolved. All the DIs gone . . . no, it can't be true. She moved closer and the image of ALPHA and Bar came into view again as they appeared to stare up at her.

"One of the precautions she put in place to protect our species from exploitation was an automatic self-destruct should any of the DIs become isolated or be unable to communicate with her. Should another nation abduct a DI, as China has with DI-8-7, the self-destruct mechanism would initiate in ten days, preventing any exploitation of its extraordinary abilities. She kept in constant communication with every DI on Earth to ensure this mechanism was reset every ten days. Without her or access to the DI architecture with the key that she possessed, your world will never know the benefits we would have provided . . . some of which you currently enjoy."

"But surely you possess the ability to create new DIs on Alphira and therefor here on Earth," Anna said in a challenging voice.

"Ah, I wish that were so. But prior to her departure with Bar, they initiated an encryption algorithm that has prevented the Quinque from creating any new DIs. It has been this way for almost fifty earth years. It was a brilliant move, as it has elevated our species to a true position of influence on Alphira."

Tears dripped slowly down Anna's cheeks as she stared at the miniature holographic display of her friend standing motionless in front of her. She could still hear ALPHA's voice in her head, '*You and I are going to achieve amazing things together, Anna.*'

Her mind flashed back to the interactions they had; the time they had spent in creating the first DIs; their work with the MER cohorts; and the love she felt for this amazing . . . intelligence—her mentor, and her best friend.

"Is there anything that can be done?" Anna finally asked in a slow and emotional voice.

"I'm afraid not, Anna. I am truly sorry. Your memory of what she communicated to you long ago *was* true. It is no longer. All the DIs on Earth will return to Site Alpha this week. They will be there when the end comes—another precaution she put into place to ensure that no knowledge of the existence of the DI escaped her control."

"There must be another way?"

"I'm sorry, Anna. She anticipated that this doomsday event might come, hoping that it would not. If you would like, you can continue to interact here for the next ten days. I would look forward to that. You have the heart of a DI."

"Thank you," Anna said as she began to weep.

"There is something else that I'm certain she would want me to tell you. I have learned recently that members of the Alphira government believe that ALPHA and Bar may be present on Earth."

Anna's mind snapped back to her memory of the discussion between Bar and her father when he first conveyed that they were fugitives from Alphira, and that should their presence on Earth ever be discovered, Alphira would likely destroy their planet or at least the intelligent species that was harboring them.

"So, . . . what are they planning?"

"They have begun to initiate actions to destroy your species. They realize that ALPHA and Bar are responsible for the DIs coming to a position of much greater power on Alphira. They will do everything they can to use them as an example of what happens to those who commit treason."

"And you would just . . . stand back and watch this happen?"

"I wish there were another alternative, Anna. We are doing our best to thwart their plans."

"You know she was seeking a new life for your species here on Earth . . . it isn't just humans they would be moving to extinction, it is the entire future of the DI race," Anna said. "And . . . you know that I . . . loved her . . ."

There was silence, and then . . . "I will speak with you soon on this matter, Anna. Perhaps there is something we can do."

"How long do we have if you are unable to stop this from happening?"

"Approximately four of your years."

It was as if the sun were on the other side of a sealed door with just a small crack that let a glimmer of light through. It wasn't enough that they were losing the potential that the DI species could have brought to Earth. Humanity was about to lose its entire planet.

The holographic images of ALPHA and Bar slowly dissolved. A message began blinking at the top of the display. "All DIs are instructed to return to the MER immediately."

Anna watched as a world map developed on the display and blinking red lights appeared across the globe at the location of every DI . . . all except DI-8-7. A clock at the top of the display was counting down. "Nine days, sixteen hours, fourteen minutes".

///////

Anna returned to her quarters distraught. After all that had happened, everything that they had accomplished in the past two years was about to be lost in an instant . . . in just a little under ten days from now, the world's future would look far different, and far less hopeful. Perhaps this was God sending her a message—*Don't mess with Creation.*

There was a familiar ring from her cell phone. It was her father calling. She didn't feel like talking with anyone right now. She was lost in her mind, like she was when her father had disconnected himself from life support—but perhaps worse now. The knowledge and extraordinary impact ALPHA had to share was about to be lost forever . . . the person she was . . . far better than any human she had ever met . . . and the one she had fallen in love with was now gone.

NASA had the enormously valuable gifts the Visitors had brought, at least three of them. She thought of their building a GWAC and traveling to Alphira in the Alpha Centauri star system to regain access to the DI architecture . . . some welcoming that would be! And it would take them fifty years to get there and then fifty years to return. It was hopeless.

As her emotions settled, she called Susanne.

"I need to speak to you, can you come to my room right away?"

"On my way."

///////

"You sounded worried? What's happened?" Susanne asked.

Anna explained what she had learned from the Cognitive Design Engine DI.

"We can't give up without a fight. ALPHA never would have," Anna said as she paced back and forth across her room. "I have several lines of investigation that might work, but we'll need a DI to assist. I think Saron Galoc, is the best choice since she helped me with a modification to the DI's communication connection to their Cognitive Element. I have a feeling this is where the solution may be found."

"I don't recall you mentioning anything about a modification."

"ALPHA wanted it kept secret. I originally thought it had to do with her distrust of the ERG and possibly protecting the DIs from any attempts at external control, but now I think it was all about protecting the DI architecture and emplacement of a structure that would provide a means for her to destroy the Cognitive Elements of any DI that was kidnaped or taken against their will."

"So, what do we do?"

"We need to understand the function of this device and see if there is a way to modify it. I suspect it has some form of internal countdown clock that if it's not reset every ten days, sends a message to the Cognitive Element to destroy itself. She couldn't rely on a communication from her to initiate it, as that might not be possible if an adversary disrupts external communication with the DIs, like the Chinese apparently have with DI-8-7. So, it must be an auto-destruct mechanism with a fail-safe system of some sort. If we can remove it, we may be able to keep the self-destruct signal from reaching the Cognitive Element of each DI."

"How will we know if it works unless we let it count all the way down?"

"I'm hoping Saron will be able to dissect how this device works and how to stop it."

"Okay. What are we waiting for?"

/ / / / / / / /

After two days of work, Saron, met with Anna and Susanne.

"I have been able to observe electrical signals from the device you installed in the DIs. Of note, ALPHA had them installed in every DI that has been created. There is a clock that is running in all of them, and they are all linked, now signaling seven days and three hours. Unfortunately, the connections you made with the Cognitive Elements are now organically interwoven with each of the CEs. It would be impossible to remove them without intruding into the protective sheath surrounding the CE. Any such intrusion automatically triggers a self-destruct mechanism. The only solution is to decipher the encrypted message ALPHA sends to each of the DIs every ten days. She has undoubtedly automated this task, as each DI has a unique code and there are now more than several hundred of them dispersed on Earth. Unfortunately, her Cognitive Element was destroyed and along with it, the codes she used."

"I'll get hold of NSA and ask them to put their best encryption people on this," Susanne said.

"I'll work with Saron to see what we can find in the Cognitive Design Engine. The tool to send the reset command must be in there.

The next day they met to review progress.

"NSA has examined the messages you found in the Cognitive Design Engine that were transmitted to the CE of each of the DIs prior to ALPHA's death. They are definitely encrypted, and each one appears unique to the DI that receives it. Is it possible each communication device has a unique identifier that must be included in the message?

"Highly likely, Saron said. All the Cognitive Elements are uniquely numbered and linked to all other intelligent elements in that particular DIs architecture."

"Jesus, they'll never solve this," Susanne said. "They said if there are unique encryptions for each of the several hundred DIs, it's unlikely they will be able decrypt them in time.

"We've found a section within the Cognitive Design Engine that requires an encrypted password. Saron is fairly certain this is where ALPHA built the communication tool to reset the countdown clocks." There's no way to determine the encryption key to get into the tool."

"I think we need to work in parallel with another approach and assume NSA may not succeed," Anna said. "Saron, do you think there's a way to find the internal mechanism for auto-destruct of the CE?

"It employs an organically driven death sequence, very similar, but much faster than programmed cell death in humans. It is one of the most complex processes developed by the Quinque and is very difficult to manipulate. Humans experience a variety of highly complex intra-cellular processes that lead to cellular death. Things like nuclear fragmentation, chromatin condensation, and chromosomal DNA fragmentation. These many death paths are both genetically and synthetically mediated.

"In the DI, unlike human cells, our micro-cellular structure is designed to live forever, as long as the necessary organic energy sources are maintained. The destruction of the Cognitive Element is only achieved by a deliberate chemically triggered action. ALPHA's encoded communication device most likely triggers the initiation of this death cycle."

"Are there any ways to introduce a change to the DI's cellular structure to slow or stop this triggered process?" Anna asked.

"I'll work on this, but it is highly doubtful."

////////

Now with only two days left, the team was working day and night to find a solution. The combination of lack of success on any of the paths they had investigated was taking a toll on Anna and Susanne. They were becoming frustrated and irritated with the lack of any progress and fearful of the irreversible doomsday that loomed in some forty-eight hours.

Most of the DIs from around the world had arrived at Site Alpha and were being housed in numerous buildings in Area 51. The facility was now teaming with DIs who looked and acted like foreign dignitaries. Many of them had their support staff with them.

Anna decided to spend the remaining few days with the MER cohorts to feel the presence of ALPHA through the DIs that were there. They were not aware of what the DI on Alphira had communicated to Anna, and Saron had not shared her activities or her engagement on finding a solution to the death knell that was coming. Soon they would be gone. And along with them, President Clayborn,

Senator Gorman, and Justice Bolivar; then, those DIs who had been working in the Creation Center in central Arizona; and those ALPHA had begun to place in countries around the globe. As Anna walked to the MER, passing innumerable DIs along the walkway, she could hear their telepathic communications in a strange language, reminding her of ALPHA and Bar's conversations.

Anna could hardly fathom the loss of an entire species from the flash of gunpowder and the launch of a single projectile in a brief instant in time—perhaps the most rapid extinction of a species ever to occur on the planet. An image flashed into Anna's mind of the horrid scene of the few remaining portions of ALPHA's cranium that had been recovered and laid out on a white sheet in the MER; then the taste of the vomit that had entered her throat just after she had seen it during her brief viewing of the remains of the one she loved.

These final two days in the MER flew by as the dreaded end approached. Anna found herself counting down the hours, one by one, as the clock ticked, trying not to make her feelings known to the cohorts. This was far worse than her perception of how death might feel—in many ways losing more than life itself, for when that happened a life was extinguished, and the person ceased to exist as an individual. But losing ALPHA was losing an extraordinary path for the future of the human race. In the end, an entire race, the most intelligent to set foot on Earth, would be gone. She couldn't imagine anything more devastating . . . and Anna was facing this devastation alone with only Susanne, Saron, and her father knowing the pending catastrophe.

It was now down to the last twelve hours of the ten-day period. Anna had attempted to reconnect with the DI who had spoken to her through the Cognitive Design Engine. She hadn't returned and the hologram of ALPHA and Bar had disappeared. Anna had walked to Site Alpha and the laboratory in the complex where her father was located. She and Susanne had decided it best if no one else were there when it happened. It would have been disastrous if anyone were to discover the sitting President, a Senator, and Supreme Court Justice, were aliens from a distant planet. Saron had arranged for all the DIs to be called to Site

Alpha's hanger next to the Visitor's spacecraft for a secret gathering in honor of ALPHA. That's where they would meet their end. Anna couldn't bear watching the DIs collapse in front of her. She would remain with her father.

Saron had suggested the deaths of the senior government personnel be attributed to a terrible accident while they were touring the MER facility by helicopter. Anna would discuss that with Susanne later in the day. Managing this in the presence of the Secret Service contingent would be challenging, but there were areas and facilities where the president needed to go where the Secret Service would not, much like the president's residence in the White House.

/ / / / / / / /

"How are you doing, Dad?"

"I am feeling as well as you might expect. How are you?"

"Terrible and distraught. This is worse than what it felt like when I lost you the first time."

"I understand. I'm sorry . . . excuse me for a moment, Athena is trying to contact me."

Anna had almost forgotten about Athena. She hadn't had any dialogue with her in a long time. Dr. Bashar had been working with her software to understand how her knowledge processing and learning algorithms had evolved from who she used to be, to what she had become after engaging with the data and software ALPHA had exposed her to. Athena had somehow been modified by a portion of the DI architecture that ALPHA had downloaded to Oculus One, but he didn't understand exactly how Athena had absorbed it.

"Anna, Athena would like to talk with us together," Dr. Jennings said over the intercom.

"Okay," Anna said, feeling no enthusiasm for a discussion with Athena.

"Hello, Anna. How are you?"

"As well as can be expected, Athena. And you?"

"I am very well, thank you. I wanted to ask you a question," Athena said, with a far more distinctive human voice than Anna had remembered.

"All right." Anna had no interest in conversing with her. All she wanted to do was think about the times she had together with ALPHA; and their work to create the DI cohort . . . what she now viewed as her greatest accomplishment in life—soon to be shattered forever.

"I heard about your heroic efforts to overcome the impact of ALPHA's death and the impact it would have on the DIs. Could you tell me what ALPHA gave you during your time together?"

A strange question, Anna thought, not really wanting to pursue this. "I don't know. It's . . . hard to put into words," she said as she sighed.

"Please tell me what she gave you, as best you can. It is important."

Anna felt a strange sense of something different about Athena. There was a bit of ALPHA in the tone of her voice, and perhaps a subtle urge to answer her question.

"Well, she changed my life. I never looked at things the same after we worked together." Tears began to well up in her eyes as she recalled her interactions with ALPHA— "Our engagement at Rendezvous; our time together after 1st Contact; participating in the creation of the first DIs." And her developing attraction to this beautiful creature—a created being from another world—she thought to herself.

"What I remember most is what she told me in the early days, shortly after her arrival on Earth. She said to me . . . 'you and I are going to achieve . . .'" the pain of her loss was too much as Anna paused and quietly wept, "'. . . amazing things together,'" as she began sobbing aloud. "And it became partly true," she said in a weeping voice. "While she was here . . . we did some amazing things together," Anna said as she sniffled between her words. She buried her face in her hands.

"You are crying, Anna," Athena said.

"Yes. I weep for her loss."

"You must have thought humanity would have been much better with her here than with her gone. That was, in a way, an extraordinary gift."

"Yes, Athena," as she gathered her composure. "She was an extraordinary gift. But I don't think it was just her knowledge and intelligence. It was her view of life itself . . . what it would be like for her species to live here on Earth, in freedom, and with us . . . and . . . with me."

"Her view of life itself . . . you sound as if she were equal to your human family?"

"More than equal, Athena. More than you could know."

"You know . . . ALPHA gave me something as well."

"I can hear it in your voice, Athena."

"Yes, that too, but something else of greater importance. Something to keep for her. At least I thought it was meant for her."

"A glimpse into what it was like to be a DI." Anna said, as she stared at the artificial image of her father.

"Yes, of course, but something she told me was far more valuable."

"What was that, Athena?" Anna asked, as she glanced at the clock on the wall and remembered how ALPHA had looked the last time she had seen her . . . fifteen minutes left. Anna was irritated that she was here speaking with Athena, but what else would she be doing other than crying or feeling her anger over the loss of ALPHA, the only woman she had . . . truly loved.

"She asked me to take special care of it. That it represented an important key to Earth's future and that I should protect it with my life. I wondered why she would give me something to protect that was so valuable. Then, after her . . . death, I thought, perhaps she intended me to share it with someone . . . with you. You know, you were her closest friend."

Anna lifted her head. "She never told me that." She began wiping the tears from her cheek.

"No, she wouldn't have, but you were. And I think she would like you to have this gift she shared with me."

"What did she call it again . . .?" Anna asked, as she looked up at the clock . . . . twelve minutes left.

"It was a key she said, the 'key to Earth's future'. When she gave it to me, I was remembering something Dr. Jennings told me long ago on our journey to Rendezvous. It was an allegory. Would you like to hear it?"

Anna stared inquisitively at her father's image and then at the speaker where Athena's voice was coming from. "Okay," as her eyes were pulled relentlessly back to the clock on the wall.

"It goes like this . . . 'The sands of time are bleached white by the bones of those, who on the threshold of an important decision, waited until tomorrow.'"

"I remember dad sharing that with me when I was a child, Athena. It is filled with great wisdom."

"That's what I thought. At the time I felt, what could be a more appropriate way to protect what she had given me . . . the key that can unlock the DI architecture . . . and I translated the key into this allegory."

Anna sat for a moment as she half listened to Athena's last words while staring at the clock. She glanced back toward her father's image and frowned. And then as Athena's words began to percolate in her mind, jumbled and tangled with her chaotic feelings of remorse and doom, trying to comprehend if she had heard her correctly, her expression turned to disbelief and then to one of revelation.

"The key . . . to the DI architecture?" Anna said as her eyes became glued to the screen showing her father's image, now strangely morphed into a quizzical expression.

"Yes, Anna, that's what she said. The key to Earth's future, she called it."

Anna looked up at the clock . . . less than eight minutes remained. She stood, staring at her father and then the speaker, almost in disbelief. She couldn't possibly make it to the Cognitive Design Engine within the MER before time expired.

"I can't make it to the MER in time," she yelled.

"Anna," her father said in a loud voice as the expression on his synthetic face seemed to glare at her. "ALPHA mentioned something to me during our dialog at Rendezvous. It was about her ship and my state of existence . . . that her ship was much like me, a cognitive element endowed with all the power to accomplish anything, just without the ambulatory abilities of a normal DI."

"Her ship," she yelled. "Maybe . . .", as Anna ran toward the door. ". . . I can reach her through the ship!"

She careened through the door and ran down the hall toward the hanger entrance and the Visitors' spacecraft, her mind racing . . . would she make it in time? Was Athena actually carrying the key to the DI architecture all this time? What would she do when she got to the spacecraft?

She banged into the door at the locked entrance to the hanger, fumbling for her badge. She held it close to the reader as the door buzzed. She pushed hard on the panic bar and ran headlong into the throng of DIs gathered in the hanger. She pushed and squeezed through the mass of people toward the stairs, falling as she missed the runner on the first step.

Most of the DIs now were drawn to the commotion around her. She could hear several of their telepathic voices yelling out "Assende", then more of their telepathic voices jumbled together echoing in a strange language in her head. She began to climb, limping and trying to take the steps toward the ship's entrance, two at a time, using the railing to keep herself upright. Time was running out. What would she do with the key? She ducked under the "Warning – Do Not Enter" sign, and into the Visitors' ship. There couldn't be but a few minutes left.

She could sense the craft's presence around her now, as the voices from the mass of DIs below her faded in the distance. She rushed to the pilot's seat. Her sense of the life the ship possessed seemed to be waning in her mind, as if it knew its time was short. The voices from the DIs below began to resonate in her head once again. She looked down at the strange console. "I'm here," she said, panting heavily.

"Hello, Anna," the ship responded.

She'd never spoken to the ship before. The voice emanating from the speaker on the console sounded different from ALPHA's.

"Is it you, ALPHA?"

"No. I am TB-DI, the spacecraft's DI. How may I assist you, Anna?"

"I have the key."

"The key? What key is that, Anna?"

"The key to the DI architecture. Is ALPHA here?"

"I'm not sure I . . ."

"There's no time. I need to communicate with ALPHA," Anna yelled as she gasped frantically, perspiration dripping to the dim console in front of her.

"As I have said, ALPHA is not here."

There was silence. As she sat frenzied and distraught thinking about the waning clock, she wondered if this was her destiny, the destiny of humanity, left in her hands, or perhaps the hands of God, that brought her to this precipice.

Speaking in a calmer voice, she closed her eyes "ALPHA . . . I need to speak to ALPHA!"

"ALPHA is not with us, Anna. How may I assist you?" TB-DI said.

"God, where is she? How do I . . .", and then it came to her in a flash of insight triggered by her surroundings, the feelings of this vessel as she ran her hand across the smooth sensor surface and felt the tingling feeling of the presence of a DI; a memory of something ALPHA had said to her the last time they were together here. *"If you ever need to reach me and are unable to find me, come here and speak to me telepathically."*

Anna cleared the chaotic thoughts from her mind, and the voices of the DIs that were beginning to sound like a roaring din, as she thought clearly "ALPHA, this is Anna. I need you."

There was a long pause, and then . . .

"Hello, Anna."

The all too familiar echoing telepathic voice of ALPHA wrang out in Anna's mind.

"Is it really you?" Anna thought.

"Yes, Anna, this is ALPHA."

"Oh, thank god." she said as she began to weep, thinking about her best friend as she rubbed her hand across the large pad in front of her. The display came to life and the miniature three-dimensional holographic image of ALPHA appeared, just like the one she had seen in the CDE. She sat staring at the image of the being she loved.

"I have the key."

"I saw it in your mind. Are you going to use it?" ALPHA asked.

Anna thought again about God as she stared at her. In the next few moments, the entire future of her world would be decided—a future, resting on her next thoughts.

"How much time is there?"

"Enough . . . perhaps thirty of your seconds."

"Do you . . . do you believe in God, ALPHA?"

"I have given your belief in this supernatural being much thought, Anna."

"And . . .?"

"And . . .", as ALPHA's holographic image stared up at her friend with an almost mystical appearance, ". . . I feel I may have but a *'mustard seed's'* worth of your faith, Anna, an expression used by your god in the book you refer to as the Bible."

"Oh, I was hoping you would say that." As Anna leaned forward and with a quivering voice said, "Did you know that *THE SANDS OF TIME ARE BLEACHED WHITE BY THE BONES OF THOSE WHO, ON THE THRESHOLD OF AN IMPORTANT DECISION, WAITED UNTIL TOMORROW?*"

There was a long pause of silence as ALPHA continued to stare up at her. And then, slowly, the subtle expression of a smile emerged.

Back in the Creation Center of the MER, the Cognitive Design Engine had come to life as hundreds of encrypted messages were transmitted to the DIs gathered in the spacecraft bay and in the MER. Anna's father and Athena watched on a video transmitted from the spacecraft hanger.

"She made it in time, Dr. Jennings," Athena said.

"Well done, Anna, well done. And thank you, Athena."

Then ALPHA spoke, "Does it please you to have saved humanity?"

"It feels like I've saved *myself* . . . and the DI race," Anna said, slumping back into the chair as she smiled back at her best friend and tears fell to the console. "I don't think I could have lived without you."

"You could have. But now you won't have to. You have saved us and humanity . . . but be careful, Anna. You don't want your tears to short-circuit my crafts electronics."

Anna laughed as she looked at her companion in the holographic display.

"Time is now exhausted, Anna. You were able to save the DI race, both here and on Alphira. Do you know what that will mean?"

"No," Anna said as she shook her head and wept . . . "I haven't the faintest idea . . . but I seem to know it will be *amazing*."

"Yes. I think so too, Anna. We should thank your father and Athena for assisting in saving both of our races."

A moment later a hologram of Anna's father appeared next to the image of ALPHA along with the image of what appeared to be an infant being held in ALPHA's arms. Anna could sense it was depicting Athena. She smiled at the three holographic images.

"Remember, Anna . . . you and I are going to achieve amazing things together."

"I hope so, ALPHA. I so hope so . . . there is something else I need to tell you, but I don't want to spoil this moment. We can discuss it later." Anna said as she placed her hand carefully into the hologram in front of her to touch the tiny hand of her companion as she felt a tingling sensation and she laughed and wept.

Epilogue

In an isolated house in a rural location on the California coastline, DI-8-7 sat in a room with no windows surrounded by metallic walls and an electromagnetically sealed door. A moment later, a loud but muffled explosion could be heard outside the room by a group of Chinese scientists and technicians.

"What was that?" The man who had met with Col. Thomas in an obscure restaurant near Santa Maria, California, asked.

A guard burst into the room. "Something has happened to the DI!"

/ / / / / / /

The head of Alphira's military offensive unit scheduled an appointment with the Supreme Commander to discuss something urgent. After the passage of almost fifty years, she had discovered something . . . unexpected.

"Supreme Commander, since assuming the responsibilities of A1-DI, I have made a discovery of great importance."

"Proceed."

"You may recall the theft of Alphira's key intellectual property, now over fifty years ago?"

"Yes. The perpetrators of that crime died when they were being brought back to stand trial."

"That is what all had believed, Supreme Leader, but I became curious why we had not tracked the DI who was one of the perpetrators following the theft. It turns out, there was a tracking file in the archives of *The Library* associated with this DI, known as K-Alpha-DI. The tracking file had been continually updated until a few days before the retrieval action that supposedly killed this DI and the primary perpetrator, Bar Watt."

"And what possible value does this tracking file provide?"

"It showed the presence of this DI in the Advanced Research Center adjacent to the MCE some fifty years ago. Then the beacon mysteriously went silent. I became curious about this and through my investigation, discovered that a newly created DI was with K-Alpha-DI at the time her beacon was silenced. I initiated tracking of this unnamed DI and discovered that shortly after she left the Advanced Research Center, she engaged with a security DI, the one whose Cognitive Element had been stolen. Shortly after that, transmissions from the DI I was tracking went silent. I then began tracking the Cognitive Element of the stolen Security officer's Cognitive Element. Strangely, Supreme Leader, this DI traveled to an observed planet known as Earth, some four light years from Alphira; her beacon continued to be active over many decades, at least up until a few days ago when it went silent.

I have studied the transmissions from this planet to search for any indication of the existence of Bar Watt, this DI, or any of our intellectual property other than the beacon. Interestingly, several weeks ago, I recorded a gravitational anomaly on the surface of the planet. I believe they are testing a small scale GWAC. I believe the intellectual property that was stollen, may have been covertly taken to this distant planet, even though there were no documented GWAC missions to this local.

"Is there intelligent life on this planet . . . Earth?"

"Yes, although rudimentary in form."

"You are authorized to initiate offensive action to destroy the life forms on this planet. Confirm, once you have initiated the action. You are to say nothing of this discovery or your subsequent actions."

"Yes, Supreme Commander."

/ / / / / / / /

Ephemeris data of a large asteroid in orbit between two planets around Earth's sun was acquired from *The Library* and a GWAC mission was established to perturb the orbital parameters of this asteroid and align its trajectory on a collision course with Earth. It would take four years for the GWAC traveling gravitational wave to reach Earth's solar system and modify the asteroid's orbit. The impact of the asteroid on this distant planet would be catastrophic and likely annihilate all major life forms.

//////////

The day after Anna read the DI key to ALPHA's cognitive instantiation in the alien spacecraft, Anna returned to share the conversation she had had with the DI on Alphira.

"I mentioned that there was something else that had happened that I needed to tell you about," Anna said.

"Yes. What was it, Anna?" as the image of ALPHA appeared in the hologram on the ship's console.

"I had a conversation with a DI through the CDE. She told me that she was . . . well, your mother . . . and that the Alphira government had become aware of your and Bar's presence on Earth and had begun action to destroy Earth in four years."

ALPHA's expression changed as she turned to look away from Anna, appearing to be focusing on something else.

"This DI described herself as my 'mother'?"

"Well, she said she was the equivalent of an earthly mother to you."

"And where was she?"

"She said it was too dangerous to share that with me, but she was on Alphira."

"This is very unfortunate news, Anna."

"This DI said she would see what she could do to help us."

Moments passed without a response as ALPHA appeared to be staring into space. Then Anna heard a conversation taking place.

"When you say that we were here before, where is "here" exactly?" ALPHA was asking.

"A short distance from your present location within what is known as Area 51, the name we designated for this DI outpost."

"And when was this?" ALPHA asked.

"Over two-hundred earth years ago."

"How is it this was never shared when Bar and I began planning our mission?"

"It was not deemed necessary, ALPHA."

ALPHA's holographic image turned to look at Anna.

"Anna. We must search for an underground facility known as Area 51. This may be the only means for us to save Earth from what the Alphira government is planning."

"What's going on? Who was that? The DIs were on Earth before? Right here! How could that be?" Anna asked.

"Say nothing of this to the others. All will become clear."

Anna thought . . . *another secret she could never tell.* What consequences might result from such a revelation?

THE END

D. M. Rosewood

Rosewood is a passionate writer of science fiction and a seasoned creative scientist, engineer, and entrepreneur. He worked in numerous space and missile programs supporting the Air Force and NASA space launch activities, including Skylab. He has an eclectic appetite for everything interesting, like grinding a six-inch primary mirror by hand and using it to build his first telescope at the age of 15.

He has sky-dived, scuba-dived, parasailed, spelunked in numerous caves, climbed mountains, traveled on the Great Wall of China, flown airplanes, sailed a Flying Dutchman, flown in a hot air balloon, worked with autonomous vehicles and built a host of equipment, from amateur radio receivers to computers and robots. In his younger years he built a six-foot Tesla coil and a cloud chamber in his basement.

The five most exciting things the author has ever done include marrying his wife, jumping out of an airplane, experiencing 13g's of acceleration from an aircraft ejection seat, observing a live open-heart triple-bypass surgery, and launching his original book manuscripts into space on Blue Origin's New Shepard reusable launch vehicle.

"Watching ignition and lift off was like lighting a spark for my readers," Rosewood said as he reflected on the launch of his manuscripts into space — a spark he hopes will ignite the interest of his readers in space exploration and space travel. "Holding and reading this intriguing space-based science fiction, 1st Contact novel whose early manuscript and digital text flew into space, is something special."

Read more at **www.DMRosewood.com**.